HOW DOES IT FEEL?

Katherine took another sip of vodka. *Ask him,* she thought. *It's sick but it's what you really want to know most of all, isn't it? So go on and ask him. Truth or lie you want to hear his answer.* She lit a cigarette and shook out the match.

"So you didn't tell me, Ray," she said. "What did it feel like?"

"Huh? I did tell you."

"You told me how it felt after. Not then. Not at the time." She took another long drink and looked at him.

"Not when you were out there killing people."

"Jesus, Kath." He looked uncomfortable as hell but she noticed that the spark had come back to his eyes. "You really want to know this?"

"I guess I must. I'm asking."

The house was silent. She could hear the ice clink in his scotch as he tipped the glass and drank. She felt absurd for a moment and a little frightened. Like they were sitting around a fire and she was about to hear him tell a ghost story.

He pushed himself up on the couch. He wouldn't meet her eyes.

He spoke slowly, carefully. . . .

The Lost

Jack Ketchum

LEISURE BOOKS NEW YORK CITY

A LEISURE BOOK®

May 2001

Published by

Dorchester Publishing Co., Inc.
276 Fifth Avenue
New York, NY 10001

ISBN 0-8439-4876-0

The name "Leisure Books" and the stylized "L" with design are trademarks of Dorchester Publishing Co., Inc.

Printed in the United States of America.

Visit us on the web at www.dorchesterpub.com.

Thanks to Neal McPheeters, Charlie Grant, Neil Linden, Robert Murphy, and Theo Levine for the info and especially to Marie Jones of the Cape May County Public Library, who I pestered quite a lot. To the folks at Manhattan Vet for the cat stuff, to Paula White for the read, and to Christopher Golden for the jump-start.

The Lost

"We all hope for a superior brand of madness but our wounds are considerably less interesting than our cures."
—Jim Harrison, *The Beige Dolorosa*

Prologue

"This world is long on hunger,
This world is short on joy."
—Jackson Browne

June 1965
Sparta, New Jersey

In the glow of the campfire he saw them kiss. Just a peck on the lips, nothing much and only once before sitting down cross-legged by the tree to what looked like a dinner of franks and beans.

No big thing. A kiss. But damn, he hated to see it.

"Christ," he said. "Lezzies. Man, that's disgusting."

Tim grinned. "Come on, Ray. You don't know they're lezzies. Maybe they're sisters. Or it's like a friendly thing."

"You ever kiss a girl like that, Jen? Ever touch a girl's hair the way she just did?"

" 'Course not."

"You ever walk around naked when there's another girl around like she was doing before? I mean forget about showers in gym class. You got no choice there. I mean just because you feel like it."

"Would you come off it, Ray?" Like she'd never dream of it. Not Jennifer. Her voice was slurred. She

13

was a little tanked. He guessed they all were.

"See? I told you. Couple of lesbos."

He'd seen the brunette walk stark naked except for a pair of flip-flops out of one of the campground outhouses around two this afternoon. He'd needed to take a crap. Practically tripped over her. Damn near got an old outhouse door shoved in his face. He didn't know who was more surprised, the brunette or him, but he knew who liked it more.

He'd laughed. *Got a cigarette?* he said. *Whoops, guess not.*

My god, she said, *I thought we were* alone *up here! I'm sorry. God!* She was trying to cover her tits with one arm, cupping the one on the right and trying to get the left tucked in under her elbow while the other hand grabbed for her snatch. The left tit wasn't cooperating and he could see the brown puckered edge of the nipple there. The girl had a body on her, that was for sure. Tall and full and firm, just the way he liked them. Face wasn't bad either.

He didn't like the voice, though. Something about the way she talked, the accent, like the girl wasn't from around here. The voice seemed to hint that Daddy had bucks.

Sorry if I scared you, he said. *I just, you know, had to use the facilities.* He also hated the *you know*. It wasn't like him. Something about the voice had done it to him. Usually he was a whole lot slicker. But he smiled at her anyway and made as though he was going to walk into the outhouse and do his thing. The girl smiled too and nodded in an embarrassed way and turned to trot away down the path.

The ass was nice too. It jiggled side to side when she ran. Just a little extra fat on her. Not much.

He figured that his shit could wait a while. He kept tight to the bushes along the narrow, winding path and followed her. She was headed over the hill down toward

14

the lake. Going downhill was always harder on his feet inside the boots than uphill was but as usual he ignored the pain.

I thought we were alone up here.

He wanted to find out who the *we* was.

We turned out to be a pale slim redhead, thick pink nipples and a long kinky cloud of hair and a lighter carrot-colored snatch. Gold necklace glinting in the sunlight. Gold bracelet on her wrist. He couldn't even see the face for all that hair. But he could guess what the brunette was saying to her. *There's someone here, we have to put our clothes on.* Because the redhead sat up from where she was lying sunning herself by the water's edge and you could see she was arguing in a half-hearted way, gesturing, like, *So what? Who cares?* but the brunette was already into her jeans and buttoning her sleeveless blouse, and he watched the redhead sigh and give in and reach for her T-shirt.

He slipped away.

He went back and took his shit in the damp, reeking outhouse and then walked back up the hill to the Big Rock where Tim and Jennifer were sitting in the shade smoking Marlboros and drinking Colt .45s. He popped a can and picked up the sleek walnut Remington .22 and leaned on it like a cane while he told them about it. He made the two girls sound prettier than they were, exaggerating, especially the redhead, since he'd never even really seen her face. Making them prettier for Jennifer's benefit. He liked to keep her on edge a little, a little jealous, fan the old flames once in a while.

And now crouching in the brush in the dark with the two of them beside him he was disappointed, almost angry at the two girls. Because of the kiss. Who could stay jealous over a pair of goddamn lesbos? Jennifer sure as hell wouldn't. Not to mention that he'd worked himself up to wanting to fuck the brains out of the

brunette in the *worst* way. So that was damn disappoint-
ing too.

Because seeing them now at their campsite and fully
dressed confirmed his earlier impression. The impression he'd got from her voice. Money. Plenty of it. He
wouldn't have had a snowball's chance in hell of making it with her anyway. He knew the type, all right.
Brand-new jeans to go camping in for chrissake.
Expensive-looking equipment. High-end insulated tent
from what was probably L. L. Bean, little portable shiny
butane stove, big brand-new Coleman lantern.

A couple of Daddy's Girls. Probably up from the
City.

Couple of queers.

He fucking hated queers. There was this kid in his
eleventh-grade English class back when he was in
school who was queer, kid named Billy Dultz. Dultz
would suck your cock for a five-dollar bill or a punch
in the face, whichever you cared to give him. He knew
guys who'd paid in either currency, sometimes both.
Give him a five for starters and punch him out later just
for fun. Not Ray. There was no way in hell he was
going to let some guy jerk him off or suck him off and
for sure nobody was going up his asshole—that was
fucking *sick*—and in his book the same held true for
lesbos. Any girl who'd rather eat pussy than suck a dick
deserved to curl up and die.

Piss me off, he thought.

He let go of the handful of brush. Who wanted to
watch a couple of rich bitches eating their franks and
beans?

The dogs smelled good, though. He was hungry.

He picked up the Remington.

"Know what we ought to do, Timmy?" he said. "We
ought to pop 'em."

"What?" He could tell by Jennifer's voice that he'd
managed to scare her. He liked that. It made him grin.

That big wide Elvis grin that contained a subtle sneer. He flashed it at the both of them. He liked Jennifer scared even more than he liked her jealous. He couldn't say why, he just did. Tim said nothing but that was because Tim was basically too chicken. They were both just a couple of kids when you came right down to it. He decided to push it some.

"Pop 'em." he whispered. "Hey, me and Tim even talked about it, couple of times. Right, Tim? What it would be like to pop somebody. See, you never hunted, Jen. You don't get it. You never shot a rabbit. Me and Tim have though. You see it in their eyes. One minute everything's fine. Hey, we're hoppin' down the bunny trail! Next minute, rabbit hell. And you caused it. You took him there and he ain't coming back. So you got to think how it would feel to shoot a person. And lezzies, screw 'em, they're barely human anyway. They're never gonna have kids, right? Who's gonna miss 'em?"

"Ray, for godsakes, you don't know they're lezzies. Not just from a kiss and getting naked together you don't."

He could hear the anxiety in Tim's voice. He liked hearing that there too. A little too much of it, though.

"Keep it down, for chrissake, will you, Tim?"

"Okay, all right. But you *don't* know they're lezzies. I hear people in Europe get naked together all the time. I hear girls hold hands in the streets over there. It's an affection thing. Maybe give one another a kiss now and then right out in public. Maybe they're European."

He could barely keep from howling.

"Tim, you are *so* full of shit. European!"

"Well, you don't know, do you?"

"That brunette's no European. That brunette's home-grown American as apple pie. Got money up the wazoo, too. So what do you figure? Pop her or fuck her?"

"Jesus, Ray."

He shrugged and smiled. "You got to figure the options, Timmy. You got to always figure the options."

"You're a beautiful girl for godsakes," Elise had said to her. "To hell with Phillip. You'll find somebody who's a whole lot better, you'll see." And then reached out and touched her long dark hair and gave her a little kiss.

It was just the kind of kiss goodnight they'd always given one another when they were little girls just before the lights went out at bedtime. A sleepy, sleep-over kiss and it was a comfort to her.

And right now she needed some comforting.

The sun had helped and the cool clear water of the pool had helped. Hell, even the franks and beans were helping. It was getting out of Short Hills for the day that was important and Elise had been the one to realize that. It figured it would be Elise. Of the two of them she was the strong and certain one, the one apt to take charge. Though she certainly didn't look it, slim and frail-looking as she was, with all that frizzy red hair.

She finished the last of her hot dog and wiped her face with the napkin.

"I wish I could just completely hate him, you know?" she said.

"I wish you could too. Tell you what. Suppose I hate him for you?"

She smiled. "You already do."

Elise tossed a twig past her into the fire. "Look, Lisa. You fell for a cute guy with a shiny red Corvette and a good, sad line of bullshit and it was spring. Okay. So then you find out that behind that great big smile and the poor-me what-a-sad-childhood act there's a nasty drunken bastard. A guy who likes his frat parties too much, likes his beer too much and likes to punch people out when he's had a few. Particularly people weaker than he is. Particularly woman. What's not to hate?"

"I know. It's just that he's always so damn sorry after."

"Sorry, hell. He's done this twice, Lisa. And in this case I don't think three's the charm."

"I know that too."

It had always been this way between them. When Elise moved in next door she was seven years old and Lisa had just turned eight. But it was Elise who seemed to see things more clearly right from the start. That they each had fathers who were far more comfortable on a golf course than sitting over Sunday dinner, for instance. That they were each only children by design and not by accident. That they would never have sisters or brothers.

Their parents traveled in wholly different circles, Lisa's Russian Jewish liberals a few years out of Manhattan and Elise's strict Irish Catholics from Baltimore. But neither set of parents were opposed to the two girls more or less adopting one another. So they did. They were almost never apart. They traded sleep-overs almost every weekend and throughout most of every summer and continued straight through high school. Arguments were rare and quickly settled.

It was as though each had found the sister she longed for. And if Lisa seemed to blunder through puberty and Elise seemed to ride it like the crest of a wave, each forgave the other her predispositions.

Elise and Lisa. Lisa and Elise.

Even their names were practically sisters to each other.

They went off to school together. Wellesley. Contrived to be roommates there. Lisa's major was education, Elise's finance. They still had plenty in common. They each liked the Beatles and Dylan and Judy Collins—though Elise said that Judy Collins lacked a sense of irony. Irony, she said, was what the cat knew that the dog didn't. When they adopted a cat they named him Dylan.

They both liked Julia Child and Betty Friedan but *not* Helen Gurley Brown. Neither would be caught dead in a topless Rudi Gernreich bathing suit but both were comfortable with their bodies. They'd seen one another naked since they were kids. And neither was exactly a virgin anymore.

They shared a liking for simple quiet times and places.

Like now. Like camping in the woods.

Tonight at Turner's Pool was the third time they'd been out this summer and the only time it hadn't been pure simple fun.

The reason for that was Phillip. Him getting in the way.

She swatted a mosquito.

"I hope we're not gonna get eaten alive tonight," she said.

"I packed the bug spray."

"Good."

She tossed her paper plate into the fire, watched the edges curl and the dark bloom at the center.

She realized she was frowning. Elise noticed too. She watched her sigh and lean back against the oak tree, her long slim fingers picking the bark off the trunk.

"Even if he hadn't hit you it wouldn't have lasted. You know that."

"I guess."

"You guess? You remember Johnny Norman back in high school? He was the *same type*, Lisa. Cute and popular as hell and so full of himself you couldn't *stand* him after what, two months? Only difference was he didn't go ballistic when he drank. But he *did* drink, and too much."

"You're right. I don't get it. Why do I keep doing this to myself?"

"Hey, you're in there pitching and there are a lot of guys like that in the ballpark. You sympathize with them—no, you *empathize* with them—and then they use you. What are you supposed to do? Stop caring? Stop trying? Dry up like this poor old scraggly patch of grass here? You're doing the right thing. You're just not doing it with the right person yet, that's all."

She could feel herself poised on the verge of tears. She didn't want to cry again, she'd done that to Elise one too many times already over the guy but she kept seeing his face going red that night and his lips pulled up into a sneer screaming at her to *shut up, shut up* and seeing his right hand ball into a fist and she couldn't help it, she'd *cared* for the sonovabitch. She'd *cared*.

Elise opened her arms.

"Oh, come here, will you?"

She went to her and hugged her and let the tears happen to her again, not sobbing like last time but letting them flow against the neck of Elise's yellow T-shirt. She felt Elise's fingers in her hair and heard the crackling of the fire and crickets in the dark grass and the frogs bellow down by the lake.

"You're who you are," Elise said. "You're fine. I mean, we'll make plenty of mistakes. How old are we? Who doesn't? But not all guys are jerks. We'll find some. You'll see."

Lisa felt something strike the back of her shoulder, *an acorn falling from high above*, she thought, *from the tree*, but knowing even then that something was wrong, that whatever it was had struck her too hard and then instantly heard the crack, like someone stepping on a branch in the brush out there in the dark and at first there was no pain, it was only startling, a sound out of sync with the world. But she turned at the sound and at the sudden wet feeling on her shoulder.

And that was when her face exploded.

Her teeth shattered the bullet. Fragments of teeth and

bullet drilled her cheekbone and poured out through her cheek.

Had her neck been turned a quarter of an inch to the right the third bullet would have severed her jugular, would have cracked her larynx a quarter inch to the left. Instead it entered and exited clean and thumped into the tree beside Elise's shoulder.

She screamed, turning, falling to her side on the hard earth and heard the scream come out all wrong, a gurgled cough that sprayed Elise with blood and bits of teeth, sprayed face and neck and chest and ran in a dark thin drool down Lisa's chin. She swallowed, the taste of it rich and sickening, overwhelming.

Had she not fallen, the fourth bullet would have taken her in the spine.

Instead it slammed into Elise's head below the hairline just over her left eye and threw her back against the rough bark of the tree. Blood washed down her forehead and into her eyes, washed into Lisa's own blood spackled across her cheek. Elise shook her head like a wet startled dog and raised her hands to wipe away the blood from her eyes, to clear them and Lisa watched the fifth shot enter her just below the breast. A sudden dark hole in the T-shirt welling blood. A sudden desecration.

Cover, she thought. *Hide!*
The tree was cover.

Elise looked dazed, amazed, like a child whose toy has just fallen from her hands and lies inexplicably broken in front of her, her eyes open wide and blinking against the steady wave of blood. Lisa rolled and stumbled to her feet and took her by the arm and started to drag her. She was aware of someone shouting somewhere in the brush, of the blood nauseating in her mouth, gagging her and of the jagged broken edges of her teeth.

"Elise!" she said. "Get up! Elise!"

Her voice wasn't hers anymore. What came out of her mouth was all but incomprehensible. She grabbed Elise's other arm and pulled with all her strength and Elise slid along with her and then they were on the other side of the tree hidden for a moment from whoever was out there doing this, but she knew they had to run and she knew that Elise *couldn't* run, couldn't even seem to move or stand, she just kept blinking and the blood from her head was all over her, rolling into her eyes and down her neck, soaking the T-shirt, glistening on her jeans in the moonlight.

She had to go find help. She had to go find somebody but she couldn't stand to leave Elise this way, she was afraid Elise was dying on her, that her friend was dying right in front of her but she was also afraid to stay. Because they were still out there.

They'd come finish what they'd started.

They almost had to.

Oh my god, Elise.

She couldn't stay.

They'd both bleed to death if she stayed.

She'd heard them only seconds ago through all her panic. She wasn't imagining. Out there in the dark. Like they were arguing. At least two male voices and a female voice out in the brush.

They'd stopped.

Maybe they got scared, she thought. Maybe they ran away.

If they had so could she.

She had to try.

She reached down and gave Elise's hand a squeeze thinking how small it was and how fragile and then let go of the hand and the letting go was itself a kind of death, a surrender that made her sob aloud in the suddenly quiet forest.

She peered around the tree.

In the glow of the fire the last thing she saw was a

man she vaguely recognized from somewhere sighting down the barrel of a rifle not three feet away.

And her very last thought was *why?*

Ray was a little pissed off.

His shooting was usually better. But after the first shot Tim and Jennifer set up this fucking racket and it unnerved him. So that he had to go in up close after the first five shots and they'd moved around the tree by then and he didn't like that, that was dangerous because who the hell knew what kind of condition they'd be in, whether they'd have enough left in them to try to fight or run or what? But he was lucky. The one still standing had given him a clean clear head shot and he'd taken her out with a single shot to the eye.

The other one, the redhead slumped against the tree wasn't going anywhere.

He was surprised, though. It wasn't like the movies.

People took a lot of killing.

Six shots counting this one. Four for the brunette alone. *Shoulder face neck eye.*

He doubted he'd need a seventh for the redhead.

"What're we going to do, for god's sake?" He was fucking tired of Tim asking him that. If he hadn't felt so basically good at the moment, if the whole thing wasn't so goddamn *cool* he'd have been annoyed. But you had to be patient with Timmy.

"We're gonna bury 'em, Tim. Then we're gonna pack up all their gear and dump it. Nobody'll ever know they were even around here. That sound like a plan to you? Huh?"

"I want to get out of here," Jennifer said. She was standing to one side and wouldn't even look at them, wouldn't even look at the body. *Bodies.* While he could hardly *stop* looking.

"*Bury* 'em? Bury 'em with what?" said Tim. "You see any shovels around?"

"You and Jennifer are going to take the Chevy over to my place. There's a spade and a pitchfork in the storage shed. Nobody's home so don't worry. Meantime I'll tidy up. Get their stuff together. Kill the campfire so it won't attract attention. Gimme your flashlight. Look, here's the keys. This one's to the storage shed. Remember to lock up when you're done. And Tim, you drive. I think Jennifer's a little upset at the moment. And you drive *carefully,* you hear? You keep to the speed limit and take your time. Don't go fucking up on me."

"I won't."

"I want Tim to drop me off at my house."

"No you don't. You just think you do." He went over and hugged her. "Listen, Jen. You're a part of this. *I want you* to be part of this. It's important to me. You've never done anything like this in your whole life and you probably never will again. Me and Tim, we could still get drafted, who knows? And then you never know how many people we'd have to kill. But for you this is a first-and-only. You're gonna remember tonight for-fucking-*ever.*"

"I don't want to remember."

He leaned in close and whispered in her ear.

"You will, Jen, once we're through. I *promise* you."

He cupped her face in his hands and kissed her gently on each eyelid. It almost always worked. It always seemed to soothe her.

"Now you guys get out of here. And be careful."

He watched them walk down the path and disappear into the dark. He didn't worry about them finding their way without the flashlight. They knew the place almost as well as he did. They'd do what they were told and they'd do it quietly and they'd do it right and that would make them accomplices. Accessories to murder, which was exactly what he wanted.

It occurred to him that he had a couple of slaves now.

He checked in on the redhead. Her breathing was shallow. She hadn't moved. You could see her tits through the blood-soaked T-shirt. From the waist up she might as well have been naked the way the shirt was plastered to her body. They were good tits. Small but not half bad.

It would be interesting to see how long she took to die.

He'd shot a rabbit once, blew the hell out of its high-quarters and he'd done that, watched and waited. The rabbit took maybe five, six minutes to die and started twitching at the end like somebody had plugged it into a wall socket.

He took a walk around the campsite. They didn't have a lot of stuff. Probably just here for the night. There was the tent, two new sleeping bags inside along with a second good new battery-operated lantern which he thought he just might keep and a knapsack with nothing but clothes in it, two different sizes, expensive and clean and neatly folded.

Bitches. Lesbo assholes. They never would have given him the time of day.

They wouldn't be able to now.

Just outside the tent there was another knapsack containing a can of *Off* insect spray, a paperback of a book called *One Flew Over the Cuckoo's Nest* and another called *Death in Venice*, a writing pad and pen, an old, beat-up Swiss army knife, paper plates and plastic forks and knives, an unopened pack of Wrigley's Spearmint which he pocketed and a half-full pack of Juicy Fruit which he didn't. They had a cooler with three Pepsis inside and four cans of ginger ale, an open pack of hot dogs wrapped in cellophane and another of burger meat, rolls to go with each, a plastic bottle of mustard and another of catsup, a can of beans and a can of sauerkraut.

Not a goddamn beer anywhere so he popped a Pepsi.

He checked on the redhead. Still breathing. No twitching.

Tough little fucker.

Tougher than the rabbit, anyway.

He didn't want to miss it when she started twitching.

He finished off the Pepsi and put the empty back in the cooler and pulled the sleeping bags out of the tent and rolled them and tied them off, set the lanterns and knapsack aside and struck the tent and threw the wooden pegs into the fire. The fire reminded him that he was hungry. The fire was still going pretty strong so he unwrapped two of the hot dogs and found the same sticks the girls were using and threaded one stick through each of them and shoved the sticks into the spaces between the rocks they'd used to surround the fire so that the hot dogs would hang over it but wouldn't fall in. He unwrapped two rolls for when they were ready and unpacked the bottle of catsup.

Most people liked mustard. He didn't.

He gathered together the tent, cooler, sleeping bag, knapsacks, lanterns and his .22 in a nice neat easy-to-handle pile for when Tim and Jennifer got back and by then he figured the dogs needed turning so he did that and popped another Pepsi.

He checked the redhead.

Still breathing. Hadn't moved. He watched her for a while.

Still no twitching. Nothing. Even with the nice tits the girl was fucking boring.

He ate the hot dogs squirted with plenty of catsup, wishing halfway through the second one that he'd bothered to toast the rolls but figured fuck it and finished off the Pepsi. He was feeling pretty good about what he'd done here and was still doing so he took time to sort of savor it. Then he kicked away the stones around the fire and turned on the flashlight and kicked dirt over the logs and embers until the smoke was just a thin white trickle in the surrounding darkness and both his feet hurt inside the black leather cowboy boots. Then he went to check the girl again.

The girl was gone.

Not *dead* gone. Gone.

Off in the fucking *woods* somewhere.

She was head shot for chrissake! How could she fucking *do* this? How come he hadn't heard her? He felt a rush of pure animal panic until he saw the drops of blood leading off through the woods and realized that she couldn't have been gone long or got far, not in that condition and felt the panic turn to anger then because he realized that the girl had fucked him over royally anyway.

Fucked him over *just by getting away.*

He had to follow her, he had no goddamn choice but to follow her but in the meantime the problem was that what the hell were Tim and Jennifer going to think when they got back and found that both he and the girl had gone? They were due back pretty soon now. They could freeze up. Go bullshit on him. Take the car and just drive the fuck away. He wouldn't put it past them. They were just *high school kids* for chrissake. Without him around to tell them what to do they might easily screw up and leave him alone out here to deal with this all by himself.

His prints were all over everything. They *had* to dump all this stuff. And to dump it they needed the car.

Shit!

You bitch, he thought. *Wait till I get my hands on you. No rifle this time. You'll wish you* had *died.*

All this stuff, my fingerprints over all of it and he thought of all he'd touched and then he thought of the knapsack and the writing pad and pen *inside* the knapsack and realized that he could still tell them what to do even if he wasn't here to tell them so he ran over and tore the thing open and found the pad and pen and wrote STAY PUT! in the biggest letters possible and propped the pad up on the ground with the knapsack in back of it to hold it in place and got the battery-operated lantern and turned it on so that the pad was flooded with light, you couldn't miss the goddamn thing unless you were blind and he picked up the rifle because you never knew, he intended to kick the shit out of her, absolutely, do her with his bare goddamn hands but he might have to down the bitch first again, the smart-ass lesbo cunt and then he started after her.

Part One

"Mary McGrory said to me that we'll never laugh again. And I said, 'Heavens, Mary. We'll laugh again. It's just that we'll never be young again.' "
—Daniel Patrick Moynihan, November 1963

Chapter One

Friday, August 1, 1969
The Cat/Schilling

The cat dodged Charlie Schilling's feet as he made his way across the parking lot to Panik's Bar and Grille. The cat was two years old, amber-eyed and mostly black except for a patch of white to one side of her nose and white paws and another white patch on her belly. She was hungry but then she was mostly hungry and had been for three months now since her owners, two young newlyweds from Hopatcong, had driven her to Sparta and dropped her off on the quiet street behind Paul's Deli and driven away. Their new baby daughter was allergic. The cat didn't know about allergies, only that where once she'd been well-fed and warm and cared for by humans whose presence rather comforted her now she was alone and cold nights and nearly always felt a rumble in her belly. She dodged Schilling's feet because Shilling was a big man and unfamiliar and big men had been known to kick.

* * *

33

Schilling wouldn't have dreamt of kicking her and certainly not today.

He walked into the yellow twilight of the bar and Ed Anderson was just where he'd expected him to be, down at the end of the bar leaning over a Bud and talking to Teddy Panik, who owned the place. It was four-thirty, Happy Hour, and it was Ed's practice to leave no Happy Hour at Panik's Bar and Grille until six o'clock when it was over. Ed called it Going to the Meeting. He'd never attended a business meeting in all his fifty-two years but celebrating that fact was precisely the point.

He walked past Dave Lenhart and Phil Preston and said hi to Billy Altman and Sam Heinz and Walter Earle who interrupted their conversation about who made more money, Willie Shoemaker or Lew Alcindor to say hello back to him and sat down on the stool next to Ed. Teddy poured him his usual Dewar's and soda and both he and Ed knew Charlie well enough to see that something wasn't right, to let him have a while before saying anything. It was Ed who finally asked.

"She died," Charlie said.

"Who?"

"Elise Hanlon. Life support all these years and what was the point. Word came to the station a little after noon."

"Aw hell, Charlie. I'm sorry to hear that."

"You know I went to see her about a month ago and it looked to me like she was *already* dead. Nothing but skin and bones. But she wouldn't let go. Or they wouldn't let her let go. Another one, Teddy."

"Sure."

He stared straight ahead at the faded blowup of Bogie as Sam Spade over the register. Bogie was flanked by Gehrig and Mantle. Behind him over the cigarette machine the neon Miller sign was buzzing again. He thought that Teddy should either fix the damn thing or throw it out. The buzzing was a pain in the ass. But

Teddy was partial to Miller and sold a lot of it. Everybody seemed to want to drink Miller these days, everybody but him and Ed. It called itself the Champagne of Bottled Beers but to him it tasted like panther piss. Weak panther piss at that.

He wasn't going to kick a cat but trashing a neon sign probably would suit his mood exactly. Except he couldn't do that to Teddy. Teddy was hooked on panther piss and they paid him to hang the sign.

"We worked like hell on that one, Charlie. You know we did."

"Yeah, we did. And look where it went. Down the toilet."

"Absolutely true."

"My partner along with it."

"Absolutely *un*true, my friend."

Charlie looked at him. Ed was the most decent, honest guy he'd ever met and he'd never known him to kid himself about anything. Well, maybe about one thing— Sally Richmond. But he thought he was kidding himself about this.

"What are you telling me? That's not the reason you left the department? Come on, Ed. Bullshit."

"I left the department because I was tired. Not because of Elise Hanlon or Lisa Steiner or even Ray Pye."

Pye was the kid they'd tried to nail on it. Except that Pye wouldn't nail.

"We've had this talk before, Charlie. I'll give it to you one more time. I won't say it wasn't a factor. Sure it was a factor. But I put on the uniform ten years earlier than you. Plus I've got *six* years on you age-wise. Let me refresh you, my friend. When I started out in this town you didn't lock your doors, you left 'em open even if you weren't home in case the neighbors *needed* something, pliers or a cup of milk or something and you weren't around to loan it to them. You didn't worry about stealing. Hell, we're lakes district, half the homes in town are closed up all winter. But you didn't worry about break-ins in the wintertime, you worried about the *pipes freezing*. From fifty to fifty-nine we had exactly one homicide. And that was Willie Becker and his wife both drunk as Chinamen slugging it out in the living room, him nailing her with an uppercut he probably never knew he had in him.

"Ten years, fifteen years ago a cop's job in a town like Sparta was mostly helping people, not chasing after punks and bad guys. You made sure the kids got to school all right mornings and stayed there and that the drunks got home to their wives at night. You cleaned up after traffic accidents, fender-benders mostly for godsakes and stood in the street directing traffic during Kiwanis Karnival or heavy weather. You worked with the volunteer fire department and the first-aid department. Sure, there was the occasional assault and battery, the occasional store theft, the occasional vandalism. But, Charlie, we were *helping cats out of gutters*. See what I mean? I didn't sign on for the reason the kids do now, to catch the bad guys. I signed on because it was a good thing to do and a way to do a little good.

"And then the world went and changed on me. Since Kennedy died, maybe a while before, I dunno, things seem all shot to hell."

Ed ordered another beer and Teddy poured it. Teddy was listening in on them but you'd never know it. Not that he was nosy. Teddy just wanted to know what his patrons had on their minds. He wasn't a particularly smart man, but you could count on him to be curious and you could count on him to be discreet.

"I didn't want to be that kind of cop, Charlie. I didn't want to look at Lisa Steiner's shot-dead body four years ago and I didn't want to look at another. Not ever. I know you've seen some since then. That's not for me. I'm not sure it's for you exactly either, you want to know the god's honest truth. But that's your business, old buddy, your call. Teddy's got a good corned beef sandwich with potato salad at two-twenty-five today. Nice and lean. I recommend it highly."

There was a clock on the wall next to Gehrig with a plaque under it saying IRISH TIME, but no clock with the real time. Schilling stared at it without really seeing it. Teddy was Polish but he'd bought the bar from an Irishman and never bothered to change the clock or anything else about the place. He wondered if Teddy knew what time it was in Poland.

"I've got to go talk with the mother."

"No you don't. Why?"

"You know why."

"It was four years ago, Charlie. She stopped calling, what, two-and-a-half years ago? Let it ride."

"It's the least I can do."

"You already did the *most* you could do for chrissake."

"You don't get it."

"Okay, I'm a dope. Tell me what I don't get."

"I don't care anymore, Ed. Most of the time I just don't give a shit. I used to want to nail that Pye kid real bad. I went from that to figuring he'd slip up one of these days and I could wait. I went from that to figuring we'd *never* nail him, not for anything. Not even for a parking ticket and guess what? We didn't. I had a woman couple of nights ago over on Cedar Street, little white house next to the corner. Noise complaint, two in the morning. She's new here and I think there's something going on between her and the neighbors, bad blood or something.

"Anyhow the uniforms go over and she's lying on the floor unconcious, stark naked with her panties pulled over her head. She's been raped so bad she can barely stand. A year ago, two years, it would have made me mad as hell. Now it's like it's the ass end of another real bad day, you know?"

"See? Same kind of blues I got. Only you got it a little later."

"No. You're wrong. You're telling me you quit because the job description changed, you didn't want to chase the bad guys. I'm staying on because I *do* want to chase the bad guys, I always did, but jesus, I need something to shake me."

"They catch this joker?"

"Jokers. Three mean boozers from Dover. One of them's her ex-boyfriend and the other two are his army buddies. She ID'd them right away. And all I'm thinking is, these guys are incredibly stupid. They should have killed her. Now how about that? I'm thinking if they killed her they might have got away with it."

"Shit, Charlie. That's a hell of a thing to say."

"You get no argument from me. That's my point."

Altman, Heinz and Earle had moved on to a loud discussion about who was the better fighter, Joe Louis or Mohammed Ali, who Altman still insisted on calling Cassius Clay. The juke was blaring out a Frankie Valle tune.

It was like the sixties had never happened in Panik's joint.

They had definitely happened to Schilling.

"Pye, the mother and Elise Hanlon were the last ones who really got to me. I want to touch bases with her."

"Phone her up."

"Won't do."

"You're telling me you're gonna drive all the way to Short Hills?"

"Soon as I leave here."

Ed nodded toward the scotch glass.

"You better go easy, then."

"I can drive on three."

"You can drive on five. I was your partner, remember? But I'd just as soon you didn't."

* * *

It was two hours from Sparta to Short Hills, out of the lakes district down through rolling hills to flatlands and once he hit Route 10 he took his time. He could drive on three but two would push him over the Breathalyzer limit and cop or not it would not be a good idea to get himself pulled over down here. Not in Short Hills anyway. The town was about as prosperous as New Jersey got and despite what most out-of-staters thought that was considerable. Their police were entirely by the book and their chief an irascible old son of a bitch in Schilling's opinion. Besides, it was getting on to dark and his night vision wasn't exactly what it used to be.

Number 245 Old Short Hills Road looked pretty much the same as the last time he'd seen it maybe a year ago. Except that the big black Lincoln wasn't there anymore. The husband, the lawyer, had held on to that and the word was not much else, leaving Barbara Hanlon the big white house on the corner, the three-acre plot behind it and presumably a settlement large enough to cover Elise's medical expenses and for Barbara to go on living in the style to which she'd become accustomed. In place of the Lincoln there was a dark blue Ferrari now. The Ferrari looked lonely on the long wide blacktop and dwarfed by the house.

Barbara Hanlon had told him once that theirs had been a happy marriage and he'd believed her. He guessed that too had taken a bullet in the head four years ago though nobody had been aware of it at the time. Elise had outlived her parents' marriage by just under a year.

The lawyer'd remarried. The wife hadn't.

He parked behind the Ferrari, got out and took the winding walkway up the hill through the carefully tended lawn and shrubbery to the steps, wond ring just why he was here now that in fact he *was* here and what in hell he was going to say to her. He hadn't rehearsed this. During the drive his mind had been mostly a blank, focused only on the road ahead, on the process of getting there. Probably he was defending himself against something. He didn't know. Right now he felt like a toad on a four-lane expressway. Something just might roll him over. He probably should have taken Ed's advice and phoned.

He crunched the last of his peppermint Lifesaver with his front teeth and swallowed it against whiskey breath and climbed the steps and rang the bell.

She took a while coming. He almost rang again. He had time to think that maybe there was nobody home. But the living room lights were on and there was the Ferrari sitting in the driveway.

He needn't have bothered with the Lifesaver. The woman who opened the door was one he almost didn't recognize. The Barbara Hanlon he knew, even in her grief, even in those awful first days and nights at the hospital, had been proud and strong and very nearly beautiful, the length of her chin almost, but not quite, spoiling her elegant patrician features. As the investigation faltered and finally died she would visit the station trying to urge them on, eyes flashing with a fury only barely restrained by her sense of dignity and sheer will. It was always clear she shopped the best stores. Her grooming dotted all the *i*'s and crossed the *t*'s. She struck him as a tough lady and Schilling admired her.

There was nothing tough about her now.

This Barbara Hanlon was a mess.

She'd gained maybe twenty pounds since he saw her last. That was very clear to Schilling because beneath the thin satin robe she was also clearly naked. The robe didn't do much in the way of obscuring the fuller breasts and belly. Her face looked puffy and her makeup smudged. The long brown hair was lank and needed brushing. Her eyes were red and he was betting it wasn't tears that got them that way.

She held both sides of the doorframe for balance. As

drunk as Schilling had ever been in his life and that was
going some. She stunk of gin and cigarette smoke. She
stood in the doorway polluting the Short Hills air.

"Christ," she said. "It's you."

Even the voice had changed. Like she was living with
a permanent head cold now.

"I heard about Elise, Mrs. Hanlon."

"You did."

"I thought I'd come by."

She nodded. Weaved. Everything he'd said so far
sounded lame to him but he had to wonder if she even
noticed.

"I wanted to say I'm sorry."

She stared at him. Empty-eyed and then not. As
though some sort of light upstairs kept blinking on and
off.

"Hon? Who's that?"

The voice was a man's and it was every bit as slurred
as hers was.

They'd been having a little party here.

On the eve of her daughter's death.

He appeared behind her barefoot, wearing wrinkled
slacks and nothing else. He was fastening his belt. He
had a bony chest and thin pale arms and he'd needed a
shave since yesterday.

"Policeman, Eddie. Sparta Police. Come to see us
'bout Elise. Detective Charles Schilling. The gen'lman
who investigated the case. This is Eddie."

"That's awfully nice of you," Eddie said. He reached
out and Schilling shook his hand.

He didn't know what to say. He felt suddenly very
weary. He didn't know whether he was disgusted or sad
or angry with her or exactly what he was. Maybe he
was all those things at once or maybe none of them.

"She died eleven thirty-five this morning. They called
me. Said she passed away."

"I know, Mrs. Hanlon. I'd asked the hospital to phone

41

me at the station if and when, so they had a note on the chart to that effect. I guess I learned a little while after you did."

"I'm a little drunk, y'know?"

"I figure you probably have a right to be."

She started to cry. The man behind her put a hand on her shoulder. The man looked both befuddled and sincere.

"Thing is, I been a little drunk a lot these days. I never did drink much before 'cept maybe a glass of wine but now I do. With Eddie. I met Eddie . . . where did we meet, Eddie?"

"We met at the Standish House, Barb. At the bar there."

"That's right. We met at the bar. Thing is, see, it's not just today. You understand?"

"I understand."

"It's good of you to come by, Officer," Eddie said. He had both hands on her shoulders now. She was quietly sobbing. Her face was red and streaked with tears.

"It's not just 'cause Elise's gone. I wish to hell I could tell you that it was."

"Elise's been gone a long, long time," Eddie said to him. "Y'know?"

There was nothing he could do here. Not for himself and not for them. He knew about drunks. When Lila and the kids had left him he'd taken to starting the morning with a couple shots of vodka and then nipping from his flask all day and passing out at night. The usual sad and stupid story. It was Ed who threw his ass into detox, telling the chief he was visiting a sick brother in Florida. Which turned out to be a poor choice of places to lie about when he returned without so much as a hint of a tan.

"If you need any help with this," he said, "with the drinking I mean, give me a call. Either of you. I know a good place. I've been there myself. Anything I can do, you call me. I'm truly sorry about your daughter, Mrs. Hanlon."

"Me too," she said. "Real sorry."

It should have sounded silly. It didn't.

It sounded like a voice up out of a well.

"Thanks, Officer," Eddie said.

He turned and walked down the steps and heard the door close behind him and thought that he'd probably interrupted them fucking, or drunk as they were, trying to fuck and that it probably wasn't a bad idea on a night like she was having to be fucking or trying to fuck, that it was flesh on flesh at least and that was something. He got in the car and headed back to Sparta and one or two more drinks at Panik's.

His visit hadn't worked. He felt nothing.

Chapter Two

Tim

Tim Bess thought that probably he was in love with Jennifer Fitch but lately, over the last year or so, she kept making it harder for him to *stay* in love with her. It never had stopped him in the past that *she* was crazy about Ray. That was a given. She'd been crazy about Ray for years. And she wasn't alone, Ray being who he was. She was only one of many. But it wasn't her thing with Ray that bothered him.

Stuff was just *happening* to her.

It was only ten past midnight and here she was drunk on beer and stoned on dope already. They were waiting for Ray by the baseball field behind the high school and Ray was forty minutes late as usual but this time Tim was worried. He wasn't going to like seeing Jennifer the way she was. It was going to piss him off. Hell, she had to hold on to the wire backstop to keep from falling. The only time she let go was to reach down for another bottle of Miller. After two beers and a half-dozen tokes

44

of homegrown Tim wasn't exactly stone-cold sober himself but he had it to where he could handle it and Jennifer didn't.

You couldn't even talk to her much lately, she was so loaded half the time. But talking to her was something to do other than bouncing chipped pieces of the fence's concrete base off the pitcher's mound so Tim figured he'd try it anyway.

"You ever wonder what happened to Brian Wilson?"

"Huh?"

He tossed a big chunk of the concrete and saw the dust fly. They'd have to clean up the mound for the game tomorrow. Big chunks of the stuff all over the place.

"*Hello? Earth to Jennifer?* Brian Wilson? The Beach Boys? Ever since *Pet Sounds*, all you get is this hippie-dippie Beatles rip-off shit. *Wouldn't it Be Nice, Sloop John B.* I just don't get it."

Hell, he was talking to himself. She swigged the beer. Despite her grip on the fence she was starting to droop again.

"You better finish that one and then lay off. Ray's gonna be pissed at you."

"Ray couldn't care less."

"He's gonna care if you puke all over his boots."

"Ray doesn't care *what* I do."

"He'll care if you puke."

"I'm not gonna puke."

He tossed another, smaller chunk. It fell short. He had to pry them out now with his fingers. He swatted a mosquito on his neck. In this humidity the little fuckers were everywhere. The palm of his hand came away sticky with his own blood. And probably somebody else's. He hated that. He wiped it on his jeans.

He watched her tilt the bottle up and drink. He had to admit, he still thought she was pretty as hell after all these years, even half in the bag. It was hard for him to figure Ray, who didn't seem all that interested anymore. But Ray had other girls. He had the gift and Tim didn't.

He wondered how much she minded. About Ray having other girls. You could tell she did mind but she'd never say how much. He'd never seen her go after Ray about it, not ever, though there was no way to know what she said to him in private. According to Ray she'd never said a thing but you couldn't tell with Ray. She might have.

There was no way he could ask her. They didn't have that kind of open thing together.

He wished they did and wondered why after all these years they didn't. He wished he could really talk to her about some of the important stuff. About Ray. About minding.

About the other thing.

The girl had died. Word traveled fast in this town, and he guessed it was all over summer school. He and Jennifer had been hanging out in the parking lot after the 3:15 bell waiting for Suzy and Dan and Sheila and whatever other kids would want to score a joint or two and the whole damn lot was buzzing over it.

He still remembered that night four years ago as though it had happened yesterday. Specific events would come back to him at peculiar times. He'd be sipping a cherry Coke at the counter of a soda fountain waiting for Ray and he'd remember pulling up and finding them both gone and finding the note telling them to stay put and he'd remember Jennifer's panic, not knowing what in hell had gone wrong but both he and Jennifer scared to drive away, scared of Ray and just as scared to stick around some dead girl's body. Not knowing what to do, whether to load the tent and all their gear into the car or not and consequently not doing anything, just waiting by the cold remains of the fire.

He'd be walking toward the school with half an

ounce of pot rolled into joints in a plastic Baggie in the front pocket of his jeans and he'd remember the way Ray looked when he returned without her. Somehow she'd made it to the road, stumbled out in front of a car, he said. Ray had crouched in the brush and watched two men load her into the backseat of a Mercury and drive away. He was furious, fucking crazy. And Tim could see that he was scared too.

He'd remember all this in glimpses, blinks in time that would catch him unawares. The panic to load their stuff into the trunk and the long drive west all the way to the Delaware Water Gap so they could dump it. The drive back. Jennifer crying. Ray fidgeting behind the wheel, saying how he should have kept the lantern, dammit, the lantern was brand new and expensive. The long heavy silences.

He avoided silences now.

Like this one.

"So. You thought about it yet?"

" 'Bout what? Brian Wilson?"

"Nah. About what you want to do tonight. Me, I still say Don's."

Don's was a drive-in restaurant just out of town, one of the last drive-ins in the lakes area and, he guessed, one of the last in the state. But they served great chocolate egg creams and it made a good change from the beer. Good burgers too. He watched her finish her bottle and toss it into the grass under the bleachers.

He considered going after it, putting the empty back in the six-pack but decided against it. He'd look like a wuss.

"Doesn't matter what I want to do," she said. "Or what you want to do. It's what Ray wants to do."

"Sure."

"It's true."

"Bullshit. He always asks."

"Yeah. He asks. Then he does whatever he wants to do."

He looked at her. Propped up against the fence, staring up into the moonlight. At least she wasn't reaching for another bottle yet.

"Shit. Whatever," he said.

He stooped and tried to loosen another piece of concrete. The problem he had was that he always bit his fingernails, so the concrete wouldn't come free. He stood and kicked at it with his heel a few times and that did it. He popped it off the pitcher's mound. He was fucking bored to tears. He didn't even feel like drinking. It would just screw him up for later.

For *what* later? What comes later?

Same-old, same-old? He pushed the thought away.

Come on, Ray, he thought. *Could you hurry it up a little, please?*

"Fuck Brian Wilson," she said. "You ever think about Twiggy?"

He grinned and shook his head. Now at least she was talking.

"No. Not lately."

"Know what her real name is? Lesley Hornly. Hornsby. Something like that. No ass, no tits, arms and legs like sticks so they call her Twiggy. Makes millions of dollars and I bet you wouldn't even want to fuck her, would you."

"No." Though there were plenty of times he figured he'd fuck pretty much anything.

"*That's* what I don't get."

"What? The money thing?"

"Yeah. Why's she make all that money? When a guy wouldn't even want to fuck her."

"I guess some guys would."

"Who?"

"I dunno. Some hippie would I guess."

"Not even fucking *hippies* would want to fuck her.

She's got no *tits,* man! Janis Joplin's got tits. Whatser-name, Grace Slick's got tits."

"Yeah, but not big ones like Joplin's."

"She at least looks like a woman for godsakes! What's all this bullshit with Leslie Hornsby?"

"Little girls."

"Huh?"

"Some guys like little girls. They like kids. Look it up in your Funk and Wagnalls."

She didn't laugh. Didn't even smile. Instead she reached down for another beer. *Oh shit.* That killed the first six-pack, four for her and two for him. Good thing they had another. Ray'd be pissed if there wasn't one for him when he arrived.

"Sick," she said. "That's sick."

They saw the headlights in the distance moving down Hanover Road, slowing, the car beginning to turn into the parking lot and he got the six-packs off the ground, the empty tucked under his arm and the full one in his hand and with the other hand he took her arm. He prac-tically had to pry her off the backstop.

"C'mon, Jennifer!"

"It's just Ray."

"Jennifer, you're not stupid. You know the drill. It might not be Ray and it *could* be the Man. Now c'mon!"

They headed for the entrance gate next to the bleach-ers. She was staggering, bumping up against his hip. If they had to run she was going to get caught. But he was the one with the beers. And he could outrun any cop, especially through the woods behind the gym which he knew like the back of his hand. If he had to he'd take the open bottle from her hand and all they could get her for was trespass. Unless she got hostile which nowadays with Jennifer was perfectly possible.

Then it was drunk and disorderly.

The arc of light swept over them. The car pulled up in the middle of the lot.

Ray's Chevy.

And about goddamn time.

He could feel her straighten up beside him and let his hand drop from her arm and looked at her. Her eyes seemed brighter, clearer, less the drunken slits they'd been just a moment ago. Ray's magic working in her. Even her face seemed to have softened in the moonlight.

He wished he could have that effect on somebody. Especially her.

He had to admit it to himself. For him it was still Jennifer.

The car door opened and there was Ray with his strange listing gait coming toward them through the headlights. Ray'd told him once that a couple of mafioso types had shot him in both legs years ago when he was still just a kid, like twelve years *old* or something. He'd been running away from a drug deal gone bad and even shot the way he was he'd still managed to get the hell out of Dodge.

That was the reason he walked funny to this day.

Tim didn't know whether to believe him or not. On the one hand Ray had dealt dope for a long time, both on the street and out of his parents' motel and if you were dealing you could easily run into some pretty rough characters now and then—though the twelve-years-old bit was hard to swallow. There was also the fact that, like Tim, who had a genuine heart murmur, Ray hadn't been drafted. He hadn't passed the physical. On the other hand Ray could definitely exaggerate. He loved turning stuff into drama, loved to scare the shit out of you when he could and loved his bad-ass image.

Tim had considered asking him once if he could see the scars but that would be like saying he didn't believe him.

"You guys been here long?" He was smiling.

"Few minutes." Jennifer shrugged.

"Long enough, Ray."

"Sorry about that, Timmy."

He put his hand on Tim's shoulder and leaned over to give Jennifer a kiss.

"I got hung up over at the motel. Ice machine's out again and the people in 409 are throwing themselves a little party if you know what I mean, couple of babes, so I had to send Willie over to the Seven-Eleven for a bag and you can't leave that fucking desk alone for a minute, y'know? C'mon. I got somebody here I want you to meet."

They walked toward the car and Ray lit a cigarette and so did Tim. They leaned in through the driver's side window and Tim took a breath, inhaled the smoke too fast and right away started coughing like he'd just come down with TB, which made him feel like a total jerk because there in the passenger seat was the most beautiful girl he'd ever laid eyes on unless you counted the movies.

This amazing girl. Smiling at them. Big wide grin.

"Tim, Jennifer, I want you both to meet Katherine. Katherine just moved here from San Francisco. How 'bout that? Her car's got a flat back on Mulwray Road. She was hitching into town and I stopped and thought well hell, we're *going* into town, why don't we just give you a lift."

"Tim thought maybe Don's Drive-in," said Jennifer.

The drive-in was on one side of the lake, town was on the other.

"Nah. We *been* to the drive-in! The drive-in's *for kids!*" He clapped Tim on the shoulder. "We're goin' into *town!* Hit the bars. *Part-eee!*"

Tim wondered if the girl was old enough to drink. She didn't look it. He guessed it didn't matter. Both he and Jennifer were a year short of twenty-one too but in a lot of places Ray had clout or to be exact his dope had clout so it didn't matter. He glanced at Jennifer.

"Whatever," she said.

The light in her eyes was gone again.

He looked at the girl, this amazing girl. And then he looked back at Jennifer.

No surprise.

Chapter Three

Saturday, August 2
Anderson

It was strange and maybe even ridiculous the directions sex could turn a man, he thought. Ever since this thing with Sally started he found himself gardening again, something he hadn't wanted to do with Evelyn while she was alive but did only at her urging because Evelyn was a Brit and the Brits did dearly love their gardens. But now here he was, digging in the dirt just for the hell of it. An ex-cop, six-foot-three and two-hundred pounds, sweating in the sun over a patch of violets by the back porch stoop.

When the cat came by as she usually did around this time, Ed filled the empty water dish with fresh cold water from the outdoor tap and went inside for the Friskies dry he'd bought her the other day and kept for her in the cupboard. The cat was already drinking when he returned. He set the bowl of cat food on the stoop and watched the cat chow down. Friskies was noisy food, all hard little pellets. He enjoyed the crackling sounds and supposed the cat did too. He thought that they probably reminded her of tiny bones breaking, of who she was down deep.

The cat never left a crumb in her bowl and when she was finished she went back to the water, eyes narrowing, concentrating, quick pink tongue darting out maybe three or four times a second. Very efficient animals, cats were. Very well put together. The pebbled tongue that was good for both cleaning and trapping water was only one example. Anderson could respect a cat. He wondered why he didn't just take this one in and get it over with. She'd been coming around for about a week now and he had to admit he didn't mind the company.

Evelyn hadn't wanted animals, said they just kept on dying on her; she kept on outliving them and she hated that. But Evelyn wasn't with him anymore. Evelyn had done six years' time with bone cancer and finally gave in to the inevitable. Gracelessly, as you almost had to with that disease. She died lost in a morphine haze, her rear end covered with bedsores despite the best efforts of Ed and the hospice people. Less than half her fighting weight at the end, hairless and gray as a slug. He'd never loved anyone more and knew he never would again. He loved her much the same way she'd loved her flowers, he thought. As a quiet, pacific force of nature.

And maybe that was why he was out planting again this summer, maybe it was that and not Sally or both. People were complex creatures, walking, talking rag quilts, youthful dreams and hopes and fears and middle-aged indiscretions, aging aches and pains and losses, the whole damn kit and kaboodle, mended here and tattered there. People were pushed and pulled in all sorts of directions and did whatever it was they had to do for balance.

So here he was this summer, down on his knees with

the trowel, patting at the loose earth surrounding the tender shoots *just so*, the way Evelyn had taught him, wiping his hands on his dirty white T-shirt. The cat nosed around awhile and then lost interest, heading out over the lawn to the woods. He watched her black tail disappear waving flaglike into the brush.

He ought to take the cat in. Before she got hurt out there. It was a rough precarious life. The weather could take you. A coon or a dog.

He resisted, though. Maybe he'd simply had it with taking on the responsibility for another life for a while after Evelyn. Any life. Had it with responsibility in general.

This thing with Sally now, that sure wasn't too responsible. He knew that.

Charlie would get on his case about it every now and then and there was no way Ed could get mad or even annoyed at him. Hell, Charlie was right. He was practically old enough to be her grandfather, a year short of fifty to her eighteen. Two years less and you were talking jailbait. But when she was with him he didn't think about that much. Sure, she reminded him in a thousand different ways just how young she was. But most of those ways he relished. He could teach her things. Tell her about the old days. She was a smart young woman and she always listened and she always had a damn good question or two besides.

And she didn't remind him how old *he* was. That was part of it too. Quite the opposite.

He'd look into the mirror mornings and he'd see the slight paunch that persisted despite his daily workout, the extra meat on the strong, wide shoulders, the graying hair. He wasn't blind. But he never did feel his age the way some men did. He'd always had good health. In hospitals he'd never been more than a visitor. Despite the fact that he sometimes drank too much and *always* smoked too much for his own damn good. Either it was genes or so far he'd been just plain lucky.

The smell of her hair, the touch of her skin and he could feel the years peel away. He was halfway back to a kid again.

Middle-age crisis was what Schilling called it. It didn't feel like much of a crisis to him. After all those years of helplessness and sadness and rage dealing with Evie's cancer it felt like a godsend. And he'd resolved not to think too hard on it, not to worry the thing to death. Not even to worry about Sally's mother and father too much, though her father was a man with some clout in Sparta and with a notable public temper. He'd resolved to be happy. Just that. And to hell with the rest.

Speaking of happy.

It was four o'clock. It was time to clean up and head on over to Teddy Panik's place. He was pretty much done here anyway.

He patted the dirt around the last of the violets and sprinkled it with water, picked up their plastic containers and walked across the driveway to the garbage cans and threw them away. After the good clean smell of fresh-turned earth the cans smelled especially foul. Tomorrow morning was pickup. He had to remember to set them out by the curb tonight.

After Sally came by.

There were weeds in the wheelbarrow—he'd dug them up and turned the earth for the violets—so he wheeled that back to the pine trees ridging his property and dumped the weeds behind them. He put the wheelbarrow, trowel, spading fork and sprinkling can back in the garage and slid the door down and locked it. Locking it, he thought about what he'd said to Charlie yesterday about the way the town had changed. He thought it was a goddamn shame. When the Palmers lived next door Al Palmer used to come by regularly to borrow his spade and pitchfork. Never asked, just put them back clean when he was through. It was understood they were his to borrow whenever he wanted.

Now he hardly knew his next-door neighbors. Their names were Patowski, a good-looking couple in their early thirties and they had two young boys, seven or eight and no dogs or cats that he'd ever seen and that was about all he knew about them. They came and went like ghosts, vanishing into the car or appearing out of it with barely a nod or a wave.

He showered and shaved and dressed and by then it was four-thirty. He left his car where it was in the driveway and walked the three blocks over to Teddy's. On the way he saw the cat again, crossing warily over Linden Avenue.

He wondered if Sally liked cats or even animals in general. He suspected she would but they'd never talked about the cat, the cat was still his sentimental little secret so he couldn't be sure. He'd have to ask her. Be a shame if she didn't.

He thought it was a good idea. He really ought to take her in.

Chapter Four

Sunday, August 3
Katherine

He wasn't tall the way she liked god knows and maybe
not as smart as he thought he was and probably a little
crazy. But he was cute and funny in a way and a pretty
good kisser. And she was probably half crazy herself.
Or there were times she absolutely had been. So who
was she to talk?

She sat cross-legged on the bed smoking one of his
outrageous joints, bigger than a filter-tip cigarette and
listening to the Stones' "Jumpin' Jack Flash" on the
radio for about the billionth time and considered the
guy. Was she going to stick around with him for awhile
or look farther? For sure he was eccentric. He didn't
even like the Beatles, for god's sake. Made a whole big
deal about it.

Who didn't like the Beatles? Even her father did.

And that weird walk of his—what was *that* all about?

His hair was long but it was more like the way Elvis

was wearing it these days minus the great big exaggerated sideburns than like anybody truly hip and she suspected that like Elvis, he dyed it. The mole on his cheek was definitely enhanced by eyebrow pencil. And she'd be willing to bet he was using eyeshadow on the lids.

The guy was definitely a little wacko.

She might just give it a shot, though. See where it led. It wasn't the most interesting town in the world, god knows, not after San Francisco, and at least he was different, more like the guys she knew back home than anybody else she'd come across here in Sparta. A character. With the black leather pants and jacket he looked a little bit like a biker. Not the bikers she knew in Frisco or Berkeley. They were the real thing. This guy drove a Chevy. But he drove it fast and hard and his dope was fine and he got her into the bars at night and bought the drinks.

She figured Ray got a guarded *maybe*.

Over the blare of music she heard a knock at the door.

Shit, *her father.*

"Wait a minute, hold on."

She didn't have to worry about the smoke. Her father had a sinus condition so bad that if the house caught fire he'd see the smoke before he smelled it. She just had to ditch the roach. She stubbed it out in the ashtray and put it in her jewelry box along with half a dozen others and put the box back in her top dresser drawer. The drawer had all her bras and panties in it, and she liked the idea of her underwear smelling like dope. Her boyfriend Deke back home liked it too.

She unlocked and opened the door but it wasn't her dad, just Etta, the maid, who could smell the potsmoke perfectly well but could be counted on not to say anything. She'd caught Etta firing up in the basement a month ago while the maid was doing the laundry. So they had themselves a little agreement here.

"Hey, Etta. What's up?"

"Your daddy says he wants to see you."

"Trouble?"

"Don't think so. Why? You been in some?"

She gave Etta one of her *who me?* smiles.

"Where is he? Study?"

"Workshop."

"Ugh."

It was the only place in the house that was dirty. Even if it technically wasn't in the house but beside it in a converted garage. He would never let Etta clean it, just swept it up himself from time to time. Which to Katherine's way of thinking wasn't nearly as often as he should have.

She hated dirt and she hated dirty people.

Like that drunken Jennifer Fitch and Tim Bess. She'd bet her weekly allowance money that neither of them had showered yesterday. They smelled like dope and sour beer. At least Jennifer hadn't hung around for long. Ray drove her home after they left the first bar. By then Katherine was amazed she could even walk. But Tim had stayed for the duration. Mostly just looking at her like she were some sort of exotic animal—though she guessed she was more or less used to that with guys—and playing straight man for Ray. He wasn't even that good a straight man. If she was going to go out with Ray on anything like a regular basis he was going to have to rethink his thing with those two.

Katherine personally showered twice a day. Once in the morning and once before bed at night. Before a date she showered again.

Ray said he did too.

"Okay. Just let me get some shoes on."

She slipped into her new leather sandals and walked down the stairs and the length of the hall through the living room. Etta walked along behind her. The living room was cavernous and practically empty. An overstuffed chair, a sofa, a table her dad had built years ago in California and an end table with an ashtray by the chair. No paintings on the walls, no photos or mementos over the fireplace. Her parents' homes had been that way for as long as she could remember. Her dad was president of the First National Bank of Sparta now and he still lived like a monk. She was used to it but anybody else usually thought it strange. She guessed it was.

But they didn't know the reason. She did.

She opened the screen door to the porch—also unfurnished except for three aluminum beach chairs and a plastic table with a see-through top and one lonely spider plant dangling by a chain from the ceiling—and went down the stairs across the cobbled walk to the shop. The day was warm and smelled of fresh-mown grass.

Her father was at the workbench with his back to her. He had a plank of pinewood in the tail vise and was working its edge with an electric sander, a sound that always reminded her of a huge drunken bee. Dust bloomed off the wood. It covered his hands and forearms and sprinkled his dark curly hair.

"That you, hon?"

Whatever had happened to her father's sinuses in Korea had not effected his hearing. His hearing was amazing.

"Hi, dad."

He turned and grinned at her and turned off the sander and released the paper clamps on both sides of it, tossed the used sandpaper on the concrete floor in front of him and inserted a fresh piece cut to size. Then he put the sander on the workbench and brushed down his hands and forearms and the front of his T-shirt. He still was covered with the stuff.

"I won't ask you for a hug."

"You better not."

"Got a minute?"

"Sure. I guess."

"Let's go out to the porch. I could use a glass of lemonade."

She followed him back.

"Etta?"

"Uh-huh?"

She was in the kitchen. Katherine could hear her turn off the water in the sink.

"Could you bring us out some lemonade?"

"Sure can. Be right out."

They sat and her father sighed. He brushed off his slacks. The muscles jumped in his forearms. He was a big man and his body was tight and toned as a teenager's despite the desk job. It was the workshop that kept him fit. He was always building things and giving them away. Half the people they knew back in San Francisco had a table or chair of his and some had two or three. He was a perfectionist so he kept almost none of what he finished. One table, one end table and the desk in his study and a chair. That was it.

"Next weekend," he said, "I'm flying back to see your mom. Want to come?"

"No."

"You sure?"

"Why would I want to do that?"

"She's your mom, Kath. It'd only be the weekend but I thought we could look up a few friends too. As long as we're out there. You could go see Deke."

"You don't like Deke."

"I don't have to like him anymore. He's there, we're here. I guess you could say absence makes the heart grow fonder."

"Very funny, dad."

Etta arrived with two tall glasses of lemonade. She put coasters in front of them and served them off the tray. Etta made lemonade from scratch, grating the rind down fine and mixing it with sugar and a half cup of water, stirring it into a paste and letting it sit overnight in the refrigerator before combining it with more water and the juice the following morning. It was tart and sweet and aromatic. Over ice on a hot summer day there was nothing better.

"Enjoy," she said and disappeared back into the kitchen.

Katherine sipped her drink. "You go, dad," she said. "I'm not interested."

"The thing is, Dr. Greenberg says she's gotten a lot worse. That she's almost completely nonverbal now. Says all she does is watch TV in the dayroom. She's not eating right either. That's why he's asked me to come on out. He thinks maybe it might help. Pull her back some. Might help her to see you too."

"It's not gonna help, dad."

"We can't know if we don't try."

The last thing in the world she wanted to do was fly to California to visit her ghost of a mother in the funny farm, and they both knew that seeing Deke was just a carrot. Though if her mother had really gone wholly nonverbal, it must at least have cut down on the rages. But she'd mostly stopped thinking of her mother *as* her mother years ago. She'd gone from *mom* to *that screaming crazy bitch* to pretty much *zero*.

Where once her mother was a fire inside her now she was barely embers.

There were times she was furious with her father for relocating them to this nowhere town, times she absolutely *longed* for San Francisco because San Francisco was a happening town and this was not, this was just hills and lakes and long winding roads. There was no Fillmore here, there was no Telegraph like there was in Berkeley, no music scene and hardly any dope scene but going back for a weekend wasn't going to cut it with her, wasn't going to make up for anything. Especially if it involved her mother.

She shook her head. "Sorry, dad. No way."

"Is it the place or is it her, Kath?"

"I guess it's both."

"It's a nice place."

"It's all *dressed up* like a nice place. It's still a place where everybody inside is crazy."

Her father sighed again and sipped his lemonade. There was no denying the truth of what she said and he knew it. He wasn't the sort of man who would argue with her just to get his way.

"You'll be all right alone here?"

"Sure. Etta'll be around."

Etta would be around during the *days*. The nights she'd have to herself and that was fine. It presented possibilities. They had only been in town since the end of the school year, a little over a month and she didn't know much of anybody. But there was Ray now for one. And the best way to get acquainted with somebody, she thought, was to dive right in.

"Well, I guess what I'll do is book a flight for Friday after work, come back some time Sunday night. Sound all right?"

"Uh-huh."

"You sure you won't come along with me, Kath?"

"I'm sure."

They finished their lemonade and her father went back to his shop and she climbed the stairs to her bedroom. The shop, she thought, was part of the way he dealt with things.

Dirty or not, the shop was good for him.

She found the number Ray'd given her in her wallet and lay down on the bed and dialed.

"Bates Motel."

"Huh?"

"Did I say Bates? I meant Starlight. Is this who I think it is?"

"You always answer your phone that way?"

"I gave you my private number. On the other line I do it straight."

"Oh."

"This is great! You called me!"

"You're surprised?"

"Yes and no."

"Which yes and which no?"

"Hmmm. Well, now you got me in a kind of a position here."

"How's that?"

"Well, anything I say is going to make me look sort of egotistical."

"Which is to say you're not egotistical."

"Let's just say I was hoping you'd call because you wouldn't give me *your* number. And then I would have had to find it out myself."

"You wouldn't have found it. It's unlisted."

"I'd have found it. Vee haff *ways*. Or else maybe I'd have had to stake out your house for a couple of days, accost you on the street, you know, that kind of thing."

"I don't know if I'd have liked that."

"Doesn't that sort of depend on how I did the accosting? Like with a dozen long-stem roses maybe, a bottle of champagne, couple of tickets to Paris?"

"It might make a difference."

He was making her smile and that was good because now she felt more secure about what she was going to suggest to him. It was treachery. But only *small* treachery. Her father'd never know.

"You busy Friday night, Ray?"

"Hold on, let me check my calender. Let's see, Monday night, nope. Tuesday night, busy. Wednesday night, unh-unh, busy again. Thursday night, nope. Friday night—I'll be damned. It's free."

"Clown."

"Joker. There's a difference."

"Pick me up at eight."

"Are you gonna tell me what you have in mind?"

"I don't think so. And do me a favor?"

"What."

"Make it a solo appearance. No little groupies, please."

"You mean Tim and Jennifer?"

"Yes."

"Who are Tim and Jennifer?"

"Good. See you then."

"Not before? Friday's a long way away."

"Your schedule wouldn't permit it."

She hung up feeling pleased with herself. She *did* like the guy, quirky as he might be. Quirky as he definitely *was*. And it was good to be skipping lightly over the rules again.

Since moving she'd been such a *good* girl.

She didn't really think it suited her.

Chapter Five

Ray

Perfect timing, he thought. He no sooner got off the phone with her than Jennifer came padding out of the bathroom. A couple seconds earlier, he'd have had to have used a little finesse talking with Katherine on the other end. Not necessary. Jennifer was wrapped in a white motel bath towel. As usual she didn't look as good to him after a fuck as she had before one. But it was like that with most of them anyway.

He went to the refrigerator, opened it and popped a beer.

"Who was that?"

"Huh?"

"Heard you talking."

"My goddamn mother. Just some scheduling thing we're having at the front desk. What else is new."

She pulled off the towel and began to dry her hair. Her hair was long and she would always bend over and towel dry it in front of her. He wished she'd do it in private but she never did. There was a crease in her belly when she bent over like that that hadn't been there a year ago and that he didn't like to see.

He pushed some Batman comics off the Naugahyde chair and sat down in front of the TV set and turned it on. He reached over and skimmed the channels. There was some kind of news summary on NBC. Lindsay was bickering with Rockefeller over municipal funding. Pope Paul VI was celebrating a mass in Uganda. Nixon was winding up his tour of Asia. Who could possibly give a flying shit?

About the only remotely interesting story was that some court had denied an inquest into the carwreck out at Martha's Vineyard, the one where that girl got her ass drowned after partying too hearty all night with that ugly fuck Teddy Kennedy. He wondered if Kennedy had been fucking her. It sounded that way. The thought of Teddy Kennedy fucking *anything* was revolting. Guy looked like a chipmunk. He turned the dial. There was a Bowery Boys movie and *Way Out West* with Laurel & Hardy but he'd already seen them. There was a Mets game being broadcast from Montreal. Baseball bored him to tears. He decided on the Bowery Boys. You couldn't hate Huntz Hall.

The phone rang again and this time it really *was* his mother.

"I want you over in nineteen. Now."

"Why? What's the problem?"

"Carla says the toilet's backed up. Says it's all the hell over the place."

Carla was one of the part-time maids. Eighteen, with a cute little ass on her. He'd already fucked her twice and one of these days he just might fuck her again. He decided to throw her butt out of the unit before he got down to work. Toilets were gross and he'd have to be digging around in there. He didn't want her watching.

Spoil the image.

"Great," he said.

"Hurry up and get over there before it ruins the rug." His mother's voice was harsh with too many Kents over too many years.

"All right. I got to get dressed, though."

"I don't care if you run over in your goddamn birth-day suit, Raymond. Just do it. Quick."

He wished his father were around. If his father were around it would fall to him to plumb out some guy's latest healthy turd. But as usual on Sundays his father was down at the Sparta Lanes bowling with the boys. His father was in a league. He bowled every Sunday. His mother allowed him that much, anyway.

Bowling, for god's sake. How lame.

He cradled the phone and pulled on his jeans and a denim workshirt and slipped his feet into a second pair of socks and then pulled them into his boots. The extra pair of socks were necessary to cushion and protect his feet from the crushed beer cans and newspapers stuffed into the bottoms which, combined with the two-inch-high heels, gave him the four more inches in height than his actual five-three.

He never took the boots off until he was in bed with a chick and never got out of bed until they were on again. So none of them ever caught on. Jennifer was the only exception to that but Jennifer could give a damn and knew well enough to keep that particular piece of information all to herself. She was not even about to tell Tim about it and she and Tim were pretty tight.

She was lying on the bed in her white bra and panties, eating Fritos out of a bag and watching Huntz Hall.

"Your mom *again?*"

"Big fucking emergency in nineteen. Toilet duty. You want to go on over for me?"

"Oh yeah, sure. Swell."

"Like my mother's a goddamn cripple. Like she couldn't go over there herself."

"Hell, Ray. You think of it, why should she? She owns the place. You're the assistant manager. She pays you, gives you this apartment. I wouldn't go plumb out a toilet bowl if I was her either."

She was right of course though he didn't have to like it. His mother paid him pretty well in fact, enough so that with his paycheck along with the dope money his pad looked like something out of *Playboy* only smaller, complete with state-of-the-art Magnavox turntable and speakers, twenty-one-inch TV, a small mahogany wet bar, black satin sheets and a brand-new waterbed.

Originally the room had been a storage space behind the management office, but they'd added sixteen units in '63 and a bigger storage space behind them in order to maintain the whole thing. When Ray agreed to come on as assistant manager his father, who was pretty good with his hands if not for much else in Ray's opinion, had converted the old space into a two-room apartment with cherry-paneled walls and a kitchenette and added the requisite plumbing.

Ray having his own apartment was part of the deal. It got him out of his parents' house up on the hill above the complex. The house that had made him laugh like hell when he saw *Psycho*. He now had a pad you could bring any babe to and feel good about yourself.

When it was clean and tidy. Right now it wasn't too clean and tidy but that was because hell, it was only Jennifer.

"Okay. Be back in a flash. Don't eat all the goddamn Fritos on me."

"I won't."

He meant it. Jennifer was turning soft on him. Slack in the belly, a little puffy in the thighs. She was still a damn good fuck though and she knew that thing he liked which most of his other girls didn't know, not unless they found it out for themselves because he didn't really like to tell them. That thing about slipping a finger or two up his asshole right before he was going to come. It drove him fucking crazy.

But you couldn't just up and tell them.

He got the plunger out from under the sink because who the hell wanted to bother with the storage space just for that and walked out into a blast of warm humid air and crossed the macadam lot around the side of the pool to number nineteen. He glanced over his shoulder and through the plateglass window saw his mother at the front desk registering a middle-aged couple. Their van was parked out front.

Sundays were the only days his mother would consent to sit desk duty. The rest of the time he split with his father and Willie, their old part-timer, supposedly about fifty-fifty but it didn't work out that way because his father had no life. Shit, you could buy Harold Pye with a clap on the back and a smile and a fifth of J&B and he'd gladly handle the overtime.

Inside the unit he found Carla in the bathroom trying to stem the tide, dipping a pan into the filthy water and emptying it into the sink. There were rolled-up towels on the floor by the entranceway. She'd managed to protect the green wall-to-wall carpeting anyway.

"I'll take it from here," he said. "I'll have her call you when I'm through."

"Thanks, Ray."

She was grateful. This kind of job? She damn well should be.

Twenty minutes later he had the water running clear again and a soggy brown Kotex in the sink. Fucking women. Some of these women were fucking *animals*. You posted a sign in every unit telling them not to flush the goddamn things, provided disposable bags but they went and did it anyway. He cleaned and rinsed the plunger in the tub, dried it with a towel and headed out to the manager's office to get Carla for the final cleanup.

His mother was sitting in the swivel chair behind the desk with a pretty young blonde standing in front of her who turned and smiled at him briefly as he walked in. His mother did not smile. She rarely did. On the television behind her they were showing clips from the moon landing. No sound. His mother thought sound intrusive in public places and in bad taste. At home she'd blast the sucker.

"Ray, meet Sally Richmond. Sally, this is my son Ray. He manages the place along with my husband Harold. Sally's coming on in housekeeping tomorrow."

Housekeeping. His mother called them housekeepers. They were maids for chrissake. In some other town they'd all have been black. Sparta had no blacks. Not so far at least. So far the niggers were at bay.

"Hello, Sally. Good to meet you." He extended his hand and she took it. Her grip was surprisingly firm, her hand not nearly as soft as he expected. He exerted just the right amount of pressure and then let it fall away.

"Hello, Mr. Pye."

"If you're going to be on staff here it's Ray, okay?"

"Okay. Ray."

"Nine o'clock, then," his mother said.

"Sure. Nine will be fine."

"Monday, Tuesday, Wednesday. We'll give you three days to start with and then see about extending you."

"Fine. Tomorrow, then. Nice to meet you, Mrs. Pye. Nice to meet you, Ray. Thanks."

"See you tomorrow." He smiled at her and she returned it brightly. It was no more a shy smile than his was. The girl was pretty and knew it and didn't mind somebody appreciating the fact.

She walked past him out into the parking lot and he told his mother about the Kotex in the toilet and that the room was ready for Carla and his mother said she'd page her. And that was the extent of their conversation. When he stepped out of the office again Sally Richmond was just pulling out into traffic in a blue Volkswagon Beetle.

The girl was interesting. Very interesting, he thought. Slim but not fine-boned. Tall too. And pretty. Not as pretty as Katherine Wallace was but that was going some. Long blond hair and big green eyes.

And not shy.

She'd be coming in tomorrow. Tomorrow was Monday and that gave him four days and four nights before his date with Katherine on Friday. He could get rid of Jennifer easily enough whenever he wanted to. He had Jennifer pretty well trained by now. She came and went pretty much on his say-so.

A lot could happen in four days. You never knew.

He crossed the hot macadam to his apartment. He hoped Jennifer would be dressed by now and ready to split. It would be nice to take a long, hot shower, find Tim and maybe Lee and some of the other guys and hang out for a while and smoke a little dope and tell them about Katherine and this new girl Sally and he couldn't do that with Jennifer tagging along.

Fact was, Jennifer was getting to be something of a drag on his action lately. Katherine obviously didn't like her *or* Tim. He wondered what he should do about that, if anything. He didn't know. Keep them separate anyway for now.

Divide and conquer.

It always worked for him.

Chapter Six

Sally

"You know one thing I love about you? Your hair."

"Hair? I don't have hardly any."

"Sure you do. It's fine as baby's hair."

"And there's just about as much of it."

Ed lay on the pillow under her arm. She stroked his head. When he turned toward her she could feel his beard against her breast. The beard was thick and soft, not at all prickly as she'd first expected and she liked the feel of that too.

She stroked his powerful shoulders, his strong arms, the soft smooth lightly freckled skin.

"What time you have to be at work in the morning?"

"Nine."

"I wish you'd told me what you were planning to do and where you were planning to do it. I couldn't forbid you god knows but I sure as hell would have tried to talk you out of it. Harold and Jane, they're all right I guess, though I don't really know the mother too well.

But that goddamn Ray. I dunno, Sally. Were you listening to what I just said? We had the guy prime on a *murder* charge. Charlie and I still think he's guilty as sin. Or at the very least knows who is. You sure I can't get you to rethink this thing?"

"Cut it out, Eddie. You're trying to spook me."

"Damn right I am."

"It's just a job, Ed. I'm not going to marry the guy."

He was making her uncomfortable, though. It was the first she'd known Ed Anderson to make her uncomfortable about *anything*, and certainly not on purpose. She needed the goddamn job. There weren't that many of them open for kids this late in the season. She'd left the last one, the Dairy Queen, because her boss had accused her of stealing from the till. And even though they went through the receipts again and they'd tallied and even though he'd apologized *sort of* she'd never stolen a dime from anybody and wasn't about to work for someone who thought she might be capable of it. The Dairy Queen was a lousy job anyway. On your feet all night long, five to midnight. Though she didn't expect that changing sheets and doing people's dirty laundry would be a whole lot better.

But it was something. And her father had made it clear to her that if she wanted college next year she'd damn well better pull her weight. And she wanted college very much. So she was going to pull her weight. She'd have done it anyway even if she hadn't been accepted at B.U., if for no other reason than to make enough money to get out of town like her older sister Ruthie'd done. There was nothing about Sparta with the exception of Ed to keep her here and she expected to be free of her father and his precious Sparta Realty and all her parents' self-important phony *connections* as soon as humanly possible.

"I committed myself, Ed. I told her I'd be there. Listen, I can handle Ray."

"The best way to handle Ray Pye is to keep the hell away from him."

"I can do that too. It's a motel for godsakes. This time of year there are people all over the place. What's he going to do, attack me in the laundry room in broad daylight? You're a sweet silly man and you're crazy about me, aren't you."

She kissed him and gave him a hug.

"I love you," she said. "I could eat you up."

She reached down under the covers and he *was* up, or well on his way up. Ed was no fifteen-minute man but he was a *half-an-hour* man and she supposed that at his age that was really not half bad at all.

She stroked him. His lips traced the side of her breast.

"You remember the day we met, Eddie?"

"Mmmm-hmmmm. Strawberry shake."

"And you asked for crushed pineapple in it, three spoonsful in the shaker and I thought you were crazy. Then you made me try it and it was delicious. And you got this great big smile on your face and said, *I wouldn't lie to you. Why would I lie?* And you've never ever lied to me since, have you."

"No."

"Then tell me the truth. Are you going to be sad when I leave?"

"Tonight?"

"I mean when I leave. Will you?"

"Yes."

"Are you going to handle that okay?"

"Hell, Sally. I'd never have expected you in the first place. I surely never expected you to stay. You're young and you're too good and too smart for this little town. You've got all sorts of places to go. I'm happy taking you day to day."

"Then you know what?"

She shifted slightly away from him.

"What."

She climbed over and straddled him, sunk him into her slowly and then deep and began to gently rock.

"That's what," she said.

Chapter Seven

Monday, August 4
Tim

Tim crossed the Andover Post Office parking lot, opened the door and stepped into the blast of air conditioning and used his key on the box. The package from Sammy was there just as he'd said it would be along with a handful of junk mail. He took it all out and locked it again and walked out the door into the sun. Simple as that. Sammy worked the mailroom for the First National Bank of Irvington so the hash was packaged like a box of checks, which for a pound of the stuff was the perfect size.

He dumped the junk mail in the basket at the curb and got into the car he'd borrowed from his boss at Center Hardware where his father had his shop. Gene was a pretty nice guy. Gave him an entire hour for lunch which was just what he needed to drive to Andover and back and still stop by his house for a few minutes in order to drop the hash. He put the box in the cluttered glove compartment and drove back to Sparta, careful to obey all the lights and traffic signs and stay within the speed limit.

His father's battered truck was parked in front of the hardware store exactly as he'd thought it would be. His father almost always brown-bagged his lunch and he'd done so today. His mother's old Plymouth was parked in front of the A&P where she worked as cashier. He stopped at the light and went on.

On his lawn the grass needed cutting. The shrubs were looking scraggly and needed watering. The pavement was cracked where the cement met the brick-and-mortar steps and there was a half-piece of brick missing out of the bottom one. You'd have thought his father, who was supposed to be so all-around handy, would have gotten around to both these things long ago.

He used his key in the door and smelled last night's ham and cabbage wafting toward him from the kitchen. He went upstairs to his room, sat down on the bed under the poster of John Lennon in his granny glasses—a photo Ray despised—and opened the package. He had plenty of time. He needed to check the weight. He got the scale out of his dresser and took the two layers of foil off the tarry brown brick of hash and placed the brick on the scale and saw that the weight was fine.

He went to the bathroom and got one of his father's double-edged Gillettes out of the medicine cabinet. This was the part that always got to him, always made him excited, the part that always scared him. Not the pickup and the drive but this. Getting the razor blade. Unwrapping it. Going back to his room.

It was almost sexy.

If Ray knew he'd absolutely shit. It was one thing to cut a dime bag or two out of a pound of grass for his own use. But hash was harder to come by these days and Ray's personal favorite. So hash was another thing entirely.

He sat down on the bed again, set an old dog-eared copy of *National Geographic* on his lap and began to shave the sides of the brick, just the thinnest of cuts on all four sides. Ray would never miss it. He never checked the weight. Either he trusted Tim as much as he said he did or figured that Tim would never dare to cross him.

But he'd been shaving the stuff for months now. What was the point of muling for Ray, doing pickups of both grass and hash, handling the risky stuff, if you couldn't take a bit off the top? His cut of the profits was good but it wasn't near what Ray was getting, it was half that, because Ray had all the connections and he didn't.

He knew that one day Ray might check the weight and he didn't like to think what would happen then. He might get away with saying that his scale was fucked, say that it was Sammy who'd short-weighted them and that the scale hadn't caught it. He *might* get away with that. But then he'd probably have to deal with Sammy. He didn't even know Sammy. Sammy was just a voice on the phone. But it was a mean voice and Ray said that Sammy came from Newark originally and everybody knew that Newark was one tough city.

No matter how you looked at it shaving the hash was dangerous.

And maybe that was why he was doing it in the first place, something strictly for himself that had nothing to do with any considerations for Ray, to strike out on his own for something *he* wanted. Which you couldn't do without getting into some kind of shit, without some risk, without some potential danger. He sure wouldn't admit it to Ray and would hardly admit it to himself except at times like this but he felt like his whole goddamn life was under Ray's thumb sometimes, he had since they were kids. But especially after that night in the woods. He'd felt the tilt in their relationship even then. He'd thought it would go away. That things would tilt back to normal again. They hadn't. It was four long years ago. Far too long for it to still be affecting his life the way it did.

And it wasn't right.

He hadn't done the shooting, Ray had. So how come he felt like *he* was the guilty party while Ray didn't even seem to think about the goddamn thing or mention it unless he needed something from Tim or Jennifer? How come he felt all tied up by this fucking secret to the point where he always seemed willing to do exactly what Ray wanted him to do, went where Ray wanted to go and when he wanted to go there?

He guessed this could count as his own little rebellion.

It was probably about all he could muster.

And Ray was basically pretty good to him, right?

Sure he was.

Fuck it, he thought. *You think too much. Just deal with the hash.*

He smoothed down the edges of the brick with his thumb so they wouldn't look so cut so recently. Wrapped the shavings in one piece of foil and rewrapped the brick with the other. He put both in his drawer behind his sweatshirts. He'd deliver the brick tonight. They were supposed to go to the movies.

He took the razor blade into the bathroom and washed it in the sink, dried it and replaced its paper wrapping and put it back in its box and closed the cabinet. As always it amused him to know his father was going to shave with that blade one of these days and if he knew where the blade had been before he put it to his face he would have gone ballistic.

So that he had a secret from Ray and one from his father too.

These were the kind he liked. Secrets were a kind of power.

Ray always said so.

You owned them.

He went downstairs and locked the door behind him and drove to Center Hardware. By the clock on the wall he was ten minutes late returning from his lunch break. Neither his father nor Gene seemed to care.

Chapter Eight

Schilling

He sat at his desk, worrying the thing like a dog with a knotted rope in his teeth.

He couldn't shake Barbara Hanlon.

Last night trying to sleep he kept seeing her standing drunk and half naked in the doorway with her drinking buddy Eddie. Then he'd picture her four years back. He'd got to thinking how fragile people were. You could kill them with guns or cars or whiskey or just enough despair. A life could turn over in a second or it could grind down over the course of years, so slowly you barely even noticed.

He had to wonder how his own life was doing.

There wasn't a whole lot in it.

The case he was working sure didn't help. This one was as stupid as they got.

Sixty-five-year-old guy by the name of Cooley is having a yard sale. All kinds of junk spread out over the lawn. His neighbor, one Michael Allen Nicholas, thirty-five, comes over and accuses Cooley of selling some of his dead father's stuff. This hammer and that chisel and this lawn chair. They all belonged to his dad and now Cooley's selling them out there in front of the house. Cooley denies it. At which point Nicholas grabs him by the throat, throws him to the ground, grabs a meat cleaver off one of the fold-up card tables and threatens him with it. Then he evidently decides that maybe the cleaver's going just a bit too far so he tosses it away and starts beating up on this guy who's thirty years his senior, starts choking him, until another neighbor, a woman who is more like Nicholas' age but only half his weight, pulls him off, by which time another neighbor has called the police.

He was calling this the *Attention Shoppers* Case.

According to Nicholas, all he did was push Cooley.

According to Cooley's bruised face, bloody lip and swollen black eye and the strangulation marks around his neck, he did slightly more than that.

The truly weird thing was that nobody could find the cleaver. The last thing anybody remembers was Nicholas tossing it over his shoulder in the general direction of the house. Did somebody *steal* the thing while all this was going on?

Where in hell was the cleaver?

It was exactly this kind of detective work that could make you want to go home and pull up the covers and spend the day in bed.

He'd asked Barbara Hanlon to call him if and when she decided she needed help with the drinking but he wasn't holding his breath. He thought there was probably only one real way he could help her anyway and that involved Ray Pye. But as far as the department was concerned Pye had been a dead issue for years now.

Pye had marched into the office one day, every inch the concerned citizen and admitted to being in the campground the afternoon of the murder. Though not, he said, that night. Even admitted to seeing the two girls and talking with them and then, he'd said, he'd moved higher on up the mountain in order to give them some privacy. Which was how he explained the match of the footprints on the packed earth of the campsite to his damn-fool cowboy boots. But there were too many footprints at the site so Schilling didn't buy a short casual visit. Pye had hung around a while. Of that he was sure.

He'd allowed them to search his apartment.

They found no .22 rifle in the apartment and Pye denied ever having owned one. His parents backed him up on that. And they found nothing that might have belonged to Elise Hanlon or Lisa Steiner. Questioning known acquaintances produced nothing though he and Ed had both thought Tim Bess might have known something, that he seemed a little squirrelly. If he did he wasn't saying and with nothing on Pye to go on there was no real way to press him.

They never found the camping gear. Not a scrap. They combed the woods for days. A whole team of cops and helpful citizens.

Pye expressed concern. He was alone that night he said, in bed reading a book, sacking out early after a long day hiking various sections of the campgrounds. He even produced the book, a Louis L'Amour western novel. Schilling doubted Pye was much of a reader but he'd managed to read that one anyway. They practically made him write an essay on the thing.

The bottom line was they couldn't shake him. The guy was good. He and Ed came back to him over and over again for months because basically they had nothing and nobody else until finally the mother complained—the mother, not Pye. Pye stayed even-tempered and cooperative through the whole damn thing. The chief ordered them off and made it clear that the order was final.

End of investigation.

Jack Ketchum

Pye was a punk and a senior-year high-school dropout whose buddies were all kids younger than he was
and who they suspected was dealing dope to those same
kids and other citizens on a pretty regular basis. But
they couldn't get him on that either. Drug busts were
few in Sparta and none of the dope they did confiscate
had been traced to him. They shook him down personally on two occasions in the high-school parking lot and
both times he wasn't carrying. That didn't mean it
wasn't why he was hanging out there. The fact that he
held down a job at his parents' motel didn't mean a
damn thing. The motel was a nothing situation. A bone
his parents were throwing him to keep him off the
streets that was only halfway effective.

Schilling had wondered at the time why the kid
hadn't been drafted. So he called up the local draft
board. Pye was too short, they said. Pye was five feet
three inches tall. Which explained the high-heeled cowboy boots.

The kid was nothing if he wasn't vain.

It occurred to him that they had a new chief these
days. Tom Court had retired a month ago and the new
man, Jackowitz, was an import from Newark PD and
wouldn't know a whole lot about the case except that
it was an unsolved murder, fairly rare in these parts.
But there were plenty of other things more urgently de-
manding his attention. He wouldn't know much about
Pye either. Probably that left him free to take another
crack at the kid if he wanted to just for old times' sake.

He decided he did want to.

He kept visiting Elise's drunken mother in his head.

He wondered if Ray had a .22 rifle lying around these
days. Maybe the kid had relaxed his guard.

At five Schilling filed the Attention Shoppers paperwork
in his drawer, got in his car and drove the four blocks
over to Teddy Panik's.

As he pulled into the parking lot Lenny Bess was just getting out of his pickup. Lenny was a carpenter and restorer who rented a shop in the back of Center Hardware from Gene Huff. Lila had used him once to repair the legs on the pie safe they'd inherited from her mother, and he'd done a good job. Lenny saw Schilling's car pull in and waved and waited for him at the door.

Schilling greeted him and they shook hands and together they went inside. For a Monday evening the bar was crowded. He saw Ed down at his usual spot at the end. He knew Lenny would hang around up front with his buddies Walter Ursul and Fred Humbolt so he stopped a moment just to be polite.

"How'd you get the stitches, Len?"

It looked like four of them, beginning at the widow's peak and then up into the thin gray hair. Bess smiled.

"Two-by-four fell on me off the goddamn stacks at the yard. You'd think I'd know how to juggle 'em better by now, huh? How's the pie safe holding up?"

"Holding up just fine."

It had gone to Arizona with Lila and the kids. He had no idea how it was doing.

"Do me a favor, will you? If you've got any more work for me or if you hear of any, I'd appreciate your giving me a call. Money-wise the whole damn winter was a bitch and I'm still behind."

"Sure. Be happy to. Tim working?"

Bess shrugged.

"I got him something at the hardware store. He works a couple of weeks, doesn't show up for a couple of weeks. Gene's a prince to put up with him. Kids, y'know? What can you do."

"I know. Listen, Lenny, you have a good one."

"You too, Charlie."

You couldn't help but feel bad for the guy. Lenny was a hard worker just trying to get by. Not many folks around here had reason to hire a restorer. Most of the year-round locals could do their own light carpentry. So jobs were always scarce until the summer owners arrived needing this or that repair and Lenny had plenty of competition from younger men even then. His wife held down a checkout job at the market. They needed the cash. The kid did nothing.

The kid hung around with Ray Pye.

He walked down to the end and shook hands with Ed and Teddy across the bar. There wasn't a seat vacant so he stood beside Ed and ordered a Dewar's rocks and Teddy poured one. Ed didn't look real happy. He didn't look drunk—Ed was never drunk—but he didn't look happy.

"What's up, buddy?"

"Ah, just an old ex-cop with a worry."

"So what's the worry?"

"Sally's working at the Starlight. Today was her first day."

He nodded. "Jesus. Ray Pye."

"Right, Ray Pye. I tried to talk her out of it but you know Sally."

He didn't actually. Only what Ed had told him about her. But he did know about kids.

"They all figure they're invincible," he said.

"And we know that they're not."

"You tell her that Pye might be a double murderer?"

"I told her. I think I even managed to scare her a little. But I don't think I scared her near enough. Maybe I should have gone into all the grisly details."

"Maybe you should have."

"Christ, she's just a kid, Charlie."

"You know better than that. We scare kids all the time. Helps 'em think sometimes. You just don't want her to see what you used to do for a living every goddamn day right up close and personal. I don't guess I blame you. You want me to talk to her?"

He looked at him and nodded again and sipped his beer. "Yeah, Charlie, I think I do."

"No problem. In fact it sort of fits in with some other plans of mine."

It took him a moment but Ed got it. "You saying what I think you're saying?"

"Got a new boss, Edward. He hasn't chewed my ass yet. I figure it's time I gave him the chance to."

Chapter Nine

Jennifer and Ray

"I really think this stinks, Ray."

"So? You think it stinks. Okay, fine. I don't fucking *feel* like it, get it? End of subject, all right?"

They were supposed to be seeing Raquel Welch and Jim Brown in *100 Rifles* at the Colony tonight with Tim and Hanna and Phil and now here he was breaking the date. Just because he was pissed that this new girl, this Sally whatever, wouldn't go out with him. Ray was the one who had the car. The Griffiths' was in the shop again and Tim had had some kind of fight with his mother last night so she wouldn't lend theirs to him. If Ray didn't go, none of them went. All Ray wanted to do was drink beer and smoke dope and crank up the music in his apartment. She was getting sick of the Rolling Stones and especially sick of *Their Satanic Majesties Request* and she was tired of hanging around drinking. She was drinking too much these days anyhow.

She grabbed a beer and popped it open.

"She's a Rainbow" was *really* getting on her nerves.

"How come you listen to this psychedelic crap anyway? You hate hippies." She practically had to shout.

"It's the Stones."

"No it's not. The Stones is 'Get Off My Cloud.'"

"That's old Stones."

"It's *good* Stones. This is junk."

"Look, anything the Stones do is fine by me. The Stones are *bad,* man. Just like Elvis is bad and Jerry Lee."

"Elvis? Elvis is a goddamn mama's boy."

He waved her off. "That's all just publicity shit. Like he doesn't smoke or drink. You tell me Elvis doesn't smoke or drink or chase the babes. Come *off it.*"

"What about all those stupid musicals? What about *Girls, Girls, Girls*? Singing to little brats for godsakes."

"Yeah, well. They have kinda de-balled him lately. It's still Elvis."

He was pacing the apartment, beer in one hand and joint in the other, singing along with the music, snatching at a line here and there, swigging the beer, pulling on the joint. She had to admit he had a real good voice. Sounded a little like Jerry Lee. But you couldn't communicate with him when he got like this. He was pretending to be lost in the music, pretending everything was cool. When it wasn't cool. All over some new potential piece of ass.

Why she kept on putting up with him she didn't know.

She loved him, that was why.

Even though he fucked her over constantly.

Like now.

But the fact of the matter was that in the long run it didn't matter *what* she did or didn't do, she was damn well doomed anyway. And doom was the right word for it—she wasn't being melodramatic. Her whole damn *family* was doomed. Heart disease or cancer, one or the other, was going to get all of them sooner or later. Her mother had died of breast cancer when Jennifer was six. Her big brother John had a heart attack at the age of twenty-six. Dropped dead right in the middle of cleaning his customer's windshield. He wasn't even overweight. She was eleven years old. Her father died of lung cancer when she was ten and her older sister Ann had been diagnosed with a brain tumor just last year. The tumor was in remission but Jennifer knew it wouldn't last. It couldn't.

Something very nasty was going to get to her too. It was only a matter of time.

When something like that was waiting around the corner for you she guessed you could pretty much put up with anything.

The foster homes. Ray. Anything.

But this, the way he was acting—it was just so goddamn *boring*.

"Come on. Forget about this Sally person, will you? Let's go out and have a good time. Let me call Tim and Phil and tell them you changed your mind. Come on. Please?"

She was whining. If you could whine and try to shout at the same time, then she was doing it.

She hated herself for the way she sounded.

"Why should I let you call and say I've changed my mind, Jennifer? I *haven't* changed my mind. *Fuck* Jim Brown and *fuck* Raquel Welch. I am not in the mood. Period. It has nothing to do with Sally."

"Oh, no?"

"No."

"Ray, you only get this way when there's something you want and can't have it. Sally whatsername's not it? Then tell me what *is* it."

"Get off my back for chrissake."

She walked over to the stereo and turned it off.

He looked at her like she was crazy. She guessed it *was* a little unusual for her to stand up to him.

"What the fuck do you think you're doing? I'm into that."

"I want to get out of here, Ray. Anywhere. I want to go to the movie. Can we please just go to the movie? I want out of this apartment!"

"You want to get out of the apartment?"

"Yes."

"There's something wrong with the apartment?"

"No."

"What's wrong with the apartment?"

"Nothing. I didn't say there was anything wrong with the apartment."

"Then what the fuck *did* you say?"

"I just . . ."

He drained the bottle of beer and walked over to the sink. She was glad to have the distance between them when he got nasty like this. He stubbed out the joint and placed the roach carefully on the edge of the ashtray.

"What's wrong with the apartment, Jennifer? You don't like the color? You want me to paint it for you, maybe? You don't like the decor? You want me to redecorate?"

"Jesus, Ray. I just . . ."

"I want I want I want."

"What?"

"I want I want I want. You want to get out of the apartment? Then get your fucking ass out of the apartment."

"C'mon, Ray. I just want to see the movie, y'know?"

"Here's the movie, Jen. *I'm* the fucking movie. The movie's *right here!* You get it?"

Then suddenly he was moving, smashing the bottle on the edge of the sink and coming toward her with the broken green neck of the thing held in front of him like

a knife and she backed away from him all the way to
the door, not really thinking he was going to use it on
her but scared of him anyhow, it was absolutely right
to be scared of him when he went into a rage like this
because you couldn't tell what he'd do, it all came on
so fast and furious. He reached into her hair and pulled
her head back to the door and held it there and pressed
the broken bottle sideways to her cheek. She smelled
the dregs of beer inside flat and sour.

Her cheek was wet but it was only beer. He hadn't
cut her.

He let go of her hair and dug into his jeans.

She didn't move a muscle. The bottle lay flat against
her cheek.

He took out his keys and handed them to her and
then he lowered the bottle.

"Here. Take the fucking car. Call your little friends.
Get your sorry ass out of here."

"Ray, I . . ."

"You put the slightest nick on that car and you are
screwed, you got that? Screwed."

She nodded. She wanted to say she was sorry. But it
wasn't going to do any good now. It was better just to
shut her mouth and leave. At least she was going to get
to see the movie.

"I, um . . . I need some money."

She hated asking him. She *always* hated asking. But
if you were a girl and a high-school dropout in this town
with no particular skills like typing or anything you
were practically unemployable except in the shittiest
jobs and the ones that were lowest paying. She made a
little selling his dope, a ten percent cut but she at least
should have finished school like Tim.

But after what had happened with those two girls in
the woods that night she couldn't stand to go back to
school. She felt so exposed. Every time some kid even
looked at her in the hall she'd think, *he knows*. Some-

how he found out. Somebody told. She felt as though her soul were showing and it wasn't a good one, it was a very bad one and everybody could see it.

"You need money. Figures," he said.

He dug out his wallet and handed her a twenty. She stuffed it into her jeans.

She swung the door open and looked back at him over her shoulder. He was already in the kitchen at the refrigerator reaching in for another beer. Maybe he'd be passed out cold by the time she got back, asleep in front of the TV. Maybe the booze and pot would mellow him some.

And maybe you shouldn't come back at all, she thought.

Sure. Right.

You need him and he needs you.

And then there's that other thing. That night in the woods.

She couldn't leave him if she wanted to. Not unless *he* left her first.

It was all this new girl's fault. If this Sally Richmond, that was her name, if she had just agreed to go out with him once or twice none of this would have happened. They'd have gone to the movie and had a good time together. She could stand sharing him with other girls, she knew she didn't have that much to offer when you came right down to it and she'd been sharing him for as long as she could remember but when these moods came on that was another thing. She couldn't stand these moods. They seemed to happen more and more lately. She bet this new girl was college-bound, that the motel job was just a stopover, some summer thing. While they were stuck here, her and Ray.

Her sister was no help. Her sister was married with a kid and probably dying and didn't want her. The Griffiths, her foster parents, were nice but they were no help either.

They were all they had together. Her and Ray.

She'd find some way to make it up to him.

She stepped out into the driveway and headed for his car.

No dings, she thought. No fender benders. You have to be very careful.

He lay down on the waterbed. The record was over, but now that Jennifer was gone he didn't mind the silence. He thought about Sally, about their little talk on the second-floor landing.

He'd waited until four o'clock to make his move. Figured, let her settle in, get comfortable. He walked up the steps to 208 where she was changing sheets and waited outside beside the laundry cart. When she came out he was smiling at her. Great big grin.

"Hey, Sally, how's it going?"

"Not bad."

In fact she looked a little beat. The first day on the job they always overworked themselves. If they didn't, you knew they wouldn't last long, wouldn't go the distance. His mother demanded hard work from all the girls.

"Not the most interesting job in the world I guess."

"The interesting jobs are usually taken."

She closed the door and pushed the cart down to 209 and unlocked the door. He followed a few steps behind.

"You got that right. Assistant manager's not exactly thrill-a-minute either. Pays the bills, though, I guess. Gets you a night out now and then. You going to school?"

She nodded. "In the fall."

"New York I bet."

"Boston."

"Boston? Great town."

"Oh? You know Boston?"

"Nah. Just what people tell me. My dad was stationed

there in the navy. Said it was pretty cool, though. Other guys say so too."

This wasn't going all that well. She wasn't warming up to him. He'd yet to get a single smile out of her. Whether she was overworked or not, that bothered him. He waited while she walked inside and stripped the bed and pillowcases and collected the dirty towels and brought them out to the cart.

"I figured I'd just hold on to the job for a year or so. Get myself a nest egg, y'know? Then try out NYU maybe."

"Uh-huh."

"Or Columbia. Columbia art school, I figure. What're you going to major in?"

"Photography. For starters, anyway."

"Really? You're a photographer? That's terrific."

She brought the clean linen in and set it on the chair and proceeded to make the bed. He stayed at the door. He didn't want to go inside. He didn't want to look too forward or anything.

"Listen, maybe you'd photograph me one day. See, every now and then I jam with some friends, y'know? We're getting a band together. So we could use some photos. For promotion, publicity. Think you might want to do that?"

"Actually I just do landscapes."

He laughed. "So do a landscape. Only put *me* in the landscape. Put the band in the landscape. Could be cool, right?"

She tucked in the corners of the sheet, moving swiftly around the room from one side of the bed to the other.

"I'll think about it. Okay?"

And now she did smile, bending, looking up at him. Not much of a smile. But something.

"You know, a whole bunch of us are driving up to the Point tonight, drink a beer, relax, have a look at the sunset. Really terrific sunsets up there. Want to join us all after work?"

She plumped the pillows. "I don't think so."

"C'mon. It'll be fun."

"You're my boss, remember?"

"So? There'll be a bunch of us. No big deal." He laughed. "Besides, my *mother's* the boss. I'm just an employee. Just like you."

"You're the manager, Ray. Sorry. I couldn't do that. But thanks for asking."

She was trying to let him down easy with last comment, he knew. *Thanks for asking*. She wasn't fooling anybody. She was giving him the brush. Fine. Chalk it up to first-day nerves. It pissed him off but he figured that tomorrow was another day. Right now it was time to retreat. As gracefully as possible.

"You're welcome, Sally," he said. He smiled again. "I'll leave you to your work. Just think about the photos, okay? We really, honestly could use them. Have a good day."

Thinking about it now the encounter pissed him off even more. His position as manager usually gave him the upper hand with the new girls. Not the opposite, not like in this case. Here she is, changing dirty sheets for a living and acting like *she's* got the upper hand. Snotty little shit.

He wondered how to work her.

At least Jennifer was out of his hair for a while.

Jim Brown. Fucking spade for chrissake.

He got up and walked into the bathroom and had a good long look at himself in the mirror. The face looking back at him was boyish and handsome, a dark-haired version, he thought, of James Dean. He smiled. The smile in the mirror was bright, the teeth even. He opened the medicine cabinet and took out the eyeshadow, eyebrow pencil and mascara, pancake, blush and lip gloss, closed the cabinet door and began with the pancake and blush. He was good at this. Better than most women in fact. A lot of them looked like clowns or sluts but Ray knew how to make it subtle. Very few people would even notice he was wearing it and his story if they did was that when you played in a band you had to know about things like makeup and hair color, it went with the territory, part of being serious about what you did.

There was something very comforting about applying the makeup and as he worked on the eyes he felt himself relax for the first time that evening. By the time he got to the mole on his cheek, darkening it with eyebrow pencil, he was humming.

He'd find a way to get to her. Miss Sally Richmond.

There were still a few days before his Friday-night date with Katherine. He liked to keep his plate as full as possible.

He was Ray Pye, man! He'd find a way.

He always did.

Chapter Ten

Tuesday, August 5
Schilling

He dialed the Starlight Motel from his desk and when Ray answered Schilling hung up on him. He gathered together the file on Billy Shade, child molester, rapist, in jail over six years now. He took it out to his car, protecting it with his jacket against the light warm misty rain. He drove to the motel, parked, took the photo of Shade out of the file and slipped it into the pocket of his jacket.

What he was about to do wasn't anywhere near kosher and would definitely get him a reprimand if Jackowitz got word of it but he doubted that would happen. Even if it did Schilling figured it was worth it. He wasn't going to get fired over the thing. He got out of the car and crossed the steaming macadam to the office.

Ray looked up at him from behind the desk and his face went totally blank. He'd seen him wear that look before. Plenty of times. Too many times.

"Ray."

"Detective Schilling."

"Not much of a day so far, is it."

He shrugged and closed the accounts book and placed his hands flat on the desk. "We needed some rain."

"We do? Hell, I don't." He smiled. "But maybe you've got a little vegetable garden out back. Tomatoes and cucumbers. Little maryjane on the side, maybe."

Pye smiled back. "You know me better than that, Lieutenant Schilling."

"Yeah, but you know how kids are today. They're all of them into the stuff. Silly of me for even giving it a thought, though. What can I say."

"I'm not exactly a kid, Lieutenant."

"No. That's true. You're not."

He reached into his jacket and pulled out the photo and placed it on the desk.

"Seen this guy?"

Pye frowned and picked up the photo and studied it. Then he put it down.

"No. Never. Why?"

"Very interesting actually. He's wanted for murder over in Hopatcong and naturally we're cooperating. Seems he shot and killed two teenage girls, campers, in the park overlooking the lake. Interesting because we had a shooting a whole lot like that a few years back. Also in a park, up by Turner's Pool. You remember that, right?"

"Of course I do. You and Detective Anderson questioned me about it a few times."

"A few times, yeah."

"And some friends of mine."

"You don't resent that or anything, do you? I mean, I'm hoping there's no hard feelings."

He shrugged. "I walked in. Told you I'd been there. I guess I made myself conspicuous. No hard feelings. You were just doing your job."

"That's right. You got that right exactly."

"That second girl from that night, she just died recently, didn't she? I think I heard that someplace."

You little fuck, he thought. *You cold little piece of shit.*

Schilling slid the picture back across the desk away from Ray and appeared to study it himself a moment.

"Yeah, Ray. She just died. Guy looks a bit like you, don't you think?"

"This guy? Not really."

"Have a look again." He handed it back to him.

He'd chosen Billy Shade precisely because he remembered Shade *did* look a lot like Pye, young and dark and good-looking if you liked them on the sleazy side.

He wondered how Shade was doing in the joint these days. With all those good looks.

"Okay. I guess. A little." His face lit up suddenly like a kid who'd just been handed a brand-new bicycle. "You think maybe he could be the *same* guy? I mean the same guy who shot those girls over here?"

Schilling gave it a beat, staring at Pye straight on and then said, "Anything's possible. But no, Ray. We don't think he's the guy who shot those girls over here. We think that was some other guy. We're actually pretty sure of it."

He reached for the photo and Ray handed it to him. His face had gone blank again. Maybe it could only be animated by lies.

"Can I see your registry for today?"

"Sure."

He pulled it out of the desk drawer and opened it and found the page and turned the book toward Schilling. Schilling ran his finger down the page, pretended to look.

"Who else is on today? Besides you?"

"Two girls on housekeeping. Pool man was in this

102

morning but he's already gone for the day."

"Your father?"

"Not till tonight."

"Okay if I talk to the two on housekeeping?"

"Sure. No problem."

Schilling got out a pad and pencil. "You want to give me their names, Ray."

"Ginny Robertshaw, she'd be on the second floor. First floor's Sally Richmond. She's new, though."

"We'll take the new girl first. Where'd I find her?"

"You want me to show you?"

"Nah. You just hold the fort here, Ray. General location's fine."

"She'd be working the right side of the pool. Ginny will be over on the left side. Sure you don't want me to come along? It's no trouble."

"No thanks, Ray. I'm a detective, remember? I gather information for a living. I find things, people. Sometimes it takes me a while because I'm kind of slow. But usually I find them eventually. You have a nice day, Ray."

He found Sally in the very last unit. Ed Anderson had told him she was lovely and he wasn't kidding. She reminded Schilling of a doe you might surprise in a clearing. Everything about her looked soft and feminine and gentle but you could see raw natural power running beneath it and know there wasn't a spare ounce of fat on her body.

"Sally Richmond?"

He held out his shield. She put down the two rolls of toilet paper and the tiny bars of soap and brushed at a loose strand of hair.

"Yes?"

"I'm Detective Charlie Schilling. A friend of Ed's."

He saw that it was possible for her to blush. But also that she recovered quickly.

"He's mentioned you. Often. My god! This isn't about him, is it?"

The concern in her voice was absolutely genuine. He decided right then and there that he liked her.

"No, Ed's fine. He's a little worried about you, though."

She looked puzzled at first but she was quick.

"You mean about the job. You mean Ray."

"I mean Ray. He come on to you yet?"

She laughed and nodded. "Yesterday. My first day here. Can you believe it?"

"I can believe pretty much anything about Ray Pye. What did Ed tell you about him exactly?"

"That he was a suspect in that murder a few years ago. Your main suspect."

"Two corrections, Sally. First, it's not murder, it's murders. Elise Hanlon died just a few days ago. Second, Ray wasn't our main suspect, he was our *only* suspect. Both of us liked him for it from the get-go. In an interview situation that boy's eyes would go empty as a blue summer sky. I just found out they still can. I'm morally certain he's our guy, Sally. So is Ed. We just couldn't put it on him. And now you're telling me he's come on to you. And I'm wondering if he didn't come on to one of those girls back then and she told him thanks but no thanks, and that's why they're both of them dead now. You see what I'm saying?"

She saw, all right. He knew he'd disturbed her.

But disturbing her was the point.

"I *need* this job, Mr. Schilling."

"No you don't. There are other jobs. Suppose I told you I'd make it my business to try to find you one?"

"At anywhere near the money? I understand what you're telling me and I'm not a fool. I'd probably jump at it."

"Good. In the meantime think about this. Whoever shot Lisa Steiner shot her in the shoulder, in the mouth and directly into her left eye from not three feet away. Elise Hanlon was shot in the head and just below the breast. This was cold-blooded as it gets, Sally. From all I could learn they were a pair of nice young women. No enemies. Nobody *needed* to do this to them. Somebody just felt like it. I don't mean to frighten you but you'd do well to stay as far away from Ray as possible until we get you out of here."

"Okay. Thanks, Mr. Schilling."

"It's Lieutenant Schilling. But to you I guess it's got to be Charlie."

He pulled the photo out of his pocket and held it out to her.

"Ever see this guy around here?"

"No, sorry."

"I didn't think so."

"Looks a little like Ray, though. Sort of."

He grinned and put the photograph away.

"Yeah," he said, "does, doesn't he."

He walked away to find the other girl Ginny. It was all smoke and mirrors just in case Ray was paying attention and to cover the fact that the real reason he was here was Sally. That and to shake Ray's tree a little.

When what he really wanted to do was bulldoze his tree to the ground.

When he was finished going through the motions he went back to the car and slipped the photo in the file and drove on back to the office. He really did wonder how Billy Shade was making out in jail. Because however he was doing, a punk like Pye would probably do just as badly.

Ray, he thought, *don't lose your looks. Hang on to 'em a while.*

Chapter Eleven

Katherine

By noon the gray rainy mist had burned away but the sunlight felt thick with humidity. There was the lake or Alpine Pool. She'd been told there was another bigger pool somewhere up by the State Forest campgrounds but she didn't know the campgrounds yet or how to get to the pool and it was far too hot to go hunting around. The lake would be crowded with tourists and summer people. There would be motorboats and fishermen and kids and radios. Alpine Pool was up in the hills, not much more than a swimming hole really, filthy after a good hard rain but probably fine after a light one like today. The pool was mostly used by the locals. Katherine decided she was a local now, like it or not.

She drove to the ridge off Summit Road which was the nearest you could get to the pool by car and parked the little black Corvette her father had given her for her seventeenth birthday on the gravel shoulder. There were only three other cars there besides her own so she figured she could expect some privacy. She took her blanket, towel and beach bag off the passenger seat and headed down the narrow trail through the woods.

It was cooler in the woods but it was a damp cool and it wasn't long before her skin felt sticky with the breath of all that vegetation. Crossing the wide granite shelf that was open to the sun was better and she might have stopped there on another day and set down her blanket but today she wanted the water. The trail turned rocky and steep. She moved slower, more carefully, aware of her sandals and thought that next time she'd remember to wear tennis shoes instead.

When she reached bottom she knew she'd got it right, taking the pool over the lake. There were only about a dozen to eighteen kids scattered across the wide pebble beach, all of them her age or slightly younger. Not a little kid with a pail or a parent in sight. Only one radio and that was way down the far end where most of them were grouped together. From here she could hear it only faintly. Just four people in the water. The water looked a little silty but not bad at all.

There was just one downer. The single person at the pool who was more than only vaguely familiar to her happened to be Tim Bess.

He was sitting with two other guys about forty feet away. He was wearing yellow boxer trunks and she could see the ridge of spine down his pale skinny back. His shoulders were already burnt and he'd spread them with zinc oxide. He hadn't noticed her yet but he would. On a beach that size it was inevitable.

Live with it, she thought. *Do what you came here to do. Get cool and wet.*

She slipped off the short terry-cloth robe. Her blue bikini would probably have appalled her father but there were girls on the beach wearing less. Skin was in this year.

The water was cold at first because of the rain but

she dove under and dove again and cold turned to refreshing. She stood and pushed back her streaming wet hair and started swimming. She was a good strong swimmer. Her mother in far saner days had taught her how. Crawl, backstroke, sidestroke left, sidestroke right, breaststroke, butterfly. She alternated them three times each going halfway across to the muddy steep bank opposite and back and then dove and swam underwater toward the beach until she was only in up to her waist, and then she surfaced.

When she wiped her eyes she saw Bess and the other two boys roughly five yards away up to their knees in the water and wading. Bess was talking to the kid with curly red hair and hadn't seemed to have noticed her. The other two had, though and the guy with the red hair nodded in her direction so that Tim turned to see who or what he was looking at and that was when he saw her. He waved and smiled.

"Hey, Katherine."

"Hello, Tim."

Her greeting wasn't exactly friendly but it wasn't unfriendly either. It struck just the note she wanted. She dove again. In the opposite direction, giving them a brief view of her butt flashing out of and then back into the water but also telling them that she wished to be left alone, thank you very much. When she surfaced she'd put six more yards between them and she was into deep water. She turned briefly and saw them laughing and splashing at one another near shore and thought, my god, *boys* and began to swim away, the crawl this time, taking the pool lengthwise.

She did this twice until her muscles began to ache and then turned over on her back and headed for shore. Taking her time, stretching out the burn in her muscles with the backstroke. She was nearly to where she knew she could probably stand and wade the rest of the way in when a head popped up to the left of her not three feet away and of course it was Bess, wearing a great big stupid grin and wiping the water from his eyes wiping his runny nose and sputtering.

Gross.

"Hi again," he said.

"Hi."

She was aware that her nipples were erect. Also that he couldn't seem to keep his eyes off them as he paddled along beside her. *What an asshole.* She pushed one more time and got to where she knew she could stand and rolled over facing him. The water was up to her neck and cloudy. He couldn't see much of her nipples anymore. She figured she'd just stay there awhile.

"Where's Ray?" she said. It was really all she could think of to say to him.

"At work."

"Ah. Right. Work."

And that about ran her out of conversation with the guy.

"Look, Tim, I don't mean to be unfriendly or anything but I came down here to be alone for a while, you know? Relax, take a swim, get some sun, do some reading. Know what I mean?"

"Sure. No problem. I'm just hanging out with the guys over there. Just wanted to say hello. Drop by later and I'll introduce you if you want. See you."

He stopped paddling and stood and started splashing his way toward shore.

"Enjoy," he said.

She didn't answer. She waited until he was on the sand and toweling dry and then walked out of the water. She realized that while she was swimming the other two boys had relocated slightly—instead of being forty feet away from her blanket and towel, now it was more like thirty. That was a whole lot closer than she'd have wanted but she was damned if she was moving. She was aware of their eyes on her as she toweled off and settled in on the blanket. She rolled the towel into a ball as a pillow for her head and dug her sunglasses and copy of Anais Nin's *House of Incest* out of her bag and started reading.

The book was too surreal for her tastes but her rule always was, you start a book, you finish it. This one had the virtue of being short at least and Nin wrote about her fiction so much in the *Diaries*—which she far preferred to this stuff—that she'd thought she'd ought to give it a try. Now, though, she was bored with the thing.

She glanced across the beach and saw that Bess was faced in her direction and caught him watching her. *Damn this kid!* He was making her uncomfortable. Which also made her angry. Couldn't a woman just lie on a beach without some dipstick kid gawking at her, wishing he could crawl all over her?

Go get yourself laid *for godsakes.*

His eyes darted away. They'd be back though. She'd bet the farm on it.

Okay, schmuck, she thought. *I'll give you something to gawk at.*

She dug into the bag for the suntan lotion and took off the cap and set it beside her on the blanket. Then she reached around in back of her and unsnapped the clasp to her halter and slid the straps down off her shoulders. It was the first time her breasts had seen the sun this year though not nearly the first time they'd seen the sun. But they were pale and they'd burn quickly without the lotion and besides, she had the feeling that watching her smooth the lotion over them would unravel Bess completely so she did it slowly, taking care not to look at him, *Bess wasn't even there,* feeling the nipples stiffen under her fingers. As in more ways than one, she rubbed it in.

When she was through and her breasts were glistening she lay back on the blanket and closed her eyes.

Shutting him out. Shutting everyone out. Feeling the nipples slowly soften again. She wondered how many women went topless here. It was no big deal in California but it might be here. She wondered if word would get around. She wondered if he'd tell Ray and if he did, what he'd think.

She decided she really didn't give a damn on any of these questions and took the sun.

Chapter Twelve

Schilling

Evenings were the worst times, not the nights.

Nights he could lose himself sitting in front of the television set with a couple of beers and it was fine even to fall asleep that way sitting in his chair, feet up on the hassock. He didn't need the bed.

But evenings like this after leaving Teddy Panik's the sheer goddamn emptiness of his days would wrap around him like a dull soft glove. The glove concealed a fist. One that could hurt him. He made it a rule not to have more than three or four tops at Teddy's bar because more than that and he knew he'd be nothing but a drunk again. They were calling them alcoholics these days but that was bullshit. What they were were drunks. The problem was that three or four wouldn't get him past the glove, that sense of uselessness that had settled over him since Lila took his son Will and daughter Barbara to Arizona to live close to her parents in Mesa.

Will was eleven when that happened and fifteen now. Barbara had just turned seven. It struck him as very interesting that Barbara was Elise Hanlon's mother's name too and he wondered if that had anything to do with the bug up his ass on this one. But he didn't know from psychology and it probably didn't matter anyway one way or another. The bug was there. Sometimes he thought since Elise died it was just about *all* that was there.

Ed Anderson called it obsession but there you went with the psychology again.

He'd been a lousy father, he knew that. A slightly better husband. *Slightly.* There had been so much physical going on between him and Lila that it had the power to smooth out a lot of the rough spots. The sex was wonderful, had been ever since they met in high school. And so was the tenderness. Their sensitivity to each other's touch remained a constant between them no matter why they were doing the touching, whether it was for reassurance or just holding hands or foreplay. The touch. They'd never lost that. Not until the distance between Jersey and Arizona made it impossible to touch.

He remembered seeing her off at the airport. They were wildly early getting there for some reason that neither of them could quite understand but that would eventually become clear to them and the kids had gone on ahead a week before with their grandmother. So they sat for over an hour and a half at a table in the crowded airport bar, Schilling drinking scotch even though that was a good part of what had got them there in the first place and Lila drinking vodka tonics and they couldn't keep their hands off each other. At first it was across the table and then he slid in beside her into the booth and they held one another and kissed and cried and tried to fathom what had happened here, what kind of beast had savaged them and what this meant. How could two people have no future together when they clung so ferociously even at future's end? It made no sense. Even in their final hour and a half as a couple there was a sweetness he would not know again. He was aware of it even then. To deal with that fact, to experience it fully was why they'd arrived so early at the airport. Somehow they'd known they'd need the time.

You could not love like this more than once. It would never happen to either one of them again.

But at least he'd had that much with her. At least they'd had the touch. He was never even in the ballpark with the kids. Probably he wasn't meant to have kids in the first place. His job was his passion and second to that was Lila and third to that was drinking, a product of the first passion probably mixed with plain old genetics he guessed. His parents had had that problem too.

His kids had got the short end.

Will had been difficult from birth and did not get any easier. He talked to Lila and the kids on a weekly basis and it was still true. Will was angry and defiant and running with an equally fuck-you crowd and Lila was worried. Schilling had treated him with very little patience and had always wanted more from him self-discipline-wise than the kid was prepared to give. He loved him but the fact was that Will exasperated him and stirred his anger, and it had always been that way and no matter how he tried to hide it, it always showed.

With Barbara he was a little better. Barbara was a quiet little girl by nature, an early reader who spent more time with her books and toys than with other kids. She'd sit outside by the brook all day with a well-thumbed book and be happy as a clam. The problem was that when Schilling finally got around to admitting it he realized that his daughter really didn't interest him. He was proud of her reading skills and delicate fair good looks—she got that from her mom—but he probably didn't understand young girls enough to wonder much about them or about what was on their minds. She was not the kind of demonstrative child who always wanted to sit on her father's lap or have him tell her a story at bedtime. She didn't ask and he didn't volunteer. So largely he guessed he ignored her. He was ashamed of that, but it didn't stop him knowing it was true.

He'd been a lousy father, a slightly better husband and what he had for his thirteen years of married life was empty hands and memories and a woman who had once been his lover who was now his friend and a heart that rarely even ached anymore. He hadn't had a woman in years. Not since Steiner/Hanlon.

At first after he realized Lila wasn't coming back to him he'd searched out women with a kind of manic fervor like someone dashing around the house scrambling for gauze and bandages after shooting himself in the foot. That had lasted a few months. He couldn't sustain it.

After Lila it was mostly nonsense to him. The touch was gone.

It occurred to him that he was probably still in mourning.

Since then he'd had plenty of offers, bold and subtle. That wasn't the problem. You drink in a bar, unless you're Quasimodo you get offers and maybe you get them even then. He didn't have the energy most of the time even to want a woman much less court one.

Someone once said that in matters of love we never renounce our loved ones. Instead we replace them.

He realized that he didn't want to replace Lila.

So he was stuck with his job, his bar, his television and *the glove,* his long empty evenings like the one facing him. Ferlinghetti had talked about waiting for a rebirth of wonder. Schilling would have settled for a rebirth of practically anything.

He was working on it with this Pye business.

Jack Ketchum

It was really all he could think to do.

He pulled into the driveway and cut the engine and stared at the house, as though trying to figure out who exactly lived there and then he went inside.

Chapter Thirteen

The Cat/Sally

The cat sat perched on the windowsill peering in at the sleeping man and woman on the bed inside.

The man was the one who fed her.

She wished the man would wake and feed her now. Since sundown half an hour ago she had felt that familiar ache in her belly. The ache was insistent and would not let her sleep. All day long the cat had wasted her store of energy chasing birds but she wasn't good at chasing birds and it was possible she never would be. Still the hunger and their chatter in the trees drove her to try.

She placed both front paws on the windowpane, stood on her hind legs and scratched at the glass. The woman inside moved in the dark, coughed, shifted to her side. Encouraged, the cat scratched harder. The woman had never fed her but she lay beside the man who did. The woman shifted again and then lay still and the cat sensed she was deep asleep now as the man was.

She leapt from the windowsill to the branch of the tree, dug in with her back claws and placed her front paws down along the tree trunk, dug in with those claws too and inched herself forward until she felt secure she could safely make the drop, let go and fell through the thick humid air to the dewy grass and began moving slowly, watching for movement, for something smaller than herself of which she could make a meal, stalking in the twilight.

Sally registered the sounds at the window and dreamt she was in school only ten years younger, just a little girl. Sitting at her desk watching a teacher she didn't know and had never known, a small mousy woman writing on the blackboard. The class was quiet and well-behaved. She turned to her left and saw Jack Wolff and Larry Pierce sitting with their hands politely folded on their desks in front of them which in life they had never done. In life Jack and Larry were a pair of cutups. Class clowns. She felt disoriented, as though she didn't belong there and sad too because her parents had simply left her in this room, just dumped her here and she knew in her heart that she was stranded, that they weren't coming back.

The mousy little teacher had her back to the class and was still writing. Long loopy letters in an elegant hand but which, because she kept on moving back and forth in front of them, Sally couldn't read. Cindy Wildman, the prettiest girl in the school, sat to her left. Sally looked over at Cindy and tried to smile in a friendly way, but her heart wasn't in it. She felt close to tears. Cindy leaned over and whispered, *it doesn't matter, she'll be gone before you know it,* which made no sense to her but scared her somehow because if the teacher was gone then who was left to help her? And then the teacher turned away from the letters on the blackboard, standing to one side of the letters and facing the class and smiled and Sally could read the words that said *put me in the landscape* over and over and then she did start to cry because she knew that the words were meant to frighten her and as soon as she did she felt a hand on her shoulder, someone standing behind her and she turned and it was Ed. He was smiling and he gave her shoulder a tiny squeeze. *You take it easy,* he said. *You'll be fine.*

The dream twisted and folded into another dream, this one she felt of little consequence. She was in a garden sorting through a bale of apples picking out the good ones and slept quietly from then on until the clock inside her did what it always did, said it was getting late, it was a weeknight and her parents would wonder, it was time to go. She woke and dressed in the moonlit dark and Ed continued to sleep. Before she left she kissed him on the forehead, very softly so as not to awaken him.

She remembered neither dream at all.

Chapter Fourteen

Wednesday, August 6
Anderson

He was thinking about Steiner/Hanlon. Thinking that if Charlie couldn't leave it alone after all these years then neither could he exactly, though he wasn't going to tell Charlie that. Wondering if there was anything they'd overlooked back then, sorting it through, thinking how Charlie and he were somehow still linked at the hip in so many ways, all this was going through his mind when he pulled in and parked the pickup outside Kaltsas' Drugstore.

So he didn't see Bill Richmond's big white Caddy at the curb two cars down. Not until he was halfway up the stairs and by then he was committed. He wouldn't necessarily have avoided either Bill or June but he might have wanted to prepare himself somehow. Though how he might have done that he didn't know.

He stepped inside and thought that Dean was over-doing it with the air-conditioning. The place felt only slightly warmer than a meat locker. He could see Bill Richmond down at the far end by the pharmaceuticals counter talking to Dean and putting his wallet back in his jacket pocket. Dean was in his hospital whites as was his habit. Bill had on a slick tan suit that, cost-wise was probably the equivalent of Ed's entire wardrobe less the L. L. Bean hunting boots kept oiled and polished in his closet.

As he approached the counter Bill turned abruptly and almost walked into him. He laughed.

"Whoops. Sorry, Ed. Hey, how've you been? Haven't seen you in a while."

Aside from Sally he and Bill had only one thing in common and that was that they were both VFW. Though Ed hadn't used the bar or pool table or been to a meeting all year long.

Richmond shifted the small white pharmacy bag from one hand to the other and then extended his right hand and Ed took it. Bill was always one for shaking hands upon meetings or departures. It was like he was running for town councilman and Ed sometimes wondered why he hadn't done that already. It felt strange to touch the father's hand when the daughter's hand knew every inch of him. He thought that it was a good thing he wasn't made for blushing.

"Got a little summer cold, Bill. Hard to get rid of. Otherwise, all's well."

"You too? Sally and June have both got colds. June got hit pretty hard with it. I hope I don't catch the goddamn thing. A day out of work would cost me plenty."

Nice to be reminded you're successful, that you have money. Thanks, Bill.

"I guess it would. Here's hoping. I'll keep my fingers crossed for you."

Bill smiled again. Despite the frigid air he was sweating and Ed thought he could stand to lose some weight. Forget catching a cold. A heart attack would put him out of commission a whole lot longer. Richmond patted him on the shoulder.

"I sure *am* hoping and that's a fact. Listen, Ed, I'm sorry, but I gotta run. You take care now. Dean, take care."

He shook Ed's hand a second time and waved at Dean behind the counter without a backward glance and walked briskly down the aisle. A man with meetings to run, deals to make, a man of importance. Ed thought, *That sure is a damn nice suit.*

And he hasn't got a clue, praise the lord.

He ordered some Dristan and a two-dozen pack of Trojans and took a box of Vicks cough drops off the rack. If Bill had stuck around he would have had to skip the Trojans. Dean didn't smile when he handed them over; Dean never did and Ed was glad of that.

Sally had wanted to go on the Pill a few months back, but Ed didn't trust the Pill for health reasons or an IUD either for that matter, he'd read about them both and he was skeptical. Even if Sally wasn't. Even though she laughed at him. He didn't want to be the cause of harm to her. Some would say that they shouldn't have been doing this in the first place, that he was putting her in harm's way just by being with her, a middle-aged man and a young girl. He half agreed. He knew he was out on a limb here. But Sally had some say in that too as long as he respected her thinking on it and he did. They'd break when the time came and they'd both know when that was. In the meantime he still felt safer sticking with the Trojans.

He stood at the counter and he and Dean talked about retirement awhile because Ed was retired nearly four years now and Dean wasn't, though he wanted to be, he wanted to move to Florida. He even had a town picked out, a place called Punta Gorda which was Spanish for Fat Point. Why anyone would want to retire to a place called Fat Point was beyond him. He pictured a town full of 300 pounders in bermuda shorts and Hawaiian shirts and sunglasses living on a diet of Big Macs, thick shakes and fries. But Dean had visited his brother there and said it was very nice.

He walked out of the store into bright morning sunlight and going down the stairs he glanced across the street. There were still two old houses there that had yet to go commercial sandwiched between a bakery and a woman's clothing shop. One belonged to Harry Dietz, retired chief of the Fire Department and the other to an elderly widow named Betty Knott who'd been Ed's third-grade teacher in a little six-room schoolhouse over on Bound Brook Avenue, now a professional building renting space to an assortment of doctors, dentists and attorneys. Reportedly both Betty and Chief Deitz had been offered a bundle for their property but refused to sell. He knew from Sally that at least one of the offers had come from Bill Richmond.

Betty Knott was sitting on the porch now with her old mongrel dog. Both of them fast and peacefully asleep in the shade, almost comically so, the widow leaning in her rocker with her mouth open wide and the old dog sprawled at her feet. And seeing them there made him smile and then unexpectedly saddened him with a sudden forceful clarity. It was as though he had looked behind the scene on the porch across the street into some terrible scene in the future. Because they each were all the other had in the world by way of comfort and it was possible for him to understand in that moment the cruel eventuality that was blooming there. They were both so damn *old.* He sensed a sort of fate about them and sensed too that it would descend upon them soon, that soon either the woman would lose the dog or the dog would lose the woman and they had been together since the dog was just a pup. When death came to one the other would be left alone, no familiar hand to pat the dog or cool wet nose to nuzzle the hand,

and there would be no consoling either dog or woman, something fragile lost forever in some awful rending.

He looked away and wondered why this thought had come to him. If it was because of Steiner/Hanlon and Schilling or if perhaps it was his wife Evelyn he was missing or maybe even Sally, missing her already. Looking down the road. But whatever the reason he couldn't let go of it, not getting into the pickup and starting the engine nor driving away down the sunny, familiar streets. He felt fragile himself and strangely close to tears, and that happened to him only very rarely.

He had hoped to escape the sight of death by taking early retirement from the department but death had found him on a sick bed with Evelyn as easily as it had found him with Steiner/Hanlon and now in a quieter way death had found him here.

Death was everywhere.

It was only hiding.

Chapter Fifteen

Sally

The girl behind the counter was a familiar face, a freshman or maybe a sophomore at Sparta High but Sally didn't know her. The two- or three-year gap in their ages was still unbreachably wide. She must have been new working in the place, though. Slightly overweight, a pretty redhead, the zits on her chin marring what was otherwise very nice clear skin. The girl smiled and asked would there be anything else right now and put the ham on rye with mayo, lettuce and tomato and the glass of ice tea down on the counter in front of her. Looking at Sally as though she recognized her too. Sally said that was fine, thanks, and the girl smiled again and moved away.

She was actually a little jealous of the girl. If she'd known that there was an opening here she'd have grabbed it in a minute.

At lunchtime you could count on the Sugar Bowl to be jammed and today was no exception. People eating standing two deep behind those seated at the counter. You were expected to share enough of your space so that somebody else's cold drink or coffee mug could rest a little to the left or to the right of you. Takeout business was brisk.

The food was good. And cheap. Homemade soups, stews, cakes and pies, fresh breads and pastries from Manger's bakery and cold cuts from Paul's Deli both right across the street. The big wide grill sizzled in plain sight so that if the short-order cook fouled up your order, broke an egg yolk that was supposed to be over easy you knew it right away. But the short-order cook was also the owner Mr. Fahner and he practically never did. She could smell eggs frying and ham and bacon and burgers and pea soup on the burner and steaming hot coffee. The mingled scents always pleased her.

She'd asked Mrs. Pye if she could take her lunch break at one-thirty instead of noon because she liked to eat in this place and the main crunch at the counter was between eleven and one. By now things were beginning to slow down a little so that with some luck it was possible to get a seat without waiting. She liked the easy mom-and-pop feel of the place. She'd been coming in for a soda or a dish of ice cream with her parents ever since she was a child, then alone or with friends all through high school. Mr. and Mrs. Fahner had always called her by her first name and over the past two years, since she was a junior, had insisted on her calling them Pat and Winnie.

If you ordered a milk shake or a malted you drank off the glass and they poured you what was left in the shaker. If you were a regular you were apt to get a third scoop on your two-scoop sundae.

She wondered if the place would change by the time she got out of college. So much was happening in the world beyond Sparta. Race riots. Flower power. Vietnam. Pot and Timothy Leary. A luncheonette-slash-soda-fountain, even as busy as this one was, was practically an anachronism now. It almost had to be. How could the simple pleasures of a milk shake stand up to a hit of acid? She wondered if the kids who were freshmen now would still want to sit around over a couple of cherry Cokes all night—or at least till the place closed at ten—hanging out together the way she'd done with her own friends, passing the local gossip, falling in and out of love with one another, reading comics and magazines off the rack and spinning around on the revolving stools like they were rides in an amusement park. She suspected she could guess the answer. It was too bad, she thought. They'd be missing out on a lot of fun. And something she felt a lot of affection for would have disappeared.

She'd finished half her sandwich, aware that the din had lessened considerably, when someone slid onto the open stool beside her, and she glanced over and there was Ray Pye.

Great, she thought. Just great.

He was smiling at her, one eyebrow cocked at her as though he were Errol Flynn in that movie *Robin Hood*. The grin was borrowed from somebody too. *I don't know if he kills people like Ed says,* she thought, *but this guy sure does give me the creeps.* He had a slim hardcover book in his hand roughly the size of a paperback and put it facedown on the counter.

Ray reads? I doubt it.

"Hi," he said. "So you like this place too, huh?"

She'd never once seen him in the Sugar Bowl in all these years. It was a small place in a small town and every face here was familiar. Was she supposed to figure this was just a coincidence? He was lying through his teeth.

She nodded and took another bite of her sandwich. The urge to just finish it and get the hell out of there was strong, forget the ice tea. She remembered what

Charlie Schilling had told her. *Shoulder, face and left eye from not three feet away. Head and chest, just below her breast.* The thought made her shudder. *Somebody* had done it. Why not him? You didn't expect the world to thrust a murderer into your face. But unless you were a child or a fool you knew it happened.

"Man, I really love the food here."

She didn't answer.

"I'm glad I ran into you, you know? I'm throwing a little party tonight. Whole bunch of people. Food, drinks, music. All the latest sounds. You ought to come. Really. You'll have a great time."

"Sorry. I already made plans."

"Change 'em."

"Sorry. I can't."

"You sure? I'm telling you, it's gonna be fun. By the way, you look great without the uniform."

"As I say, I've got plans."

"That's too bad."

She was very aware of him looking at her.

"Well, maybe some other time then."

The red-haired waitress came over and she was grinning.

"Hey, Ray."

"Hey, Dee Dee. Good to see you." Turning all the fake charm on Dee Dee now like a spotlight. The girl was actually blushing in its glow.

Wait a minute. He *knows* her, Sally thought. Not from here certainly because the girl was new and he was no regular anyway. *No. He knows her from somewhere else. Plus the girl's got an obvious crush on him. Ray's somewhere in his twenties, right? A grown man. She can't be more than sixteen. Jailbait.*

What a guy.

"What can I get for you?"

"How about a Coke and a burger, medium."

"Sure. Fries?"

128

"Hold the fries, Dee Dee. Got to watch my figure."

"Nah, Ray. Not you."

She almost laughed. Now he's *flirting* with her! Oblivious to any impact it might have on Sally sitting right beside him with whom he had *just been* flirting. It was as though it was some sort of compulsion with him. He couldn't *not* flirt. Dee Dee smiled and turned to call the order. Sally finished her sandwich and went to work on the ice tea. She wasn't going to run off because of this guy but she wasn't going to stick around any longer than necessary either.

"Ever read this?" he said.

The spotlight was back to Sally again. The cocked eybrow. The grin.

He turned over the book.

The Prophet by Kahlil Gibran.

And she came *this* close to snorting a mouthful of tea out of her nose. What she did do was laugh out loud. This time she couldn't help it.

"You're kidding."

"It's a great book. I've read it half a dozen times." The smile had faltered when she laughed but there it was again, all 2000 watts of it. *Six times?* He was trying to bullshit her again. The book was brand new. If he'd read it half a dozen times then he'd read some other copy. The jacket was immaculate.

So she'd caught him in two lies. The Sugar Bowl and now the book.

Just to be sure she took it from him and cracked it open. Binding intact. She sighed and picked a passage at random and read aloud.

" *'Work is love made visible. And if you cannot work with love but only with distaste, it is better that you should leave your work and sit at the gate of the temple and take alms of those who work with joy.'* Jesus. What incredible *crap.*"

She was angry. She knew she shouldn't be. Or at least

shouldn't show it given what everybody seemed to think he was. But she couldn't help that any more than she could help laughing. This unctuous little prick kept insulting her intelligence every which way.

The smile vanished. He kept staring at her like he was waiting for something.

Well, she'd *give* him something, then.

They were in a public place. He wasn't going to harm her.

"You realize what this guy is saying, Ray? That if you don't like your job it's better to be a leech on the rest of society and let somebody else do all the work. Let's only do the jobs that make us happy. Oh sure. Let's have a world without garbage collection, or better yet, of *happy garbage men*. Or how about happy executioners? For that matter happy *beggars*. Anybody over twelve who reads knows that Kahlil Gibran is completely full of shit, Ray. Even the prose stinks. What's next, Rod McKuen?"

She put a five-dollar-bill on the counter, enough for a healthy tip for Dee Dee who at that particular moment was making a point of not watching them and slid off the stool. She realized with a bit of a shock that she was fuming.

Cool it, she thought. *Take it easy for god's sake.*

"Bye," she said.

It was the best she could manage under the circumstances.

She snatched her purse off the floor and walked the length of the counter and out into the parking lot and she was almost to her Volkswagen when he caught her and grabbed her arm and spun her around.

If she'd been mad before she was furious now. He'd actually *touched* her! *How dare he?*

And scared. She had to admit that she was scared too.

"Let go of me, Ray!"

She hated the quiver in her voice.

"You go off on me like that? In *public?* What the hell is wrong with you? Who do you think you are? Look at me."

She refused to. His eyes were scary. She tried to pull away from him but he wouldn't let go so she stopped trying. *All right,* she thought. *You're scared. Probably you have a right to be scared. So what? Go for it anyway. Scared or not, give it to him. The little bastard. The little bully.* There were too damn many of him around.

He'd grow up to be her father, only worse.

Give it to him.

"What the hell's wrong with me? What's wrong with *you,* Ray? You come on to me my first day on the job and I make it clear to you I'm not interested. Then you follow me my *second* day on the job and come to me again with some stupid line about some stupid book you probably don't even know."

"I don't like being insulted in public, Sally."

"Well neither do I. And you following me to a place I've known for years pretending that, gee, it's your favorite place in the world and then throwing these ridiculous moves on me, that's damn insulting. Grabbing my arm is insulting. What you're doing right *now* is insulting. Why don't you go back to your burger and your underage girlfriend and just leave me the hell alone? Tell your mother I won't be coming back after lunch. Tell her I quit. And I wish I could be around to hear whatever idiot lie you use to explain it.

"You see that car? Right there? You see these people pulling in? Let go of me Ray or I swear to you I will start screaming *right now.*"

He glanced at the car and relaxed his grip.

"You little bitch. Fuck you!"

"No, fuck *you,* Ray. Let go!"

He flung her off like her arm had suddenly burst into

flame. And that was all she wanted, that was just fine, so she got into the Volkswagen and turned the key in the ignition and saw him stalk back through the door into the luncheonette. She felt light-headed, trembling with rage and fear and thought it was completely possible she might lose her lunch if she didn't manage to keep on moving.

She put the car into reverse and then into forward. *One step at a time,* she thought. *You're doing fine.* She drove out of the parking lot headed toward home and thought, *Well, that was easily the shortest job of your entire life but to hell with it.* The guy was crazy. Killer or no killer Ed and Charlie had been absolutely right to warn her.

After a while the trembling stopped but she drove home on total autopilot, registering almost nothing, her mind still back in the parking lot working it over. She thought she'd done all right. She'd handled the little bastard and told him what she thought of him and that was that. Before she knew it she was there.

Her mother's Chrysler was in the driveway. She pulled in behind it.

As she opened the door her mother was just coming out of the living room, moving toward the kitchen. She had a glass of what appeared to be sherry in her hand and when she heard Sally shut the door behind her she turned and smiled and Sally saw that her eyes were glassy and sparkling.

It was two in the afternoon.

"Sally! What are you doing home so early?"

She didn't want to deal with her. Not now.

"How was the luncheon?"

A question that was practically guaranteed to divert her.

Her mother wore an elegant tan silk dress belted at the waist. Today it had been a benefit for the American Legion. Tomorrow it might be the NAACP. The next day, who the hell knew? It was all part of being Mrs. William Richmond. What was clear was that she'd already had a few and was not at all opposed to another. It was happening more and more lately. Her mother was well on her way to becoming a full-fledged drunk and her father never even seemed to notice.

The question did its job though.

"Oh, the luncheon was lovely, though the chicken was a little chewy, we thought. Betty Morrison says the chef is new, which doesn't bode well for the future I suppose. By the way, she's throwing a pool party for her daughter Linda next Sunday. Would you like to come? I think it would be nice."

The Morrisons had more money than god, more than even her father and they raised beagles as a hobby. A pool party at their house would be all baying, barking and howling. No thanks.

"I'll think about it. Listen, mother, I've got a splitting headache. I want to lie down for a while, okay?"

Headaches her mother understood.

"Are you all right?"

"I'm fine. Just a headache."

"Take some aspirin, dear."

"I will."

"Take three. Two never works. That's just what they say on the bottle. Take three."

"Okay."

She walked upstairs thinking that it was not surprising at all that her mother had never come back to her original question about why she was home so early. Whether it was the liquor or the self-absorption Sally had managed to head her off at the pass again with the usual ease and speed. The very normalcy of the exchange—her mother asking, Sally evading—had served to calm her.

She sat down on the bed and considered calling Ed but thought it might be a bad idea. Ed might be mad enough to do something that could get them all into trouble. It was better to come up with some other reason for quitting the job when she talked to him, something simple like *Ray just gives me the creeps, that's all* and then ask him to see if Charlie Schilling could try to make good on his promise to find her some other kind of work as soon as possible. For now she decided to let the whole thing rest. Let *herself* rest. Maybe she'd phone him later.

She turned on the reading lamp beside her bed and leaned back and took her copy of *The Magic Mountain* off the bedside table. She looked at the bookmark with satisfaction. She was nearly halfway through. She held it to her nose and smelled the good musty scent of print and paper. She opened it and began to read. She found that it was indeed possible to read, to lose herself, and then she had to laugh.

Kahlil Gibran, she thought.
Jesus.

Chapter Sixteen

Ray

It was time to seriously party.

Screw Sally Richmond.

He set it all up from the desk, no problem. There were interruptions. Three pairs of guests checking in, three families and a couple checking out. His mother all in a huff about Sally, who had disappeared after lunch without so much as a word. Ray faking phone calls to her house to "check up" on her while in fact he was doing no such thing, then locating a temp replacement. In the meantime he dialed his own numbers and assembled his admirers.

Telling Sally he was throwing a party had been nothing more than a spur-of-the-moment inspiration. Now, even though it hadn't worked on her it seemed like a good idea. He needed a lift. Hell, he deserved one.

By five he'd reached pretty much everybody. He'd tried to get Kath in on the thing but she was being sly and mysterious, telling him to wait for the weekend, he should be patient, *it would be worth it.* He thought he heard a distinct promise there and decided that sure, he could do that. The phone call excited him and took the edge off that other shit earlier.

He tried all day to purge Sally Richmond from his mind. You couldn't have everybody, that was what he told himself. She was probably frigid anyway. But it bothered him that she seemed to see through him so easily. So he hadn't read the goddamn book. He'd just heard about it. Heard everybody was reading it in college so he went out and bought a copy. He'd thought it would impress her.

The snotty little bitch.

He was doing just fine without her. The party was going to prove it.

His father relieved him at five-thirty. He decided a little nap would be in order. Nobody was expected till ten so he could catch up on his beauty sleep. He lay down on his bed and set the clock and picked up the day-old edition of the Newark *Star Ledger* folded open to the article about that girl Elise Hanlon finally dropping dead and recapping the four-year-old murder of Lisa Steiner. The article wasn't real long. He read it over and over the same as he had yesterday. It scared him. Also thrilled him.

He was reading about himself again.

What he'd done.

He was practically famous in a sort of way.

Like Jack the Ripper was famous. Nobody knew who he was but they sure knew what he did.

He fell asleep with the paper on his lap. When the alarm woke him at seven-thirty it was getting close to dark.

He wanted a couple hours to get ready.

Chapter Seventeen

Schilling/Ray

It was about quarter after eight when the phone rang. By then Schilling was already into this week's episode of *The Virginian* so he almost didn't answer. But there was a Marlboro commercial on when the phone started ringing and he hated the Marlboro man. Some phony Mad Ave cowpoke with a smoke in his mouth. So he got up to take the call. Turned out he was glad he did.

It was Ed Anderson.

"Listen, Charlie, I just talked to Sally."

"Yeah?"

"She quit the job."

"Good. Good for her."

"Yeah. She said just being around Pye was getting to her. So I guess I got to thank you again for putting the fear of god into her."

"My pleasure."

"You said something about trying to find her work, Charlie?"

"I did, yeah. I forgot to ask her, though, any special skills I should know of?"

"She can type."

"Good again. That makes it easier. You think she'd have any objection to working for the department?"

"I doubt it." He laughed. "She doesn't exactly seem to mind cops."

"No, I guess she doesn't. She'd need to pass the civil service exam."

"She'll pass."

"Okay. I'll ask around tomorrow and see if I can come up with something."

"That'd be great. One other thing. She told me Pye invited her to a party he's throwing tonight."

"Persistent little bastard, isn't he."

"So are you. That's probably the only thing you've got in common. Anyway she told me he said there'd be a lot of people there. Drinks, music. And I got to thinking."

"You did, huh?"

"Yeah."

He knew exactly where Ed was going. And he liked it.

He liked it very much.

"Pye hangs around with a pretty young crowd usually. Might be minors there. Might even be drugs."

"And I know you *do* hate the corruption of minors, Charlie."

"I hate it worse than taxes, Ed. Thanks."

"Don't mention it. You have a good night, now."

"I'm having one already. I'll be in touch."

When he hung up the show was on again so he sat down to see how things were going at Shiloh Ranch. Trampas was in trouble again. What else was new. During the next commercial he got up and got himself a beer from the refrigerator. He figured one wouldn't hurt.

He nursed it until the show was over at nine-thirty, turned off the set and headed for his car.

He drove through the hills to the Starlight Motel and parked across the street and waited. He smoked a few Winstons. Around ten o'clock cars started pulling into the lot, parking around back. He saw kids get out and counted heads as best he could from that distance and when he made it to twenty it was still only ten-thirty. By eleven he'd counted at least thirty. Pye's apartment wasn't very big. At this rate the party would be crowded.

Perfect.

He started the car and drove a few blocks to the all-night diner and ordered a large cup of coffee to go, black, from a sad-eyed girl with frizzy hair, overweight, a mouth-breather, clearly not one of those elect who'd be favored for Ray's party. He drove back and found the same spot vacant so he parked again and smoked some more cigarettes and sipped the coffee. More cars pulled in. Nobody left. He waited until just after midnight and then drove back to the diner and got out of the car.

There was a pay phone just outside the diner and he used that. He dialed the department. He recognized Evanson as the dispatcher but didn't let on, simply filed his noise complaint like any ordinary citizen and when Evanson asked his name, told him that his name was Robert Hall, which went completely over Evanson's head, that he was staying at the motel on the ground floor in Room 2A and that he'd already called the desk but the desk wasn't answering. He was a businessman trying to get some sleep but with all that racket, hell, he couldn't.

When he got back to the motel his space was gone so he parked a half block down and waited. Fifteen minutes later he saw a green-and-white cruiser pull into the motel lot. It paused a moment in front of the office and he saw the uniforms inside take note of Harold Pye sitting at the desk and then move on toward the back. The moving on by was critical. If they chose to just register the complaint with Pye's old man this wasn't going to happen. But either it was a slow night for the department or the uniforms were eager beavers. He waited until they got out of the cruiser and then drove slowly in behind them.

Just happened to be passing by, guys. Saw you fellas pull in. Thought maybe I could lend a hand.

He was going to enjoy this completely.

Six girls, thought Ray, *I've fucked* six *of the girls in this room and still they come around. Because I got the juice, that's why, I got the animal magnetism, I got them all coming in their fucking pants to get fucked* again *one of these nights and they don't even care about the others being there too. They keep coming back for more of old Ray. Can't help it.*

He watched Judy hand her beer to Roger, his sometime drummer in his sometime band Silver Web, they were sitting on the sofa and she was flirting with Roger, but that was fine. Roger knew enough not to fuck with any of the girls he'd fucked, knew that Judy was private territory whether Ray particularly wanted her or not that night or any other night. She was strictly off-limits. Cross him and no more pot, no more hash, no more speed, no more parties, no more getting into bars. They all knew it. Jennifer was his and Judy was his and Cheryl and Sylvia and Rachel and Linda.

The party was jamming. His parties were *always* jamming. He was doling out a sufficiency of dope and they had enough beer to float a cruiser. The place was wall-to-wall kids. Mostly high-school kids but *his* kids. Smoking *his* dope if they were lucky and he favored them with a hit and eating *his* cheese spread. They were there because he called them. He was toastmaster. He was the glue. Sally Richardson could go fuck herself with a plunger. He felt very happy. Very content. That may have had to do with the fact that his own dope was Panama Red and not the Jersey homegrown he was handing around to the others or that Ray was drinking Chivas, not Schlitz. But mostly it was just the party. The Magnavox was cranked. Tom Jones was belting out "Delilah." Suds were flowing.

The only thing that slightly bummed him was Jennifer over by the window with Tim, standoffish from the others. What the fuck was it with those two? They were acting like the party was some sort of personal betrayal, as though he didn't have the *right* to party, as though they owned *him* and not the other way around.

So what that he'd canceled on yet another dumb movie that night in favor of the party? He had them in his fucking pocket and always would, and they should be remembering that and doing what he wanted them to do, having fun, having a good time. Not sulking.

Especially fucking Jennifer. Jennifer was acting like her goddamn mother died. Which was pretty funny since Jennifer's mother was already dead, she was a foster-home brat and as far as he could see the only family she *did* have aside from some sister somewhere was good old Ray. He was the only one looking out for her.

So she comes here and acts like this. Ungrateful little bitch.

You could always go to a movie for chrissake.

Well he was not going to let her spoil things. For sure not while Dee Dee was around. Dee Dee was definitely in love with him. When he asked her at the Sugar Bowl if she wanted to come to the party she'd damn near wet her panties. He could do without those zits on her chin and she could stand to lose a pound or two of baby fat around the waist but otherwise she was a looker. Big tits and not-too-big ass and a long pale neck that just begged you to give it a hickey. He had his hand on that nice firm ass right now, moving her through the noisy crowded living room toward the kitchen to get her another beer from the fridge and fill his glass of Chivas.

He thought maybe he'd send Jennifer back to the Griffiths' place tonight and fuck Dee Dee instead, zits and all. Who cared if she was underage? Half the girls he fucked were underage and he liked it that way. Already she was a little drunk. Couple more brews and she'd fuck a three-toothed Georgia nigger.

He got the beer for her and popped it and handed it over to her and turned back to the crowd, to *his* crowd and that was when he saw Tim running to the Magnavox, a worried look on his face and suddenly the Magnavox went silent. Tim hissed *Cops!* at him and Ray thought *Shit!* but didn't miss a beat, he went right into action. He grabbed the beer out of Dee Dee's hand and set it on the counter. *No goddamn underage kids with booze.*

"Everybody! You got a roach, swallow it. Dump the beers. Timmy, handle the door. *Ashtrays! Toilet! Now!*"

He was the first one in there, fishing the bulk of a dime bag of prime Panama Red and over half a lid of homegrown out of his jeans and emptying them into the bowl, glad he'd thought to sift off the twigs and seeds because twigs and seeds floated and were fucking hard to flush and at the same time pissed that he was flushing good dope in the first place especially the Red. He heard the doorbell ring and whispering and feet moving across the floor and the windows in back thrown open and then the music was up again a little—somebody, probably Tim, had the sense to make things seem nice and normal out there and then there were kids behind him dumping ashtrays into the water swirling down the toilet, watching with scared excited fascination.

"Out! Outa here!" he said and pushed them back out

of the doorway and slammed the door in their faces.

Some of the shit was still floating. He had to wait for the water to rise again so he could flush again. It seemed like a fucking eternity.

The cops were in his face again.

Shit! Dammit!

The uniforms were Shack and Hallan, two good kids only a few years out of high school themselves and they readily accepted that his being there was nothing more than happy coincidence. He let them do the work initially. Tim Bess opened the door. Shack and Hallan stood on the threshold peering in.

"Excuse me, sir," said Hallan. Hallan had been taught to be polite, giving Bess a *sir* though Bess was just a kid. "We've had a noise complaint. This your place?"

"Unh-unh. Belongs to a friend."

"May I speak to your friend, then, please?"

"I think he's in the john."

"He's in the john?"

"Yes."

"Would you get him for me, please?"

"Sure." He turned to go.

"Do you mind if we come in?"

"I think . . . I think you'd better wait and ask Ray. Ray Pye. I mean, it's his apartment."

"Then would you get him for me, please?"

"Sure."

Except for the music the room had gone dead silent. Tom Jones was warbling some love song in a baritone so forced and labored it sounded like he was giving birth to twins. The kids were all either watching the cops or making an elaborate show of not watching. Schilling saw some familiar faces. Also saw that about half the kids were under the legal drinking age just as he'd suspected they'd be. None of them had a bottle in hand though. He guessed that was too much to ask.

Pye came to the door elaborately adjusting his jeans. He wondered how much dope had just gone down the crapper. He hoped it was plenty.

"Officers? Is there some problem?"

Schilling figured it was time he stepped in.

"Hi, Ray. Mind if we all come in and talk a moment?"

"I don't guess you have a warrant."

"Why would we need a warrant on a simple noise complaint? Nah, just a little chat like we had yesterday. Remember yesterday? You know, the guy killed those two young girls. The guy who looked kinda like you?"

He sent *that* out to the entire room.

Ray flushed and then turned to the uniforms as though to say, this guy is nuts but from regular fellas like they were he expected some sanity.

"Listen officers, we're having a party here. We'll turn down the volume, okay? We're sorry if we disturbed anybody."

Shack and Hallan just looked at him. Giving him nothing.

Good boys.

"You smell anything funny, guys?"

"I kinda do," said Shack. "Now that you mention it."

"You smoking a little weed, Ray?"

"Nope. I guess what you smell is just cigarettes. Oh, and we burnt a pan on the stove. Making popcorn."

"Making popcorn."

"Yeah."

"And you burnt a pan."

"That's right."

He nodded. "Uh-huh."

And then he just stared at him. Ray stared back awhile and then looked away, glanced over at Tim.

So Schilling had won *that* pissing contest, anyhow.

"Okay," he said, "party's over."

There were groans from the crowd.

"You can't do that."

"Sure I can, Ray. I think I see some minors here. I can definitely see beer cans and bottles from right where I'm standing. You want us to start IDing everybody? Have them walk the line? It'd take a little while but we don't mind, do we fellas?"

"IDing everybody'd be fine," said Shack. "Recite the alphabet. Stretch out your hands, touch the tip of your nose. All of that, sure. We got plenty of time."

"Jesus," Ray muttered and shook his head.

He was very pissed off.

Excellent.

"What's that, Ray?"

"Nothing."

"I thought you said *Jesus.* Which some people could definitely construe as a curse word. Used in the presence of officers of the law. You cursing in the presence of officers of the law, Ray?"

"No. All right." He turned abruptly. "You heard the man. The party's over."

More groans, a lot of muttering. But they collected their sweaters and jackets anyway and filed out the door. Schilling and the uniforms stepped back to let them through. Tim Bess was the last one out, looking back at Ray, and he read the clear silent message between them that Bess was wanting to stay. Ray shook his head no.

Finally there was only Ray and a girl Schilling remembered as Jennifer something.

"You too, miss."

"I'm . . . I'm staying here," she said.

"Permanently?"

"Tonight."

"Your parents know about that?"

The girl sighed, impatient with him but nervous.

"I'm twenty years old," she said.

"May I see some ID, please?"

She sighed again and went to get her purse off the kitchen counter. Ray just stood there with his arms folded staring at the shelf filled with records, not looking at the records but just glaring in their general direction, his lips pressed together in a thin tight line. Schilling thought that at the very least he'd gotten beyond Ray's cute little bland facade tonight.

Hey, it was a start.

The girl handed him her driver's license. As he'd figured she was telling the truth. She was twenty. A shame though because moving her out of there would have managed to annoy Ray further.

"Okay. Sorry to have troubled you, miss. See you around, Ray."

He figured it had to be taking all Ray's willpower not to slam the door behind him.

He would not have wanted any daughter of his to be in that little girl's shoes tonight. Unless he missed his guess she was going to catch a lot of flak, a lot of anger. He thought she was nuts to stick around.

"What was that business about some guy killed a couple of girls? Somebody who looks like this asshole?" Shack asked him.

"Ray's got an interest in police detection. We had a little talk, that's all. What do you think? Would you want to have him in the department?"

"God forbid. I'd just as soon not have the little dickhead in the same town as me, let alone the department."

Schilling patted him on the back and smiled. "I like the way you think, Officer Shack. You'll make detective one of these days. You just wait and see."

Chapter Eighteen

Jennifer

She didn't know why she was staying but something told her she should, something instinctive saying that Ray was very vulnerable now so it was a perfect opportunity to wean him back away from this Katherine person he was so interested in, away from that stupid Dee Dee and the rest of them including this new girl Sally. She suspected a storm from him but also suspected she could weather one.

She was an old hand at weathering them by now.

She hadn't expected him to trash the place.

She sat rigid on the bed with her back pressed to the headboard and her hands balled into fists while he toppled the kitchen table, beer and pretzels flying all over the kitchen and the table slamming against the wall, kicked over the kitchen chairs and stomped them, cracked their ribs, broke records over his knee and threw them spinning against the living-room wall, ripped the wires out of the turntable and heaved it all the way across the room, tore his Stones poster down and ripped it in half, smashed glasses and half-empty beer bottles in the sink, against the cupboard, against the wall, all the time cursing the cops and Schilling and whoever the fucker was who'd called and turned him in and his *fucking mother* and his *fucking father* neither of whom had done a thing as far as she could see, his hair streaming down his face, screaming and jabbing his finger at her like it was her fault though of course it wasn't, she knew it wasn't, she was just there in the room and human and that was plenty.

She remembered the jagged edge of the beer bottle against her skin.

She stayed put.

She watched it all with a kind of awe, like watching a hurricane from what might or might not be a safe distance. Scared of him and scared *for* him, scared that the police would come back because if the party had been loud the party was nothing, absolutely nothing compared to this. It was as though he was actually daring them to come back. And if they did she was afraid he might go after them. It almost seemed he'd have to he was so mad.

You could get yourself killed that way.

She'd seen him mad before but not this mad, never, so that when finally he exhausted himself and fell back across the bed she was afraid to go near him, afraid he'd go off again for some reason so she stayed huddled right where she was, knees hugged up to her chin, back tight against the bedboard, fingernails digging deep into the palms of her hands as though the reality of pain might make everything she'd just seen and heard bearable, might bury it like a nasty dream.

She was barefoot and glass was everywhere.

He was breathing like a long-distance runner. Staring up at the ceiling, face contorted as though from some massive migraine headache.

"*Ray?*"

She had to try. It was what she was here for. To reach out to him.

To be there.

What did the actors say? That was her *motivation*.

"Ray?"

It was as though she weren't there. She knew the feeling. He'd done it to her before, cut her off like this and it hurt worse than anything.

"Come on, Ray. Talk to me," she said gently. "I know how you feel, I really do. It was a great party too, before they came along. They really screwed you. I don't blame you one bit for being mad. Hell, I'd be mad. Anybody would. Just talk to me and maybe in a while we'll clean up the place and forget all about the goddamn stupid cops. Plan another party, maybe for the weekend. Throw an even bigger party. That'd show them, wouldn't it?"

"You thought it was a really great party?"

He said it so low she almost didn't hear him.

"Sure I did. Everybody did."

"Then what were you doing the entire time standing by the fucking window sulking with Timmy?"

And that she *did* hear. His voice like a razor sometimes. Cutting deep, scraping bone.

"I was just a little tired, Ray. I wasn't sulking. Honest."

He reached over and grabbed her by the front of the blouse and pulled her across the bed, not even moving off his back, until she was face-to-face with him and sometimes his strength simply amazed her, you wouldn't think he was that strong because he wasn't that big and she was scared of him again.

"You're a lying little bitch, Jennifer. You don't lie to me. You don't lie to Ray. You tell Ray the fucking truth. I *saw* you. You were fucking sulking. Why the hell was that? At *my* party?"

Her blouse had pulled up out of her jeans. She could feel cool air from the open windows across her stomach. He had the collar balled up in his fist. There was something thrilling and sexy about it huddled inside the scariness.

"I . . . I guess I got a little depressed, Ray. I mean, I saw all those other girls there. You know. And that Dee Dee. I'm sorry. But you know how I feel about us, Ray. I couldn't help it. I got a little depressed, that's all. It was dumb I guess because I love you and I know you love me back but . . . I'm sorry."

He looked her in the eye a moment and the eyes were hard and mean and then suddenly he let her go.

"Take off your blouse. I want to see your tits."

This was more familiar ground and she did as he said. Kneeling in front of him, slowly unbuttoning the blouse from the bottom up, not the top down, doing it the way he liked. She knew her breasts were good and she was proud of them and of their power to excite him. He always wanted to see her breasts and squeeze and bite and suckle them like a baby. She slipped the blouse down off her shoulders.

"Undo me."

She unfastened his belt. She unzipped his fly and he raised his hips so she could pull down his jeans and his BVDs.

"You want them all the way off?"

"Did I say I wanted them all the way off?"

She knew sometimes he didn't. She pulled them down to his knees. His cock lay flaccid against his thigh.

"Suck it."

She put it in her mouth and sucked up and down until it was gleaming wet with her saliva. She could smell his mustiness and taste it. She took the shaft between her thumb and forefinger and stroked halfway upward while her lips moved down tight over his glans to meet them halfway down. Most girls didn't know how to do this right Ray said, they'd move fingers and lips both in the same direction but Ray had taught her.

She sucked and stroked and licked and nibbled his balls but he wouldn't get hard. And this had never happened to them before, only when he was blind drunk which he wasn't now and she started to panic. She sucked harder, cheeks beginning to hurt and neck beginning to ache, slobbering him with her saliva so he'd stay good and wet and her hand wouldn't hurt him, being careful with her teeth. She put the forefinger of her other hand in her mouth and then moved it down under him and slowly and gently probed his asshole, her fingernails on that hand kept closely clipped for exactly that purpose and this had *always* worked, *always* even when he *was* blind drunk but nothing was happening, not a thing, she was into him up to the knuckle moving in and out, and he was wide enough, but there was no response at all.

"Fuck it. Forget it. Get the fuck out of here."

"Ray?"

"Just fuck it. Get dressed. Go home."

He pulled up his BVDs and jeans.

"C'mon, Ray. It happens. You know."

"It doesn't happen to me. Not to me it fucking doesn't. I mean it, Jennifer. Just get the fuck out of here and leave me alone, all right?"

She felt bad for him. It meant a lot to a guy, this kind of thing. But it didn't make any sense for her to have to leave him just over that.

"Look. I've got an idea. Why don't you let me help you clean the place up? When we're done, we'll take another shot at it and you'll be fine. You'll see."

He shot bolt upright and grabbed her neck.

"No we *won't* take another shot at it, you hear? All *right*, Jennifer?"

He was shaking her. The waterbed shifted beneath

them like a flimsy rubber raft in a wind-tossed sea.

"All right?"

"Okay, okay! Whatever! Let go, Ray! Jesus, you're hurting me!"

He let go and fell back to the bed. Silent again, staring at the ceiling.

She watched him for a moment, hurt but mostly bewildered, *she really didn't understand him at all* and then she got off the bed and tiptoed to the closet where she'd left her sneakers, mindful of the glass on the floor and put the sneakers on and then returned to the bed for her blouse. She watched him while she was slipping it on and buttoning it but he hadn't moved, he was still staring up at the ceiling like he was just tired out, like nothing had happened whatsoever between them, like it was just another long and tiring day.

At least he looked calm now.

She got her handbag from the kitchen counter. She walked to the door, glass crunching underfoot.

" 'Bye, Ray."

He said nothing.

She wondered what he was thinking, what in the world was going on in that brain of his that would allow him to let her leave him this way without even so much as a word after all they'd done and been together over all this time. She wanted to cry but she wouldn't, wouldn't give him the satisfaction, she didn't want him to see.

She'd save that much for herself, anyway. That much dignity.

That if nothing else.

Chapter Nineteen

Ray

He couldn't get it up.

What the fuck was wrong with him?

You can't get it up, you're nothing.

He should have let her stay and clean the place. Now he'd have to do it himself. But the thought of her sucking his dick and *nada, zilch* disgusted him. He didn't want to look at her. Or look at her looking at him. Pitying him, maybe. Trying to make light of things that were not to be taken lightly.

Lying there in bed he kept playing it over and over in his mind; the fucking images and feelings wouldn't go away. Her head bobbing, tits bobbing, the bed moving beneath him. Her finger up his ass, his dick slimy wet and rubbery. And him feeling nothing, feeling completely empty inside. No excitement. Not even rage. He should have grabbed one of her tits and squeezed it as hard as he could, he should have hurt her and maybe that would have got him hard, it had in the past but tonight he didn't want to touch her. He just wanted her to suck his fucking dick and she couldn't even get that right.

Jesus! This entire day was *fucked!*

First Sally Richmond in that stupid greasy spoon and then the cops and having to flush perfectly good dope some of it expensive and now this shit with Jennifer.

He could have had Dee Dee if the cops hadn't busted him but he didn't even really want Dee Dee all that much. She was just another slit basically and an underage slit at that. And when you thought about it, what the fuck kind of name was *Dee Dee?* Here's my girlfriend, Dee Dee. The girl I'm poking these days is Dee Dee. Screw that. Dee Dee was just a fat little whim with pimples and that was all she'd ever be.

The one he wanted was Katherine. Kath or Sally Richmond. Either one would have got him hard.

But Sally'd told him to go screw himself.

He'd get her for that one of these days. She hadn't even given him a chance the stuck-up college-bound bitch.

Realistically speaking that left Katherine.

Which when you came right down to it was the one he wanted most anyway. Kath would have got him off. No question.

Tomorrow was Thursday. Maybe he could get her to move up their date a night but he kind of doubted it. He had a feeling she was hard to push. In a way it was something that he liked about her. It was different. It made her a challenge. And maybe it was best anyway that he wait a day. He had to get the place in shape, for chrissake. Get his father to fix the chairs he'd busted and he was probably going to have to take the Magnavox in for repairs or maybe even replace it altogether. He regretted heaving the Magnavox but that goddamn Schilling had got to him.

Schilling. Another one on his list.

He didn't know how you got to a cop but he'd find a way sooner or later, and then it was *fuck you, Detective Schilling, fuck you for getting in my face all the time and fuck you for busting up my party. You remember my party, Charlie? I flushed maybe an ounce of dope at that party you cocksucker.*

Sally. Schilling. Jennifer. They'd all managed to screw him. All in one day.

She'd had her finger up his ass and still *he couldn't get hard.*

Jesus wept.

Whatever was happening to him Katherine could fix it. He knew that. He only had to wait. He'd never been real good at waiting but Kath was going to be worth it. *Sweep the place up. Have yourself a beer. Get some sleep. You can do this, no problem.*

You're Ray.

He swung off the bed and crunched a broken shard of beer bottle beneath his boot and that made him think that first he wanted a beer or two, maybe watch a little TV. At least he hadn't trashed the television.

Then he'd get around to sweeping.

First he had to clear his brain of all this crap, blot it out, but there wasn't any dope god knows and besides, dope had a tendency to make him paranoid sometimes and this was no time for paranoia. Not when there were people who really were in his way out there and people who really were out to get him. You wanted to keep things clear and calm and reasonable.

Take stock. Fix your apartment. Check your wardrobe.

Weekend's coming.

Chapter Twenty

Thursday, August 7
Tim/Jennifer

He couldn't believe this was happening.

He and Jennifer were in bed together.

It was like a dream.

He didn't ask any questions, no way, he didn't ask why him and why *now,* he just took off his clothes when she told him to, she'd said it just like that, *Take off your clothes, Tim* and he did.

It was the middle of the afternoon. He'd taken the day off, called in sick, when really all he was was a little hung over and depressed about the party. Ray was going to be hell on wheels for a couple of days, that was for sure, and it depressed him that when the cops had ordered them out Ray hadn't let him stay. Tim wasn't like the rest of those goddamn kids. Most of them just bought Ray's dope and drank his beer. He wasn't even close to the band members for godsakes, they hardly ever practiced anymore.

But he and Ray were supposed to be tight. They'd been tight since Tim was in the seventh grade and Ray took pity on the skinny pimpled wuss he was then and decked Joey Spagnoli with a single punch to the face during recess one day for pushing him around, no reason, it was just because he could, because he was big and fat and strong, a nasty ignorant wop bastard up from the slums of Newark. To Ray it was nothing. A gesture. To Tim it was everything. He never got pushed around by Spagnoli or anybody else again. It marked the end of his long sad penance. The penance of the weak.

It was the beginning of the Tim he was today.

He and Ray were supposed to be buddies. They were special.

So he couldn't help it. He brooded.

Then around two-thirty the doorbell rings and he goes down to answer it and it's Jennifer and his whole day changes just like that, like magic.

Take off your clothes.

She'd been drinking some. A couple of beers probably. He could smell them on her breath. But she wasn't really drunk or anything.

So he did what she said, did it gladly and without hesitation and now he was lying on the bed naked and a little embarrassed by his growing erection, watching her peel away her panties, her breasts beautiful and thick-nippled and softly swaying. She had a bit of a belly and her hips were a little thick but he'd seen her in a bathing suit and he already knew that and didn't mind. Not a bit.

She seemed very solemn as she crawled toward him from the foot of the bed and kissed him, she didn't smile, her thigh brushing over his cock which was fully erect by now and he thought, there's something weird about this, this is more than just sex for her. Just look at her. She's so *serious.* What's she want from me?

Whatever she's offering, take it, he thought. So he did.

Tim was very tender, not like Ray. She knew him better than almost anybody and felt sure it would be that way. It was part of the reason she was with him.

She'd felt so sad and lonely last night. As she'd figured the Griffiths were asleep when she got home but it wouldn't have helped even if they'd been wide awake. The Griffiths were nice people, they'd been good to her all the years she'd known them, not like the previous set of foster parents and it was nice of them to let her stay, a twenty-year-old now, no teenager anymore and running with a crowd they weren't particularly happy with. They treated her almost like a daughter. But even if she had been their daughter she doubted she could talk to them. Not about Ray. How could you tell anybody who didn't know him about Ray and make them understand why she stayed with him? Especially when half the time she didn't know herself.

She lay awake in bed a long time and when the tears were finished the loneliness was still there and she found herself thinking about Tim. Not about confiding in Tim though she knew he'd listen. But just once lying naked with Tim, having a warm pair of arms around her and knowing he'd be gentle. That his hands would be gentle, not ball up into fists and grab and squeeze and even strike her on a whim. She fell asleep thinking about that and in the morning when she woke the thought was still there.

She called Ray again and again but he wouldn't answer the phone. It made her mad and hurt so she had a beer or two and then thought, *fuck* this, there's got to be some better way than *this* to spend your day. She recalled what she'd been thinking the night before.

So here she was. Seducing Tim.

He hadn't taken much seducing.

She'd figured that too.

His body was so different from Ray's, almost hairless except for the light brown pubic hair and he was thin, wiry and not very muscular. He had freckles across his chest and thighs. This close to him his eyes were startlingly blue, the lashes almost transparent. She liked the almost scentless scent of him. Ray was musk and leather. Tim was summer air. The wild erotic charge she felt with Ray was missing but she was getting what she came for, something warm and comforting. He was almost shy with her, his hands moving so softly over her ass and breasts and belly it was as though he were stroking a kitten, not a woman. She felt his cock jump against her thigh but he wouldn't move it up inside her, she had to do that for him and when she did he moaned deep and low in his throat and she almost laughed because that was almost the way *she* sounded when Ray would enter her, as though she'd stepped inside a looking glass.

His strokes were deep and soft and slow. It didn't take long but by the time he came his body was shiny with sweat. He gasped and cried out, a sound that was almost a whimper. Her own orgasm was still way out of reach but that didn't matter. Because then he rolled to the side and the pale thin arms came round her and held her sweetly in the dim light of his room and the silence.

And now he *did* want to ask her why him and why now but he knew that asking would spoil it. If there was some reason she was lying here today and not yesterday and probably there was one and probably it had to do with Ray and the party he thought he didn't really need to know it. He was holding the old Jennifer—not Ray's Jennifer or the drunk, stoned-out Jennifer, but the Jennifer he'd fallen for long ago way back in the ninth grade.

For the first time in months or maybe even in years, he thought, he was really happy.

He knew he'd come too quickly and that chances were she hadn't and wondered what she thought of that, if she was disappointed in him. But he didn't wonder too long. If she was disappointed she didn't show it. She seemed just as content as he was lying there.

He was aware of the sweat drying on his body, of the softness of the flesh of her arms and the tight skin over her back, of the smell of her hair mingling with the scent of the pillow and—*thank god*—clean sheets. He heard birds calling to one another outside the open window. He felt her moist warm breath ebb and flow across his chest.

"That was nice, Timmy," she said.

He didn't need to answer. He held her and somehow knew that was what she wanted.

He felt he could stay just like this the whole rest of the day, stay like this practically forever and they did lay there a good long while, but at last she pushed gently away from him, smiling a little, turned her back to him and reached for his pack on the night table. The proverbial cigarette. She lit one and took a drag and snuggled her ass back into his crotch. Making spoons with him, settling in. After a while she passed the cigarette over and he took a drag and passed it back and they stayed that way until the cigarette was gone and she'd snubbed it out into the ashtray.

"I'm a little thirsty," she said. "Got anything to drink? A Pepsi or anything?"

"Sure. Stay there. I'll get it."

He pulled on a pair of jeans and went downstairs to the kitchen. The stairs, even the kitchen looked somehow subtly different. It was as though she'd brought something with her to the place, his own place and his parents' place, that hadn't been there before. At least he'd never seen it. As though she'd scrubbed it clean.

The sun streaming in through the window almost dazzled him.

He opened two cold Pepsis and took them back upstairs, hoping she hadn't gotten dressed, hoping she was still in bed. She was. Smoking another Marlboro. The sheets still bunched around her feet.

She smiled at him again, a slightly embarrassed smile this time he thought. He didn't want her to feel that way. Tim smiled back, not at all sure what his own smile was doing. He sat down next to her on the bed and handed her the Pepsi. She took it from him and he could see her nipples pucker, whether it was the cold soda in her hand or a breeze through the window or him looking at her body he couldn't say.

They sipped the soda in silence, neither one of them sure what to say. It occurred to him that most of what they had in common centered on Ray and he sure didn't want to start talking about Ray now, not after this and he thought that probably neither did she. When her bottle was half empty she reached down for the sheet and pulled it up and tucked it under her arms. She was frowning a little.

"Anything wrong?"

She seemed to consider this a moment, like maybe there was and maybe there wasn't and she wasn't sure.

"Nah. You know me. In one mood and out the other." She laughed. "I'm just a great big pain in the ass, y'know?"

"No you're not."

"No?"

"No."

They were on the verge of talking about Ray right now like it or not. It was Ray who had gotten to calling her a pain in the ass lately. The moment passed and he took a slug of his soda.

"You think we, uh . . . I mean, you think we might be able to do this again sometime?"

He *had* to ask. Just couldn't help it.

"I don't know. Maybe. I just needed to see, you know? I just wanted to see . . . something. I dunno."

"Sure. It *was* nice though, Jennifer. Real nice."

"Mmmm." She nodded. A breeze wafted through the room and tossed her hair. She pushed it back off her forehead.

"I don't suppose you've got any dope on you, do you Tim?"

He didn't especially want to do any dope with her right now any more than he wanted to talk about Ray but he couldn't refuse her either. Then he thought of something and almost laughed out loud. The idea was exciting because it was just a little dangerous but somehow he knew it was perfectly suited to the occasion.

"Hold on. Wait a minute."

He put the Pepsi down on the floor and got off the bed and went to his dresser drawer and opened it and dug behind the socks and took out the foil packet of hash shavings and a small wooden pipe fitted with a screen. The screen had once been gold but now was mostly black.

He handed them over to her, smiling.

"Try some of this."

She opened the package.

"Oh, hash. Cool. Where'd you get it?"

"Ray."

She nodded. "You usually don't buy."

"I didn't."

"Ray *gave* it to you?"

Ray was notoriously stingy with his hash. Everybody thought so. He'd dole it out to you once in a while but only when he was smoking too and you never got to take some home with you. Never.

"I mule it for him, right? Pick it up at the post office? So I weigh it and then I trim it. Been doing it for about a year now. Ray's never noticed."

"Jesus, Timmy." She looked at him wide-eyed and astonished but smiling too. "You've got more balls than brains, you know that? Stealing Ray's hash. Ray would have *conniptions* if he knew."

He laughed. "I know. Let's fire up."

She laughed too and packed the pipe and he lit it for her. Feeling good about the whole thing, feeling good that somebody else knew his secret, and particularly that it was she who knew.

The only thing that soured it was that there they were talking about Ray again even though neither of them wanted to. He always got into it somehow.

The guy was inescapable.

Chapter Twenty-one

Schilling

Usually he waited for the weekend to call because rates were cheaper. This time he didn't want to. He needed to hear their voices, if only for a little while. It was seven, just after dinnertime so chances were they'd be home. Lila answered.

He could tell by her voice that something wasn't right. She was trying to make small talk, something about her friend Suzi's daughter's wedding but it wouldn't wash with him. She never was good at evasion. It was one thing he was much better at than she was and except for pissing standing up he couldn't think of another. There was no point pretending to go along so he asked her.

"It's Will. They threw him out of summer school, Charlie. One of the teachers caught him with a joint in the men's room. He had another in his pocket. They called me at work. I had all I could do to talk them out of turning him over to the police. He does it again, they

164

will. And the police will send him straight to reform school they said, no options."

"Jesus Christ."

"He's fifteen years old for god's sake. He got tossed out of the last school for stealing. What's he going to be doing at twenty?"

She didn't even try to keep the anger out of her voice. But he knew her. The anger was the only drug that could smother the fear.

"He says all the kids are doing it. Marijuana I mean. He doesn't even seem to feel guilty. And now he's going to have to repeat freshman math next year. I don't know what the hell to do."

"You want me to fly out there?"

She didn't seem to hear him.

"I've grounded him. Of course. Big deal. I can't be around to watch him all the time. I have to go to work five days a week. So how can I trust him not to go out and meet his buddies when I'm not home? What am I going to do? Hire a baby-sitter?"

"What about your mother?"

"She's got dad to deal with. His arthritis is worse in both knees now. He can barely get around. I can't ask her to do that."

"I asked, you want me to fly out there?"

He was suddenly glad at the prospect of doing that and guilty about the reason why.

She sighed. "No. I don't know. Not now. Just talk to him, will you? See if you can talk some sense into him. I can't."

"Sure. Put him on."

"*Will?* Your father's on the phone."

In the silence he pictured her standing there holding the phone in a kitchen or a bedroom he'd seen only once before on one short visit. He didn't know which room so he pictured them both, a beautiful woman with a haggard overburdened look about her but still beautiful. His woman once. But now solely her own, preferring her aloneness to the company of him.

"Hello?"

The voice on the other end seemed to belong to someone much too young to be stealing and smoking dope. It was still in the process of changing. Every time he heard it now the voice was slightly different, a fact that usually pleased him. His son was growing up. This time he met that same realization again. Only this time there was a sadness about it and a very real reason to be worried. You could grow up every which way, a tree standing tall and straight in an open field or blasted and twisted on the side of a mountain.

"Hello, Will. How are you?"

"Okay, I guess."

He let it hang there.

"I guess she told you, huh?"

"Yes she did. What are you doing, Will?"

"What do you mean?"

"You know what I mean."

The voice turned whiny and defensive. Went up half an octave.

"Look, dad, everybody does it. There's nothing wrong with it. I mean, just because it's illegal doesn't mean it's *bad.*"

"I'm not going to argue whether it's bad or not. But it is illegal. As it is right now they can put you in reform school for smoking the stuff and in another year and a half you'll be seventeen and they can throw you the hell out of the system altogether. You want that?"

"So? I don't care. I'll get a job. So what."

"So what? I'll tell you so what. You ever hear of Vietnam, Will? People get kicked out of school these days, they get drafted. They get shipped over to Vietnam to bleed all over some goddamn rice paddy or lose their legs on a land mine. You don't *care* about that?"

"By the time I'm seventeen the war will be over.

There won't *be* a draft anymore. Everybody says so."

"They do, huh. Well, I don't know who *everybody* is but do they teach you about Laos in that school? Cambodia? The war's escalating, for godsakes. Do you really want to bet your life that whoever *everybody* is, happens to be right? Your *life* for godsakes? Come on, Will. You've got more brains than that."

He hoped he was keeping the anger out of his voice. He wasn't so sure.

"It's just dope, dad. God! It's not like I'm shooting up or something."

"Look, I've never smoked the stuff. I don't know what it does to your head and I don't even particularly care. But I know it could screw up your *life,* you get caught with it one more time. Permanently screw it up. You get yourself drafted, it could *end* your life. I love you, dammit. Your mother loves you. Your little sister's crazy about you. How do you think Barb would feel if it just so happens that they ship you home in a body bag one day? Her big brother? Jesus, Will!"

"Okay, dad. All right. Okay."

There was nothing left to do but let the silence do the work for a moment. He'd pretty much said his piece.

"Do the right thing, son. Don't screw up. There'll be plenty of time to screw up later, once you get out of school and all this is over."

"Okay, dad. I hear you."

Schilling wondered if he did. Somehow he doubted it. He wished he could be in the room with him, actually see if his words were having any effect at all. He felt angry at himself, frustrated. He suddenly had the urge to end the conversation right then and there. Before he said more than he wanted to.

"Is your sister around? Let me talk to her, okay?"

"She's got a couple friends over."

"I won't keep her long. Put her on. And think it over, Will. Please."

He heard him call her. He was glad she had friends there, that she was becoming more social than she'd been back in New Jersey. She needed that. Brains weren't everything. Friends were important too.

And then after a while, another disembodied voice on the phone. This one steady and small.

"Daddy?"

"Hi, darlin'. How ya doin'?"

"I'm good, daddy. I've got Linda and Suzy over. Mommy let them stay for dinner. We're making a project for science class. Are you coming to see us soon?"

"Soon," he said. "I hope. What's the project?"

"We're making a make-believe swamp. We got that big glass aquarium tank for the turtles? So we're taking the turtles out and leaving in the real dirt and real moss and stuff, but then we're making all these fake trees and bushes and vines out of papier-mâché and pipe cleaners and painting them and sticking them all around and stuff, sticking them to the glass so it looks real thick in there but isn't? And we're making this little pond with rocks all around it and then putting the turtles back in so that they look like *giant* turtles, like it's a prehistoric swamp or something. Like the jungle in *King Kong* sort of. The teacher said it didn't have to be really real."

"Sounds like fun."

"It is fun. But I gotta get back, daddy. Linda messes up if I'm not around to watch her."

"Okay. You go keep an eye on Linda. Put your mom back on, okay? I love you, Barb."

"Love you, daddy."

Silence again. Not long this time. She must have been standing there.

"What do you think?"

"I don't know what to think. I don't know if I got through to him or not."

"Jesus, I hope so. I know he's not listening to me.

All I get from him is anger, as though everything's my fault. Either that or he's just sullen."

"Listen, Lila, I know it's not your habit to, but call me. Call me anytime. I wish you'd phoned me yesterday when this happened. He's my son too and I care about him. You don't have to tough this out alone. Whenever you want to talk, give me a call. At work, whatever. I don't care. Will you promise me?"

"I . . . sure, all right. I won't call you at work, though. I know how much you hate that."

"I mean it, Lila. Anytime. At work or whenever. I don't give a damn anymore."

"Sure you do, Charlie. But thanks. I'll be in touch."

"Promise?"

"Promise."

"Okay."

The urge to say *I love you* to her was as strong as it was to say it to his kids. Probably stronger. But all he did say was good-bye and hang up the phone. He sat looking at it for a while thinking about his son and about Lila. If he were out in Arizona with them now, where would they be family-wise? Could his presence straighten Will out any? Was it really even possible to be a family again in any sense whatsoever?

There wasn't a single happy answer that came to him.

He got up and turned on the television. In a few minutes *Daniel Boone* was on, buckskins and all, saving the country for democracy, the best of a bad lot of shows this evening. He thought about the war and exactly who was saving the country for democracy these days.

Kids a couple years older than his son, that was who.

He got a beer from the kitchen and tried his best not to dwell on Will's problems. He'd either straighten out or he wouldn't. All Charlie could do was wait and see.

Chapter Twenty-two

Friday, August 8
Ray/Katherine

It was dusk and they were driving down Cedar headed for the old White Castle to grab a burger or two, Ray at the wheel and Tim riding shotgun, when the scrawny black cat with the white paws and belly walked out into the road from behind some hedges and Ray accelerated. Racing for it. Scaring the living shit out of Tim. Which was the point. Not that he'd have minded bagging some mangy cat. Especially wired on Black Beauties the way he was. But looking over and seeing Tim's face gone white as he bore down on the cat, that was the ticket, that was what made him smile. Reminding Tim of what he could do and *would* do whenever he fucking felt like it.

The cat was fast and lucky and made it past him inches from the left front tire. Ray laughed, high and clear and giddy and glanced into his rear-view mirror and saw it frozen by the shoulder and staring after them as though all the dogs of hell had just roared screeching by.

"Jesus, Ray!"

"Yeah, I know. I missed him."

"What the fuck you wanna go and do that for?"

"I'm here, cat's there. I got a car, the cat doesn't. Why not?"

"Shit, Ray."

It was always fun to give Tim the willies because you could *do* it so easily. When they'd all gone to the drive-in to see *Rosemary's Baby* last summer Jennifer said she'd caught Tim looking away during the Mia Farrow rape scene. While Ray wouldn't even allow himself to blink. That scene was terrific!

They were playing that goddamn song again on the radio, the one about San Francisco *"Be sure to wear some flowers in your hair. . . ."* Good Christ. He switched it off. You couldn't much hear it anyway with the Chevy's top down, but still it annoyed him. Fucking flowers in your hair. Yeah, right. The song was disgusting. The song was utter shit. He had a date with Katherine in a couple of hours and didn't want a goddamn thing to spoil the vibe.

"You ever think about doing that?" Tim said.

"Doing what?"

"Going to San Francisco, to the Haight. Sometimes I think we should do that, you know? You and me and Jennifer. Get out of town and head for the Haight."

"Now why would I want to do that?"

"Sex and drugs and rock 'n' roll, man!"

"Tim, we got sex and drugs and rock 'n' roll right here. Next you're gonna want to go live in some fucking commune. Eat bean sprouts and brown rice. I worry about you sometimes, you know that?"

"They do what they want there. You deal some drugs, you always got money. You don't have to work. You panhandle if you need a little cash."

"Oh yeah. I can just see me panhandling. Asking fucking college kids for money. I'd kill the first little prick who said no to me."

He would too. Just the thought of it infuriated him. Some asshole hippie with a silver spoon in his mouth telling him no. He decided to change the subject. Tim was messing up his mood just like the song did.

"You hear from Barry Winslow at all? I haven't seen him around lately. Barry's a good customer."

"See? There you go. Exactly my point. Barry Winslow went to the *Haight!*"

"Aw, jesus."

Why he hung out with all these fucking losers he didn't know.

They pulled into the drive-by window and ordered three burgers each and two chocolate shakes from the kid in the white paper hat. Three burgers at White Castle were about the equivalent of one burger anywhere else but together they were still about half the price. Ray paid. He was feeling expansive, thinking about his date with Katherine. Evidently Tim was thinking about it too, the poor horny bastard.

"So where are you gonna take her?"

He shook his head. "I dunno. She's got something in mind. I got no idea what. She's being real mysterious about it. I figure I'll play along, what the hell. If it's something stupid I'll take her back to my place and fuck her on the waterbed."

He wasn't sure about his chances of fucking Katherine on the waterbed or anywhere else on their first date for that matter, but there was no point telling Tim that. Let him think what he always thought. That Ray was Mr. Stud and got what he wanted each and every time he spread his wings to fly.

And he *was* feeling pretty good about it.

Maybe it was the methamphetamine buzzing around in his brain, but he actually felt pretty confident. The way she sounded on the phone at lunchtime. Flirting with him but something more than that. Seeming to promise something—*I've got something different in mind* was the way she put it. Fucking wasn't exactly different for Ray but maybe it was for her. Kath was younger. Who knew? On the other hand maybe she was more experienced than he gave her credit for and she'd been reading up on her *Kama Sutra* lately. He thought the *Kama Sutra* was mostly un-do-able or at the very least uncomfortable horseshit but there were a few things in there he'd definitely like to try.

That *I've got something different in mind* intrigued him.

He'd give her some rope on this one.

They finished the burgers and shakes in the parking lot and by then it was time to drop Tim off and get ready. He had to shower and shave and polish his boots and do his makeup—just a little, very subtle—and decide what he wanted to wear. He'd lay out all his best stuff on the bed and figure what matched what. He was very good at choosing colors that complemented one another. He'd learned how from his mother's fashion magazines at an early age. She subscribed to practically all of them but most of the time still managed to look like Ma Kettle on a real bad day.

Women.

Then again he might decide to go for all black. The outlaw look. She might like that. He'd decide after the shower.

Her father had driven to the airport straight from work so the house was hers for a while. She took her time in the kitchen broiling herself a steak in the oven along with some fries and tossing the spinach salad Etta had made for her that afternoon. Her father was never much for steak though he'd eat it if Etta put it in front of him. She rarely did. So Katherine would treat herself to one whenever he was away. *What kind of guy doesn't like steak?* she thought. Then again, what kind of guy spent all his free time building furniture and then giving it away? She'd never heard of either type of animal.

While she cooked she sipped a glass of Remy Martin. Another treat, albeit this one forbidden, to be savored when her father was away. When she sat down at the table to eat she poured herself another. By the time she was finished she felt a comfortable glow. Half the steak was left on her plate so she wrapped it and put it in the refrigerator for tomorrow. She'd do a teryaki marinade and slice it thin and cook it very briefly along with some vegetables and rice. She decided not to bother with the dishes. Etta could clean up tomorrow. She rinsed and piled them in the sink.

She tried not to think about her mother, about the reason her father wasn't home tonight. But it was like trying not to think about some stupid song that had popped into your head first thing in the morning. The more you tried to lose it the longer and harder it stuck.

Practically catatonic was what he'd said.

She could almost picture it, her mother crouched in some corner in a stark bare room, her mother thin and wasted, not eating, hair a mess and probably dirty. Would they have her in a straitjacket? No. That was only for the violent ones, not the catatonics. She wondered if they still let her wear her own clothes or if she'd graduated to some hospital gown open in the back so you could see her backbone and the crack of her ass.

It was not good, this kind of thinking.

She drew herself a hot bath and lay in the water for awhile sipping slowly at a third glass of Remy. Her father would never miss it. Her father drank so rarely that he never knew what was inside his liquor cabinet let alone how much of it. He ordered liquor in for entertainment purposes, for the occasional visit from a client. And when the visit was over the bottle went back into the cabinet and for the most part there it sat.

She showered after the bath and dried her hair, wrapped herself in a towel and padded into her bedroom and sat in front of the makeup table and mirror that had once belonged to her mother. It was still a wonder to her that her mother hadn't smashed the mirror as she'd smashed so much else over the years. Kath had appropriated the table and mirror the same day they committed her, moved it into her room all by herself. At first her father'd been appalled. *Couldn't you have waited?*

No. She could *not* have waited. She was going to get *something* out of the woman if it killed her. She'd made their lives such a living hell for so many years that dammit, she deserved something.

After a while her father got to thinking it was just Kath's way of remembering her mother as she was in better days, of honoring her memory and accepted what she'd done as that. She never corrected his thinking but he was wrong. Practically every time she looked in the mirror what she was saying to herself was *To hell with you mom, I survived you.* Saying it with a grim smile, as though her mother were somewhere in the mirror and could see her on the other side free while she was trapped there, trapped and able to read her thoughts. No honoring, no remembering.

Not if she could help it.

She brushed her hair and applied her makeup and dressed—one of her father's white starched Brooks Brothers shirts and a pair of tight new jeans and tennis shoes. No belt. Very simple. She imagined Ray would expect something more elaborate and didn't want to play to his expectations. She never wanted to with a boy. It was simple policy. You kept them off guard at first. It always paid to do so. She fastened the silver necklace her father had given her for her thirteenth birthday around her neck and she was ready.

From her bedroom window she saw the car roll up

in the driveway. He honked his horn once. Briefly. Politely. A single light tap.

She sat down on the bed and opened up a *Cosmo* and began to read.

It was not a good idea to hurry.

"How'd you get that walk, Ray? Mind my asking?"

"Nah. No big deal. I broke both my legs when I was a kid. You know, stupid kid stuff. I was nine, ten. There was this house under construction and a bunch of us were walking around on the frame, what was going to be the attic. They had just the bare rafters and the ceiling joists up, you know? So we're doing this kind of tightrope walk back and forth and this guy, this asshole, this asshole *pushes* me. I fall thirty feet to the ground and fracture both legs. Ten days in the hospital, compound fractures, both of them. Then the damn doctors took the casts off too early so they didn't heal right. I was varsity gymnastics that year. That was the end of that."

He didn't want to use the story about the drug dealer shooting him.

He was afraid it might spook her.

He definitely had her attention, though. He had the top down and he was shouting into the wind which was a good way to tell it. It made him seem tougher somehow, the story cooler. Elvis tooling down the highway with Lizabeth Scott in *Loving You*. Yeah, a lot like that.

They were on their way to a package store, heading down the mountain, you could see the lake glinting through the trees. She said she wanted some chips and stuff. Chips and stuff wasn't his idea of how to start off a perfect date but he wasn't going to argue with her. Even in a man's baggy shirt she looked terrific. She wasn't wearing a bra. The wind pressed the shirt flat to her tits and he could see the wind-stiff nipples. Damn! He was driving with a hard-on here. He wondered if she'd noticed. He figured it was a no-lose situation whether she did or didn't, either way.

"I got the guy though," he said. "I waited six months until he figured I'd forgotten all about it, and then one day after the movies we were all walking home, pretty much the same kids as before and I said, 'Hey, Eddie, remember that fall I took?' just a casual question and he looks at me and nods and so I sucker punch him. One shot right to the chin and he's out, bleeding all over the sidewalk. Concussion and a fractured skull. So he got to have *his* little stay in the hospital too. No, I don't mind you asking about it. Everybody does eventually."

He pulled into the parking lot and cut the engine. The lot was almost deserted, only three other cars though the package store was the biggest in the area. She had her compact out and was checking her makeup in the mirror. He got out and walked around and opened the door for her. With a girl like this you wanted to be a gentleman.

As she stepped out of the car he saw that she'd unbuttoned her blouse almost to the waist. *What the fuck?*

They walked toward the entrance.

"So, uh, what're we getting?"

"I'm getting some chips and a pack of cigarettes. You're going to steal us a couple of six-packs."

He laughed. "I don't need to *steal* stuff, Kath. I got plenty of money. I can buy us a case of it. Two cases! Scotch, bourbon. Whatever you want."

Her smile was thoroughly wicked. "What I want, Ray, is for you to steal it. Cold, please, and something imported."

They were almost to the door.

"Go on up the aisle to the left and get the beer. The chips are in the next aisle so I'll head over there. When you see me go back to the counter you just take them and walk out the door, just like that."

He laughed again. "Just like that. The guy's gonna see me."

"Ray." She put her fingers to the side of the shirt and flashed him a pink-tipped breast. "The guy's *not* gonna see you, believe me."

He had his doubts but he did as she told him. Walked down the aisle eyeing the six-packs that were ranged along the cooler until he came to the Lowenbrau and then pretended to keep on looking further until he saw her walk up to the register with four bags of chips and a box of pretzels hugged to her chest. There was one other shopper, a woman, behind him to the left checking out the wines but she and some fat guy in the vodka section all the way over on the other side of the store were the only ones he saw. *Casual,* he thought. *You can do this. No problem.* But his heart was beating fast as he reached into the case for the Lowenbrau. He had to suppress a nervous grin.

The lady was a pistol.

Halfway down the aisle he saw her point to a pack of cigarettes behind the balding old guy at the register, saw him turn and get them for her and put them on the counter along with the other stuff and then she was digging into her purse for her wallet, one shoulder cocked and the purse held low so that the shoulder pulled the baggy shirt open and Ray had all he could do not to laugh out loud just then because the bald guy's eyes were going nowhere except to what was inside that shirt, the guy did not get to see this too often, the guy was *riveted.*

He put the beer in the backseat and waited for her outside the car. Leaning on the passenger side. Very cool, waiting for her with that half-smile on his face he'd copped from Elvis. She came out with the brown paper bag under her arm laughing and shaking her head. He laughed too. It was contagious.

"That is one embarrassed old man," she said. She put the bag in back with the beer.

"How come?"

"I caught him at it. Got him dead to rights. I said, 'How would you feel if your fly was open and I could see your you-know-what and I just decided stare at it?' He didn't know what to say. I think he apologized to me five times. He got saved by some woman with a bottle of Cold Duck coming up behind me."

"You are *bad*, lady. I mean *bad!*"

"He's going to be thinking about this all night."

"Shit. He's gonna be *dreaming* about it!"

She stopped laughing then and looked at him and smiled. The same wicked smile as before.

"And what about you, Ray? What are you gonna be dreaming about?"

Her fingers went to her shirt and began slowly to button it again. He had no answer for that one. That one wasn't in the thesaurus. He just smiled at her and spread his hands as though to say *you got me, darlin'*, which was all he could think to do and then he opened the door for her and watched her slip inside.

"Take fifteen to eighty to forty-six."

"Why? Where we goin'?"

"You'll see. You'd better have a church key."

" 'Course I do."

He reached past her and opened the glove compartment. Dug around awhile amid maps and scraps of paper and came up with the bottle opener.

She cracked a beer and settled back.

"Pass me one too, will you?"

"You're driving."

"So?"

"A cop sees you with a bottle, you get arrested? You expect me to bail you out? Get home on my own? Have a joint, Ray. It's less conspicuous."

"Okay. Not a bad idea."

He reached into his shirt pocket and she watched him while he lit the joint. What to make of this strange little guy? She felt morally certain his story about the limp was just that, a story. Especially the part about decking the other kid. The limp, she felt certain, had sources which were probably a lot more mundane than that. Some childhood illness or something. The story was meant to impress her.

She didn't mind a lie so long as it was a good one. This one wasn't too bad. Not great but she liked the part about climbing around on the rafters, she'd done that herself as a girl. She'd find out the truth sooner or later if and when she wanted to. *If* she bothered to hang around that long. The jury was still out on that one.

She sat back to enjoy the view. Highway 15 rolled and twisted through small towns and long open stretches of land and thick dark forest where you had to be careful of deer at night. Where she was told people had even seen the occasional bear along the roadside. He was driving fast but he was driving well, taking care on the blind turns and hills. He knew how to handle an automobile.

She wondered how he'd handle New York City.

He was going to make an impression, that was for sure, at the place she was taking him. The duck's ass hairdo, the black leather jacket, black T-shirt and black jeans. The black silver-studded cowboy boots and silver ID bracelet, the touches of makeup.

She was testing him, sure. It almost wasn't fair to the guy.

But pass or fail on his part she had a feeling this should be kind of fun.

She wasn't saying much so he did most of the talking. About his apartment, describing how he'd furnished it and how he was planning to enlarge it by knocking out the back wall—actually something he'd only just thought of that minute. He could probably get Tim to do most of the work in exchange for some hash. Not a bad idea. About his band and his wanting to become a rock star. About his expertise with the flying and still rings back in junior high. About the drag races in the hollow. She seemed particularly interested in the races. A whole lot more than his opinions of who was hot and who was not in music these days. He told her about the time Bobby Sylvester'd lost control and drove his Ford off the road so deep into the woods that he'd startled a mother raccoon and her three cubs fishing in a stream.

He told her he'd take her there sometime. She asked if she could do the driving. He said that first he'd have to *see* her drive but maybe.

You couldn't promise them everything right up front.

By now he knew where they were going. They'd been on the road about an hour and fifteen minutes and were on Route 3 headed for the Lincoln Tunnel. He thought it was *very* cool of her to have thought of driving into the City but wondered exactly what she had in mind. A movie, maybe, at one of the big movie palaces? Some bar? He seriously doubted it was going to be a topless bar but he had the sense that with this one you never could tell. Even that was possible.

It was her call.

Traffic was heavy but he kept it at an even sixty until they hit the Tunnel and then he had to slow to thirty-five. He hated tunnels, especially this one. It was one of the reasons he didn't go into New York too often, to tell the truth. The Chevy always seemed too big and wide for the narrow lanes. Especially when you were shoulder-to-shoulder with some goddamn Greyhound bus. The tunnel had been built for the smaller cars of another time. The light inside was piss yellow against piss-yellow exhaust-stained tiled walls and tended to do more to distort your vision than to aid it. There was the sense of falling, of moving far faster than the reading on your speedometer. The fact that he was buzzed on the joint and the meth didn't help any. He couldn't wait to get the hell out of there.

"Turn up Tenth."

He pulled into uptown traffic. Felt much better now.

"I got a question. How's a California girl get to know the city?"

"My dad used to fly us here on vacations. He was born and raised in South Orange and used to like to take these sentimental journeys across the river. So I got to know the Tunnel pretty well. We'd stay at either the Olcott or the Sheraton so I got to know the Upper West Side. Think like a cabbie, Ray. You're going to make a right turn on Sixty-eighth."

"Like a cabbie?"

She laughed. "My father always says that. 'You're all right driving in New York if you think like a cabbie.' That means you drive defensively, you watch out for the other guy but you also drive like hell, you find the holes in traffic. You don't bother signaling, you don't worry about the speed limit, you just find the hole and *move* it."

He grinned. He could do that.

He shot up the hill, saw a van pulled over curbside on the right and darted left between a beat-up '65 Buick and a Checker Cab. *This was fun!*

"That's it. Stay at roughly this pace and you'll hit green lights all the way uptown."

Evidently everybody else on the street had the same information. They kept the traffic moving. At Sixty-eighth he slowed and took a right. By contrast crosstown traffic crawled.

"Look for a parking space. Anywhere around here."

He got lucky. Two and a half blocks down just a few yards from the corner of Columbus Avenue a steel-blue Corvette pulled out in front of him. It was going to be a tight squeeze but parallel parking was something he was good at. He got in at the first pass and straightened out. Turned off the lights and pressed the button to put the top down and cut the motor. He grinned at her.

"How'd I do?"

She leaned over and gave him a peck on the cheek. "You did just fine."

He had too. The whole drive. So far, perfect performance.

"I guess we'd better stash the beer though."

She nodded. She'd only had two of them along the drive. He took the six-packs and the empties out of the backseat and opened the trunk and put them in and was about to close it up again when she appeared behind him with the paper bag full of chips and pretzels.

"These too. This neighborhood's pretty quiet generally but in this town they'll break into your car for a subway token on the driver's seat."

He put them in and closed the trunk and fastened the clamps on the canvas top, slipped off his leather jacket and slung it over his shoulder, then turned to her.

"Okay. Where to?"

"Give me your arm."

"Huh?"

"Give me your arm."

He did. They strolled the line of vine-covered brownstones. The street was noticeably clean. He always pictured New York City as filthy. Small lean struggling trees studded the curbside every building or so, fenced in against the inevitable dog piss. The air was thicker here than it was up north in Sparta, more sticky and humid but there was a breeze that made it tolerable. A real nice summer night. He felt like a million bucks walking with this girl on his arm, here in the Big City. He couldn't wait to tell Tim and the guys.

He hoped he had enough cash. New York could be expensive, depending on what it was she wanted to do.

He'd taken fifty out of his account that morning. Which, after gassing up, left him thirty-five or so. He figured it ought to be enough. He knew she'd probably have her own cash on her but to run through his and have to ask her for some would be humiliating. Especially here where everybody had money. Just to live in one of these brownstones you had to have money. They were a long, long way from Times Square. Which was basically all he knew about New York City.

A horror-movie double feature at Forty-second Street.

Beers at Jack Dempsey's. Pricey beers but worth it for the old-time atmosphere and all the famous stars pictured on the walls. A place where you could almost feel like a star yourself just by standing at the bar.

The pale junkie dancers with pasties on their nipples at the Metropole.

Shops that sold whoopie cushions and fake vomit, knives and handcuffs.

That was what he knew. Not even Central Park, which she pointed out they were coming up to now. He'd heard the park was dangerous at night. You could get robbed and mugged. He could see a low stone wall across the street and a lot of tall trees behind it. Like the trees were being held prisoner there. They crossed the street and walked two blocks south and she led him up a set of stairs to a well-lit cobbled walkway leading into the park. The sign by the stairs said Tavern on the Green. There were shade trees and hedges and a trellis above him and electric streetlights that looked like gaslights from way-back-when.

He saw limos and cabs in the parking lot and people standing in front wearing business suits and long fancy summer dresses and a half a dozen horse-drawn carriages all waiting on the tourist trade. There was a doorman in some old-fashioned livery and a tall hat. The front doors were elaborately carved wood with panels of etched glass, like they'd come off some English mansion.

He was beginning to feel a little uncomfortable about this but Kath walked him in like she owned the place. Walked him through the paneled, carpeted hallway to the big oak desk manned by two tall skinny guys in tuxes with Valentino-style slicked-back hair and said that they were here for drinks in the garden.

One of the guys smiled and said certainly, right this way and held the door for her. They stepped out into a great wide courtyard full of trees strewn with potted flowers and carefully tended hedges and white wrought-iron chairs and tables. There were white tablecloths on the tables and folded linen napkins. The trees were all hung with japanese lanterns, dozens of them. To his right through the wraparound windows he could see diners in the restaurant inside leaning over their dinners, bathed in an amber glow. Music was coming from somewhere, some kind of easy-listening rock 'n' roll. Ordinarily the music would have annoyed him—in a car he'd *definitely* have changed the station. Here though, it seemed just about right. He could put up with nearly anything tonight anyhow.

Look who he was with.

A terrific long-legged blonde in a white shirt and tie and tight black skirt smiled and told them they could seat themselves wherever they liked. About two-thirds of the tables were full and packed close together. Katherine took him by the hand and led him through the crowd past one tree to another slightly off to one side and they sat down.

Already they'd got some glances. He definitely felt conspicuous. A *lot* conspicuous. For one thing everybody here looked over thirty, easy, unless you counted some of the little kids they'd dragged along. The one possible exception was the couple directly to their right who were probably in their late twenties but *dressed* as though they were in their thirties, young-Nixonite conservative style.

Plus, everybody looked like money up the ass. Solid upper-middle-class or better. He guessed he could smell cash as good as the next guy. And he smelled it all around him. He shook his head. He had to laugh.

"Kath, what in hell are we *doing* here?"

"We're having drinks, silly."

"Where'd you find this place? Your dad?"

She nodded. "I've been coming here since I was a kid. See that big old oak tree over there? My mother once shattered half a glass of banana daiquiri all over it."

"What'd she do that for?"

"I guess she didn't like her drink. Or else she was pissed at my father. I don't remember. I just remember that tree with banana daiquiri running all down the trunk like some kind of milky goo."

The long-legged blonde came by to take their order. He said scotch and soda. He figured that would do the trick sophistication-wise.

Kath laughed. "Banana daiquiri," she said. "For old times' sake."

The waitress just smiled and said thank you. He guessed you learned not to question stuff in a place like this.

"You must have been embarrassed as hell. For your mom I mean."

"Huh? Oh, not really. We got used to things like that from my mother."

"You mean, like, she was just in the habit of throwing her drinks around and all?"

"You don't want to know about my mother's habits, believe me. They'd make all that pretty, wavy hair of yours stand on end."

"You like it? Really?"

"What? Your hair?" She laughed. "Sure. Though I

might go with a little less gunk on it if I were you."

"It's not gunk. Honest. Here, feel it."

He bent his head a little and she smiled and reached over and ran her fingers lightly through his hair.

He wanted those beautiful fingers all over him.

"See? Vitalis. Not Brylcream or that greasy stuff."

"You're right. Not gunk. I apologize."

"Apology accepted."

She rubbed her fingers together and sniffed them.

"A little on the oily side, though."

She dug in her purse and came out with a pack of cigarettes and shook one from the pack.

"Got a light?"

He took out his own pack of Marlboros and his Zippo and flipped back the top with his thumb and lit hers first and then his own. The click of the top drew glances. Some of them lingered. Fuck 'em.

"Want to play a little game?"

"What kind of game?"

As a general rule he didn't like games unless they were ones of his making. He was wary.

"It's called Truth."

"Yeah?"

"I ask you a question, you have to answer it truthfully. No bullshit. You have to answer completely and truthfully and give it the best shot you can. Then you get to ask me a question. Same thing. Each person has, say, three questions each for starters."

"I don't get it. Who wins?"

She shrugged and took a drag of the cigarette and exhaled.

"Sometimes nobody wins. Sometimes everybody does."

He thought about it.

"I dunno. Weird game."

"You think so?"

"Sounds like some kind of head game to me."

"No, it's the opposite. See, head games are meant to fuck you up. Head games are when you're messing around with illusion. Smoke-and-mirrors stuff. Not the truth. The truth can't fuck you up, can it?"

He thought he knew about a hundred ways the truth could fuck you up, but he didn't say so. From the look of her she did too.

She was daring him, that was all.

The drinks arrived and their waitress said she'd run a tab for them. He liked that. Back home it was strictly cash on the bar. Pay as you go. Though he did wonder what they were charging for the drinks here. It was New York City after all. Kath's daiquiri was pretty substantial but his scotch and soda could have been a whole lot bigger. He'd have to do two or three of them even to feel anything.

The daiquiri had a cherry on top and a wedge of orange perched on the rim.

"You're not gonna heave that thing at any trees, are you?"

She smiled. "I don't know. I haven't tasted it yet." She took a sip through the straw. "I think I'll just drink it for now. So what do you think?"

"About what?"

"About the game."

She had him over a barrel here. If he said no it'd look like he was chicken. Like he had something to hide. Of course he *did* have a thing or two to hide. Everybody did. On the other hand if he played along he was supposed to tell the truth to her about whatever the hell she asked him. He didn't mind doing that, depending on *what* she asked him. He wondered how good her bullshit detector was. Maybe he could finesse her.

"Okay, I'll give it a shot. Go ahead. Ask me something."

He took a hit of the scotch. She squinted, like she was considering him.

"We'll start out easy. Ray, do you dye your hair?"

He laughed.

"Not personally, no."

"Unh-unh. You're supposed to answer truthfully and *completely,* remember?"

"Okay, all right. I have this girl who does it for me once a month. A shop over in Newton. Cuts it and styles it and gives it a touch-up. I guess it's kinda unusual for a guy but shit, everything's unisex these days anyway. My real-color hair's not bad but it's a little mousy brown for me. I just happen to like this better. And then, you know, there's the band."

Not bad, he thought. In fact he thought he did pretty good. He'd admitted to an eccentricity, sure. But also to having a certain amount of taste that set him apart from other guys, guys who were just run-of-the-mill, everyday slobs sitting in barbershops. And he'd done it without sounding defensive.

Not bad at all.

"My turn now, right?"

"Right."

He thought about it and sipped his drink. The drink was almost gone already.

"Okay. What do you really think of me?"

She laughed. "Well first of all, I hardly know you. But all right. You're funny, quirky in a way I kind of like. Good-looking, conceited."

"Conceited?"

"Conceited. And in this game you're not allowed to interrupt. Let's see, what else? You're a good driver. You're a pretty good dresser though I'm not too sure about the leather jacket and cowboy boots in August. You hang around with a bunch of losers. But I can't much blame you for that. Sparta's ninety percent losers anyway from what I can see. And you have secrets. You talk a lot but you don't say much. I find that . . . kind of interesting."

"That's it? That's all?"

"For now. My turn. Are you actually *fucking* Jennifer?"

"No."

"No?"

"Absolutely not."

"Never?"

"Isn't that another question? I thought it was my turn now."

He got her. She smiled and then shrugged. "Yeah, I guess it is."

He resolved never to fuck Jennifer again, which would make what he'd said fairly close to the truth. It was no huge loss. Especially not if he was going to be fucking Katherine.

"So. Are you attracted to me?"

She laughed. "You see? I *told* you you were conceited. That's two questions and they're both about you."

"No they're not. I'm trying to figure out how you see me is all. Your own personal perception, I mean. That's different, isn't it?"

"Sure, Ray. If you say so. Okay. Yeah, I find you attractive. That doesn't necessarily say I'm going to do anything about it, you understand. But yes. In a strange sort of way, yeah, sure. I do."

He wasn't so sure about what that *strange sort of way* stuff was but now he knew at least he had her going. She sipped her daiquiri and stared at him.

"What's the worst thing you've ever done?" she said.

Maybe it was the beers and the daiquiri working on her but she said it loudly.

He felt suddenly like everybody in the courtyard was staring at him or at least stealing sidelong glances, dozens of eyes on him sitting there with an almost empty glass of whiskey in front of him, *Ray in a T-shirt and jeans with a silver chain around his neck while every-*

body else was wearing white shirts and ties, college grads for sure most of them while he hadn't even finished high school, all these people waiting to hear the answer to her question, what was the worst thing this out-of-town guy who obviously didn't belong here had ever done.

The music didn't seem loud enough. The talk and laughter at the tables didn't seem loud enough. There was no way he could tell her anyway. Though there was a moment there when crazily enough, he actually wanted to.

Which itself was fucking scary.

"I trashed a house once."

She waited for him to continue. He decided to give it to her pretty much straight.

"I was fourteen, fifteen. Me and Tim, who I guess was like, twelve, we'd both run away from home. He had his reasons and I had mine though mine were basically that I was pissed at my parents, that's all. It just seemed like a cool idea. Run away, just get the hell out of there.

"Anyhow there was no place we could crash where somebody's parents wouldn't tell *our* parents but Timmy knew of this place up on Stirrup Iron Road where his father'd done some work as carpenter. Used to bring Timmy along on weekends, show him how to hold a hammer. Some macho bullshit. Make a man of the kid, that kind of stuff."

"It didn't take, I guess."

"Hey, Timmy's all right. You just got to get to know him a little."

"Sure I do."

He decided to let it pass.

"Anyway it was way the hell out in the boonies and he knew that the owners only used it in the summer and here it was March or maybe April so the two of us broke in there. Big four-bedroom job. Rich people. So rich that now they don't even bother to use the house at all anymore or even to rent the thing out. It just sits there all year long. Fully furnished. You believe it? Sheets over all the furniture. Man, I don't get it. Goddamn fucking waste if you ask me.

"But breaking in was easy because they had these big glass double doors off the patio in back that were easy to jimmy. We stayed two, two-and-a-half weeks. All they had to eat was this brown rice and pasta, some canned stuff, tuna and fancy soup and canned tomatoes and Spaghetti-Os for their kids I guess. So we lived on that. Man, to this day I hate brown rice and Spaghetti-Os. But the liquor cabinet was full and we found a case of beer in the cellar. I figured out how to turn on the pump so we had running water but no electricity and it was cold out there in March so we busted up some of the furniture and made fires in the fireplace and by the end there wasn't much furniture left because we'd burnt it all."

The leggy blond waitress appeared and asked him did he want another drink. He decided he did and to hell with the price. He was feeling expansive sitting there in the warm night breeze, expansive because of Kath and because of the story. Kath was still sipping her drink and said she was fine for now.

The next part was possibly a little risky but he decided to tell her anyway.

"I found a twenty-two rifle in the master bedroom closet and a thirty-eight Ladysmith revolver in the nightstand along with some boxes of shells. We were amazed they'd just leave them sitting there and nobody home more than half the year. But see, the worst thing about running away was the fucking boredom. You couldn't watch television or listen to any of their records which were mostly classical anyway because there wasn't any electricity, the pool was drained in back, so all we did was smoke dope all day and drink and look at magazines and hang around the house.

"So we took to trying to pot birds and squirrels and shit out from the glass double doors. The idea I guess was to vary our diet so to speak with some squirrel-meat stew but what it really was was to relieve the goddamn boredom.

"We never hit anything. I mean, we were *lousy* shots. I got better eventually but at the time I couldn't hit shit and neither could Tim. So we started target practicing *inside* the house. Set a plate up on the mantel, shoot it. A lamp, a bottle, a beer can. Some of those dumb china figures they had. It was fun because whether you hit the thing or not, you had to dodge this bullet whizzing around after you, you had to dodge the ricochet. I guess we were pretty stupid. We could have got killed in there. But we were pretty stoned and it was a kick. We even shot the television. It wasn't any use to us anyhow.

"Anyway to make a long story short one morning we get up and realize that the house is a fucking disaster. I mean, we never washed a dish or a glass never mind pots and pans so the kitchen's a wreck, the living room's a wreck with broken glass swept up into little piles everywhere and hardly a stick of furniture, the liquor cabinet's empty and we're out of tuna and sick of Spaghetti-Os. There's no more pot, we're bored shit-less, so we said, fuck it, we're outa here."

"Where'd you go?"

He shrugged. "Home. Told 'em we'd spent two weeks or whatever it was just hitching around. We both got grounded for I don't know *how* long, but I guess they just decided to believe us. We never did get caught or anything. But that house—that house was a wreck, man. I mean, the second or third night we were there Tim had too much to drink and puked all over the bed-sheets. All he did was move to another bedroom. I mean, that house was *funky*."

His drink arrived and he thanked the waitress.

If he lived in New York he'd have chased her ass to hell and back. The waitress was a stone looker. He lit a smoke.

"So," he said. "What's the worst thing *you* ever did?"

"That would be lying to my mother."

He laughed. "Lying to your *mother?* That's the *worst* thing?"

"One lie in particular."

He waited.

"The *complete* truth, right?" he said.

"I remember." She sighed. "My mother was diagnosed paranoid schizophrenic when I was somewhere around twelve. But she was crazy long before that. I hardly remember her sane in fact. She went from being this decent mother I guess and this terrific painter, an abstractionist—she had shows in San Francisco, Rhode Island and even here in the City at the OK Harris Gallery, this real prestige place run by the guy who discovered Warhol. Anyhow she went from there to thinking the entire art world was out to get her. And not just the art world either but the cops and the Mafia, aunts, uncles, cousins. Pretty much her entire family. And oh yeah, the FBI too.

"But my father refused to commit her. I guess he still loved her or maybe he just couldn't do it. So she'd be in and out of hospitals all the time. On and off every kind of drug you can think of. You think you know about smashing up houses? My mother could have given you guys a few lessons.

"Anyhow this one Saturday afternoon, I was fourteen, my mom's in one of her rages, she's off her medication again and she's tearing up the flower garden out in front of the house, in front of the *neighbors*, it's a nice day and half the street is out there and she's insisting I help her, pulling up violets and begonias and shrubs and I don't know what else and scattering them all over the lawn and rushing over to me and grabbing my wrists and insisting I help, yelling at me to go and get the shovel from the garage goddammit because there's somebody *buried* in there. It's a plot by the police and art dealers to pin some murder on her and get hold of all her paintings.

"Finally I'd had it up to here with all this crazy bullshit so I told the lie.

"I told her my father had come into my room the night before and said that he was leaving her any day now. That he was sick of this too. And that he was taking me with him. So fuck her and her bodies buried in the garden, she could dig them up herself.

"I think I did it because it was a combination of the fact that that was what I was wishing for, that he *would* take me away somewhere, that and because I thought that she'd *tell him* what I'd said. Confront him with it. I couldn't tell him myself. We didn't have the kind of thing where I could just go up to him and say, 'Come on, dad, let's get the hell out of here, let's put her in a loony bin and split.' But I guess I thought she'd confront him with what I said to her and that way he'd know how I felt.

"But she didn't. What she did do was constantly accuse him of *planning* to leave. Like now he's part of the conspiracy against her. She'd search his drawers for maps and tickets and travel folders. Call the bank hour after hour to make sure he was actually there at work and not flown away to some island somewhere. She was driving him and his assistants bananas. Not once that I know of did she mention me saying *anything* to her or even mention me much at all. It was like I *couldn't* be part of the conspiracy, I was out of the evil loop because I was her daughter. When in fact if anybody was conspiring against her, it was me.

"Anyhow that was kind of the last straw, her not being able to trust my father. The conspiracies got crazier and crazier, with satanists involved. She's calling the cops on a daily basis only she's calling them in Orange County because all the cops in our county are all after her and crooked and finally she gets this thing in her head that my father's given her syphillis, so that she's rotting away inside.

"Medication didn't work. You couldn't medicate her because she'd hide whole bottles of pills and say she lost them and then take more than she was supposed to. Or else she'd decide she was fine and the meds were part of the problem anyway, part of the plot. So when medication time rolled around she'd hide her pill under her tongue and then spit it out when we weren't looking.

"Then one night while we were asleep she went downstairs. She went to the kitchen. We had all the knives and all the sharp stuff locked away by then. We had an electric range, though, not a gas stove. She turned the two front burners on high and waited till the coils were red and she put both her hands on the burners and held them there and woke us with her screaming. The idea was, she was trying to burn away her finger-prints. It's not even possible to do that. I remember the coils were still smoking when we got down there.

"She wouldn't let my dad touch her. Just me. But I didn't know what the fuck to do with burns that bad and basically neither did he. So we had to wait for the emergency crew, me holding her squatting on the floor while she's howling and sobbing and my dad at the kitchen table just sitting there crying into the palms of his hands. The way I knew he was crying was I could see his shoulders shake. She never painted again after that. Even though after a while she could have once the burns had healed. When she got out of emergency care and was stable enough, he finally committed her."

He sat back in his chair looking at her. He realized his second drink was almost gone. He finished it.

"Damn," he said.

She finished hers too.

"That's three questions each," she said. "You want to go another round?"

He thought it was a hell of a story. *What he had here,* he thought, *was one tough girl*.

"No. I don't think so."

"Neither do I. Let's get out of here."

She raised her hand for the waitress and asked for the check. The girl smiled and did the addition and tore the check off the pad and put it facedown beside his drink, telling them both to have a lovely evening. You too, he said and had a look at the check.

"Steep?"

He guessed she could see by his expression.

"Nine bucks. Steep where I come from, anyway."

"Leave her a dollar."

"That's only ten percent. You sure?"

"No. I mean leave her a dollar, period."

"Huh?"

"The blonde you've been eyeing every damn chance you get, Ray. Stiff her."

"Why?"

"Because I'm asking you to. Will you do that for me?"

He wondered what they did to you walking out on a check in New York City. But okay, he thought, we'll play that game too. He reached for his wallet and saw that the blonde was taking an order from a table to the left, she was leaning over a fat man with a mustache and mostly had her back to him. He pulled out a dollar and put it on top of the check and put the ashtray on top of that. He stood and shook his head.

"You're something," he said. He meant it. He'd never met one like this before. "Let's go."

Somewhere inside the Lincoln Tunnel she thought how odd it was that she'd told him as much as she had, in such detail and that telling it still hurt. She thought of her father visiting her mother in the hospital tomorrow morning and that what he'd be visiting would be a vegetable, basically, a catatonic. Somebody who sat there and rocked and stared and maybe moaned but that was all and who used to be her mother.

He'd asked her to come along.

She was glad she hadn't but maybe she should have. She didn't know.

Fuck it. She had other things to think about right now. Like this guy here smoking a joint and driving her back to Sparta.

What to do with Ray.

"I'll just walk you up the stairs. Make sure you get in okay."

She smiled at him as though to say she was a big girl and besides, the line was transparent as hell but sure, okay, why not? A complicated smile but then he got the feeling all her smiles were complicated in one way or another.

"All right."

She led him up the walkway and up the stairs and fished her keys out of her purse and then turned to him very serious and looked at him. He realized his heart was pounding. He felt like a kid on his first date ever and his first date ever just happened to be the senior prom.

"Thanks, Ray. I had a really good time."

He put on the grin. Wore it like a Halloween mask. *Trick or treat.*

"So hey. Do I get a kiss at least?"

"I don't fuck on the first date, Ray."

"I didn't say you did. Though actually it's our second date. And we kissed that time, remember?"

She laughed. "You're counting that little barhop with Tim and Jennifer? I don't think so."

"I asked if I got a kiss at least. Did I say a thing about fucking?"

She set her purse down on the porch.

"Sure," she said. "Sure you do."

She slid into him and wrapped her arms around his neck and her mouth tasted like beer and cigarettes but sweet underneath like the mouth of a very young girl. He was very aware of the trim strength of her body and even more aware that she was just as tall as he was, taller if you counted what was stuffed inside his boots and aware of her breasts beneath the man's white shirt, her breasts moving against his chest and he wanted very much to move his hand around to touch them but knew he'd better not, not this time, not unless she actually led him in that direction, which was almost like a prayer for him just then but then like most prayers he doubted it would do him a damned bit of good.

He had one arm across the center of her back and the other down lower near the base of her spine and he pressed her into him so she'd know he was hard for her even if she wasn't having any. It was a message to her, and he guessed she got it because she moaned a little and her left hand went into his hair and then through his hair and down to the base of his neck and she kissed him harder, moving against him then pulling away, nipping at his lower lip and then she kissed him again.

The kiss was softer this time and he could almost feel her drift away from him, it was a goodnight kiss, he knew one when he felt one and he had all he could do not to start mauling her then and there right on the porch, to hell with what she wanted and not fucking on the first or second date. But his good sense told him he still had tomorrow and her father would still be out of town that night as well. He was not used to waiting. But he was not used to a girl like this either.

"Good night, Ray," she said.

"Tomorrow night?" he said and that was another

prayer. He didn't know what he'd do if she refused him. She let it hang for a moment.

"Okay. One condition."

"What?"

"You pick what we do this time. And you make it interesting."

"What happened just now was interesting."

She smiled. "Other than that."

"You telling me it's out of the question?"

"Did I say that? I said make it interesting. Surprise me. Think you can manage that?"

He already had one idea in mind. It came to him as soon as she said *surprise me*. He'd surprise her all right. His grin was real this time.

"Yeah, I can do that."

"Good. Nine o'clock?"

"Nine o'clock. You got it."

She pecked him on the cheek and opened the door and stepped inside and with her back to him said, " 'Night, Ray."

" 'Night."

When she was gone it was like all the breath had gone out of him, like she'd punched him in the gut and he took a moment to collect himself and realized he still had a hard-on for godsake and then he headed for his car. Then had to sit there a while catching his breath, slowing down his heartbeat. Then he started up the car and backed slowly out of the driveway.

The wind in his hair felt like her fingers in his hair as he sped away.

Chapter Twenty-three

Saturday, August 9
The News

Jennifer Fitch was doing the dinner dishes when she heard the news. She heard it from her foster mother Mrs. Griffith who had just seen a report on television. Mrs. Griffith's opinion on the matter was that in this day and age you had to be terribly careful who you associated with. Jennifer knew that this was directed none too subtly at her but made no comment. Telling Ray about it was an excuse to phone him so she did that just as soon as she finished the dishes, feeling bad for a moment that it wasn't Tim she was thinking of calling but the line was busy and by the time she got through to him Ray already knew.

Charlie Schilling heard it earlier on the radio in Ed Anderson's backyard. It was Charlie's day off and Ed had invited him over for a barbecue that evening, said he hadn't been over for a couple of beers and a sirloin all summer long and it was damn well time he did. He knew Ed had a fine hand with a sirloin on the grill and allowed himself to be persuaded.

When he got there around five he wished he hadn't. Because there was Sally Richmond in charge of the potato salad and tossed greens and corn on the cob and taking photos of the three of them with her Nikkormat. Talking with her at the motel was one thing but partying with her when he knew what Bill and June Richmond would say about it was another. It was too late to back out now but he was going to have to read Ed the riot act tomorrow. Ed's business was Ed's business and he thought that Sally was a nice girl but two grown men drinking beer with a eighteen-year-old in shorts and halter top was not exactly kosher, not in his book anyway.

And then there was the matter of Sally's getting a job at the station. He had to discuss that piece of business with Ed too. He'd made a point of asking around on Wednesday and it didn't take long for him to see that word of Ed and Sally had made the rounds. He got a lot of averted glances. Nobody he spoke to needed anybody even on a part-time basis, though desks were stacked with paper wherever you looked. Not even Johannson, who was usually so lazy with his paperwork Schilling had gotten into the habit of going though his desk *for* him in order to find whatever file he happened to need. Most cops would bristle at such an intrusion but not Johannson. His desk was strictly help yourself. Even he didn't need anybody.

What it came down to was that everybody at the station liked Ed but nobody was going to get involved with a situation where an ex-cop was making it with a teenager. He thought of taking Sally on at his own desk but he *really* didn't need anybody. He'd been the only guy in his typing class in high school and though he took a lot of ribbing for it at the time he was also the fastest one in his class and the most accurate. A lefty who wrote his longhand painfully and badly, his grades had soared. It was what had enabled him to go on so long without taking on another partner after Ed. His own desk was clear.

Besides, as Ed's best friend taking on Sally seemed somehow wrong to him. It would indicate approval. He guessed that was part of what the others were going through too.

He decided to go to the head of the class, to Jackowitz himself. Figuring as captain he'd be the last to know. The boss usually was. Jackowitz just looked him in the eye and said *Bill Richmond's a very prominent man. I don't think it's a real good idea, Charlie.*

Jackowitz hardly even *knew* Ed, and word had got to him too.

He had to talk to Ed about it but he kept stalling. He didn't like to hurt him and this was going to hurt no matter how diplomatically he tried to put it. He certainly wasn't going to get into it here in Ed's backyard. Not unless somebody asked.

Luckily they didn't.

They were listening to the radio, some top-ten station and Ed had his sprinkler going way in back so that when the wind wasn't blowing the delicious smell of charcoal-broiled steak at you there was the fresh green scent of watered lawn and he settled in on a lawn chair with a beer and willed himself to relax and have a nice evening despite the peculiar circumstances. Sally's Volkswagen parked on the grass nearby—so it couldn't be seen from the street—seemed the emblem of his discomfiture. He'd finished half the beer when the news came on, the newscaster managing to sound both grim and all excited both at once.

When the report was over Ed flipped the steak and shook his head and said I don't know what the hell this world is coming to.

Sally was petting the stray black cat curled up purring

at her feet. Poor little girl, she said to the cat. In the Middle Ages they'd have burned you. Probably some of these creeps *still would* burn you just for fun.

Tim Bess heard it on the radio too, only half an hour later. He was sitting on a towel at Alpine Pool stewing about why Jennifer hadn't called, hadn't returned the two calls he'd made, the first one answered by Mr. Griffith and the second by Mrs. Griffith both of whom had assured him that they'd relay the message. No contact whatsoever since she'd fucked him and what the hell did *that* mean?

The beach was practically deserted. Most of the kids had gone home to dinner and so would've Tim but his ten-year-old little sister Ginnie had begged him for one more dip in the pool. And Ginnie was a pretty good kid as little kids went. So he let her. His sister was a seal in the water, a much better swimmer than Tim and he actually liked watching her out there diving and surfacing and barely making a ripple.

Besides, he had to think. And you couldn't do that home. Especially not around dinnertime. His father was okay and mostly just read the paper but his mother was a nonstop talker. Either that or she was always humming something 100 percent tuneless and whether she was talking or humming it was irritating as hell. It was as though his mother couldn't stand a silence. You couldn't think there. Here you could. So he indulged his little sister and stayed.

So how come she hadn't called?

He couldn't have been *that* bad in bed.

They'd been friends for years.

He felt confused and hurt and for some reason, he had to admit it, a little bit worried. He didn't know why. It was the way you feel when it's dark outside and you're walking all alone and you get the feeling somebody's waiting for you just around the next corner. Probably irrational as hell but maybe not.

He was thinking that maybe he'd better just drop by the Griffith house tonight and see what was up with Jennifer even though he didn't usually do that because Mr. and Mrs. Griffith obviously didn't like him. Like he wasn't good enough to hang around with Jennifer. Who wasn't even their real daughter. He thought that maybe it had more to do with Tim's being friends with Ray than with Tim himself but they still didn't like him coming over.

He was considering doing it anyway when he heard the news on the radio.

Christ, he thought. *I gotta phone Ray.*

He got up off the towel and started packing their gear. When Ginnie surfaced he called her, said it was time to go and she didn't fight him like some kids would, she just smiled and waded dripping out of the water and squeezed out her long brown hair.

They climbed the trail to his father's pickup and spread their towels out on the seats and got in the car. All the way home he had the radio on, switching from station to station but all he got was music and commercials. He went right to his room and peeled off his trunks and put on a pair of jeans. He could smell his mother's spaghetti sauce cooking on the stove downstairs but figured he still had plenty of time to phone Ray before she called him down for dinner.

He picked up on the second ring.

"Did you hear what *happened* last night?"

"No. What?"

He didn't sound bored or disinterested the way he did sometimes. Maybe because Tim's own voice was so excited.

"They killed Sharon Tate, man!"

"Killed who?"

"Sharon Tate! The girl in *Playboy*? Remember that

vampire thing in *Playboy*? That movie *Valley of the Dolls*? *Wrecking Crew*? Sharon Tate, man! Oh and man, that *witchy* thing, you know, that *witchy* thing, *Eye of the Demon* or *Eye of the Devil* or something."

"Cool down. Who killed her?"

"They don't know. But man, they think it was *satanists*. That's the really weird part. See, there was blood on the walls and stuff, writing, like it was some kind of ritual murder or something. I heard it on the radio, there was blood all over the place. She was pregnant and they like *ripped the baby out,* man. Ripped it right out of her and they found these black hoods like satanists wear and they killed this other woman, some heiress or something and two other guys, some guy who was her hairdresser or makeup guy, I dunno which. Cut the shit out of *all* of 'em."

"Shit!"

Ray was impressed he could tell. He didn't get to impress Ray real often.

"And see, she's married to Roman Polanski, right? The guy who directed *Rosemary's Baby*. Which is all about witches, right? And she was in that *Eye of the Devil* thing. We saw it at the drive-in a long time ago, remember?"

"Yeah. I kinda do. She was fucking gorgeous."

"So it's *got* to be satanists. Has to be. You gotta wonder what shit Polanski was into."

"Wild. Hey listen, I'm gonna turn on the TV. See if they show any pictures or anything. Let me know if you hear any more about it. Call me."

"Sure. What's on for tonight?"

"I got another date with Katherine. I wanna go turn on the tube. Call you later."

"Okay."

And just like Jennifer he never did.

* * *

Katherine heard the six o'clock news on TV in her bedroom.

Etta had just gone home for the evening. The smell of pot still wafted up the stairs.

In fact they did have pictures. Of the victims as they'd been in life. The attractive brunette heiress to the Folger coffee fortune standing beside her Polish jet-set lover. Publicity photos of the handsome, internationally known hairstylist, who looked to her a lot like the French movie actor Alain Delon. And of the beautiful young ash-blond starlet married to the famous director. There was no picture of the teenage boy they'd found in the car outside and no mention yet of his name.

They'd filmed an aerial view of the big sprawling house at 10050 Cielo Drive and of the winding road leading up to it and of the gate outside.

They made a big deal about Sharon Tate being eight months pregnant as though it were the most tragic and horrible thing imaginable for an unborn child to be denied its birth. Whereas as far as she was concerned the most horrible thing imaginable had happened to the actress herself, to be murdered in all likelihood begging for her life at the most awful moment Katherine could think of, full of beauty and hopes for career and family, probably in love with the guy she married and carrying his baby and maybe even at the brink of real stardom. She had to wonder just when it had become clear to Sharon Tate that none of these things was to be. That all her sweet beginnings were endings now.

It was almost impossible to imagine what she must have felt like. You thought about it and you almost wanted to cry. You wanted to smash things. It just confirmed her opinion that basically, the world sucked.

Who would do that kind of thing?

She switched the station to a rerun of "Wild Kingdom," about water buffalos of all things and finished painting her toenails. In less than half an hour "The

Dating Game" was on, a stupid show but like "Wild Kingdom" it would take her mind off Sharon Tate, which had disturbed her to a surprising degree.

She wondered why it should.

Chapter Twenty-four

Ray

He parked the car a few blocks away and cut the lights. He got out and jogged uphill to her house so that he was puffing by the time he got there and then stood awhile in the darkness beside the hedges catching his breath and looking up at the lighted dormer. Her bedroom window.

He checked his watch. Just after 8:30.

He was supposed to be there at nine.

She wanted a surprise. He'd give her one.

Incredible to be doing this on this of all nights. The night after Sharon Tate and Jay Sebring. And what a weird coincidence that he'd *thought of doing it* the same night they were getting murdered. He wondered how those guys had managed to get in. He wondered if they'd climbed a tree like he was doing now.

He'd noticed the tree right away the first time he drove her home, and more than once he'd thought about spying but this was better than spying. He wondered why they hadn't cut the branches back farther. Because you could step from one of the limbs right out onto the roof, the limb was thick and looked reliable.

He hadn't climbed much since he was a kid but this was easy, a whole lot easier than the flying rings, the tree had handholds and footholds wherever you needed them, more like a ladder than a tree with very few obstructions so that pretty soon he was standing on a limb just off the bole a few feet from the roof and slightly above it and dusting off his hands. The slope of the roof didn't look bad and the chimney was right there in front of him. He could grab on to that and from there the gable with the darkened dormer that would be the master bedroom, her father's bedroom, then slide across the few feet of shingles to the second gable where the light was burning.

Yeah, sure. A whole lot easier said than done.

The chimney was fine but he almost lost his footing getting from there to the first gable, his boots a *major* disadvantage on the shingles, and crossing from the first to the second gable he had to go flat out on the fucking roof, inching across, sweating and grunting like a pig and hoping like hell the shingles would hold or else he was going down right over the overhang into the bushes below, wondering why the hell he'd thought of this dumb idea in the first place and hoping she wouldn't hear him scraping his way along crab-wise, looking ridiculous up there, until finally he was able to grasp the corner board of the second gable, hold on to the thing and rest. By then the palms of his hands and fingers felt raw, his knees were scraped inside the jeans and probably he was filthy pretty much all over.

Some balcony scene. Some fucking Romeo.

Still, damned if this wouldn't surprise her.

He inched over and rested squatting with his back to the gable for a minute and dusted off his shirt and jeans. Luckily he'd picked black again for both. The dirt didn't show as much. He ran his fingers through his hair and then turned and looked through the window.

She wasn't there. The light on the dressing table was burning and the one beside the bed. The bathroom door was open and he could see the toilet and the edge of the sink but that was all. She could be in the bathroom or she could be downstairs. He could hear her air-conditioner humming from the window opposite just beside the bed.

If anything his heart was beating faster now than it had when he was crossing the roof. He considered the possibilities. He could try the window and if it opened, climb into the room. He could wait outside until she showed up and tap on it. It occurred to him then that if she was downstairs already she might just wait for him there and not go back to her room at all, not even to turn off the lights. Daddy had money. Maybe she couldn't give a shit about wasting the electricity. He hadn't thought of that and it was a helluva thing to have to think about now. Not only would all of this have been for nothing but he'd have to find his way down off the roof without breaking his goddamn neck.

You better check the window.

It opened. Now his choices were easier.

He liked the idea of being inside. There was still the possibility of slipping off this stupid perch of his, the very real possibility of broken bones.

He raised the window all the way and gripped the inside jambs on both sides and hauled himself in. The room smelled strongly of her perfume. The bed was made, the pillows plumped. She kept the place pretty neat. There was a fine dusting of powder on the dressing table and the poster of John Lennon in his granny glasses, the same fucking poster Tim had, was folding down off the thumbtack on the top left side. But that was about all he could find out of place there.

He wouldn't have figured Kath for a neat freak.

He sat down on the bed, smiling, *because this was gonna be good* and no sooner had he done so than she walked in from the bathroom with a towel wrapped around her hair and another around her body and jumped and gasped like she'd damn near been run over by a passing train.

"What the . . . *fuck,* Ray?"

"Hi. Surprise you?"

"*Surprise* me? Yeah, I guess you could say that. Jesus!"

"You told me to surprise you."

"I didn't tell you to scare me half to death. What the hell are you doing here?"

He pointed to the open window.

"Came in through there."

"Bullshit. I left the door open downstairs. I must have."

"Maybe you did and maybe you didn't but I came in through there."

She walked over to the window and looked outside. "You're telling me you somehow got up on the roof and opened the window and climbed in. That's ridiculous. There's no ladder out there. You took the stairs."

He stood. "Do I look like I took the stairs? Didn't think I'd get this dirty, but what the hell, it was worth it. It was fun."

It was *not* fun but she didn't have to know that. "See that tree? I climbed that and then over past your dad's bedroom and over across the roof."

She looked him carefully up and down and finally he saw that she believed him.

"You're crazy. You could have gotten yourself killed. What are you, a part-time cat burglar?"

He couldn't tell if she was impressed or peeved or what. He shrugged.

"A lady tells me to surprise her, I surprise her."

"I guess you do. So now what? You want to hang around and watch me dress? Is that it?"

"It hadn't occurred to me but sure. Love to."

"In your dreams, Ray. There are some beers and Pepsis down in the fridge. Help yourself. Where we going, by the way?"

"I thought Bertrand's Island."

"Bertrand's Island?"

"You never heard of it? It's an amusement park."

She nodded. "An amusement park, huh? They have a roller coaster?"

"Best around."

She took the towel off her head and began drying her hair. He couldn't tell what her reaction was to his plan for the evening any more than he could tell how she felt about him coming in through the window. He had a hard time reading this one, he really did.

"You hear about those murders out in L.A.?"

"Yeah. I heard on TV."

"Pretty wild, huh?"

"Wild's one way to put it. Go have yourself a drink. I'll be down in a few minutes," she said.

He was dismissed.

She looked great again. Tight black sleeveless sweater and a cream-colored miniskirt. Though this time there was a bra.

But how the hell to get to her?

He couldn't really seem to impress her tonight no matter what he said or did. At Bertrand's Island she appeared to have a pretty good time. She said the roller coaster was okay but you could see she'd been on better, you could tell by the way she said it—though she didn't rub it in or anything by naming any or saying where. Probably fucking California. They'd gone around twice on the 'coaster and did the Tilt-a-Whirl and the Wild Mouse, which dipped way out over the shore of Lake Hopatcong and swooped back in again. In between they put away a few beers dosed with Chivas from his hip flask but mostly they just walked around looking at the lights and the people, listening to calliope music and the screams off the rides. He'd shot ducks well enough to win her a teddy bear and thrown darts at the balloons well enough to win her another. Aim-wise he was in top form. The beers and scotch loosened him up. He wished he felt in top form otherwise.

She seemed to like the teddy bears and the rides but he could tell she was a little bored.

Bored with him?

It wasn't something he was used to.

When she said no to the Ferris wheel he knew he had to come up with a new idea and do it soon. The longer they did nothing but wander the grounds the worse it was going to get. The drag strip would have been perfect. But the strip had gotten busted last weekend and the Man would be watching it, so that was out. After a while he figured it.

"So. Want to split?"

"Sure. Where to?"

He grinned. "You'll see."

In the parking lot she stopped about ten feet from his car and started looking around.

"Car's over here," he said.

"I know," she said and kept looking. "You know how to hot-wire, Ray?"

He laughed. "No. I've seen it in the movies. But I wouldn't know where to begin."

"I do. I had a boyfriend, Deke. Knew all kinds of good things. Which one do you like?"

"Which *car* do I like? I like my own car."

She shot him a glance. "Fine. Then you can just drive yourself home in it. I'm thinking that little black 'Vette over there. Thanks for the teddy bears, Ray. It's been real."

And the next thing he knew she was walking over to the Corvette and trying the door handle, the teddy bears like small hostages tucked beneath her arm. He couldn't believe it. He stood there like a damn fool watching her.

"Shit. It's locked." She walked around and tried the passenger side. "Shit!"

Anybody in the lot could have heard her. He all of a sudden felt very exposed. The night air felt too damn thick and too damn warm.

"I don't suppose you know how to *break into* a car?"

"Jesus, Kath! What the hell are you doing?"

She looked around again and then walked over to a big red Caddy in the corner of the lot and tried all four doors on that one. The Caddy was locked too. Thank god.

"Oh, well. Fuck it. The rest of these junkers aren't worth the trouble. What the hell. It was an idea."

She marched back over to his Chevy and smiled like nothing unusual had happened here so he unlocked the passenger side for her, which was about all he could think to do and she opened the door and got in. She tossed the teddy bears in the backseat and then propped them up next to each other.

The hostages were passengers now. He slid behind the wheel.

Was this lady strange or what?

He couldn't tell if she was just testing him again or if she'd really have gotten him involved in an auto theft.

Grand theft auto? Jesus!

"Let's go," she said.

They rounded the corner up the hill, the dirt road winding through the thick stands of trees and when he stopped he was glad to see there were no other cars or campers anywhere. They'd be alone. He'd had a feeling that they would be. Since the night he'd done the two girls locals tended to avoid the place. Even though Turner's Pool below was a whole lot better than Alpine across the mountain. Tourists came by every now and then but even some of them got spooked away by what the locals said. As though the place were cursed or something. It was stupid.

He didn't know why he'd thought to take her here except it felt right. In a way it was his turf. And he had the feeling that they'd be alone here.

She was staring at a blackened campfire site in the headlights.

"What. We're going camping?"

"Nah. Swimming. There's a real neat pool down there. You'll see."

"You want to swim?"

"It's a warm night, sure."

"No swimsuits, Ray."

"You always use a swimsuit?"

Saying that like maybe *she* was the one who was chicken.

"No towels either."

"So? We air-dry."

She looked across the clearing and into the woods beyond and then back. Her smile was complicated again.

"You better have a flashlight."

"In the glove compartment. Same as with the church key."

She opened it and took it out.

"Okay. Swimming."

She turned on the flashlight and got out of the car and he pointed her toward the path leading down to the pool and then they were moving through the thick tangled woods and down over the rocks and she was giving him hardly any slack at all, using the flashlight in front

216

of her and only rarely sweeping it back to him but he knew this path almost as well as he knew his own apartment. He and Tim had been coming here forever. Only once did he lose his footing and there was a tree beside him to grab on to so she never even knew it had happened.

At the narrow pebble shoreline she stood there letting the light play over the black expanse of water. It sounded like a thousand frogs were out there in the darkness hidden from the beam.

"Leeches," she said.

"It's possible. That bother you?"

"Not if it doesn't bother you. I mean, the thought of a leech on your dick."

"My dick will have to take its chances."

She kicked off her tennis shoes and stepped into the water.

"Chilly."

"That should keep down the leeches."

"Enough with the leeches, Ray."

He laughed. He could tell the idea bothered her. Maybe not scared her exactly but bothered her. Close enough. He felt a slight shift in the balance of power. If you managed to scare somebody you always had the advantage. For the first time all night long and maybe both nights together he felt he had one up on her.

So push it, he thought.

"Twenty bucks says you haven't got the guts to go in first without me. Face all those nasty leeches all by yourself. Maybe even a snake or two. Who knows?"

"I thought this was your idea. Cool in the pool."

"I'll be right in after you. Twenty bucks."

"You want to watch me get naked. Right?"

He gave her the smile. "Who, me? No interest at all."

"Make it thirty and you even get to hold the flashlight. How's that for a deal?"

"Okay, thirty's fine. You want it now or later?"

"Later. I'll trust you."

She hesitated a moment and then handed him the flashlight and he turned it on her, right into her eyes to see how she'd take it but she didn't hardly blink, just pulled the sweater off over her head and dropped it onto the sand and already he had a raging hard-on. She was staring directly into the light. She unzipped the miniskirt and stepped out of it and dropped it on top of the sweater and then reached around to unhook the bra and slipped it off her shoulders and tossed it down, hooked the panties with her thumbs and skidded them down over her hips and stood there.

"Go ahead, Ray. Move the flashlight around a little. Have a good look. Have fun. You can see my face anytime, right?"

He held it on her a moment more and then moved it down. He took his time. When he got back to her face again she said, "Think I'll take that swim now."

She turned and waded into the water and he followed her with the light until she was in up to her shoulders, he was hardly able to look away from her, from her ass disappearing in front of him into darkness and the dimples in the small of her back and then he scrambled out of his own clothes and naked, plunged in after her. The water was like ice cubes on his stiff prick and had the effect of melting it but that was okay too and he swam fast and hard watching her own slow measured strokes ahead of him and soon he caught up with her.

She turned and they were only a few feet apart treading water face-to-face. He was warmer now.

The frogs had gone silent. He heard them tentatively start in again.

"Now what?"

He reached for her through the water and she pushed his hand away. She was smiling.

"Thirty bucks bought you a look, Ray. Not a feel."

"Shit, what am I gonna have to pay for a kiss?"

"You already did kiss me and it was free. But it's not a kiss you want, is it."

"It'd do for starters."

She looked at him a long moment.

"Tell you what we'll do," she said. "We'll have a little race to shore. You beat me, you can fuck me. How's that."

"What?"

"You having a hearing problem? You can fuck me."

She'd had his dick's complete attention ever since they'd started treading water and now it was close to painful. He nodded toward the shoreline.

"You mean right now?"

"If you want we can wait a couple of weeks. Yeah, right now."

"You're not just messing with me?"

"Bet's a bet."

"And if you beat me? I mean it won't happen. I'm just saying, if."

She thought about it.

"I can't think which you're more fond of Ray, your car or your boots. Suppose we say you give me your boots."

He laughed. "You sure do like your games, don't you."

"As much as you like yours."

"This one, though. You can't lose."

"Either way I win?"

"Either way."

"Maybe. We'll see. You ready? We go on three. One, two, *three.*"

And it wasn't just the prospect of fucking her that propelled him through the water though god knows that was the main thing but it was also the boots and what was stuffed *inside* the boots too, she wasn't going to get a peek inside those babies if he could help it and get a laugh at Ray Pye's expense *plus* the boots cost a fortune *plus* there was the matter of his pride so he swam like every leech and snake in Sussex County was after him, catching a glimpse of her only just slightly behind to the side graceful and barely cutting the water and gaining on him steadily for chrissake while he pounded at the water like the water was the enemy and kicked at it like it was some kid he was kicking the shit out of in a schoolyard and soon he stumbled gasping onto shore and fell to his back to the pebble beach and she fell right beside him.

"You won," she panted.

He couldn't tell if she was surprised or not. He knew *he* was. She'd scared hell out of him back there, coming up on him like that.

She wasn't as winded as he was but still she was breathing hard, she had her arms up over her head, looking straight up at the stars. He watched her breasts rise and fall, beads of water rolling down, water in the hollow of her belly, hair plastered back so that for the first time he could fully see her ears and the shape of them, to his eyes perfect like the all rest of her, looking back to her breasts and the long dark nipples, looking down to the glistening pubic hair, the proximity of what he was seeing making him start to rise again.

"You gonna cop out on me?" he said.

She still didn't look at him.

"No."

And with just that single word breathed quietly and without emotion into the still night air he went fully erect and rolled onto her.

Her skin was cool and wet like his, her mouth hot but the kiss didn't last, she turned away from the kiss and he thought in a moment of panic that something must be wrong, his breath or something until he looked into her eyes and saw that things were fine. She reached down between his legs and put him inside her and began rolling her hips and moving up and down beneath him.

She closed her eyes and turned her head offering him
her neck, and he kissed and bit the water-sweet flesh
and went suddenly to some place beyond himself, beyond sheer sensation, overriding his senses somehow, *it
was like watching himself in a movie, only not like any
movie he'd ever seen, he could see himself take her
breast in hand and turn the nipple, see his ass pumping
his back straining as though from a great height, as
though he were outside himself watching. She was silent
and he was moaning and he heard this too as though
these were two other people not Ray and Katherine and
then suddenly he was coming and that was far too real
and not part of the movie not part of the plan because
it was far too early, he'd only just begun, he'd only just
gotten a taste of her but he couldn't help it, couldn't
stop, and he groaned his disappointment and shuddered
his pleasure, both.*

When it was over he lay on top of her awhile feeling
himself shrink inside her and then slowly rolled away.
He felt the sweat drying along his chest and hips. He
was aware of his heart still racing, moving slowly from
gallop to down to canter.

"Sorry," he said.

"For what?"

"That was a little fast."

"I've had faster. Don't worry your pretty head about
it." She gave the tip of his dick a flick with her forefinger. "Either head."

But he couldn't help but worry. First Jennifer
couldn't get him hard and now this.

With the one girl he needed.

He realized that actually was the word for it. It surprised him.

Needed.

He didn't know how or when that had happened or
how it had happened so fast but right now the thought
of not having her, of losing her to some other guy and

221

maybe just because of this stupid fast fuck by the pool was unthinkable, impossible to consider. There was no goddamn way he was going to let that happen. If he did he was just another loser and probably she had a pretty long list of losers in her past, a girl like her. It was just not going to happen. Not to him. No fucking way. He had to find a way to grab her and hold her. He'd do just about anything, say just about anything to hold her.

He had to put his mark on her.

One way or another.

He had to piss on her tree.

"I never should have brought you down here," he said.

"Why's that?"

He looked away from her down along the dark narrow beach.

"Remember last night you asked me what was the worst thing I ever did? And I told you about trashing the house?"

"Uh-huh."

"It was a lie."

"Trashing the house?"

"No. We trashed the house, all right. But that wasn't the worst thing I ever did."

And then he told her.

Later driving back to her place he didn't know exactly *why* he told her. It had come crashing down into his brain all at once, the telling and the aftermath of the telling, like a movie where you already knew the ending from the first few minutes of the story. He didn't know why he told her, only knew that it had been the right thing to do. Of that he was absolutely certain now. He'd *felt* its rightness. He knew that telling her had set him apart from every other guy she'd ever met. Whether she believed him or not.

He wasn't sure she did.

Chapter Twenty-five

Katherine

This was really twisted.

She was pouring a scotch for a guy who said he'd committed murder. He was sitting outside in her living room.

She was alone.

The guy definitely had a line of bullshit and he was probably in most things an out-and-out liar. She didn't believe his story about the broken legs for one minute. So why should she buy this one?

But if this was a lie it was the strangest damn lie she'd ever heard. *Why would he tell me this shit?* Did he think it was romantic? She thought about the Tate murders on the news tonight and wondered if they'd maybe fed into his story somehow, if they'd brought on some kind of weird dark personal fantasy for him.

The guy was *strange.*

Her father would die if he knew she was sitting around with him. The truth of the story be damned.

It was late at night.

She was alone.

I should have gone with him, she thought. *I should have gone with dad.* The thought came unbeckoned and nagged her. *What kind of a daughter am I to him, that I wouldn't go too?*

She pushed the thought angrily away. She'd made her decision on that one. She'd have to stick by it. And she had enough to think about right here and now.

She could not say this was the smartest thing she'd ever done, letting him in tonight.

But the sheer *weirdness* of it. A couple of dates and the guy confesses murder. Shows her where and how he did it and how he cleaned up afterwards.

In a way it was more twisted if it was a lie than if it was the truth. You could have some motive for spilling your guts out even to someone who's practically a stranger, even to someone you've fucked only once and spent a few evenings with. But what in the world would be the motive for making the whole thing up? What in god's name could you hope to gain?

He said he cared for her. Was maybe even falling in love with her.

She thought it was a little early for that.

He said he trusted her.

Why would he trust her?

He hardly knew her.

Something inside her was inclined to believe his story. Another part of her denied the possibility, said that he was a liar.

Still another part wanted to play detective.

Maybe that third part was the reason she was pouring the scotch here.

It was the strangest thing that had ever happened to her, though. No contest. And she had to admit there was something exciting about it too and probably dangerous as well because whether truth or fantasy there *had* to be something dangerous about a guy who would tell you stuff like this.

Murderer or nutcase.

Either one could hurt you.

You're playing with fire here. Kath. You're pushing yourself again. But this is a game you should maybe think about twice, you know?

He was sitting on the couch just staring off into nowhere when she brought in the drinks. He looked exhausted. Drained. If he was acting it was easily the best performance she'd seen from him so far. She handed him his scotch and sat down across from him in the armchair. She wanted that space between them, and he looked as if he expected as much. She took a sip from her vodka and tonic.

"I don't know what to say to you, Ray. I honestly don't."

"I don't expect you to say anything."

"And I don't know whether to believe you, either."

"I figured."

"It's fucked up, though, you know? Either way."

"I'm fucked up. I been fucked up all these years. Shit, I used to think it was because I was adopted but that's not true. My parents are good to me. And the fact that I never got to know my real mom and dad, well, so fucking what? Lots of kids don't know their real parents. That's got nothing to do with anything."

That's a new one, she thought. *He's adopted. Or says he is.*

She took another sip of the vodka. *Ask him,* she thought. *It's sick but it's what you really want to know most of all, isn't it? So go on and ask him. Truth or lie you want to hear his answer.* She lit a cigarette and shook out the match.

"So you didn't tell me, Ray," she said. "What did it feel like?"

"Huh? I did tell you."

"You told me how it felt after. Not then. Not at the time."

She took another long drink and looked at him.

"Not when you were out there killing people."

"Jesus, Kath." He looked uncomfortable as hell but she noticed that the spark had come back to his eyes. "You really want to know this?"

"I guess I must. I'm asking."

The house was silent. She could hear the ice clink in his scotch as he tipped the glass and drank. She felt absurd for a moment and a little frightened. Like they were sitting around a fire and she was about to hear him tell a ghost story.

He pushed himself up on the couch. He wouldn't meet her eyes.

He spoke slowly, carefully, like he really was having to work at this.

"It felt scary," he said. "It felt dangerous and scary. But I gotta tell you, I gotta be honest. It also felt like I had all this power all of a sudden. I mean, I could scare them or just wound them or whatever. And then, even when I started shooting I could still stop and let them . . . let them live. Or I could . . . go on doing what I was doing. But also it was like I was on a fucking roller coaster, you know? I mean, part of me *couldn't* stop. It was . . . *it was so fucking* . . . it just *grabs hold of you,* you know? Jesus! I'm sorry. That's so sick. That's *so* fucked up. I'm . . ."

He shook his head. She leaned over and put a finger to his lips.

"Shhhh," she said.

She couldn't believe it. She was going to do this, she thought.

She was going to do this just once and then never again.

I dare you, she thought. *I dare you, Katherine. Double-dare.*

Ray was fucked up all right. Either way. Truth or no truth. But then so was she and here she was, about to prove it again. The fact was nothing new to her. She'd known for a very long time. She was her mother's daughter. She'd grown up practically comfortable in the knowledge. It had the familiar sting of the inevitable.

Katherine's about to screw up again.

Only question was, how bad?

She was going to do this whether he was lying or not, but do it believing he was telling her the truth because at that moment it was what she wanted to believe and the truth right now was unknowable anyway. She was going to take a certain leap into the murky waters of *what it feels like.* A place she liked to visit now and then. A place where she felt wide awake and wholly at home.

In her mind tonight and for just this one time and then never again, she was going to fuck a murderer. An enemy of human life. She was doing it just to see what it felt like inside *while* she was doing it and for no other reason than that. No good reason, certainly. Certainly not to comfort him.

Did that make them two of a kind?

Maybe.

Whatever.

She put down her drink and went to the couch and straddled him and she could feel the energy pouring off him, he was practically vibrating in the grip of it staring at her wide-eyed, unbelieving as she pulled her sweater off over her head and put her hand down onto him and found he was already hard and closed her hand over him.

And that was when the phone rang.

She turned and looked at it like she'd been bitten by a snake.

The phone was hard reality.

What she'd been doing, it suddenly occurred to her, was not.

What she'd been doing fell squarely into the category of sick twisted fantasy and that was all it was. She felt suddenly ashamed.

"Don't," he whispered. "Don't get it."

"Jesus. You know what *time* it is?"

"It's probably a wrong number."

"It's not a wrong number, Ray. Not at this hour."

She got off him, shaking now and not knowing whether it was him or what she'd almost done with him that made her shake or if it was what the call might mean. All she did know was that she was afraid of picking up that phone and afraid of herself most of all.

She picked up the receiver and listened and when she heard the voice on the other end in all its sadness and lost desolation she began to cry but tried not to show it for her father's sake. She let him speak until it seemed he was through and his voice was almost normal and then told him that she'd call right away, she'd be on the first plane in the morning and said she's better off, daddy, you know the way she suffered and he said yes I know, I know, but dammit I loved her and Katherine said, so did I and then she didn't even try to hide the fact that she was crying, the shock that it was simply true and inevitably true ran all at once too deep. All these bitter spiteful years she'd loved her and hadn't known, not really, it was a small light in a cave, a light too dim to penetrate the dark but it was burning now. She was a child parted forever from the mother she had loved and no more and no less than that and she hadn't known.

She hadn't known at all.

Part Two

"There are no intact men."
—Pete Dexter, *The Paperboy*

Chapter Twenty-six

Monday, August 11 to Friday, August 15 The Week in Review

At ten o'clock Monday morning when the phone rang the cat lay on Ed Anderson's sofa sleeping off a half-can of Friskies Buffet mixed with a handful of dry, the sleep of the not-so-innocent, since, having eaten and feeling fine, she immediately began using the leg of Ed's sofa as a scratching post, quitting only under threat of being misted with water from his flower spritzer. She reacted to the phone by opening her eyes and yawning, extending and retracting the claws of her right front paw and going back to sleep again.

It was Charlie on the line. If the cat had been awake she could have watched Ed's face fall as Charlie told him the results of his efforts to get Sally a job at the department.

Ed hung up feeling dazed and vaguely shamed. If the department knew, who else? He'd thought they were being discreet, he and Sally.

He thought about the boys over at Teddy Panik's

place. Would they know too? And why should he give a damn anyway? There wasn't anything wrong about what they were doing. Sally was of age under the law.

They cared for each other.

Aw, shit, he thought and called her.

Sally had a private line in her room so it shouldn't have been June Richmond who answered, but it was. He hung up on her and sat there a moment next to the cat just staring at the phone. He felt like a teenage kid sneaking phone calls behind his parents' back. His mother and father had been dead for eight years and seven years respectively. It was as though the sheer fact that Sally was still living with her own parents had dragged him back decades to when Ed was living with his.

He should have known that in a small town like this secrets wouldn't keep. But he'd thought that if anybody discovered them it would be somebody who had reason to care. In particular her father and mother. That it was common knowledge at least in the department surprised and bothered him.

What the hell was he doing?

The afternoon was slightly hellish.

He drove the few blocks to town and dropped off his cleaning and picked up his shirts. One of the few little luxuries he allowed himself since Evelyn died was to skip the ironing completely. He walked over to the Sugar Bowl and went to the Hallmark rack and picked out a birthday card for his sister in Wisconsin and paid the girl at the counter. He crossed the street and made a hundred-dollar withdrawal from his account at Mayflower Savings.

Then he got into the car again and drove to the A&P. From the seafood counter he got a one-and-a-half-pound lobster, a dozen mussels, a dozen medium shrimp, a dozen bay scallops and a pound of cod. He wheeled the shopping cart over to the produce department and picked out some leeks and parsley, a head of celery, a medium onion and a clove of garlic. In the aisles he got a loaf of french bread, a bottle of clam juice, crushed fennel seeds, bay leaves and a can of tomatoes. The thyme, white wine, bay leaves and oil he already had at home. He was going to make a bouillabaisse. He was a good cook, even better than Ev had been. Since his retirement it helped to pass the time.

He paid for the groceries and wheeled them to the car.

And all these people, all the way along, he knew. Most of them by name.

The cleaner, the girl he paid for the birthday card, the teller at the Mayflower, the man in the white apron behind the seafood counter, the A&P checkout clerk.

He knew them all. And they knew him.

He felt the everyday and natural go unnatural all over the course of just a few hours. As though his life were an open secret. As though he were in some way marked now. Hester Prynne in *The Scarlet Letter.*

So this is what paranoia's like, he thought.

Welcome to the Monkey House.

At home he put away the groceries and unwrapped the shirts and hung them in the closet and thought about calling her again but decided against it. He didn't want to risk getting June again instead. A second mysterious hang-up call would raise questions. He found it interesting and unnerving that all of a sudden he was worried about raising questions. But speaking to Sally could wait anyhow. She was due at seven-thirty for dinner.

He wondered what she told her parents about her apparent lack of appetite at their dinner table those two or three nights a week she ate at his place.

Then wondered why he *hadn't* wondered it before.

Questions again.

Teddy Panik's Happy Hour at four-thirty came and went. He wasn't up to it. He cracked a couple beers from the refrigerator instead and tried to read but much as he liked the book despite some of its politics Mailer's *Armies of the Night* was not about to hold him. By five-thirty he'd retreated into sleep, his second beer half-finished on the floor beside him.

He woke at six-thirty with the cat that thus far still remained nameless perched on his belly and gently kneading. The cat was looking for her dinner. Getting into the habit of easier, fatter times. He dumped the flat warm beer into the sink and opened a cold one and fed her the leftover half-can of Friskies and chopped up the vegetables for dinner.

He got Ev's big kettle out from under the sink and put it on the stove and heated the quarter-cup of olive oil, the vegetables, the thyme and bay leaf for five minutes and then added in the clam juice, wine, tomatoes and the rest of the spices and simmered them for another fifteen while he peeled and deveined the shrimp and rinsed them in a colander. He boiled the lobster, cut the raw cod into pieces and scrubbed and debearded the mussels. When the lobster was done he ran it under cold water and cracked and cleaned it and broke it into quarters. He figured he'd wait for Sally to arrive to add the seafood for the final fifteen minutes' cooking time and to slice up the bread. He turned off the burner and put the cover on the kettle and returned the seafood to the refrigerator.

He felt no better for his nap nor for the cooking so he made himself a martini, very dry and dropped in three pimento-stuffed olives. By the time he heard her Volkswagen pull around back of the house he was building himself another. No olives this time. Just gin and vermouth.

She came in wearing a smile and a halter top and a pair of cut-off jeans and carrying a bottle of Pepsi and another loaf of french bread in a paper shopping bag. He put his own bread in the freezer. Hers was fresher.

She gave him a kiss and he asked her about her day but she didn't answer, just looked at him as he took the seafood out of the refrigerator and dropped it into the kettle and stirred while he turned on and adjusted the burner.

"What's going on?" she said.

Jesus, she could read him. Kid her age, it was amazing. But there was no point lying to her or avoiding the matter.

She poured herself a glass of Pepsi and they sat down at the table while he told her.

"So you're feeling guilty, is that it?" she said.

"I don't know if guilty's the word. I'm feeling . . . I guess you'd say exposed. All day long I had this feeling people were staring at me. Here comes the dirty old man."

She smiled. "You're not a dirty old man."

"So how come I feel like one?"

"Ed, the only thing that bothers *me* about this is that school doesn't start up until September fifteenth, a month from now. And I need to make some money between now and then. I still need some kind of job. As far as the rest of it goes, so what? I don't care who knows about us. I wouldn't really even care if my parents knew about us. Except that it would make *being* us harder. Don't you get it? I'm happy with you and proud of you, you dope."

"Christ, Sally. I'm old enough to be your grandfather."

"Sure, if you'd married and had a kid at fourteen. You're two years older than my dad. I don't see that as such a great big deal."

"The town would. Your parents would. The department thinks it's a big enough deal not to hire you."

"To hell with the department." She got up and took the knife from him and finished cutting the bread. His hands were shaking. She wasn't blind. She was doing him a favor taking over.

237

He finished his martini and opened the cabinet and took out the gin.

"Are you gonna get drunk on me now?"

"Sal, I don't know why but I'm doing about sixty in a thirty-mile-an-hour zone. I'm not going to get drunk on you. I don't think I could if I wanted to."

She sighed. "Just forget about it, Ed. Let's have ourselves a nice dinner. I'll just have to do some job-hunting tomorrow, that's all."

She arranged the bread along the length of folded white linen in his wicker basket.

"The department doesn't matter. And the town doesn't matter. We do."

"Charlie thinks I'm nuts. He thinks I'm riding for a fall."

"So are you? Are you riding for a fall? Forget about what Charlie thinks for a minute. What do you think?"

"I don't know what I think. I know I've still got to live in this town once you're gone."

He saw her wince at that and instantly regretted it. He couldn't remember ever regretting anything he'd said to her before no matter how foolish. He poured his martini. He sat down at the table. She put the basket on the table and sat across from him, folded her arms and watched him.

"So what are you saying, Ed?"

"Huh?"

"You know what I mean. What are you telling me?"

"You've got your reputation to think of, Sally. I don't want that damaged because of me."

"My reputation? In a month I'm leaving it in its tracks."

"You'll be coming back. Vacations, Christmas. Sparta's your hometown for godsakes."

"I don't care about that. I want to know exactly what you're telling me. Don't fuck around with me, Ed."

He didn't think he'd ever felt so uncomfortable in all his life.

Still he owed her the truth.

"I just don't feel right about it the way I did. I don't know why people knowing about us should change anything. Charlie's known all along and that didn't change anything. But I guess I'm wondering if maybe we shouldn't . . . I dunno . . . maybe we shouldn't be doing this. Maybe *I* shouldn't be doing this. Maybe it's just not right for me to be doing this. Jesus. I don't know."

For a moment she simply stared at him. His drink untouched in front of him, his eyes not quite seeming able to meet her own.

"So what you're saying is that what we should do is, we should have ourselves a little dinner, have a little bouillabaisse and call it quits. Is that it?"

"I'm not . . . I don't . . ."

"For chrissake, Ed!"

He looked up. Her eyes were brimming with tears. He couldn't stand to see her that way. Not over him. He shook his head.

"Sal, listen, you're young. You . . ."

She slammed the palms of her hands flat against the table and stood up, leaning toward him. For a moment he thought she might hit him.

"*Don't* you say that to me! Goddamn it! Young? That's bullshit. I never would have figured you for a coward, Ed Anderson! Never. I never would have thought you'd do this to me in a million years! It's not my reputation you're worried about. It's your reputation. And you're putting that in front of us? In front of what we've got? Well *fuck* this town and your precious department and *fuck* your goddamn bouillabaisse and Ed, right now, right this moment, *fuck you!*"

When she was out the door and the house was silent he went to the sink and poured his martini down the drain and turned off the stove. The bouillabaisse was ready but he couldn't eat. The cat padded into the room, sleepy-eyed, curious about the commotion maybe or about the scent of fish and shrimp and lobster.

He couldn't quite bring himself to reach down and pet her either.

He sat back at the table and stared at his hands and realized that he really *did* feel old now. Old and as tired and as empty as he'd felt since Ev died. He told himself that it was all for the best, that it would have happened sooner or later anyway, she was going off to school.

She'd called him a coward and he guessed she'd been right about that.

Her voice inside his head now also called him liar.

She got home and shut the door to her room and sat down on the bed. The tears had subsided in the car as had the anger, enough at least so that her parents hadn't noticed anything strange about her. Nor did they question her early arrival. Her mother was half in the bag again, watching "Here's Lucy," and her father was immersed in paperwork so that probably helped some. What she was left with was a sad and unfamiliar ache inside. She dialed Tonianne Primiano, her best friend since junior high, and told her the whole sad ludicrous story.

"He's just scared," Tonianne said. "Why wouldn't he be? He'll come around."

"You think?"

"Sure."

"It's like he feels he's endangering me, corrupting me or something. I dunno. What he doesn't get is that when I'm around Ed I feel the exact opposite. I feel *protected.* He knows damn well I wasn't some sweet little virgin when we met. So what is this?"

"I think he's scared of what people will say. *Are* saying. Peer pressure and all. Give him a day or two to stew on it. Then go over and give him another chance.

I bet he jumps at it. You really called him a coward?"

"Yeah. I wish I hadn't now. He thinks he's doing the right thing."

"Sure he does. He's another generation, Sally. Jeez. Sex is something a lot of them don't handle real well. Plus he's a *man,* right? You ever meet a guy who wasn't a little screwed up sex-wise? Like I say, give him a couple days to get used to the idea that first of all, people know about you two and there's nothing you can do about it and second of all, *you're not around anymore.* Couple of days, he's gonna be missing you like crazy. You can bet on it. Meanwhile I've got some *good* news. I was going to call you tonight if you hadn't called me. They fired Liz Beach today. That means we've got an opening."

Tonianne worked at Sam's Sporting Goods out on Route 15.

"You think you can get me in?"

"I *know* I can get you in if you want it. I already talked to Sam about it. It's just a store clerk job but . . ."

"Toni, I love you. I absolutely love you! You just made my day."

"Given the givens, I'd say that wasn't real hard. Be in at eight-thirty. We open at nine. What do you suppose he'll do with the bouillabaisse?"

"Huh?"

And then wonder of wonders, they were laughing.

By Wednesday night Ray had broken his promise to himself not to sleep with Jennifer again. He told himself it was a mercy fuck. That she kept on hanging around him looking so goddamn pathetic and sounding so goddamn pathetic that what could you do? That fucking her now had more to do with his previous *failure* to fuck her did not occur to him until afterward. And even then his response was to note that he was back on track again sexually speaking and that was that.

He felt so good and expansive as a result of it though that he gave her one of the rings he kept in his drawer for just this kind of occasion. Saying he'd bought it just for her. To show how much he loved her. That she still was number-one with him.

The ring was Austrian crystal. He told her it was a diamond.

It was pretty and sparkled and she'd never know the difference. And seeing the expression on her face, you could almost believe it *was* a diamond because how could a ring you picked up for a few bucks bring on all that happiness?

He figured that took care of Jennifer for a while.

The night before that he'd slept with Dee Dee. He was disappointed to find that Dee Dee wasn't a virgin. He'd figured that somebody named Dee Dee almost *had* to be. He was even more disappointed with her performance in bed. The chick was enthusiastic, sure. But she hadn't a clue as to how to actually do the dirty deed. She kissed too hard and too wet, grabbed when she should have stroked, lay back and made him do all the work when she should have been grinding away. He figured that once around with Dee Dee was plenty and got her out of there as soon as he could. With the promise—which he'd never in a billion years think of keeping—to call her about getting together over the weekend.

Not a chance.

By the weekend Kath would be back.

At least he thought she would.

By then they'd have buried her lunatic mother and she'd be home again.

In the meantime the fact that he had no phone number for her out in San Francisco and no way to talk to her until she *did* come back was driving *him* crazy. She'd refused to give him one, saying that she and her father would be busy dealing with relatives and friends of the family. Saying it wasn't appropriate for him to call. Using that word. *Appropriate*.

Who gave a shit about appropriate?

But he'd had no choice but to accept it. Her mother was dead for godsake. He guessed you had to show some respect. But he was surprised to see how sad she seemed after all she'd said about her. About her mother being a fruitcake and throwing her drink against a tree and bodies buried in the garden. He'd have thought she'd be relieved to get the crazy bitch off her back.

He'd left her house that night feeling excited and confused again.

She'd grabbed his dick for chrissake!

He guessed that Katherine just had that effect on him. Excitement and confusion.

But this was worse than ever.

Because waiting was a total bitch. He'd come *that close* to fucking her and fucking her right this time and then she gets this phone call and it's good night, Ray, I'll call you when I get back, sure I will, of course, wiping her eyes and blowing her nose into a Kleenex. And the hell of it was that he only half believed her.

He wasn't at all sure she *would* call.

Even after what he'd told her. Even after what they'd damn near done *after* he'd told her. With Katherine you just couldn't say. You couldn't be sure.

If she didn't call he didn't know what he'd do.

They were a thing now, right?

She could have called from California. She could have done that at least.

She didn't.

He was having trouble sleeping. He *never* had trouble sleeping. He slept like the fucking dead.

He was eating too much junk food and drinking too much booze neither of which was good for his waistline and smoking too much dope and too many packs of

Marlboro and mornings he got up hacking lungers into the toilet and feeling like a large polluted stream.

He looked for distractions. What the hell else could you do?

That was what Dee Dee and Jennifer were about really. Distractions. He picked out a brand-new Magnavox on Monday over at Sounds Limited and bought some new records and dealt Ralph Dorset, who worked behind the counter, a couple lids of dope in order to cut the price in half. He got the car washed. Tuesday he spent over at Lee Seymour's house practicing with the band, getting lost in "Let's Spend the Night Together" for three solid hours. That was okay.

The band as a whole still sounded like shit, though.

He even put in some extra hours at work, surprising the hell out of his father by offering to spell him so he could get in a few practice games over at Sparta Lanes.

All of it fucking distraction. Something to do. A way to keep from thinking too much about Kath.

It only half worked.

Thursday he got stoned on some truly amazing hash and went to the movies with Tim. The Colony was showing *The Fearless Vampire Killers or: Pardon Me, My Teeth Are in Your Neck* with Sharon Tate and Roman Polanski. Tim said it was pretty fucking cynical to release the movie now after what had happened to Sharon and wondered what Polanski thought, but that didn't stop them from going, hell no, they went anyway. The movie was spooky and funny if a little lame sometimes like all European movies were a little lame but Ray definitely thought it was *too cool* to see this short guy, Roman Polanski, who had got this tall terrific perfect girl in real life and had been fucking her on a regular basis and then married her and knocked her up.

Short power! Yeah!

They were disappointed that you didn't get to see all

244

of Sharon's tits in the bathtub scene. No nips. There was too much soap.

Supposedly one of those tits had been cut off by whoever had killed her and left on the floor by her body. That was what he heard.

It was weird to see a woman, especially a gorgeous fucking beast like Sharon Tate almost totally nude in a movie and then to know that somebody had murdered and mutilated the real naked flesh of that same beast just a week or so before. It made you remember that anybody could get fucked over and killed, *anybody*. Even a movie star like Sharon. That was the kind of world it was.

He wondered if they'd raped her. She was eight months pregnant and probably fat as a house.

You probably wouldn't want to rape her. Not then.

After the movie they drove by Katherine's house. No lights were on. He'd driven by the night before too and found that it comforted him in a way. She hadn't called him because she wasn't back. Period. The dark house said it all.

If she didn't get home by the weekend he was going to go seriously nuts with the waiting.

She had to call. She fucking had to.

He woke that night at ten to three in the morning.

His head felt thick and achy from too much beer but he didn't want to be alone. He wondered who'd be up at this hour and thought that probably Roger would. Roger was his sometime drummer in the band but made his living as a gas jockey working night shift at the Esso station and had his own apartment over it. Had Roger and the apartment not reeked of gas all the time he might have been as popular as Ray was.

There would be dope there and beer and maybe even a girl or two.

He stripped to the waist and in the bathroom washed his face and hands and spread Ban Roll-on across his armpits and slicked and combed his hair. From his closet he chose a crimson shirt threaded delicately with black, 60 percent rayon and 40 percent polyester, bunched slightly at the shoulder and baggy in the arms, a lot like the one Elvis used to wear touring on the road, left the top two buttons open at the neck and tucked it into his jeans.

He checked himself in the mirror, decided he looked tired, the eyes dark-rimmed and broody. But on him the look wasn't bad. Anyhow it was only Roger and a couple of chicks maybe.

He got into his car and drove through dark deserted streets into town. There was a light burning in the apartment window over the Esso station, just as he'd suspected. He walked up the rickety flight of wooden stairs and knocked at the door. He heard Donovan on the stereo inside, "Mellow Yellow." He hated that shit. Roger thought Donovan was cool but why anybody would think a song about fake dope was cool was beyond him and maybe that kind of thing was part of what was wrong with their band.

He knocked on the door and waited and then knocked again harder this time and Roger opened it and squinted at him and grinned. He was barefoot and bare-chested, in a pair of oil-stained jeans, long lank hair ratty as usual.

"Far out. C'mon in, man."

Roger talked like that. *Far out. Groovy.* And maybe that was part of what was wrong with the band too.

"We was just doin' a little blow, man. You want to do some blow? Only thing is, you gotta help me out on the bread situation, y'know? That fuck Danski don't pay me till Saturday and I'm already, like, y'know, tapped, right? Hey, Cheryl, Sylvia, Harvey, look who dropped by for a little blow. You know Stevie Ray? His chick Marie? Nah, 'course you don't. Stevie Ray's from Morristown. My bro's main man. Just got back from Nam, right? Just a coupla months ago. But jesus this is good blow. Try some. You want a beer, man?"

"Hey, Ray."

"Hey, Ray."

"Hey, man."

They were all of them sitting cross-legged around a table that was probably already old and beat to shit when Eisenhower was in office. Its legs were cut off so that it rested about two feet above the equally beat-to-shit rug. Cheryl and Sylvia and Harvey he knew. In fact he'd fucked the first two and beaten up the third in junior high, he didn't remember why. The girls were basically dogs. Stevie Ray was a bull-necked longhair in jeans and a cutoff denim workshirt. With arms that were not quite as big around as Harvey's head. His girl Marie was blond and slim and big-titted inside the Grateful Dead T-shirt and fuckable as hell.

Man!

The lines were laid out on a cloudy old mirror beside a rolled-up dollar bill and the blade from an Exacto knife.

Roger handed him a Schlitz.

"How much?"

"Ten, man."

"For how much blow?"

Roger sat down between Sylvia and Cheryl and grinned. "Fuck it, man, bop till you drop, y'know? I mean, like, we got about four grams left. I figure about half a gram ought to sock it to ya righteously. We already done three grams of the shit tonight."

He dug into his wallet, pulled out two fives and handed them to Roger and sat down next to the girl. It felt dangerous to sit down next to the girl because of Stevie Ray there on the other side of her especially when she smiled at him but it was the only space left at the table.

The girl smelled like patchouli oil.

It was slightly better than the smell of gasoline.

"So you guys are from Morristown, huh?"

He said this to Stevie Ray. Not even *looking* at the girl. He wasn't about to get his ass kicked tonight. Not over some piece of pussy. He picked up the dollar bill and snorted a line and sniffed it up good and wiped his nose and rubbed his forefinger over his gums and snorted another. The coke rush blazed a sudden smooth trail to his head.

"Yeah."

The guy was looking at his shirt like there was something wrong with it, like he'd puked all over himself or something.

"Good town. I got friends in Morristown. You were in Nam, huh?"

"Yeah."

"How was it, man? Pretty bad over there?"

The guy kept staring at his shirt.

"See, the thing is I don't talk about it. That okay with you, *Ray?* I sure as shit do hope so."

He caught a glance between Stevie Ray and the girlfriend. On the girlfriend's part it was a worried glance.

What was this guy's problem?

He was liable to get his ass kicked just sitting here.

"Hey, whatever." He snorted another line.

Doing the coke gave him an idea. A terrific idea. An inspiration, really. Good drugs could do that to you.

"Hey Roger, how much you take for a gram of this shit? Twenty?"

Roger hesitated and stroked what passed for his chin. He shook his head.

"Like I said, man, I'd like to give it to you for twenty. I'm real tight for bread right now. I mean, like, I'd have to say thirty. You think you can go thirty? It's really good blow, man, you know?"

Roger was gouging the shit out of him but what the fuck. He dug into his wallet again and produced a twenty. Roger got up and went to his filthy walk-in kitchen and opened a drawer and tossed him a thimble-sized glass bottle with a plastic cap.

"Done, my man."

He wondered if the thirty included another line or two at the table. He decided not to push it. Stevie Ray was still staring at the red shirt like it was a fucking red flag and Stevie Ray was an angry bull.

He finished his beer and said *thanks, good to see you guys* and pocketed the coke and got his ass out of there while it still was safe and sound and the last thing he heard when the door shut behind him was Stevie Ray say, *fucking pussy in a pansy shirt*, he could hear it because the Donovan album was over by then and tears of sudden rage stung his eyes. *Get that piece of shit bastard alone with the Ladysmith and then let's see how tough he is, let's see who's the pussy.* But in a way he had to be almost grateful to this asshole too because the coke and wanting to get out of there so bad had given him the idea in the first place.

He'd go home and have a little more. Not too much. Two or three lines and the rest he'd save.

A present for Katherine.

Something to look forward to. No, *something else* to look forward to.

He knew she liked surprises.

He walked away smiling.

Once the coke wore off he'd sleep now.

Charlie Schilling was having no trouble sleeping. In fact he was sleeping away half the evening, falling out in front of the TV set. And twice there was a scotch in his hand which he found still clutched there in the morning. He was breaking his own rules drinking like this but somehow the rules didn't seem to matter enough to worry about.

When he thought about exactly why he was falling

off his personal version of the wagon he thought about his son Will and his daughter Barbara, and about Lila and fucking up with his family. He thought about Ed and Sally and felt that he was failing them too in some way though he didn't quite know how.

He thought about the felony animal abuse case he was working, where a couple named Neinhauser had dragged their black Labrador bitch behind their car at thirty miles an hour as a punishment for running away, pausing only in order to let the dog vomit. He'd found a thousand-foot trail of bloody pawprints behind their car. The dog was in a new home now and the Neinhausers were out on bail. There would be jail time and a fine, but not enough of either.

But mostly he thought about Barbara and Elise Hanlon and Lisa Steiner.

And Ray Pye.

Not even the business with the dog could touch his anger the way Pye could. It was as though Pye had been born to engage his fury and to no other purpose whatsoever. None that he could see. Pye was his White Whale, his Judas Kiss. All these years, getting away with killing a pair of kids. Riding around town in his convertable, taking in a movie, going on dates, going to parties. Basking in the fucking sun.

When the sun should burn, not bake him.

He thought *jesus christ get off of it*. Ed had found a way to leave it alone and he knew that so should he. But the only way he could leave it alone other than to get the kid was to drink and drinking would kill him eventually if he kept it up, he knew that too. His liver would fail him or his car would argue with a tree or he'd make some stupid mistake on the job. You couldn't be a decent cop and drink. Plenty had tried but to his knowledge nobody yet had succeeded.

Booze would kill him. And Pye would have outlived him.

Leave off of this, he thought.

Yet Wednesday night found him parked in front of the Starlight Motel in a half-drunk sullen rage looking for some excuse to push the kid, some way to bust the kid's balls, even just to annoy the kid. Any excuse, the kid not even around that night, his apartment dark and vacant. Schilling waiting, his radio turned up high enough to violate his town's own noise ordinances. Drinking steadily from a flask of Cutty. His ashtray filling with cigarettes and his head beginning to bob eyes wanting to close until he woke to the first rays of morning to the birds twittering in the trees and a wicked throb in his head that told him more about what the rest of his day was doing to be like than he wanted to know.

You're losing it, he thought. *You really are. You got to get straight.*

You got to stop this shit and get the kid.

When she wasn't with Ray, Jennifer spent most of the week indoors at the Griffiths' house avoiding Tim and his calls. She felt awkward and guilty around Tim now. What they'd done together was a betrayal. That was how it felt. Especially after Ray had given her the ring and told her how much he loved her. She felt guilty. She didn't know what Tim felt but she sure did. It was a beautiful ring. It must have cost him a fortune. She thought now in retrospect that she'd slept with Tim only to spite Ray, not to just be with someone tender. Ray could be tender too, couldn't he?

You're still my number one, Jen. You know that.

She figured that in time her awkwardness around Tim would fade so that was what she was doing, giving it time. She still wanted to be friends with him. It would just take a while.

She helped Mrs. Griffith with the chores, the shopping, the cooking, the housekeeping. She caught up on her magazines, sitting in her room listening to the Carpenters and the Mamas and the Papas on the stereo, neither of which Ray or even Tim could stand. Mrs. Griffith was happy to have her there and grateful for help with the chores what with her arthritis kicking in again and probably both she and Mr. Griffith were surprised to have her home so much too. It'd been a long time since they'd felt anything like a family together.

She never told them that it couldn't last.

On Tuesday afternoon Katherine slept with Deke at his place in Oakland.

On Wednesday she buried her mother.

On Friday she slept with Deke again and told him about this strange little guy she'd met who said he'd committed murder.

Chapter Twenty-seven

Saturday, August 16
Schilling

Schilling woke—*really* woke—to the world around him, surveyed it as from some great height and found it unacceptable.

Unacceptable wasn't even the word for it.

His bedroom was a tidal flat of strewn clothing and shoes and dirty sheets and pillowcases. He hadn't even bothered to shove the dirty laundry in his closet. There were books and newspapers and magazines scattered across the floor, the night table, the dresser. Coffee cups stood stained and empty. Ashtrays brimmed. His floor had a very bad case of the dust devils, compounded by paper clips, the nub of a number-two pencil, assorted pocket change, dropped gray ashes, sprigs of tobacco and the occasional twisted butt that had somehow escaped its intended target.

This at just a scan.

In the bathroom there were rings in the sink and the

toilet bowl and tub and peering into the tub he found it surprising to see just how much hair he was losing. The tub looked hairy as his chest did. His towel felt crusty and smelled of mildew. There were suspicious yellow stains on the porcelain rim of the toilet. He supposed he'd missed his mark a couple of times. Toothpaste splatters on the mirror. Yet more hair on the floor and in the sink.

The living room wasn't much better than the other two rooms.

It looked like the Visigoths had ridden through. It looked like somebody'd come in and tossed the place while he was sleeping.

But the kitchen was the worst. The kitchen was by now *abstract*. It was not his kitchen, it belonged to Jackson Pollack. Whatever havoc it is possible to wreak with empty cans, freezer wraps and boxes, tinfoil, cellophane, eggshells, apple cores, lemon peels, beer cans, liquor and soda bottles and bottle caps, Wonderbread and butter wrappers and crumbs and toast crusts, pans and knives and forks and dishes, this he had wrought and done so supremely.

He was a titan of disorder. It was summer. Flies buzzed.

Heave to, he thought. *My god.*

And heave he did.

He worked all morning long and into the late afternoon. Washing and scraping and polishing. Mop and vacuum, dust cloth and sponge, Windex and Comet, plain old soap and water. He thought at the beginning it was a hell of a goddamn way to spend your day off but by the time he stepped into the gleaming white hairless tub to shower off the muck of his efforts he felt a kind of catharsis, an actual cleansing of the wit and soul.

It had come upon him gradually. With the finding and placement of the telephone book where it belonged beneath the end table. With the folding of his socks in the drawer, the stuffing of his towel in the hamper. His house was his house again. The Visigoths were vanquished. He scrubbed his armpits singing. Tunelessly.

But singing.

You work with your hands, he thought, sometimes you work things out some. You eliminate the toxins, the confusions. Questions find—if not exactly answers—approaches to answers. And that'll do.

He didn't have Ray Pye. Not even close. But he did have a couple of names. Two names of people he knew were important to the guy. Two pressure points.

He'd always had the one. Tim Bess. Ray's best friend. Tim hadn't budged back then. But that was back then. People change over the years. It was worth a shot again and if he did it right and not just strictly by the book he might get some results this time.

He had some ideas.

But as of the night of Ray's party he had another name. Jennifer Fitch. It should have occurred to him right then and there when she handed him her ID and wanted to stay behind. And maybe it *had* occurred to him in a way because he'd filed the name in his memory. He'd just been too damn loaded half the time to figure how to use it.

The first thing he wanted to do was dig into the file and see what Jennifer Fitch had said to Ed in her interview four years ago. It couldn't have been much or else Ed would've called her in for a follow-up with Schilling and he hadn't. But anything might help. He was feeling pretty optimistic about this for a change, he really was.

He even took the time to wash behind his ears.

The tune he was singing was something he'd heard on the radio. It was catchy and popular as hell as was most of their stuff.

Get back, get back, get back to where you once belonged . . .

You got that right, moptops.

Get back *Lo-re*tta!

Chapter Twenty-eight

Ray/Anderson

"Man, put on the radio!" Tim said. "They're talking about it after practically every song."

"Can't."

Ray stood behind the desk watching the couple leave the office, the guy with a bunch of travel brochures off the rack he'd probably never use.

"Problem with the AC in some of the units and the old lady's being real hands-on about it. Watching the repair guy like a fucking hawk. So she's been in and out of here all day long and you know what a bitch she is about the sound on the TV and the radio. I don't even know why we bother to have a radio. Anyhow, who gives a shit?"

"Man, we shoulda gone. We fucked up bad. They're talking four hundred thousand people, maybe more. Four hundred thousand people! Three days and nights, man, nonstop rock 'n' roll. Hendrix, Joplin, Cocker.

Can you imagine all the dope got to be floating around?
All those chicks?"

"Tim, I gotta get you laid. I really do. Those chicks
are *hippie* chicks. Unshaved legs and armpit hair, remember? They're fucking *diseased,* man. Go listen to
your radio. It's cheaper than a dose of the clap."

"We shoulda gone. Really, man."

"Sure. I'm gonna drive all the way to Woodstock to
listen to Joan Baez and Arlo fucking Guthrie and sit
around on some farm with a bunch of dirty longhairs
and chicks with the crabs. And then I'm gonna join the
marines and get my fucking head blown off. Get a grip,
Timmy."

His father relieved him at the desk at four and he
drove immediately to her house. Her car was in the
driveway.

Finally!

The house was silent.

He considered a moment and then slid out from behind the wheel, walked the path to the steps and up
them and pressed the doorbell right away before he lost
his nerve. He waited, wetted a forefinger with his
tongue and ran it over his eyebrows. He breathed into
the palm of his hand and decided his breath was fine.

After a while the door opened and it was the man
he'd seen in photos in her living room. Her father was
a big man. That was what hit him right away. Six feet
or more. Imposing. Second thing, that the guy had been
crying. His eyes were rimmed red and puffy. That a
stranger should see him like this didn't seem to bother
him. Ray put out his hand and her father stared at it a
moment and then gave it a brief shake. The grasp was
neither particularly strong nor weak.

"My name's Ray Pye, Mr. Wallace. A friend of Katherine's. I'm sorry for your loss, sir."

"Thank you."

The man just stared at him as though dazed, didn't invite him in. Like he was waiting for Ray to do or say something else. His white shirt was rumpled and his pants had lost their crease. Ray didn't get it. The wife had died over a week ago. What would a big successful guy like this be doing still all bent out of shape after all this time? Get on with it for godsakes. He guessed Katherine got her nerve from her crazy mother.

He could see their bags in the hallway.

He guessed they'd just got in.

"Is Kath . . . is she available? I'd like to give her my condolences."

He nodded. "Certainly. Come inside."

About fucking time.

"Katherine?" He called up the stairs but she didn't answer. "Someone to see you, Kath. Please, sit down Mr. Pye."

He pointed to the sofa where a week ago she'd strad-dled him.

"I have some papers, some things to do in the study. I'm sure she won't be long."

He shuffled along down the hall and through a door-way to a room he'd never been in. Ray had the uncom-fortable feeling that throughout their entire exchange not once had the guy really seen him. Like to this guy he was invisible. Some voice on the doorstep.

He heard her footsteps on the stairs. He turned and saw her stop and look at him and then glance down the hall toward the study where her father had just gone and he couldn't tell if she was happy to see him or what so he just stood and smiled.

"Hey, Kath."

"Ray, what are you doing here? We just got back." She glanced down the hall again. "Come on, come on outside with me."

He made the smile into a grin. "I just got *in*side."

"Come on, Ray." She took him by the arm and led

him back out through the door. They stood on the porch
and he could see she was nervous. He figured some
sympathy was probably in order.

"He doesn't look too good, Kath. I guess he's still
pretty messed up about this thing, isn't he."

"Yes. He is."

Like *of course* he is. Like *it goes without saying*.

He didn't get that either. But he knew he'd better let
it slide.

"How about you? You okay?"

"I'm okay. I'm fine. But you shouldn't be here, Ray.
I mean, we just walked through the door half an hour
ago, you know?"

"I needed to see you, Kath. Man, you don't know
how much I did. Why didn't you call me? I *missed*
you."

"I couldn't call you."

"Why not? A phone call?"

"Look Ray, we'll talk. We'll talk later. I'll . . . I'll
phone you tomorrow once we're settled in, okay?"

"Tomorrow? Christ, Kath. You been gone a whole
week."

"All right. Okay, tonight. I'll phone you tonight, all
right? But you've really got to go, Ray. Really."

"What? You ashamed of me all of a sudden?" He
smiled again.

She didn't.

And for a moment he thought, *Uh-oh, she fucking is*
and then he thought, *she can't be. Not after all we did.
She's just upset about her father. That's all.*

"I'll call you tonight and we'll talk. Okay? 'Bye,
Ray."

She stepped inside and closed the door. Standing
there he could hear birds in the trees and a car a few
blocks away somewhere heading down the mountain
and that was all. He walked back to the Chevy and got
in and sat there a moment before turning the key in the

ignition, feeling a slow black suspicion creep over him like a shadow. The back of his white cotton shirt was damp with sweat.

She was playing him. Playing him like a goddamn guitar.

How the hell could that be?

You couldn't play Ray Pye. *He* did the playing.

Fuck it. Wait until tonight, he thought. She's got some explaining to do, that's all. Don't even give it a thought until then.

But he was *always* waiting on her it seemed and that was going to have to stop. He'd tell her that when she phoned him. Enough with the *wait until this, wait until that.* No fucking chick was going to keep telling him to wait all the time. Not even Katherine. She was going to have to revise her behavior.

At the red light in front of Sam's Sporting Goods he glanced in through the shop window and saw Sally Richmond behind the counter ringing something up on the register for some asshole kid in cutoff denims and a khaki fishing cap. Under the fishing cap the guy's hair was longer than Sally's was and under the hair was a bushy brown beard. Sally was smiling. So was the fucking hippie. So the little bitch had got herself another job already. Pretty fast in a town this size. He wondered who she had to fuck in order to get it.

It was nice being able to keep track of her, though. To know where she was in case he felt like fucking her up sometime. Which he just might one of these days. What he'd ever thought he needed from some snotty little cunt like her he couldn't imagine unless it was to rip her fucking heart out and shove it down her throat but he guessed that was always an option.

Fifteen minutes later just before the beginning of Happy Hour at Teddy Panik's Ed drove by Sam's too and saw Sally inside with Sam and watched her concentrating, checking off items on an invoice sheet. She had her hair in a ponytail pulled back tight. As usual she wore no makeup and to Ed it looked like her beautiful pale skin was glowing under the fluorescent lights. Not even fluorescents could paste-out Sally Richmond.

You should go apologize to her, you damn fool, he thought. *You should park the car and wait till Sam's in back and there's nobody else around and go in there and just say you're sorry and be done with it. Say your piece and walk away. Then it's in her hands as to whether you get yourself forgiven or not. There's weeks yet before she goes to school. How many really good weeks are you going to see in this life? You want to spend this next month gardening?*

You damned fool.

The light went green and he slowly pulled away.

Chapter Twenty-nine

Schilling/Tim

Most working folks in Sparta ate dinner early so Schilling gave it till six-thirty when he figured the Bess family would be finished with their meal and then drove over. He parked on the downhill side next to a scraggly old maple tree that had seen better days. The tent caterpillars were bad this year and the maple was going to have to struggle to make it through the coming winter.

The Bess place had seen better days too. Cracks on the walk and on the stairs. White paint peeling on the porch. The hedges needed trimming. Somebody'd recently mown the lawn and that was about it. He knew it wasn't that Lenny Bess didn't have the time but that repairs cost money. He remembered he'd promised him to keep an eye out for some work for him. He hadn't.

When he knocked it was Lenny who opened the screen door and let him in, Lenny smiling, welcoming, wearing a worn white T-shirt, scuffed shoes and dirty khakis, the uniform of the working carpenter, Lenny asking him would he like a beer or a cup of coffee and him refusing and it was simple guilt he guessed because practically the first thing out of Schilling's mouth was to wonder if maybe he could make a little time this week to come over to his place to have a look at one of his kitchen cabinets, it was out of plumb and falling off its hinges—true enough, he'd noticed it cleaning up this morning—but simple guilt anyway for not asking around for work for him when easily he could have and guilt for what he was about to do to Lenny's son.

Their television set was a black-and-white Zenith. The evening news was on. Their living room was vintage Sears but Clara kept it tidy. He could see her in the kitchen cleaning up the dinner dishes, unaware of him over the din of running water and the television. Lenny gestured to an overstuffed easy chair and moved to turn the news off but Schilling said that's all right, leave it on.

"It's Tim I'm really here to see, Lenny."

He watched the man's face turn serious.

"Is there some kind of trouble?"

"No trouble. Not that I know of. I just want to ask him a few questions. He around?"

"Upstairs in his room."

"You mind calling him down here?"

"He's probably got his TV on. I'll go get him."

He wondered if Tim's TV was color.

He watched Lenny disappear up the stairs and realized how strange a body the man had, thick long arms and bandy legs and stooped shoulders. The work, maybe, had a tendency to deform you. On the news they were wrapping up a story about the Los Angeles arrest of twenty-six suspects in an auto-theft ring on some abandoned movie set called the Spahn Ranch, way out in the middle of nowhere. Its owner was an eighty-year-old blind man who said he knew that there were people living on the ranch but was unaware of how many or of any criminal activity going on. The suspects had been stealing Volkswagens and converting them into dune buggies. A sizable arsenal of weapons had been found.

They were moving on to a piece about the Woodstock Festival, which looked to Schilling like a nightmare of mud, traffic and bad sanitation, when Bess came down the stairs walking behind his son. Tim was barefoot, dressed in jeans and a red T-shirt. He looked pale and startled and trying hard not to show it. They sat down on the couch across from him.

"No problem, right?" Lenny said. His smile was strained.

"That's right. Just like I said. How are you, Tim?"

Tim shrugged and spoke to the floor. "Okay."

"Working for your dad?"

"Sometimes. You know. When he needs a hand."

Schilling heard the water go off in the kitchen. In a minute Clara'd be out here. He didn't want that. It would tend to complicate things.

"Lenny, could I ask you a big favor?"

"Sure."

"Could I speak to Tim alone for a few minutes? It won't take long, I promise."

Bess didn't like the idea much, that was obvious. He sat back and spread his big scarred hands.

"I dunno, Charlie. What's all this about?"

"Trust me on this one. It's just going to be harder for Tim to speak freely to me with his parents around. You can understand that, can't you? From his point of view?"

"Sure. I guess." He hesitated. "But I dunno. I'm his father. You're sure he's not in any trouble? Because if he is . . ."

"He isn't. You have my word on it. This is all about somebody he knows, not about Tim."

Comprehension lit his face. "Ray Pye. Just like last time. Got to be."

Schilling just looked at him. "Please. Could we have a couple of minutes, Len?"

"All right."

He got up and went into the kitchen and Schilling heard murmured voices, Clara's voice worried, Lenny's reassuring. Tim was still staring at the floor. He was sprawled spread-legged on the couch, fiddling with an elastic band between his fingers. The picture of adolescent nonchalance. Which was the same as saying he was nervous as hell.

"Tell me about Jennifer Fitch, Tim."

The kid was expecting this to be about Ray. It was a curve ball and it got his attention.

"Jennifer?"

"That's right. What can you tell me about her? Where she lives. Who her friends are. That kind of thing."

"Jeez, I dunno. She lives with the Griffiths over on Poplar Avenue. Mr. and Mrs. Griffth. Jennifer's like an orphan, y'know?"

"So we're talking foster home here?"

"Yeah."

"She showed me her ID. She's old enough to be out on her own. So how come the Griffiths?"

"The Griffiths are just . . . nice people I guess. They let her stay."

"She have a job? Contribute any money?"

"I dunno. I think she works sometimes. Part-time. Stuff like that."

"You sound like you don't know her too well."

He shrugged.

"I can find out one way or another. Might as well talk to me, Tim."

"I guess . . . yeah, I know her pretty well I guess."

"She deal any drugs?"

Which got his attention a second time.

"Hell, no."

"You sure? For Ray, maybe?"

265

"I wouldn't know anything about that. Not as far as I know."

"But she's sleeping with Ray, right?"

His face went red. Schilling wondered why. He wondered exactly what Tim's relationship was with the girl. Could be he'd hit a sore spot here.

Could be he'd gotten lucky.

"I guess so. Yeah, I guess she is."

"And *Ray's* dealing drugs, right?"

"I wouldn't know anything about that, either."

"So it would make sense that if Ray's dealing drugs and she's his girlfriend, then she's probably dealing too, right?"

"Like I said, I . . ."

"You dealing drugs, Tim?"

Schilling reached over and turned up the volume slightly on the television. The opening song to "Lassie." Another, more bucolic Timmy smiling, racing across a field. He leaned in close.

"Come on. You can tell me."

"You said I wasn't in any trouble."

"You're not. I'm not after you. It's Ray I'm after. You never heard that from me but it's the truth. I want to know what you and Jennifer Fitch know. Once I'm finished here I'm going to ask her."

"I'm not dealing any drugs."

"You're not? Does that mean you don't mind if I check your room? You mind inviting me upstairs?"

"You can't make me do that."

"Are you sleeping with Jennifer too, Tim?"

"That's none of your business!"

"Okay, fine. That about answers *that* question. But the other question is, how's Ray taking it? Does he even *know* about you two?"

He'd gotten lucky all right.

"Look, Mr. Schilling . . ."

"Detective Schilling. See Tim, what worries me is

that it seems to me that Ray's a pretty possessive guy, also that he's pretty concerned about appearances. That big shiny convertible, those fancy boots—hell, they're polished so high I could shave in them—that slicked-back hair. I think he worries a lot about what people think. Don't you? And I know he's got a temper."

He was fishing on that because Ray had never shown him much in the way of temper, not even when he busted the party. But he knew he was dead on the money. Ray would *have* to have a temper. You couldn't be wound that tight without one.

And Tim was listening.

He didn't like to do it but it was time to go for the throat with him.

"I also know he killed those girls, Tim. And I think that you do too. So what worries me and it worries me bad is what a guy like him would do if he found out about you two, if he *knew*. Like if somebody were to tell him. See, I'm worried about what he'd do to you and Jennifer. Don't you think that's something *you* should be worrying about, too? I mean, I sure as hell know I would. On the other hand, I put him away for the killings, he can't do anything to anybody."

The boy just stared at him openmouthed. Then he shook his head as though trying to remember something that wouldn't come.

"Look, Detective Schilling, I don't . . ."

"Tim. Look. Here's my card. You think about this thing and call me. Remember it's not you I'm looking to nail. Or Jennifer. I will if I have to. I've got to be honest with you about that. But I like your mom and dad. I've known them both for years. I wouldn't touch you for dope or anything else unless I absolutely had to. I just want to know what you know. I think it's to your advantage to tell me."

He stood. The boy's eyes locked into his own. He could tell he'd got him thinking. Schilling turned and walked back into the kitchen. He saw two very worried parents sitting over coffee mugs at the kitchen table. He smiled.

"Talk's over, folks. Tim's been very helpful and I want to thank you for the privacy. I appreciate it. Clara, it's nice to see you. And Lenny, remember what I said about that kitchen cabinet, will you? The damn thing's going to fall off and break my toe one of these days."

"Sure, Charlie."

"Give me a call and we'll set a time. Thanks again."

He turned and walked back into the living room and nodded at Tim, still sitting on the couch and let himself out the door.

It wasn't something you could feel good about, putting the kid in this position. But the pot was stirring.

He fielded their questions with a simple lie. That Detective Schilling had asked him not to speak about it.

They couldn't argue with that. Not unless they actually talked to the guy and found out it *was* a lie. Until then they'd leave it be.

Upstairs in his room he tried Jennifer's number but all he got was Mrs. Griffith again saying she wasn't home and no, she didn't know where she was. Maybe it was true and maybe it wasn't. For once he hoped it was. Then Schilling couldn't get to her before Tim did. He told Mrs. Griffith that it was important, to *please* have her call as soon as she got in, that it was urgent. He'd never even used the word before.

She might be over at Ray's. He didn't know whether to try to phone her there or not. What could he say to her with Ray around anyway? He knew Ray was expecting a call from him. He'd picked up another block of hash today over at the post office. He'd want to know it had come through okay. Tim hadn't even gotten around to shaving it yet.

He'd been just about to do that when his dad knocked

at the door. It was sitting unwrapped on the bed right out in plain sight with his dad's fucking razor blade lying next to it and when he heard the knock he'd almost shit. Then Schilling asks to come up and take a look around.

Jesus!

Their conversation kept looping around in his head. *What if somebody tells him?* Schilling had said.

Was that some kind of threat?

Was he saying that he, Schilling, might tell him? Would even a *cop* stoop to that?

But he was right about Ray's temper. And Tim *was* a little worried what Ray might do if he found out. It had nagged at him ever since they'd slept together. Wanting so much for it to happen again, that had just overcome the worry, that was all. He told himself that Ray didn't seem to care so much about Jennifer anymore since Katherine came into the picture. Katherine was all Ray talked about. He told himself Ray would figure it was no big deal.

But Ray had this thing about holding on to what was his. However much or however little he really wanted it.

What *would* he do?

Everything seemed all mixed up inside him now about Jennifer. He still wanted it to happen again with her but now he had to be *worried* about it happening again because that increased the odds that Ray would pick up on something.

It wasn't fucking *fair*.

What if somebody tells him?

She could easily be at Ray's. He could phone there, report on the hash, ask to talk to her. But for what reason? And then what would he say to her with Ray standing right there listening?

There was just no way to do this right. He couldn't even drive over to her place and wait for her to come home. For all he knew she *was* home. And there was no way for him to ask to borrow his dad's pickup or his mother's car anyway. Not so soon after some mysterious conversation with a cop. They'd want to know where and why. They weren't stupid.

He just had to wait. Hope she really *wasn't* home. That Schilling would miss her and have to try again tomorrow.

It wasn't fair. He hated this.
Come on, Jennifer. Call me.

Schilling got the address from the dispatcher, 362 Poplar Avenue. A twenty-minute ride a third of the way around the lake through stands of fur and pine and middle-class residences that were one cut up from the Bess place. Not yet into the luxury of the hills or lakeside but nicer. It had been a long hard winter and the road around here still needed lots of patching. He drove around potholes and rehearsed what he'd say to the Griffiths.

But the Griffiths weren't there. Jennifer opened the door herself. They'd gone to the movies, she said, the eight o'clock show over in Hopatcong. It was what they always did on Saturday nights.

An old married couple who still regularly dated. How about that.

She let him in.

He sat in his second overstuffed armchair of the evening while she sat rigid on a wooden one, her hands clasped tight in her lap. He noticed the ring on the middle finger of her left hand. A bright, clear stone in a gold setting. Somewhat at odds with the T-shirt, jeans and scuffed leather sandals.

She looked far more composed and adult than Tim had. He got right to it.

"I think you're living dangerously, Jennifer."

"What?"

He sighed. "Four years ago my partner Ed Anderson interviewed you in connection with Ray Pye and his possible involvement in the shooting of Lisa Steiner and Elise Hanlon. You told him that you and Ray were friends, you knew him from school, that he seemed like an okay guy but you didn't really know him all that well. You remember any of this?"

"A little. It was a long time ago."

"You told him that the night of the shooting you were here, alone in your room watching television."

"That I remember."

"Why?"

"Huh?"

"Why do you remember it?"

"I don't know. I just do."

"Okay, let's say you do and you were. But why did you lie to him about the other thing?"

"What other thing?"

"You were already sleeping with Ray, right?"

"I was not."

"Sure you were." He smiled.

"That's ridiculous."

"Tim Bess doesn't think so. He says you were."

"That's not true. Tim wouldn't say that."

"He also says you're sleeping with him now."

"Jesus! I slept with Tim *once!*"

"Once counts, doesn't it? But the thing is, Jennifer, Tim told me you'd slept with *him*. So why would he lie about you and Ray? Doesn't exactly make him look good, having to share you with his best buddy. Why would he lie?"

She was halfway out of her chair by now, starting to protest, looking for the words. Schilling cut her off with a gesture.

"Jennifer, listen, I'm not here to hassle you. I'm going to tell you the same thing I told Tim. I know about Ray. I know he deals dope. I know he's dangerous. I think he's killed people. I think you know more about Steiner/Hanlon than you're letting on. And I suggest you think it over and tell me what you do know. Because you're playing with fire messing around with Ray. That's all I have to say to you. Call me. Think it over and phone me. But do it soon."

He stood up and handed her his card.

"Nice crystal," he said. "Ray give it to you?"

"It's . . . it's a diamond."

He smiled. "Nah. Austrian crystal. Fairly high-quality cut glass. My grandfather was a jeweler. Try hitting it with a hammer. Glass shatters. Pretty, though. So maybe you better not."

Chapter Thirty

Jennifer

The first thing she did when it was possible to unglue herself from her chair was phone Tim. He picked up on the first ring.

"Jennifer, thank god."

"Jesus Christ, Tim. What did you tell him?"

"Shit, he was already there?"

"Yes, he was already here! What the hell did you say to him?"

"Nothing. He just . . ."

"You didn't tell him I *fucked* you, Timmy? You didn't tell him I was fucking Ray?"

She was so furious with him she was trembling. She could almost hear him wince on the other end of the line.

"I'm trying to tell you, Jen. I didn't say *anything* to him. He just guessed! He comes over here, he throws all these questions at me, about you, about Ray, about me, are we dealing dope, who's fucking who. It's like

273

he knew everything already. I didn't *have* to tell him. I tried to warn you, for godsakes. I called you and Mrs. Griffith said you weren't there."

She sighed. It was impossible not to believe him. She was afraid to ask the next question but she knew she needed to ask, she couldn't stand to feel alone about this.

"Did he say anything . . . you know . . . about those two girls to you?"

"Yeah, jesus, he said he knew Ray did it. Just like that. Isn't that some kind of fucking slander or something? And he said we'd better watch it, me and you, or he'd wind up doing the same thing to us."

"That's total bullshit."

"Yeah. Sure it is. I dunno, though. I mean, maybe we should think about it a little. What *would* Ray do? If he found out about us, I mean."

"He'd be mad. He'd be mad as hell. But he'd get over it. It was only just the one time. You're his best friend, for godsakes."

"I guess." He didn't sound convinced.

"Did he seem to know . . . I mean, that the two of us, you and me . . . *jesus!* that we were with him that night?"

"No. I don't think so. Man, I gave that a *lot* of thought. Just that we probably knew something. Like maybe something Ray told us 'cause we were his friends and all. Something we weren't telling."

Thank god for that much, she thought. There was a pause, both of them considering. It was Tim who broke it.

"So how come you won't talk to me, Jen? How come they keep saying you're not home every time I call you? I know you've been there. I thought it was nice, what we did. I thought you thought so too."

She'd known it was coming. She guessed it had to sooner or later.

"It *was* nice, Tim. But see, it can only be that one time, you know? I didn't want to get your hopes up that it would be anything more than that. I mean, I'm still with Ray."

"I don't get it. Why? What in the hell has Ray done for you lately? All he does is give you shit all the time. *I'm* the one who's got . . . I'm the one who's got feelings for you. Ray's all weirded-out over Katherine."

"Katherine's just another one of his flings. My god, he's had a dozen Katherines! It's me he always comes back to. You know that, Tim. I'm still his number one. Nothing changes that."

"How do you know? This thing with Katherine Wallace looks pretty damn serious from where I'm standing, I gotta tell you."

She almost couldn't believe what she was hearing. That Tim would take it this far. That he was willing to betray Ray this way. He'd never done anything like it in the past. She couldn't believe he *ever* would. But she had to be patient with him.

"Tim, is Katherine Wallace wearing his ring?"

"Hell, I dunno. Why? What'd he do, give you a ring?"

"Yes, Tim. He gave it to me Wednesday night."

"Jennifer, I hate to tell you, he's got a *drawer* full of rings. He showed me. He's given out half a dozen of the damn things. Some diamondlike thing? They're fake, for chrissake!"

"I don't believe you."

But she already did. He was just affirming what Schilling said. She felt her face flush. Her heart was pounding.

He sighed. And then his voice went all sad and lost-sounding. "I wish you did believe me, Jen," he said. "About everything. Not just Ray. But about you and me. I just wish you did."

And then he did something else he'd never done before.

He hung up on her.

She replaced the receiver and looked at the ring, turned it between her fingers. She felt like crying but she couldn't cry. All she could do was turn the ring and turn it again, the feel of it already familiar and comforting to her. She walked into the kitchen and poured some dish detergent on her finger and turned the ring some more and removed it over the knuckle and rinsed her finger.

In the utility drawer next to the refrigerator she found an old claw hammer amid the pliers and screwdrivers and batteries and she took it out and closed the drawer. She set the ring on the Formica counter next to the sink and covered it with a frayed white dish towel and raised the hammer and brought it down and removed the towel.

And looked at the ring. And then she did cry.

It was one-thirty in the morning when she drove the Griffith's car through the winding streets down to the lake. She parked in the lot of Tony's Fish and Bait Shop, dark now and closed and walked down to the pier and sat down at the end of it. She could feel the rough gray weathered wood beneath her jeans. The night was cool with the wind off the water and she hadn't brought a sweater. She sat with one arm wrapped around in front of her, cupping her elbow tight against the breeze and smoked a Viceroy, one of two she'd taken from Mrs. Griffith's pack on the coffee table.

How weird, she thought. *The lake is so beautiful and we hardly ever use it. Tourists use it. Little kids use it like we used to once but now we hardly ever do. Like the lake would have to be a novelty, something fresh and new the way it would be to some tourist or you'd have to have the innocence of a little kid to bother.* She felt stupidly old and tired and wasted. Wasted even more than when she was drunk or stoned. She stared out at the water, starlight glinting on the waves and black and deep beneath and wondered who was out there if anybody was out there at this hour, sitting on a dock like she was across the distant shore.

Chapter Thirty-one

Katherine

Such a strange thing watching her father. So strange the choices people make and why they make them. She'd known all this week now why he'd never gotten involved with another woman. Never even so much as dated. He still loved her mother after all these years, loved her deeply. Loved her crazy or not. It was simple as that. It had never even occurred to her that he might. But then it had never occurred to her that *she* might either, that it was possible to love the person someone once had been while hating and even fearing what that person had become. It was as though the mother she loved had been trapped inside Katherine all this time just as her mother was trapped inside the insanity, a pair of flies in amber.

Strange too to be doing all these things for him. She'd arranged for Etta to come in tomorrow morning but tonight it was she who made him dinner, a salad and spaghetti in red sauce and she who served it and cleaned

up afterwards and earlier, she who poured him the un-
accustomed glass of single-malt whiskey, who sorted
through the stack of mail, opened the windows to let
some air in, cleaned a week's worth of dust off the
kitchen table and counter. He stayed mostly in his study
with the door closed. Whether he was working in there
or not she didn't know but did not disturb him except
to call him to dinner. Afterwards they watched TV until
ten. He got up and kissed her on the cheek and smiled
and said he was going up to bed. They both were
drained and exhausted. She lingered in the flickering
light until the news came on at eleven. She didn't care
to watch the usual parade of wars, crimes and politics,
the smirking talking heads. Not tonight.

She went upstairs to her own bed and sat there staring
at the phone.

The phone felt like the enemy.

What to tell him. How to handle Ray.

There was no denying she had to handle him one way
or another, and do it right away. He'd already called
once in the middle of dinner. She'd had to promise him
yet again that *she'd* call *him.* If she didn't, she wouldn't
put it past him to come over for a visit in the middle
of the night. The guy was starting to sound obsessive,
that was the only word for it and obsessive from him
was a little scary.

After what he'd told her.

How long had she known him? A couple of weeks?

His *interest* in her was way, way over the top.

Deke with his usual sensitivity said she was crazy as
her mother was if she didn't dump the guy like he was
wired to a keg of dynamite. It was not the best way to
put it at the time but she had to agree. You didn't fool
with guys like this. Though she'd never *met* a guy like
this exactly she wasn't stupid. You didn't have to shoot
yourself in the foot to know that guns can hurt you.

The problem was what to say and how to say it. To

let him down fast or easy. *If at this point easy was even possible.*

The way he was sounding she wasn't sure it was.

Just phone him and let the call decide, she thought. See where it goes. Otherwise you'll be sitting here the rest of the goddamn night.

She found his number in her book and dialed.

"Hello?"

"Hi, Ray."

"Kath! Great! How you doin'? How's your dad?"

"He's okay. Better. He did some work, I made some dinner, we watched television. Fairly normal evening."

"Yeah, he'll be okay. It just takes time."

"I know."

"What about you?"

"I'm fine. Tired. Exhausted. The flight, the drive and all."

"So I guess you wouldn't want to be going out or anything."

"Tonight?"

He had to be kidding.

"Sure. I got kind of a present for you. You're gonna like it. I know you are. A surprise. Right up your alley. I thought maybe we could . . ."

"Ray, listen, we have to talk. There's no way I can go out tonight. I've got to get some sleep. I figure I've got maybe another half hour in me and that's it. But we can't do this anymore, anyhow."

"Huh?"

"This just isn't working out for me, Ray. I'm sorry. I mean, I've been thinking. I like you and we've had a good time together but I've got to be honest with you. I really don't think we should keep on seeing each other."

He started to interrupt but she wanted to keep this rolling.

"I think you're getting too involved with me, you

know? And I don't *want* to get involved right now. I don't mean just with you. Not with anybody. I mean, you say things like . . . you tell me you're falling in love with me . . ."

"Jesus, Kath. I *do* love you."

"See? That's what I'm saying. You *can't* love me, Ray, not after a couple of weeks and a couple of dates and even if you could, you've got to understand, I don't *want* to be loved. Liked is fine, loved's a whole other thing."

"Everybody wants to be loved, Kath."

"Sometime, sure. Sure they do. But I don't want somebody loving me right now. You see what I'm saying? Not now. I don't want the responsibility. Look at it my way. I'm new in town. I hardly know anybody here. I'm heading into my senior year in a brand-new school in a brand-new town."

"So?"

"So I don't want to get into some serious thing with somebody. I'm gonna be meeting a lot of new people, I want to be able to . . ."

"Fuck other guys."

"Excuse me?"

"You want to be able to fuck other guys, that's all the fuck you're saying."

"No, that's *not* all the fuck I'm saying. You keep hearing what you want to hear, Ray, you know that?"

"So then it's college, right? Your daddy's got this great job and all this money and you're going off to college in another year like that bitch Sally Richmond and Ray isn't. Ray's some kinda loser, Ray's staying right the fuck where he is. So to hell with Ray, right? Jesus Christ, Kath."

Sally Richmond? Who in god's name was Sally Richmond?

"Ray, it's none of those things. It's just what I said

it is. I don't want to get involved, that's all. No more, no less."

There was a silence on the other end. The room felt oppressively warm though she'd opened the windows first thing and tonight was on the cool side. But there wasn't much breeze. Maybe that was it. Or maybe it was the brandy she'd snuck after dinner. But what she really wanted to do now was strip off her clothes and take a shower and lie down naked on the bed and try to relax but she had to talk to him and get this over with and until that was done the jeans and shirt seemed weirdly necessary. Protective, like second skins.

"So you want to tell me who he is?" he said quietly. "The other guy?"

"There isn't any other guy."

"Don't bullshit a bullshitter, Kath. I'll find out anyway."

"I'm telling you there isn't. There's nobody."

"I don't know why you'd want to lie to me. I mean, I've been straight with you."

"Ray, there *isn't any other guy*. This is *me* we're talking about, what *I* want and don't want. Stop trying to make more of it than it is. There's no *other guy*."

"What you want. It always comes down to that doesn't it, Kath?"

"It comes down to that for everybody, Ray. You included. Isn't that why we're having this discussion right now? Because I'm not telling you what you want to hear? I'm sorry. I'm really sorry it didn't work out the way you wanted it to. I really am. But you're not going to change my mind arguing about it. You can't *talk* a person into having a relationship with you."

He laughed. It wasn't a nice laugh. It seemed to say she didn't know what the hell she was talking about.

And maybe in his case she didn't.

"No other guy, huh."

"No."

"I figure you owe me the truth. I figure you owe me that much. You fucked somebody else out there, didn't you."

"For chrissakes, Ray!"

"One of your old biker buddies, right?"

You should hang up right now, she thought. *Don't get into this.*

"Come on. You did. Didn't you."

"What business is it of yours what I did or didn't do? What do you care?"

There was a pause and then his voice went soft again.

"Oh, I care, Kath. Believe me. I care."

She didn't like this tone of voice of his any more than she liked the nasty one. It frightened her. Like the guy was capable of innumerable instant changes. It also was making her mad and she needed to control that.

"Listen. This is getting us nowhere, Ray. I'm sorry if you feel hurt. I didn't mean to . . ."

"What do you know about hurt, Kath? You get every goddamn fucking thing you ask for. You always do, don't you? You ever get something you *didn't* ask for?"

Screw this, she thought. *You don't need it.*

"That's it. Discussion over. I'm going to bed now, Ray. I'm much too tired for this."

"You're saying you're gonna hang up on me now? In the middle of all of this?"

And now he was sounding like a hurt little boy. The guy had more faces than Carter had pills.

"We're not in the middle of anything, Ray. I've said everything I have to say. I'm sorry but . . ."

"Dammit, Kath! Will you fucking *listen* to me!"

". . . but that's the way it is. I've got to get some sleep. Good night, Ray. Good-bye."

She placed the receiver down. Then took it off its cradle and placed it on the nightstand.

He wasn't through. He'd try to call her. She knew he would.

She wondered how scared of him she should be.

She was shaking with tension. Exhausted or not she was not at all sure about getting to sleep tonight. She thought about her father's brandy and single malt whiskey in the downstairs cabinet. A glass of something would calm her.

No, she thought. Ray Pye was not going to turn her into some goddamn alky. A good hot shower instead. But thinking about a shower immediately brought to mind Janet Leigh in *Psycho*. She remembered Ray appearing in her bedroom. Scaling the roof. Climbing in through her window.

Surprise me.

Jesus. Tonight a good hot shower was not going to make it.

Maybe I should give Deke a call, she thought. *See what he thinks. It's still pretty early in California. The guy tells me he's killed two people and now he's practically threatening me over the telephone. Maybe I should phone the police.*

It was not her habit to have anything to *do* with the police. Nor was it Deke's. But maybe.

One drink does not an alky make, she thought. Not even two or three.

She shut and locked the window and then she went downstairs.

Chapter Thirty-two

Ray

Ray couldn't sleep. Though he was already halfway wasted on the last of his hash and the better part of a six-pack by the time he got her call. He wondered if she could tell he was high. If that contributed to her dumping him. He didn't think so. He'd sounded fine.

The bitch, she'd made up her mind already. Didn't even give him a chance.

He didn't even get to mention the coke.

And now her phone was off the hook. He tried her over and over again.

What the fuck was going on here?

He drank another beer and then he switched to scotch. He sat in front of the TV set without hardly seeing it. All he saw were images of her. Kath stripping off her clothes by a moonlit pool, walking through the parking lot at Bertrand's Island trying out locked car doors, showing tit to the guy behind the counter in the liquor store, Kath sitting gazing at him beneath a tree

285

lit with red Chinese lanterns in New York City, in her bedroom wrapped in a towel, in an oversized white shirt and jeans and then naked beneath him and he remembered the feel of her, the taste of her mouth and scent of her hair and alongside all these eddying images and impressions an anger flowed and a will and a yearning that almost hurt him to consider.

More scotch and the images blurred and softened, springing into focus like slow strobic light, like a knife tearing up through paper glinting and disappearing. Finally he slept.

In his dream he was in Turner's Pool.

Night in deep water.

He was swimming for his life.

Pulled down at the hands of strange maidens.

Chapter Thirty-three

Sunday, August 17
Jennifer/Katherine/The Cat

Jennifer woke around eleven with a dull throbbing headache that testified to the warm six-pack of Colt .45 from the night before, to drinking herself to sleep once she left the dock, drinking well into the morning and to a not-so-dull fury. In the shower the headache began to subside but not the anger. She dressed and had a cup of coffee and borrowed the Griffiths' car. The day was gray, a slow drizzle of rain falling, misting the windshield. The houses along Poplar and Ridge Road looked sullen and empty. People were at church. People were at home reading their Sunday papers. People were still in bed.

And all these people had lives. Boring or not.

All these people were *doing* something.

Mrs. Pye was manning the front desk as she usually did on Sundays. She drove past it and back to Ray's apartment and opened the car door and stepped out onto the macadam and leaned on the horn. She did not want to go inside. She wanted him to come *out*side and she didn't give a good goddamn who else she managed to disturb to get him out there. The horn blared its steady note through the open motel courtyard and after a moment his door opened, Ray looking pissed and only now climbing into his shirt, his hair not even combed yet. So she'd woke him. Fine.

She wondered who was inside. Who he was fucking this time. His precious Katherine? She waited until he started walking toward the car and then released the horn.

"Jennifer? What the fuck?"

He looked terrible. Red-eyed and puffy.

"What the fuck. That's exactly right. What the fuck makes you think you can use me whatever way you want, Ray? *When*ever you want. What the fuck makes you think you can just go on and on with this bullshit? I came here to tell you, I quit. No more bullshit, Ray. You hear me? *No more!*"

She was shouting. She loved it. She felt practically weightless all of a sudden. It was pouring right out of her. All the poison, *his* poison—she even imagined its color, *green,* green and yellow—spilling right out of her across the macadam between them like some kind of nasty bile.

"You crazy? You want to tell me what the fuck's going on?"

"You've fucked with my head for the last time, Ray, that's what's going on. I'm gone. You got it? History. You played me for a sucker for the last time. You know what? I don't need you anymore, Ray. I don't know if I *ever* needed you. I think you were just a real bad habit. Guess what? Habit's broken. I'm *Tim's* girl now, you asshole! And he's better in bed than you'll ever be. And he doesn't have to stuff his shoes with beer cans to make people think he's got a great big cock. So screw you, Ray! And screw your goddamn phony ring!"

She dug it out of her pocket and threw it at him hard, heard it *thunk* off his forehead just over his eye and tinkle like a bell on the ground and saw him flinch, saw the *big man, the big stud* flinch from a blow from a tiny little broken ring and it felt so good she laughed. *She laughed right at him, right into his face* and at that moment he was nothing, Ray was absolutely nothing to her for practically the first time she could remember and she knew this with a certainty she'd never known about anything in her life.

"You *fucking bitch!*"

He lunged at her, grabbed her by the arms. His breath sour with old alcohol. And then he was shaking her. The fingers hurt but she didn't care. He could slap her, punch her, throw her to the ground and she wouldn't care about that either. There wasn't a thing he could do to her, there wasn't any way he could hurt her anymore. Not in that soul-deep way he'd hurt her all these years. She'd made it past that in one big leap. *She* was done with *him* now and and not the other way around and as he raised a fist she looked him in the eye and saw the hesitation there, the moment of cowardice and doubt, almost laughed in his face again and then she heard a voice behind her.

"*Raymond.*"

She saw him glance beyond her down the drive and turned and saw his mother standing there behind her.

"Let her go, Raymond. Right now."

There was a moment when she thought he still might hit her despite the cold command in the voice and she steeled herself for that. She could take a punch. She could take whatever the hell he was dishing out. Whatever it was it had been worth it. Then the fist dropped. The fingers on her arms relaxed and then released her. She turned back to him and looked into a face so explosively red, at an expression so strained and twisted, she thought he might just have a stroke right then and there.

Go ahead, she thought. *Die.*

You damn well deserve to die.

And it was the first time she'd thought that too. Though she more than anyway knew he did.

"Get back inside, Raymond. We'll talk about this later. Jennifer, I think you should get into your car."

She took a deep breath and nodded and then climbed into the driver's seat. She didn't close the door. Through the windshield she saw him glaring at her, then turn and spit down to the macadam and as he walked back to his apartment trying to look so tough, the long strides, the fists clenched, the open shirt flapping in the misty breeze, slamming the door behind him, she thought that it really *was* a damn funny walk he had. Really, it was ridiculous.

Mrs. Pye leaned in through the open door.

"You better stay away for a while," she said.

She nodded. "Like forever."

She realized suddenly that she'd never really seen Ray's mother up close before. Not this close. His mother was always just passing by or sitting behind a desk. She was a handsome woman. Her eyes were narrow, dark. Her lips were almost nonexistent, her good skin barely lined, the nose attractive and slightly beaked, the long graying hair pulled back tight into a severe bun.

"I can't stand the temper on that boy. I'm damned if I know where he gets it from."

The eyes glittered, moved back and forth, studying her.

"I don't know either," she said. She started the car. "Thanks, Mrs. Pye."

"Jane, honey. Call me Jane."

"Thanks . . . Jane."

The eyes studied her again.

290

"You go on home now," she said and stood there watching until the car pulled away.

It was two o'clock in the afternoon before Katherine reached him on the phone. Ten in the morning California time. It sounded like she'd woken him.

"Where were you last night, mister?" she said.

"Don't ask and I won't say."

"Okay. You sound like shit though."

"Thanks, Kath. I really appreciate that, y'know?" He yawned. "To what do I owe the pleasure?"

As best she could Katherine told him about the conversation of the night before.

"What do you think? Should I call the cops?"

"Jesus, Kath. I don't know. You really want to get involved with the Man? What are they gonna do for you?"

"Arrest him?"

"For what? It's not like he showed you the goddamn rifle or something. It's your word against his. They talk to him, release him, and then he's *really* pissed at you."

"Harrassment?"

"He's not harrassing you. He's phoning you. You had a shouting match over the phone. So what? You really scared, babe? You really scared of the guy?"

"I don't know."

"You want me to drive on out there?"

"Here?"

"Sure. Big fella on a Harley. Have a little talk with the asshole?"

"You'd do that?"

"For you I would. I wouldn't drive that far to see the Pope piss on Lyndon B. Johnson's leg but for you I would. Sure."

She laughed. "I always told my father you were a romantic. He never believed me."

"They never do."

"Tell you what," she said. "Anything else happens, I might actually want to take you up on that. I'll give it a few days though, I guess. Wait and see."

"Okay. You watch that ass of yours for me though, okay? He gives you any more shit, you call me."

"I will. Love you, Deke."

"Love you, babe. Later."

She pictured Deke's Harley pulling up at a stoplight beside Ray's Chevy convertible. Ray's Chevy with the top down. Ray glancing over. Deke glancing over. The Harley's engine revving.

She couldn't help but smile. She felt better already.

The cat saw the bird flutter down into the branches of the elm tree deep in the woods behind Ed Anderson's yard. The cat was not hungry, but since her eyes had led her to the bird she crouched into the hunter's pose anyhow—head low, haunches tight, shoulders hunched—and moved slowly through the brush. The bird which was a blue jay, loud and squawking, was inattentive for its kind. Perhaps it too had eaten its fill, stolen its feed from a flock of sparrows it had frightened away. It perched with its back to the cat, long blue tail feathers hung low over the branch and bobbing. To the cat the bird was irresistible.

She judged she was close enough, poised herself, tensed and made her run. The elm tree gave good purchase. The cat was a black sudden streak up the trunk of the tree into and through the branches and the bird was barely a second from its death at the claws and jaws of the cat when the black eye flashed and the banded wings spread and flapped and it squawked and flew away.

The cat perched on the tree limb watching. Earthbound, the cat watched the bird careen through thin air. Her heart was racing. She panted with excitement. She watched the bird wide-eyed until it disappeared beyond other, smaller trees in the distance and then looked around her into the branches and the leaves and then looked down.

The elm tree was a tall tree and the cat had not realized the branch the bird was on was this high up, hadn't considered it, had only the confidence that the muscles and limbs of her body could get her to the bird, that it was possible. She had not known *she* was this high up until this very moment. The confidence and courage to climb the tree were not the same as the confidence and courage it would take to get her down again. The distance between even the lowest limb of the tree, three limbs down, to the ground beneath now seemed formidable. She essayed those three branches handily, but with only the earth below her now the distance looked even more daunting.

She stretched and placed her front paws tentatively ahead of her along the tree trunk to the left side of the branch, her claws digging into the bark, carefully scanning the terrain. The ground was rocky, hard and forbidding. She turned and repeated the maneuver on the right side. The problem was the same. She carefully paced the length of the limb studying the earth below along either side until the limb thinned and swayed underfoot and a thicket of leafy branches would not permit further passage. She returned along the limb to the trunk, sat hunched in the crook of the limb's thick safety—which in fact was no safety at all but which was illusory, the only true safety for the cat the hard earth, the known ground below—and sat shivering, tense with anxiety, attempting to determine just what to do.

The afternoon sunlight had burnt off the morning mist.

The cat opened her mouth and gave voice to her solitary grief and confusion. Her world made no response.

Chapter Thirty-four

Tim

He got the call at three o'clock and he could tell that Ray was pissed. He wanted his hash and he wanted it now, he said. Why the hell hadn't Tim called him? He made up some story about a massive headache and fever which probably was the flu, and that seemed to work for the moment.

Twenty minutes later Ray was down ringing the doorbell. His parents had taken Ginnie to a matinee of Barbra Streisand in *Hello, Dolly!* at the Colony so it was Tim who let him in. *What's up and hey and how ya doin'* and not a word from Ray in reply and they climbed the stairs in silence. Already Tim had a bad feeling about this. In his room Ray flopped down on his bed and Tim went into his drawer for the hash, took it out and tossed it over to him.

"Weigh it," he said.

"Huh?"

"Get out the scale. Weigh it."

"I already did."

"So do it again."

There wasn't any arguing with the hooded eyes or with the flat black tone of voice. He felt like a snake had just entered the room and was having a look around—he had better be careful where he stepped. He got out the scale and set it on his bureau, hoping against hope that he hadn't trimmed too much this time, not enough for Ray to notice. Ray got up and unwrapped the hash and examined it a moment and placed it on the scale. Then he looked at Tim.

"Short. You've been shavin' it on me, Timmy."

"I . . ."

"I figured."

He took the block of hash off the scale and began tossing it up and down like you'd toss a rubber ball, pacing the room from bed to bureau to window to the door like he was trying to figure something out in there, like he was concentrating and the pacing and the tossing were helping him. And the strange thing was that he didn't seem mad about the hash. Tim had no sense of that. Just concentrating, like the hash didn't matter a bit. Which for Ray was very weird. It didn't stop him from being worried about Ray's being there, though. The snake had turned into something that looked more like a caged lion, that was all.

"Had a real strange visit this morning, Timmy. I mean, *strange,* man."

Still pacing.

"Yeah? From who?"

"Jennifer."

He thought, *Oh shit.*

"See this little scratch here?"

He walked up close and pointed to his forehead, a tiny red pinprick scab there. Then he started pacing and tossing again.

"She threw my fucking ring at me. Said that you were

295

screwing her and threw my ring right in my face. Said she's through with me and fucking you and made jokes about my dick. About my dick, man! You believe that shit? This kind of shit I'm getting from *Jennifer?* If my mother hadn't come along I'd have killed the little cunt right there in the goddamn driveway, I'd have killed her fat flabby ass right there, no doubt about it. I'm telling you, Timmy, I've had it up to here with them. I've had it with every one of these bitches.

"Fucking Katherine, right? Fucking Katherine Wallace won't even talk to me. Says she doesn't want to see me again, gives me all this bullshit about not wanting to get involved with anybody, won't even discuss it. And I go out and buy coke for her. Me. I get fucking *coke* for her! You believe that? What am I, nuts? Fucking whatsername, fucking Sally Richmond, talking to me like I'm pond scum. Now Jennifer Fitch! You believe it? *Jennifer* fucking *Fitch?* I mean it's incredible to me. You tell her about the rings? I guess you did, right. I mean, fuck 'em, you know? Fuck *all* of 'em. You know what I'm saying? That's it. That's really *it.* That's fucking plenty. That's enough. Don't you think that's enough, man? I mean, *I* think so, jesus, what do you think?"

He had the strangest sensation.

It was like Ray was talking to him but Ray wasn't really *in the room* with him at all. Ray was somewhere else. He heard the voice, he saw the pacing. But it was like Tim was watching a movie. Like Ray was somewhere inside his own personal movie screen and all Tim was *supposed* to do was watch. He wasn't supposed to answer. And what was *really* weird was that he still had no sense of danger.

He'd shaved Ray's hash for chrissakes and Ray knew it.

He'd fucked *Jennifer* and Ray knew it!

Dropped that little bombshell like some guy reporting the weekend weather.

What the hell was going on here?

Whatever it was, it was scaring him. The air felt thick and close and he could smell Ray's sweat, sour and strong like salty soup. If the rage wasn't there—*and it wasn't, it wasn't, this was just some kind of crazy rant*—if it didn't look like Tim was going to get beat to shit over this, that sure didn't stop it from being scary. Because this wasn't like any *version* of Ray he'd seen before. Not even drunk or stoned. Ray was always *there* at least. Even his unpredictability had its ranges and Tim thought he'd seen all of them by now.

But he didn't know this weird, pacing zombie looking pale and sick like'd he'd just thrown up, didn't know him at all and when he stopped in front of his bureau and balled up his fist and suddenly screamed *fuck me!* and put his fist through the white plaster wall right next to Lennon in his granny glasses, hit the wall so hard he rattled the scales on top of the bureau, Tim's *own wall* in *Tim's parents' own home* which he *never* would have dared to do at any other time in all the years he'd known him it almost didn't surprise him. It was like Ray was pounding at his own big wide silver screen and who the hell cares where or whose house it was.

And he'd have thought *that* at least would have taken some of the steam out of him, punching the fucking wall. But it didn't.

He wasn't tossing the hash anymore. He was squeezing it in his fist like a ball of clay. Moving faster, wobbling in his boots, spit flying out of his mouth and going on about fucking bitches and fucking cops—*jesus, did he know about Schilling too?*—like he'd lost it completely, not angry like when he'd hit the wall but talking, talking nonstop, talking to somebody inside himself or in that silver screen of his but not to Tim, not looking once at Tim the whole time until finally and without any reason or warning he flung open the bedroom door and tromped down the stairs and out across the lawn, the block of hash still clutched in his hand.

Right out there in the open, right in plain sight. Carrying his hash to the car.

Tim didn't so much as move till he heard it pull away.

His legs felt weak, like it was he who'd been doing all that pacing. He sat down on the bed.

Who to call.

Somebody.

What to do.

Something.

How to explain the goddamn hole in the wall to his parents.

He sat there and stared at it and wondered.

Chapter Thirty-five

Happy Hour

When Charlie Schilling walked in Ed was glad to see him. The mood in Teddy's was way, way off today. Nobody even bothering to feed the jukebox. Not even Teddy, who usually could be counted on to pick up the slack if his customers weren't parting with their change. He watched Charlie walk the length of the place greeting some of the regulars and saw his smile turn to a frown along the way.

He picked up on the mood right away. He always was a quick study.

"Christ, Ed. What's up? Joint's like somebody up and died today."

"Somebody did die, Charlie. Ray Hardcuff's oldest."

"Danny Hardcuff?"

"That's right. Lance corporal in the Marine Corps. The VC shot his chopper down. Teddy says he was crew chief, supposed to soften up the landing zone with M-sixty fire. I guess it didn't soften."

"Aw, shit, Ed. Has anybody seen Ray?"

"Teddy talked to him on the telephone this morning. He asked Teddy to pass the word around for him. He doesn't want any calls for a while. I guess Dot's taking it real hard and so is he."

"They've got another boy, right? Younger boy?"

"Two. But one's not young enough. He's over in that shitstorm too. Andy I think his name is."

Teddy came over and nodded and Charlie ordered a scotch.

"Ed fill you in?" Teddy said.

"Just now."

"I talked to him this morning. Said Dot's sister's flying in from Seattle to handle things for a while."

"That's good."

"He was engaged, y'know, Danny was. Girl by the name of Cathy Stutz."

"Christ, I know her too. We busted her for popping a beer in public once. Remember, Ed?"

"Sure I do. Nice girl. It was just that one time. Never had any trouble with her again."

"Damn."

"That's four from this town that I know of," Teddy said. "Town this size, four's a lot."

They drank awhile in silence and then Schilling ordered a second scotch and told Ed about his visits to Tim Bess and Jennifer Fitch.

"I don't get it. What are you trying to do?"

"I'm trying to scare them into talking to me. They know something. I want to hear it."

"You saying the kids were in on it?"

"I don't know. I doubt it. But Ray brags. Maybe he bragged about it to them."

"Think he's that stupid?"

"He might be. The tough guys usually tend to be. Anyhow I got the same feeling from both of them. They both know more than they're telling."

Ed finished his beer and ordered another and Schilling wondered how many he'd had already. He was slurring his words a little and that wasn't like him at all.

"You're really pushing the envelope with this, you know that. We're talking harrassment, slander. All that shit."

"I know. Anything comes of it, it's worth risking."

"You sure?"

"I'm sure."

He sighed and hunched over his beer. "Hope you're right, partner."

Schilling looked at him. "What's going on, Ed? This isn't just Danny Hardcuff on your mind. It's Sally, right?"

Ed sighed again and shifted on his barstool. "Yeah. I been a hell of a fool, Charlie. Thing is, I figure I'm damned if I do and damned if I don't. I ask her to come back and she *does* come back, which she might or might not do at this point, I'm gonna feel guilty all over again. If I don't ask her, I'm just gonna feel *bad,* period."

"Guilt's for suckers, Ed. Or the guys who are guilty. You're neither one."

There was a fine irony here and Schilling was well aware of it. *All along I'm worried about Ed seeing this girl much too young for him and now I'm trying to convince him to start seeing her again. I'm worried about him* not *seeing the girl.*

Go figure.

The irony wasn't lost on Ed either.

"You're telling me I should call her? I'm really hearing this?"

"Yeah, Ed. I'm telling you you should call her. And wipe that goddamn smirk off your face. Whoever said I had to be consistent? If I were you though, I'd wait till the beers settle. Have some dinner. Do it stone cold. . . ."

301

"Sober. Yeah, you're right about that. You really think I should call her, huh?"

"Yeah. I do."

And Schilling had to laugh. Not just at the look on Ed's face, like a guy who's just been told he's *not* going to jail after all, he's going to Palm Springs instead all expenses paid but also at the thought that it was impossible in life to predict anybody's behavior. Not even his own.

He wondered for just a moment if the thought should have any wider application for him, one he somehow wasn't getting.

But by then the third scotch was down and working in him and the moment fled into the whiskey like a rabbit from a hunter on a winter day and disappeared.

Chapter Thirty-six

Sally

"*I* was going to call *you*," he said.

It was so good, she thought, to hear his voice and even better to hear him say what he was saying. She lay back on the bed and relaxed.

"You were, huh?"

"I just finished dinner. I was going to clean up and then phone you."

"Bouillabaisse?"

"What?"

"For dinner. Bouillabaisse?"

"Oh, I threw that out. Some I gave to the cat."

"Shame."

"The cat didn't think so."

"So what were you going to say to me?"

"You called me, remember?"

"Let's hear it, Ed. Indulge me."

She heard him clear his throat. It made him sound

stern and gruff, which was the last thing he was and which now amused her.

"I was going to say that I acted like a goddamn dope and that I've been hurting for it ever since. I was going to say I'm sorry."

"That's it?"

"Okay. That and that I'd like to spend the rest of this time with you, what time you have left here. That you're an adult and I don't have any right to say what you should or shouldn't be doing. That I miss you. And that I don't give a damn what people are saying about us. That I want you around if you still want to be here."

She gave it a beat. Figured let him stew a second.

"Gee Ed, that's a lot. I was just gonna say I forgive you."

"You do? Well hell, that's plenty!"

They laughed.

"Can you come over?"

"Can't. Not tonight. I promised Tonianne I'd take her out for burgers and a movie. Sort of a thank-you for getting me the job."

"How's that working out?"

"It's not the most interesting thing in the world. But Sam's a nice guy and an easy guy to work for. And it's fun when Tonianne's around. You know. We get in some girl talk. It's a whole lot better than making beds and vacuuming floors and collecting dirty linen. I could come over tomorrow if you want. After I finish up there."

"Good. I'll make us dinner."

"No you *won't* make us dinner. You'll drive us over to Hopatcong for a couple of steaks. Deal?"

"Deal. Sal?"

"Yeah."

"I just can't say how glad I am we talked. I mean, lord, what a relief!"

"I am too, Ed. Real glad."

"So you have a good time with Tonianne tonight. I'll see you tomorrow."

"See you tomorrow. Good night, you."

"G'night."

She hung up and thought, *Well that was easy.* They were back together.

Just like that.

She felt warm and snug and safe again.

She also felt like an ice-cold Pepsi. With a wedge of lemon to cut the sweetness. There was always a lemon or two in the fridge for her mother's vodka tonics. She crossed the room barefoot and smiling.

Her father was standing just outside the doorway.

The door had been open a crack. It wasn't a mistake she usually made. Had he opened it without her hearing?

"Daddy?"

He'd obviously just come from the bathroom. He was standing in the hall flossing his teeth, one of the many habits of his she casually detested. Flossing wasn't a thing you did in public, even with family. You kept it in the goddamn bathroom.

"Who's Ed?" he said "And why in god's name are you going all the way to Hopatcong for a steak? Perfectly good steak at the White Horse Grill. Plus we know the owner."

"You were *listening* to me?"

He shrugged. "Just passing by."

She'd always wondered how he'd come so far in real estate. As far as she was concerned he was a lousy liar. There wasn't any point calling him on it though.

"So. Who's Ed?"

"A man I know."

"A *man* you know? How old a man we talking about?"

She had the feeling she understood where this was going and felt a chill that he should know. If he did it couldn't be helped. It wasn't going to change anything. If he was only fishing she wasn't about to help him. She decided to try cutting this off before it went any farther. It was usually as easy to get around her father as it was to get around her mother.

She didn't want to know what or how much he knew. She didn't care.

"Men my age aren't *boys* anymore, daddy. Try to move a little with the times, okay? And it's none of your business anyhow. I'm leaving for college in a month or so. You going to want to know who I'm seeing in Boston too?"

"Maybe."

"Well I won't have any more intention of discussing it with you then than I do right now. At the moment I'm thirsty. Excuse me."

She walked around him and down the stairs. Left him standing there, floss dangling from his fingers.

"And the steaks at the White Horse Grill are awful," she said.

Chapter Thirty-seven

The Cat

It was dusk. With dusk the need to get out of the tree had conquered all her apprehension. Her belly rumbled. There were night predators far more suited to trees than she was.

She chose to go down on the same side she'd come up. As she had done many times before she placed her front paws against the bark and dug in with her claws as best she could and inched along, only this time when she'd stretched her full length down along the tree trunk she retracted the claws and allowed herself to fall. She arched her spine and raised her head and lowered her shoulders, her legs seeking the ground. For a moment she felt sudden wind and perfect balance and then the jagged earth hit her and she yowled in pain.

The cat had great tolerance for pain but this was unlike any she'd ever had before. A deep dull throb ran from her right front foreleg to her shoulder. When she placed the pad of her foot tentatively to the ground the pain became an electric red-hot streak that dizzied her so much that she fell sideways onto her hip into tall tufts of scrubgrass and then awkwardly had to work her way up again.

The right front leg was useless to her.

Her only thought was to get back to the house where the man was and where there was a comfortable place to lie down.

She was deep in the woods.

She hobbled three-legged in the house's direction. Each footfall brought new pain, a combination of the bone-deep throbbing and a lesser version of the earlier sharp agony that had caused her to fall to her side into the grass. She felt thirsty now, not hungry and made her way slowly through the woods. No longer quite herself anymore. Not quite the same cat she had known herself to be.

Diminished.

Chapter Thirty-eight

Ray

Black.

All black.

Black silk shirt buttoned to the neck, tight black jeans, black string tie, shiny black boots, onyx ring in a silver setting on the index finger of his left hand.

He looks into the mirror and sees a handsome young Black Knight freshly showered and shaved, teeth brushed, hair combed and patted gently into place and sprayed to hold. His eyeliner, shadow and mascara are somewhat heavier than usual though still in very good taste he thinks so that the eyes are the first thing you notice, their dark glitter the first thing you see. A touch of rouge on the powdered cheeks. The mole carefully painted with the tip of an eyebrow pencil wetted with his own saliva—his witch's mark, his Mark of Cain.

He removes the mirror, turns the four silver clamps that hold it in place so that they no longer do so and sets the mirror on the floor so that it leans against the toilet. In removing the mirror he reveals a large, deep hole and inside the hole, a horizontal brace against a vertical stud. Along the length of the brace there lies, first, a .38 Smith & Wesson Ladysmith revolver with a frosted stainless finish and a rosewood grip. Behind it are two full boxes of cartridges, one for the Ladysmith and the other for the Remington bolt action .22 long rifle with the beautiful checkered walnut stock that lies behind them.

Each day as Ray has been looking into the mirror he has simultaneously been looking at these.

No one, not even Tim, knows they are there. Tim thinks they're long since thrown away. Ray has oiled, cleaned and polished them once a year on the anniversary of the night at Turner's Pool and then thrown out the materials he purchased to do so. He has covered his tracks.

He takes out the Ladysmith and the boxes of shells and places them on the toilet seat. He reaches in deep and grips the Remington by its smooth slim stock and stands it by the sink. He picks up the mirror and clamps it back in place. He opens the box of .38 shells and sets it on the sink and picks up the Ladysmith and watches himself in the mirror as he loads it.

Empty, the Ladysmith weighs only a pound and a half, its barrel just two inches long. But it feels heavier in his hand. A thing of fine balanced weight. He slides the five bullets into the cylinder and when he is finished snaps it shut.

He closes the box of shells and puts those and the handgun back on the toilet seat and opens the second box of shells, picks up the rifle and releases the magazine and fills it with four shells and slides it back into the magazine floor plate. To do this he must pay attention to the rifle and not himself in the mirror. When he's through he slings the rifle over his shoulder by its soft leather strap and closes the second box of shells

*and picks up the Ladysmith and then his gaze returns
to the mirror to his reflection in the mirror to the Black
Knight in the mirror to Ray, Death-Ray in the mirror
and the now-empty hole behind the mirror, he regards
all this and then takes up the boxes and turns away
smiling the Elvis grin, the Evil Elvis grin and walks out
of the bathroom and through his bedroom and living
room past his waterbed and his television and his stereo
set and his wet bar and out his door into the brightness
of the motel-parking-lot lights to greet his defected fans.*

Chapter Thirty-nine

The Lost

Ray walked from his car to the top of the hill and clicked off the safety on the rife and watched the lights from the television flicker in the living room. He walked through the door to the big house where his mother and father had raised him and saw her sitting on the sofa watching Ed Sullivan. Ed was talking with Dinah Shore following her number, and the audience applauded and his mother blinked at him standing in the doorway and frowned and started to say something as Dinah exited and the audience applauded and Ed went to a commercial waving to the audience and Ray shot her through the heart and threw the bolt. The .22's spent cartridge made no sound whatsoever on the welcome mat and he raised the rifle and sighted and shot her again.

He walked back down the hill to the car and as he did so threw the bolt and heard the cartridge ping on the flagstone walkway. The sound was satisfying. He clicked on the safety. He opened the door to the Chevy and got in and slid the rifle over into the passenger seat next to the Ladysmith and boxes of shells.

His father was in the lighted office staring at the television which would have the sound off and he wondered if his father was also watching Ed Sullivan only without the sound. His father looked up and smiled and waved at him as he drove past and Ray returned the wave. He pulled out onto the street wondering where to first and then realized he was hungry and thought it would be a damn good idea to get some food in him before proceeding any further.

He drove through mostly empty streets with only an old Ford proceeding him and two pair of headlights behind him moving over the hills and pulled into Don's Drive-In. The drive-in was crowded for a Sunday night, the first row of spaces completely full of cars with trays hooked to their driver-side windows so he drove around them and turned moving slowly along the second row, and then saw an empty space but before that saw something else that made him forget all about his hunger.

He pulled in anyway.

Parked the car and thought a minute.

There was a waitress taking an order two cars down to the left of him. The driver had just turned off his lights at her approach. Ray did the same. He took his keys out of the ignition and opened the car door and walked to the back of the Chevy and noticed a dark splotch of bird shit splattered drying on the trunk which he would have to go over with a rag later on. He opened the trunk and took out the tire iron and jack so that only the spare tire remained. He left the trunk open and walked around to the backseat of the car and tossed the tire iron and jack down on the floor through the window. Went to the front and took the Ladysmith off the seat and holding the gun at his side walked down the row of cars.

The girl in the passenger seat of the Volkswagen was

someone he had never seen before but he didn't care
who she was, it didn't matter. Her window was open
which did matter and she glanced up at his approach,
turned her head toward him slightly which made the
angle fine for him, perfect, so that he brought up the
.38 and fired directly into her right eye from just inches
away, driving her exploded head into Sally Richmond's
lap and her blood and brains all over her sitting with
her chocolate shake and she immediately began screaming, the shake falling out of her hand, Sally Richmond
trying to push the girl's head off her and at the same
time open the driver's side door.

He got around to the door just as she managed to
throw it open and put the gun to her wet glistening
belly.

"Shut up," he said. "Shut the fuck up." His voice was
very calm.

She stopped screaming with the gun pressed into her
belly but kept sobbing and noisily trying to get her
breath but he guessed she couldn't help that. He
grabbed her arm remembering that other parking lot
when he'd grabbed her arm which seemed like only
yesterday. Only this time she didn't pull away. This
time she didn't mouth him. He turned her around and
shoved the muzzle into the small of her back.

"Move. Wipe that shit off your face. Come on."

People were standing outside their cars or climbing
out of their cars, mostly guys and one of the waitresses
stood frozen in the middle of the lot but nobody tried
to stop him. He kept the gun just above the crack of
her ass and walked her to the rear of the Chevy. The
adrenaline rush was truly one hundred percent amazing.
He pointed to the trunk.

"Get in."

She was trying to wipe the blood out off her hairline
but only managing to smear it across her forehead and
didn't seem to understand him.

"Get in there. Get your ass in."

She turned and looked at him with the blood smeared all over her face and the tears running down and her whole body shaking tits shaking nipples practically popping through the bloodsoaked once-white short-sleeved blouse, and he put the gun up under her chin and used it to tilt her head back.

"Get. In." he said, nice and quiet. And if *he* was not his voice was still calm which amazed him.

He was practically coming in his pants here.

She turned and did as he said. He slammed the trunk door shut. The door sounded as loud to him as the shot had been. People were staring. He could feel their eyes crawl over him. He could hear low murmurs and the squealy voices of little girls. The voices made him want to laugh but he didn't laugh. It would spoil the effect he wanted. He walked slowly around and got into his car and shut the door. He turned the key in the ignition and revved the Chevy hard and then eased up and put it into gear and pulled away past faces pale in the fluorescent light past the long row of cars and the red and green flashing neon sign above the entrance to the Drive-In out into the streets of Sparta.

He laughed and shook his head and pounded the wheel at his amazing good fortune.

Gradually his hunger returned.

But that would have to wait now.

Inside the trunk Tonianne's blood was sticky on her hands, sticky on her chest and skirt, sticky in her hair. She lay jostled in a fetal position in the dark, her hip pressed against a tire, unable to stop shaking, eyes blinking uncontrollably and the eyelids too sticky with blood. She could smell exhaust fumes and rubber and dirty metal and her own faint perfume and she could hear the hissing of the tires moving over the road and something metallic rattling on the floor of the backseat a few unreachable feet behind her back. When the car turned abruptly she put her right hand down to the floor of the trunk for balance and the hand came away with some kind of wrapper stuck to it, some kind of cellophane and she picked it away revolted like the wrapper was a spider she had crushed burst across the palm of her hand.

Her mind played the scene over and over again vivid and sharp and she couldn't get it to stop. She kept thinking how Ed on the phone had asked her out tonight and if she had only gone Tonianne would be alive *her oldest girlfriend would still be alive* and she wouldn't be here in this dark close rattling box, that this never would have happened because Ed would have protected her and she kept calling silently for him to come protect her now, needing to believe for the first time in her life that such a thing as telepathy might exist but despairing that it did, the tires on the road sibilant as a snake beneath her.

Schilling was dozing through the last ten minutes of Ed Sullivan when the call came. There were no premonitions, no warnings, no feelings about the phone call whatsoever. It was Jackowitz.

"Don's Drive-In," he said.

"What about it?"

"I hear you worked a homicide a few years back, suspect was a guy named Ray Pye. Ring any bells?"

"Rings all my bells, cap. What's up?"

"You're not gonna like this, Charlie. Pye's been ID'd by two eyewitnesses as the shooter of a girl named Tonianne Primiano about fifteen minutes ago. Uniforms just phoned in their report. Girl was sitting in the passenger seat eating her burger and fries and up walks Pye and blows her brains out. The driver he kidnaps at gunpoint and forces into his trunk and drives away with her. They're telling me it all went down in about two minutes flat. We got an all-points out on his car."

"Her?"

"Car's a Volkswagen Beetle. I hate this the worst, Charlie. It's registered to Sally Richmond."

It felt like somebody had hit him in the chest with a bowling ball. He sat down on the sofa. He didn't know what to say. But his thinking was clear. Stunningly so.

You did this, he thought.

You had to push him. You goddamn idiot.

"I don't know how well you know the girl personally, Charlie. But Ed . . . I mean . . . it's got to be a helluva thing for him. A helluva thing."

You pushed him and he went off. Just like that. Only not the way you thought he'd go off. Not the kind of slip you wanted. You smart-assed stupid obsessing son-ovabitch drunk you were playing with lives all along here. You asshole.

"You want to go over there? I mean, you want in on this one? You want me to phone Ed?"

"I want in on it. But I'll tell Ed. I'll do it right now while I've still got the guts to and then head on over to the Drive-In. Get a car over to the Starlight Motel right away. Pye has an apartment in back. Tell them to watch for him but not to approach. There's a file on Pye on my desk. Inside are two names, Tim Bess and Jennifer Fitch. Send uniforms over to their addresses too. Have somebody call and tell them to stay put and not open the door for anybody until we get there. Especially not Ray Pye."

"You think Pye might be making a night of it?"

"Yeah cap, I think maybe I do."

"Jesus. Okay, we'll get on it right away. Charlie listen, when you talk to Ed tell him for me, I mean, tell him for everybody here . . ."

"I know. I will. Thanks."

*   *   *

Ed placed the phone in its cradle and sat staring at his hands a moment, as though the hands didn't belong to him and were not the hands that puttered in the garden or the hands that had stroked her. He rolled them into fists and unrolled them. The hands were cold and clammy and he didn't like the feel of them.

He got up and walked to the bedroom and opened the drawer to his nightstand and took out the .38 special and checked the chamber to be sure it was loaded even though he knew it was. He took the gun and the box of bullets back into the living room and set them on the table while he pulled on his jacket and then slipped the box into one pocket of the jacket and the gun into the other and went outside and locked the door behind him.

The cat was approaching the rear of the house when she heard the front door slam and the key in the lock and the man's heavy tread across the walkway. She had become accustomed to the pain to the extent that the pain was part of her now and not a foreign thing as at first, the pain was simply part of her being. But it would not permit her to move swiftly and that was part of her now too. She hobbled around the side of the house past the hedges and heard the car door slam and the engine roar and for a moment found herself bathed in headlights as they swept over her and the car pulled out of the driveway and the man drove away.

She listened to the house.

The house was empty.

She moved back to the dark protection of the hedges, moved carefully between and into them and lay down on her uninjured left side and waited for him to return.

A few moments later she smelled *dog* and heard a snuffling sound and peered out from between the hedges. She saw it large and shaggy sniffing at the base of the streetlight a block away, sniffing and moving on along the grass between the sidewalk and the street and headed in her direction.

She crept back farther and hunkered down.

He parked two doors down from Jennifer's house and reloaded the rifle and the single empty chamber in the Ladysmith. He climbed out of the car and stuck the Ladysmith in his belt and grabbed hold of the rifle. He listened for noises coming from the trunk but there were none. Maybe she was dead of exhaust fumes. It happened. He closed the car door and walked up the street. Opened up their door and came upon a family tableau.

Mrs. Griffith was just putting the phone down, she was standing by the sofa and the end table, a worried expression on her face, and she struck him as so *old*, he'd never realized how old these two fuckers were, old enough to be her grandparents not her parents which of course they weren't anyway and Mr. Griffith sitting skinny and hunched and balding in the armchair was the first to see him, Mr. Griffith startled, rising and you never knew not even with these old guys so he shot him first with the rifle assuming the stance and firing, shattering his glasses *he was getting all eye-shots tonight* and Mr. Griffith falling back into the chair like somebody'd pushed him except his eye was a wide red hole pumping blood all over his shirt. Then Jennifer was running up the stairs which was stupid and fine with him so he turned to Mrs. Griffith who was screaming high and whiney and holding her face in both withered white hands which looked deformed to him for some reason and he didn't even bother aiming, he just pointed the rifle at her midsection and shot her in the stomach and she went down onto the carpet writhing, moaning, trying to crawl.

He ejected the cartridge and stepped over her and climbed the stairs.

Jennifer was in her bedroom. He tried the doorknob

and the door was locked. No problem. He slung the rifle over his shoulder and pulled out the Ladysmith and shot twice at the lock just like they do in the movies the Ladysmith loud as hell in the hallway and kicked the door and again, just like in the cop pictures the door flew open and there was Jennifer at the wide-open window, half in and half out of the window and he crossed the floor in three steps and grabbed her arm and hauled her in.

"Where you going, Jen?"

He thought she said something or maybe she was just whimpering, but his ears were ringing so he couldn't hear. He pulled her to the doorway and out into the hall and down the stairs. She didn't fight him. She was scared and crying and now he could just barely hear her say, *don't hurt me, please Ray please* which was exactly the kind of thing he wanted to hear from her. Mrs. Griffith was crawling toward the kitchen, trying to make it to the back door he guessed. The blood trail behind her skinny legs looked like the kind a slug or a snail would make only red.

He decided not to shoot her again, to give her a fighting chance.

She was old. She'd be dead soon anyway. Fuck her.

He hauled Jennifer out the door and down the street to the car. She was sobbing and she looked like hell, her face all red and blotchy. When they got to the car he put the .38 to her cheek and she stood there while he fished out the keys and opened the trunk and *surprise surprise!* Miss Long Tall Sally was still with them not dead of carbon monoxide poisoning blinking out at them covered with dried and drying blood and trying to get up so he stood back to where he could shoot both bitches if he had to.

"You stay right there, hear me? Jennifer, get in. You'll be nice and cozy inside. Kind of a slumber party. But hey, you don't really know one another do you?

Sally, Jennifer. Jennifer, Sally. Get in Jen. Don't make me shoot you in front of the fucking neighbors."

She did as he said, the two of them curled up playing spoons in his trunk. He had to smile. It was a tight fit. Kind of like boots were a tight fit when you first bought them but then you broke them in.

He was breaking them in.

He closed the trunk. He got into the car and drove away.

The patrol car pulled up to the Griffith house five minutes later. The front door was open wide and Officer Bill Klossner thought *what the hell?* and then *oh shit* because he'd been standing right there at the desk listening when the lieutenant called to warn them.

They had the area roped off and were working crowd control on a lot of curious teenagers and taking statements from the kids who claimed to have seen the shooting as Schilling pulled into the lot. He talked with Fisher and Bartel, the first team of officers on the scene and the two kids who'd ID'd Pye, a tall sandy-haired kid with a brush cut named, appropriately, Sandy Zulof and his girlfriend Barbara Toss both of whom were certain it was Pye because they knew him from the high school parking lot, one of his favorite hangouts when school was in session. They got his car right and his description right down to the mole on his cheek and Schilling had one of the patrol cars take them down to the station to record their statement in full and lifted the tape and stepped inside the perimeter.

Tonianne Primiano's body lay face-up, her head wedged between the driver's seat and the brake. Her long dark hair was spread out above her and matted in a pool of blood. She was wearing short cutoff jeans and a tie-dyed red-and-blue T-shirt. Her calves and right forearm still sprawled along the seat of the Volkswagen and her brand-new tennis shoes looked jarringly white and pristine, not a spot of blood anywhere on them nor even a spot of dirt. He looked more closely at the wound and figured it for a .38. The burns made it point-blank range.

Fisher stepped up behind him and told him that forensics was on its way and that the captain was on the radio wanting to speak with him. He walked over to the patrol car and talked into the unit.

"I'm having a real bad evening, Charlie, I gotta tell you."

"I'm listening."

"Our boys pull up to the Griffith house and door's wide open. They go in and there's Harry Griffith shot dead in his chair and his wife gut-shot, passed out on the kitchen floor."

"Jennifer Fitch?"

"Not a sign of her. Except the lock on her bedroom door's been shot too."

"Is the wife going to make it?"

"Too early to say. The first-aid crew were hopeful. The good news is that the other kid, Tim Bess? He's safe and sound."

"Good. Where's he now?"

"Kid and his parents are sitting right out here in the hall. Figured it was best to just bring 'em on in."

"He know why he's there yet?"

"Nope. Not exactly. All our boys told him was that it was for his own safety. All three of them guessed it had something to do with Ray Pye, though. And the kid's definitely worried about Jennifer Fitch."

"He should be. Listen, I want to speak to forensics and get a quick look at the car and run through their purses and then I'll be right over. We'll seal up the Griffith place and leave it for later. Talking to Tim Bess is top priority now. How are Lenny and Clara holding up?"

322

"The parents? Nervous. Fine."

He signed off and replaced the unit and was headed back to the Volkswagen when he saw Ed Anderson's car pull up beyond the taped-off area and Ed get out and approach one of the officers on crowd control, a new kid he didn't know. The officer was shaking his head and Ed was jabbing a finger in his face and then pointing to the Volkswagen. Charlie walked over.

"It's okay. Let him through."

Ed ducked under the tape.

"You sure you want to see this?"

"I'm sure I *don't* want to see this. But I figure I ought to."

They walked toward the car.

"You're carrying."

"Huh?"

"Jacket's a little heavy. I don't guess you got bags of peanuts in there. You're carrying."

"Okay, Charlie. But I'm not just carrying. I'm out for bear."

"I shouldn't be letting you do this, you know."

"Yeah, I know."

"Listen, Ed, what I said before . . ."

"What you said before was bullshit. I told you that. You're not responsible for somebody like Pye. There's no way in hell you could be. If you didn't push him over the edge then somebody else would have. I helped you bust up his little party, didn't I? Blaming yourself or me blaming myself is like putting the blame for all the murder stats on kids watching TV and the movies. It's bullshit. *We* didn't make Pye. Pye made himself."

Schilling thought that he was right as far as that went but that it didn't go far enough. He wondered if in his heart his friend felt the same but was only trying to let him off the hook. Because people like Schilling were supposed to *un*make people like Pye. Not kick them into gear for yet another set of atrocities.

They looked through the window into the car.

"She was pretty," Ed said quietly.

"You knew her?"

"Sally pointed her out to me a couple of occasions. She was her best friend since way back when. Sally must feel awful about her."

He thought that this was the way it was among decent people. People who had respect for life and living. Ed was thinking about Sally as though Sally were still alive even though she might not be and part of what concerned him was the pain she must be feeling for her friend. The dead could not be helped. The living demanded the highest degree of empathy you were capable of committing to them and that was what Ed was doing. It was what made him so different from people like Pye. He reflected that he had not thought of that aspect of the killing at all himself and wondered where Charlie Schilling fit in on the scale of human decency in the range from Ed to Pye.

"It won't work. I already tried. You can't get leverage."

Jennifer was on her hands and knees pushing up with all her strength against the lid of the trunk. Trying desperately to pop it open.

"All you'll do is hurt yourself."

She collapsed and rolled to her side. She could feel Sally's breath on the back of her neck. Along with the other smells she could smell the dried blood on the girl like spoiled meat. Her throat felt raw from the crying and the shouting and the exhaust fumes.

The hysteria was gone. What was left to her was wholly empty.

She felt dazed. The girl behind her was silent.

"He just walked up and shot her? Your friend," she said.

"Yes. He just walked up and shot her."

* * *

When they came through the double doors Bill and June Richmond were standing at the dispatcher's booth talking to Jackowitz. Bill looked pale and anxious but his shirt was crisp despite the heat and Ed wondered if he'd changed to come down here. June was observably halfway in the bag, swaying beside him which under the circumstances might be all to the good. They turned when Charlie and Ed walked in and Ed could see his eyes flash. He moved fast for a heavyset man and Ed stepped back and Charlie stepped between them.

"Hold on, Bill."

"*You,* you sonovabitch. I knew damn well it was you!"

"I'm sorry, Bill. I probably can't say anything to you right now except that I care for her very much and I'm very worried."

"You goddamn *lecher!* You're disgusting! I ought to have your ass thrown in jail."

"Come on. She's age-of-consent, Bill," Charlie said.

"So that makes it okay? This sonovabitch dares to come around here? To come around here *now?* Throwing it right in my goddamn face?"

"You heard him. He cares what happens to her. We all do. So do I."

"What? What are you telling me, Charlie? *Are you fucking her too?*"

They all saw June flinch at that little zinger.

Ed sighed and stepped out from behind him.

"Listen, you're way out of line here. What beef you've got, you've got with me and only me. I hope we can talk this through. But I'm thinking we've got more important things to deal with now. We've got to find Sally. Fast as we can. We need to talk to that boy over there."

He nodded toward Tim sitting with his parents watching all of this from down the hall.

"That okay with you, Bill?" Charlie said. "Ed's right.

This can wait. Finding Sally can't. You'll agree with me on that, right? I want you to let me do my job now, okay?"

They watched the man fold. It wasn't pretty. It was graceless and small and defeated. June appeared behind him and touched his shoulder as though she knew it was all right and safe for her to do that now and not before. She glanced at Charlie and then at Ed and neither glance was unfriendly.

"He's right, Bill. Please. We need to get our Sally back. Let them help us do that."

Her eyes were brimming with tears but she did not appear to notice, as though tears were part of her natural condition. Bill turned and looked at her and at first they could read disgust on his face pompous and ugly and judging her as weak and then watched his expression change and melt to something infinitely more tender and vulnerable. It was like looking at each of them twenty-five years younger. Before whatever had changed them had begun.

"Can we get a room for these folks to rest up awhile, cap?" Charlie said.

"Sure. Come on along with me. We'll get you some coffee."

He moved them down the hall past the Bess family and saw Bill hesitate a moment and look at Tim as though wondering what this boy, this stranger, had to do with his daughter and the finding of her and then continue on.

"I want in on this, Charlie."

"I figured. But you know that Jackowitz will have something to say about that. You're a citizen now."

"Whatever Jackowitz has to say, I can answer."

He smiled. "You probably can. Let's go talk to Bess."

Harold Pye was puzzled and a bit confused.

He'd called up to the house fifteen minutes ago to

see if Jane might fix him a sandwich. He was *starving*. Jane had wanted Chinese for dinner and he didn't really care for Chinese. Chinese to him was like a bunch of crunchy wormy things in salt sauce poured over taste- less chewy rice. The ribs were more like candy than honest meat. He always picked at his food when she ordered Chinese and now he was hungry again so he phoned her.

He could see from the rear window of the office that the lights were on in the bedroom of the house and there were flickering lights in the living room so she had the TV on which meant she was in there. But she wasn't answering. He'd tried three times already.

He called Ray's apartment but got no answer there either, though he hadn't really expected one. He'd seen Ray drive away and hadn't seen him return again.

But that she wasn't answering seriously puzzled him. Could she have the TV up *that* loud? Was there some- thing wrong with the phone? Could something have happened to her, a heart attack, a fall or something? Jane had always had her health but they were no spring chickens, either one of them.

The confusion part was what to do about it. He wasn't supposed to leave the office. That was the rule. It was Jane's rule actually. He didn't really know what she was afraid of—whether it was that somebody would break in and steal the cashbox or that somebody'd want a room and no one would be there to rent them one or or that somebody'd need change for the Coke machine or what the hell it was she worried about. But that was the rule. He'd never broken it.

Meantime his stomach rumbled.

It was the stomach more than anything else, more than any real worry about her, that decided him.

It would only take a minute.

He took the keys for the office off the rack behind him and locked the drawer to the cashbox and turned

off the silent TV. Raised the desk gate and walked
around the desk and out the door and double-locked it
behind him. He crossed the parking lot and walked past
Ray's apartment which was dark. He climbed the walkway up the hill to the house.

He was going to catch hell for this.

But it would only take him a minute. Maybe five
minutes when you figured in the ham and cheese sandwich.

His stomach said it was worth it.

Ray parked the car directly in front of Katherine's
house. The reason was her father. He remembered
clearly that her father was a big man, and you had to
wonder how many shots it would take to bring a big
man down. He remembered the girls in the woods who
had taken more shooting than expected.

Kath knew his car. It was possible that she'd see it
parked here with the lights on and the motor running
from inside the house and come out all angry and pissed
at him and then it would be a simple thing and not a
more complicated thing like dealing with her father.

He debated.

Tim was scared so he was easy. He told them what had
elapsed since Schilling's visits to him and Jennifer. The
telephone calls. Jennifer's telling Ray off at the motel,
throwing the ring at him. Ray punching a hole in his
bedroom wall. Even about the hash he'd been muling.
Schilling hadn't promised him immunity. They hadn't
promised him a goddamn thing. They'd Mirandized him
and that was all they did. It was as though something
wound tight had snapped in the boy and now his pro-
peller was spinning all by itself.

He told them about the night four years ago. His own

and Jennifer's part in it. The boy was in tears by then. The boy was remorseful.

He could see that Ed was moved by that.

Schilling wasn't. Fuck this kid's remorse. Two more people were dead because it didn't kick in quite quick enough. Too little and far too late.

He didn't show his feelings to the kid. He wasn't going to show him anything.

"So where would he take them, Tim? Where would he go?"

"His apartment?"

"We've had a car there since the first shooting went down. He hasn't shown."

He shook his head. "I dunno. Turner's Pool, maybe? Where he did the ... other? Jesus, I dunno *how* he thinks anymore. I used to figure I did. *Oh jesus.* Oh my *god!*"

"What?"

"Kath. Katherine Wallace. It wasn't just Jennifer he was pissed off at, or Sally. He was maybe pissed at Kath more than *any* of them. See, they'd gone out a few times and Ray really liked her and then Kath's mother died and she went to California and when she came back she wouldn't go out with him again, said she didn't want to get involved with anybody, he was telling me all this shit over at my place too and Ray ..."

"Where's she live?"

He told them. Schilling looked at Ed.

"New player," he said. "We better go."

Ray was sick of waiting. It was a long shot she'd see him out here anyway. He was wasting his fucking time. And a .38 wasn't the same as a .22 in terms of stopping power. A .38 was truly *mean.* He'd seen that once tonight already. He spooned another snort of coke out of the small brown bottle and turned off the engine and cut the lights. Got out of the car and shut the door. He heard the girls pounding on the hood of the trunk. It didn't annoy him. It amused him. The girls weren't going anywhere. Nobody was going to hear them. There wasn't a soul in sight. The girls were playing drums to his lead guitar, that was all.

He shouldered the rifle and as he climbed the steps kicked off the safety on the pistol. He reached for the gleaming polished doorknob. And turned it. And smiled.

Her father was talking in his sleep again. Kath closed the copy of *Cosmo* and tried to make out the words coming from his bedroom down the hall. There were times he spoke so clearly in his sleep it was startling. This wasn't one of them. One night in their room in California she'd awakened to hear him say *she's what she is, she can't help it* and wondered who the *she* might be and if her mother was peopling his dream or if she herself was. This time all she heard was something like *amoomphanawful* but listened further just in case. It seemed important for some reason to have more clues about him now.

He was sleeping a lot the past few days. All the way home on the plane and then a long nap yesterday afternoon and tonight he'd said he wanted to lie down for an hour or so just after finishing Etta's good roast chicken and here he was still sleeping. More than three hours later. Probably it was the tranquilizers. She wondered if all this sleep was good for him. If it was avoidance or healing or possibly some strange mix of both. She'd read a little psychology but mostly it was about sex. Not the loss of a loved one. Not death.

She listened a few moments longer and then went back to her magazine. The article was stupid. Something about the usefulness of keeping at least one rich boyfriend around for special parties and social occasions even if you were dating somebody else you liked better. As though most girls had either of these options. She was only half-reading it anyway. She'd found that no-brainers could be soothing sometimes plus she still was keyed to her father, to whether he'd speak again more clearly this time, and that was the reason that she heard the soft footsteps in the carpeted hallway and why she leapt out of bed.

Jackowitz took the call. It was Patrolman Shack on the line and he was calling from the living room of the Pye residence. He and Patrolman Hallan had Harold Pye with them and Pye was in a bad way. They'd been watching the motel through a pair of binoculars from their patrol car parked along a side street when Hallan saw him come running down the walkway from the house like the man had a pack of wolves at his heels, stumbling and off balance like the wolves had already halfway gutted him. They got out of the car and went to his aid.

He brought them up the hill and opened the door and they saw what they saw.

Pye had passed out on seeing her a second time and Hallan was working on him with an ice pack. They'd already called in an ambulance. And what Shack wanted to know right now was, once they got Pye off to the hospital, did they go back to staking out the motel or what?

Jackowitz said you bet you do. And you don't seal up the place either. Leave the place just as it is, lights burning and everything. Go back to what you were doing on the off-chance the crazy little bastard decides to come home again.

And now he had to tell Schilling.

He'd left the force in Newark for a nice quiet town in the lakes district.

He thought that maybe there weren't any nice quiet towns anymore with what was going on in this country.

Maybe the days of nice quiet towns were over with.

So what he'd do was, he'd try to put a muzzle on this one at least temporarily.

"Get me Schilling," he said.

She didn't know how she knew it was him but she did and she hit him full speed in the chest with her shoulder and knocked him down flat to the carpet and when she saw what he was carrying, the pistol and the rifle on his back there was no further question but that his story was true and she hesitated because her father was in the next room vulnerable and asleep, and then thought *no, it's you he's after, he doesn't give a damn about your father,* understood that in the certainty that she also understood his cowardice, that he would not make a move against her father unless he had to, unless her father woke, that he was fine if she just got out of there *now* and she leapt over him, over his legs sprawled beneath her as he whipped around and lunged for her, she could almost feel his hand claw for the loose shirttails billowing out behind her, could almost see it happen. And then she was past him running down the hall down the stairs and heard him hit the stairs too but she had the distance on him, she held the moment, he couldn't run in those goddamn boots of his and if he didn't shoot her *right now* this very second she was going to be out the door.

She grabbed hold of the handle and twisted and it was then she almost screamed, it was only the father upstairs sleeping in his room that kept her from screaming because Ray was smarter than she'd thought he was and the seconds she'd bought hitting him knocking him down were suddenly denied her.

He'd thrown the lock.

He'd locked the door behind him.

Locked them in.

She reached down and threw it to the open position but by then it was far too late and she knew it, the despair was already upon her and when she felt the cold steel of the pistol jab painfully into the back of her neck it had the force of inevitability behind it, the touch of a dark reckless god who it seemed had stalked her all her life.

"Gotcha," he said.

His breath was rank with some kind of drug.

He reached around her and opened up the door.

She heard footsteps shuffle across the landing above and a muttered *whaa?* and he turned and fired even as she shoved him against the doorjamb and fired again and then the hand that held the gun arced toward her and the world went black.

Chapter Forty

Schilling/Ray

In all probability he'd killed Ed's girlfriend. Jennifer Fitch too. Tonianne Primiano and Harry Griffith.

Now Pye's mother.

Ed was right. He should have quit this job long ago. Taken half pension and retired. He'd been nothing but an accident waiting to happen and now the waiting was over and innocent people were paying for his arrogance and stupidity. The fact that he'd been correct about Pye and Steiner/Hanlon all along carried about as much weight for him now as a fly splattered across the windshield of his car and the results were a whole lot messier and worlds more important.

They hadn't spoken a word to one another since Jackowitz's call about Jane and Harold Pye. For the first time he could remember he hadn't the slightest idea what Ed was thinking. In the past it had been easy to know, intuitive, the way it was with the best partners.

Now he hadn't a clue. He couldn't read anything in the set of his face but anxiety.

Ed said he wasn't to blame.

That was what he *said*.

They pulled into the Wallace driveway and saw that the lights were on inside.

"Wait here," he said.

"Like hell."

"You're a civilian."

"I just heard you deputize me."

Schilling looked at him and nodded. They walked up the stairs to the porch and he rang the bell. No one answered. He ran again. And now he had a bad feeling about this one too.

He slipped a plastic Baggie on his hand and used the doorknob. They drew their weapons and walked inside.

The hall and living room were neat and tidy and practically empty of furniture, the home of some rich ascetic. They saw him on the landing right away. A big man in rumpled white shirt and trousers sitting propped against the wall, a long smear of blood against the white wall where he'd fallen. There was a dark hole in the man's chest and the smear was the exit wound. He went up the stairs while Ed proceeded through the house making sure it was clear. The man's eyes were blinking in tiny rapid flutters and he looked up at Schilling stupidly as though trying to figure what in hell had happened to him. His breath came in shallow gulps.

Schilling stepped over him and moved carefully down the hall. The first bedroom door was open and he looked inside half expecting to see yet another body. He checked the closet and under the bed. The girl's room was empty and so was the bathroom. The second bedroom door was shut and he opened it and had a look around inside and the father's room was empty too. He walked back to the man and crouched beside him.

"We'll get you some help, sir. You hang in there."

He'd seen a phone in the girl's room so he used that to call first aid, who were having a helluva busy night and then Jackowitz and by the time he got back Ed had the man leaning against his shoulder and was tying a bath towel tight across the entry and exit wounds.

"How bad?"

"Guy's in shock and he's lost a lot of blood. The shot won't kill him, the shot's clean. The shock and the bleeding might though. You see the bullet there?"

He did. The bullet had passed through the guy and into the wall at just about the level of Schilling's hairline. Which meant it had been fired from downstairs.

"Any sign of the girl?"

"Nothing."

"Dammit. You know what this guy's doing, Ed? This guy's *collecting.*"

"Yeah. And we got to hope for two things. That he's through with that part of it for now and that he wants to keep his collection intact awhile."

"We'll wait for first aid and then I want to head back to the station."

"Tim Bess?"

"He's all we've got."

He was climbing through the northern hills where the houses and grounds got bigger and there was still raw acreage between them. He kept an eye on her in the seat beside him. When he saw her start to come around he parked the car by a low stone wall, took the keys out of the ignition and walked around to the passenger side. He made sure that the first thing she saw when she opened her eyes was the Ladysmith pointed at her forehead.

"Slide over. You're driving."

"Fuck I am." Her voice was thick. Like she needed a drink of water.

He smiled. "You're gonna have a helluva lump on your head in the morning, Kath. You want another one? Slide over."

She looked at him a moment, a look of hate and disgust that he didn't like to see there but she did as she was told. He got in and handed her the keys. She started the car. He swatted at a gnat buzzing around his head. They were out in full force this year.

"Where to, Ray? Back to the campgrounds so you can dump the body?"

"What body?"

"My body."

He smiled. "No campgrounds. You'll know when we get there. Just drive the car."

"Did you kill my father, Ray?"

"Maybe yes and maybe no. You won't know either way unless you do what I tell you though, will you?"

"If you did then you better kill me. Or you'll be watching your back the rest of your life. I swear it."

"I don't know what I'm gonna do with you yet, Kath. That's my business. Your business is just to drive. Simple, right?"

He realized that he really *didn't* know what he was going to do with her or with any of them for that matter. There was no particular plan. He had some ideas, sure. Of course he did. And he had a destination. That much he definitely did have. He guessed it was plenty for now. He felt happy as a kid again in the car with her and holding the Ladysmith on her—her driving away because he said so, understanding he'd gut-shoot her in half a second if she didn't—only this kid also had an erection. He had the other two in the trunk and her not even suspecting they were there. This was really too cool. He felt like all of this was exactly as it ought to be. Like getting a song down exactly right and perfect.

Too bad Tim wasn't around to appreciate it. He was a fucking artist and there was nobody around to see. He couldn't be mad at Tim. Tim was just a guy like he was trying to get by, trying to get a little pussy now and then. He kinda missed Tim.

But Tim would just go sissy on him at this point like he had over those other girls and besides there was Jennifer tucked away in the trunk. He wouldn't like that.

Tim and Jennifer. Tim and Jennifer *fucking*. Unbelievable.

What a world.

Chapter Forty-one

Jennifer

She was dying in there. They both were.

She wasn't at all sure but that Sally Richardson wasn't already dead. She hadn't moved in the longest time and trying to shake her or talk to her got no response at all. Her throat felt so raw she could hardly talk anyway so she stopped trying.

She couldn't breathe. She couldn't get a proper breath. The smell of gas fumes was like a hand clamped tight over her mouth and nose, like the fumes were inside her skin, invading every organ in her body. Her legs had cramped up bad earlier but now she couldn't even feel them anymore. For a while her head had ached worse than she'd ever thought possible, so much pressure she'd thought it would burst. Now even that was gone. She fought constantly against the drowsiness.

Sleep would kill her.

She thought about the Griffiths. It wasn't right. What

had the Griffiths ever done to Ray? He hardly even knew them.

What had *any* of them ever done that was so awful?

To make him do this.

She saw Mrs. Griffith crawling. A bright trail of blood behind her.

And surrendered.

Perhaps it was that image that caused her to surrender. The old woman bleeding, dying, crawling toward the kitchen. Because this was better than what had happened to Mrs. Griffith. That was *pain*. This was just sleep.

She closed her eyes and the darkness fell and then lifted some unknowable time later into some other, brighter darkness that was the real dark and not the dark of sleep and she realized that her eyes were open and the trunk was open and she was breathing real air and pain hit her suddenly like blows from a hammer, a crack to her head and a crack to each of her legs and then descended into her belly and she turned her head and vomited into the dirty rusted hub of the spare tire.

She heard Sally Richmond coughing and vomiting too and stared up at him frowning outside the car, him standing with a gun in Katherine Wallace's belly, stared up at the moon and stars that framed him, the brightness far beyond him huge and clear and open.

"Look at the mess you guys made! Shit."

The pain didn't matter. Neither head nor legs nor stomach. She actually welcomed the pain. She'd been wrong about Mrs. Griffith.

Pain meant you were still alive.

Chapter Forty-two

Sally/Ray

"You look like shit," he said.

However she looked it was nothing to the way she felt. She'd never been so sick in her life. She had no idea where they were or how far they'd gone or how long they'd been driving. She had no idea where her brain had taken her in the interim, only that she was weak and sick and that her mouth tasted of vomit and gas fumes and under all that, horrified at what he'd done and scared of what he *was still* doing.

"Get the fuck out of there."

She slung her legs one by one over the rim of the trunk and pushed up with her arms until her ass scraped over it and she was standing wobbling in front of him.

"You too, Jen."

She heard Jennifer moving around behind her but didn't look. Her attention was focused on the pistol he was shoving into this third girl's stomach. It was the same one he'd shot Tonianne with. The girl was a stranger to her, extraordinarily pretty, wearing jeans and a man's white shirt. She could see a livid welt on her forehead. The shirt was stained with dirt.

Who were these people and why was she, Sally, suddenly and out of nowhere with them? Because of a single argument in a parking lot?

And Tonianne? Shooting Tonianne? It defied understanding.

We think he kills people, Ed told her.

And he did.

She had better get straight. She had better be aware of everything any of them did if she was going to get through this.

The first thing was, where was she? She had to force herself to take her eyes off him and off the gun and take a look around.

They were parked on a narrow dirt road at the base of a hill. Off left on the car's passenger side were deep thick woods as far in and up the hill and down along the road behind them as she could see. Off right what in the moonlight appeared to be a wide field of tall, long-untended grass. Beyond it, more woods. Leaves and branches in dark silhouette against the sky.

They were parked in the middle of nowhere.

She considered which would be worse, a run through the open field or a scramble through dense scrub and thicket. In each case a gun would be aimed at her back. Neither choice was a good one. She couldn't afford to panic. Running wouldn't work. She'd have to wait and see.

She heard a metallic rattle and turned back to Ray.

Something gleamed and dangled in his hand. He was holding it out to her. It took her a moment to realize he was offering her a pair of silver handcuffs but he was speaking to the new girl.

"Know where I got these, Kath?"

The new girl's name was Kath. Kath and Jen. Who

was she? *Sal?* Did everyone in this guy's world have a diminutive?

"*New York City*, Kath. Times fucking Square. Remember our date at Tavern on the Green? Where you told me about your sorry sick fuck of a mother? And I told you about the worst thing I ever did? About trashing that house? 'Course I lied about that being the worst thing. But this is where it all happened! Right up there! That's where I got my firepower. House right at the top of the next rise, you can't make it out through the trees."

He laughed. "Scene of the crime, babe, scene of the crime."

He gestured with the handcuffs. She was supposed to take them.

"I figure Kath's gonna be the one wants to give me the most trouble and I only got one pair. So do the honors for me like a good girl."

She took them. The girl Kath held out her hands. The girl managed to look both furious and disgusted with him. She had to be scared, there was no way she couldn't be scared but she wasn't showing him that. She thought, *good for her.*

Ray shook his head.

"Unh-unh. No way. What the fuck's wrong with you, Kath? You ever see a cop cuff somebody that way in the movies? Huh? You got shit for brains? You cuff the hands *behind* the back, not in front. Jesus! You see somebody do that in the movies, you know you got one fucked-up movie. You just wasted your dollar-fifty. You know the guy's gonna bust heads, cuffs or no cuffs. Man, it's bullshit."

Kath turned and stared him straight in the eye and then folded her hands together behind her back. He swatted at something in front of his face and looked at Sally.

"Flies, man," he said. "Whole fucking town's infested with flies. They come off the lake this time of year, buzz around your apartment."

Sally stepped over.

"I'm sorry," she said.

"Not your fault," Kath said. "It's okay."

She said it as though she meant it too. Sally suddenly liked this girl. Liked her quite a lot. And hated what she was doing.

Snapping the handcuff home around her delicate wrist.

"Katherine, is it?"

She nodded.

"I'm Sally."

And saying that and snapping the second cuff shut was like throwing a bolt on some prison cell and she felt the sob catch in her throat and she was silently crying again, no stopping it and Kath turned and looked at her and she raised her own eyes and looked back and saw an unexpected gentleness there, knew that the forgiveness was real. The girl smiled sadly.

"If I could give you a hug, hey, I would," she said. "It's okay. You understand?"

"Uh-huh."

"Good."

"All right."

But it wasn't all right. It was awful.

She glanced at Ray, and Ray was smirking at them. *You bastard*, she thought. *You little weasel. If Ed were here . . .*

Ray waved his pistol.

"Okay, ladies, on up the hill. Mush."

She turned and saw Jennifer hesitate, afraid to go and afraid to stay, saw that Jennifer was terrified of him, her face pale as death and the eyes deeply hooded and shadowed, dark circles like bruises beneath them and red-rimmed and she wasn't surprised when Katherine stepped out ahead of her to lead the way instead. Something in the line of her back maybe, in her steady gait seemed to give Jennifer the nerve to follow and then catch up with her so that they were walking side by side with her trailing a few steps behind and she could hear Ray, rifle over his shoulder and gun in hand, shuffling in the dirt in back and a little to the left of them where he could keep an eye on each of them.

It was only as they reached the crest of the hill that she heard him pause.

"What the fuck?" he said.

Through the thick copse of trees they could see the house ahead.

A porch light burning.

Fuck this, he thought. This was *his* place *his fucking place* and he wasn't turning around, he wasn't piling them all in the car again and driving someplace *else*.

It was supposed to be empty. He was damn well *staying*.

He marched them past the Dodge wagon in the driveway and up the stairs to the porch and reached past and through them and *these people, these fucking stupid people up here they* never *lock their doors, they all think they're living in the fucking '50s for chrissake, they deserve whatever the fuck they get* and he pushed open the door and pushed Kath and Jennifer in, Jennifer skidding to her hands and knees and then pushed Sally. Through to a brightly lit dark-paneled hallway leading to a brightly lit living room, bare bulbs blazing on lamps without lampshades, cardboard boxes all over the place, chairs piled on top of one another and tied with twine, photos and paintings bundled together, sofa and armchairs covered with sheets tied round with more twine.

And in the middle of the room two startled people in the act of wrapping some stupid blue-and-white seascape in a sheet of brown paper, the woman holding the painting and the guy on his knees taping the wrap.

Ray showed them the gun. Waved it like a football pennant and slammed the door behind him.

"Who the fuck are you!" he said.

The guy started to stammer and moved to rise.

"Don't. Stay right where you are, man. Don't you fucking move! You either, lady. Now who the hell are you?"

The guy had his hands up. *I surrender*. The guy was stammering again.

"Take a deep breath, asshole. You three, over against the wall."

They did as he said. Stood where it looked like a great big circular mirror had been until just recently. A pure white moon on the faded wall.

His ducks all in a row.

"We . . . my father's sold the house. There are movers coming tomorrow and we're . . ."

"Packing things up," the woman said. The woman jittered. Like she had to go to the bathroom. He hated the bitch immediately. Let her go in her fucking pants if she had to.

"That's right. Packing things up."

"Uh-huh."

He looked them over. The guy had short brown hair, blue jeans with a crease in them for godsakes, a checked short-sleeve shirt. Twenty-five-ish, thin. He was not going to be a problem. The woman wore gold wire-rim glasses, long hair in a kind of asshole Jackie flip, no makeup, pretty if you liked the type, about the same age as Mr. Cleanjeans. Her sleeveless pale blue blouse wasn't tucked into her skirt, it just hung there. Not quite covering up the fact that she was sporting a tummy on her. The bitch could definitely use some exercise.

"What's your names?"

"Ken. Ken Wellman. This is my wife . . ."

"Don't tell me. *Barbie*."

"Her name's Elizabeth. Liz."

He couldn't believe it. His joke was totally lost on the guy. What a putz.

"You got movers coming in tomorrow?"

"Yes."

"What time?"

"Eight o'clock. Listen, I don't know what you want here, but please, for god's sake . . ."

He was looking at Katherine's handcuffs like he'd seen them for the first time and thought that maybe the cuffs were going to jump off her wrists and bite him.

"Hey, don't worry, Kenny. Be cool, my man. You just do as you're told and you'll be okay. You and Lizzy here. My business is with the girls, you know? Ain't they pretty?"

"I . . ."

"C'mon. You don't think they're pretty?" He laughed. "Well, shit, I have to admit they've looked better. They've been through some heavy stuff tonight. But *basically*, y'know? Doncha think? These are all my girls."

The man shifted, uncomfortable on his knees. Uncomfortable as hell with *all* of it and scared.

Good.

"I . . . yes. They are."

The guy was trying to placate him.

"You're goddamn *right* they are!"

He looked at the wife. The wife was standing still now. Rigid. With her shoulders hunched and her hands clasped in front of her down in front of her snatch like she was secretly praying and looking at the hands and what was behind the hands it suddenly hit him.

"Hey, Kenny! Your old lady! She's *pregnant*, man. Am I correct?"

He hesitated, glanced over his shoulder at his wife and nodded.

"That's cool, man! Hey, good for you, Ken. Good for you. You know why guys like pregnant women or women with little kids? I thought about it. It's easy, man. It's because a guy looks at a pregnant woman or a woman with a little kid, he knows that at least *somebody's* fuckin' 'em, that they can *be* fucked, know what I mean? So how far along're you, Lizzie?"

"I'm . . . three . . . three and a half months. A little over that."

He grinned. "Shit, that's great. And I bet you folks want a boy, right?"

She tried to smile. It didn't come off.

"We don't care. I mean, either way. We're happy either way."

"Sure you are. You're happy either way. Listen, I want you to help me out here. You got all this twine here and that's just what I need. See, I want you to give me a hand with the girls. I got some serious talking to do to them and I don't want 'em runnin' away on me, I want 'em to pay attention, see what I mean? Hey, all this twine, all this tape you got? Shit, it's lucky for me I ran into you. I mean it. Will you give me a hand, Ken? Lizzie?"

He watched the man look over to the girls standing against the wall. Jennifer had begun quietly sobbing. Ray hadn't noticed. He looked back to the guy. The guy looked paler, less healthy-looking than when they'd first come in. He guessed it was understandable. He just hoped the man wasn't gonna upchuck on him too. He'd shoot the fucker dead on the spot. He'd seen enough puke for one night.

"Whaddya say, Kenny?"

The man looked back to his wife for an answer but Lezzie-Lizzie with the fucked-up Jackie-do just spread her hands and shook her head like she didn't know what his answer should be and now he could see that she was crying too.

What was it with gash anyway? All these fucking *tears*.

348

"Did you know that Sharon Tate was pregnant, Kenny? You know, Sharon Tate? The movie actress just got herself killed? Amazing, terrific piece of ass. Kath here kinda reminds me of her except Sharon has red hair and Kath's younger of course and her tits are a little smaller. I think she was farther along than Lizzie though. I don't remember. Hey, whatever. Who cares? She's dead, right?"

The guy just looked at him wide-eyed and then stared down at his hands.

"I'm waiting, Kenny."

"Mr. Wellman?" It was Katherine. "I don't know what the others think. I can't speak for them. But I think that for now you had better just go along and do what Ray asks you to do. I think that's probably your best bet for now."

He didn't like all those *for nows* but what the fuck. Kath was making sense, basically. Whatta girl. He guessed Ken thought so too.

"All right."

"Lizzie?"

She cleared her throat. "Yes," she said. "All right."

"Good. So let's get to it. You guys don't know about Sharon Tate? That's fucking amazing. Where you been? You guys get to work and I'll tell you all about it."

Chapter Forty-three

Anderson

Ed lied. He did lay some of the blame on Charlie. Himself too for not seeing something like this coming. When you decided to pressure a man you had to watch him like a hawk and neither of them had done that. Granted he hadn't done much pushing of his own except to encourage Charlie to bust Pye's party. His own sin was mostly one of omission—he'd not *dis*couraged him. But you couldn't put responsibility in neat little packets, this much for Charlie, this much for him. Charlie at least had the excuse of having a job to do. He didn't.

But he blamed this kid here across the desk from them a whole lot more than either one of them.

Tim Bess could have turned Ray in right after Steiner/Hanlon. Same with Jennifer Fitch. Instead they lied for him. Covered up. Fitch was paying for that now but what was this kid going to pay? He'd been a minor at the time.

Nothing. A goddamn slap on the wrist.

He did look scared as hell though. Scared was good he guessed. Scared was something. Kept moving around his half-empty can of warm Pepsi in his hands and staring at it frowning as though he'd find some sort of answer there.

"Man, I still can't believe it. I still can't believe he did this."

"Believe it, Timmy."

"I mean, the other two maybe. I can see that, from Ray's point of view. You could maybe expect it. But Jennifer? He's been with Jennifer *forever.*"

Schilling and Ed exchanged glances. Bland glances. Glances that said *it would be nice to pummel this kid.*

"Think, Tim," Schilling was saying. "Anybody at all."

"That's hard, man. There's his drummer Roger. They're pretty tight. But see, Roger's deep into drugs. I mean, I can't see him risking having Ray there and guns there and three kidnapped chicks. I can't see him doing it. The only other guy I can think of is Sammy Nardone, he's the one who sends us all the hash and stuff. Supposed to be some tough street guy, that's what Ray says. From Newark and all. I dunno. I never met him."

"You know their addresses?"

"Street addresses? Sammy's in Irvington. I know where Roger lives, I mean I could take you there. But not the exact address. I got them at home, though."

The kid brightening, thinking he was maybe going home to have a look through his address book. Ed knew he wasn't. Schilling pushed the phone across the table along with a yellow pad and pencil.

"Okay. Call your parents. Tell them to look up the addresses and phone numbers and you write 'em down for us. Lieutenant Anderson and I will be outside. We'll be right back."

Jackowitz had sent the Bess family home half an hour ago. Bill and June Richmond too, thank god. He didn't look forward to seeing Bill and June again soon no matter how this all turned out. Both families had State Police cars parked outside their houses. Just in case Ray wasn't finished yet.

"You want anything?"

"I could use some smokes, yeah."

"Okay, sure."

They walked outside and closed the door. Ed smiled and shook his head.

"Lieutenant Anderson?"

"I know, I know. Force of habit."

Schilling lit a cigarette. Ed noticed he hadn't offered one to Bess. But then he knew Schilling felt the same about Bess as he did.

"So let's look at this. We've got every available car on the street. We've got State Police patrolling the highways and the lake, the campgrounds around Turner's Pool, we'll have dogs for the woods in about half an hour. And now we've got two names."

"I don't think much of the names, tell you the truth. Bess is right. Who's gonna let this kid in the house with three scared girls held at gunpoint? You'd have to be nuts. Unless this Nardone character's some real hardcase. Maybe then."

"If he's still in the area and if he's still cruising around in the Chevy we'll get him."

He nodded. "Yeah. Question is when."

The door opened. Bess was leaning out at them as though afraid to step over the threshold. But the look on his face was excited.

"I think I know," he said. "I think I know where he might go. *I think I know where he'd take them!"*

Chapter Forty-four

Jennifer/Katherine

"So why you doin' all this work anyway? Why not just let the movers pack the stuff?"

Jennifer was sitting in a spindle-back chair facing the front door. Her right wrist was tied to the armrest and the man was working on the left. Triple strands of twine wound around the back of the chair and just below her breasts. Katherine sat to her right tied to the chair's twin. The only difference was that Ray had told the woman to loop the twine around the chain connecting the handcuffs and tie them behind her to the middle spindles of the chair so that Katherine sat slightly forward on the seat.

The twine was itchy but the man hadn't made it too tight.

"We're supposed to be taking some of it for our apartment. Those boxes over there and . . . these chairs." He nodded toward the ones they were sitting in and two others stacked beside her. "And some paintings."

"New apartment?"

He nodded again. You could see the man was very uncomfortable having to talk to him.

"Where?"

"South Orange."

"Classy, Kenny. Very classy. So let me guess, you guys are newlyweds or something, right?"

"Six months in September."

"And what do you do for a living, Kenny? I mean, if you don't mind my asking."

He kept waving the gun around gesturing and every time he waved it toward the man he flinched.

"We're . . . teachers. I teach math and science. Elizabeth's home ec."

"High school?"

"Yes."

"Damn. I never finished high school. You think I should've?"

The man didn't seem to know what to say to that. So he said nothing. She wished that Ray would stop pacing. She wished he'd stop waving the gun. The man finished the knot on her left wrist and stood. Ray upended a third chair.

"Her next."

He waved the silver pistol toward the man's wife.

"What?"

"Lizzy. *Eliz*abeth. Her next. C'mon, Ken. Look how jittery she is, your wife. She looks like she could bolt and run on me any minute."

"I won't. I *won't run!* I promise!"

"You say that now, Lizzy and I believe you because I'm standing here. But if I turn my back for a minute, who knows? Kenny, you know you can't trust a woman especially a nervous woman and especially a nervous *pregnant* woman, I mean they're *supposed* to be unpredicable, anyway that's what I hear, wanting pickles and ice cream in the middle of the night and everything.

So just have a seat and let Kenny tie you down, Lizzy, not too tight, don't worry. And that way I know you won't run. I mean, I'm not gonna hurt you or anything."

The woman looked at Sally. "Why not *her?* Why *me?*"

Ray turned and looked at Sally too. Looked her up and down.

Jennifer hoped to god he never looked at her that way.

It was like he was looking *inside* her, looking to find the fear. As though fear were an organ. Locating it like you would locate heart or lungs or vagina. He took his time.

"Oh, I got something planned for Sally. You wouldn't like it, Lizzie. Ken wouldn't like it either. But I think it's pretty small of you to suggest it, don't you? Now *sit down in the fucking chair!*"

He pointed the gun at Ken the barrel only a foot from his head, and she barely heard him when he spoke again.

"*Or I kill daddy.* With daddy's *daddy's* own gun. How about that? It's the truth! This belonged to your mom and dad once, Kenny. That's right. Rifle too. 'Member somebody trashed this place a few years back? That was me. Me and my buddy Timmy who unfortunately is not here to reunion with us. Lizzie, please be seated."

The woman took a deep breath and wiped her cheeks and moved slowly around the chair and sat.

"That'sa girl. Much, much better. Look, she's all settled in. Kenny?"

The man hesitated and then stooped and picked up the ball of twine. Held it in his hand a moment as though the twine were some object wholly unfamiliar to him. He unrolled a length of it and dug into his pocket for the red Swiss army knife. Pulled open a blade and cut the twine.

355

She wondered if the blade was big enough to kill a man.

He walked over to his wife, hesitated. Looked into her eyes.

And then he just stood there.

"Kenny? Hey, Kenneth? You're not gonna go all Steve McQueen on me, are you?"

The man still held the knife. The red knife open in his right hand and the twine dangling from the other. He stood and looked at his wife. His eyes were the saddest eyes on a man she'd ever seen.

As though he *knew.*

"Fuck it, Kenny. I didn't like you anyway."

A sound like a bomb going off in the room then and the back of the man's head was suddenly mud flung over the faded white wall in front of him and he jolted into the wife's lap, the wife screeching, trying to reach him and missing her grip so that he slid off her and crumbled into a fetal position on the floor. Sudden movement to her right and in front of her and Jennifer saw Sally bolt for the door, Ray stepping over one long step and hitting her sidearm in the head with the barrel of the gun, driving her first against the wall and then down to the floor . . .

. . . and Katherine thought, *you son of a bitch, fuck you! you think you got me? you think I can't* hurt *your sorry ass?* and rose chair and all, handcuffs cutting into her wrists and whipped around fast, to hell with the pain, the legs of the chair slamming into the back of *his* legs just below the knee and she heard him grunt and fall, heard the pistol hit the floor and she knew what to do, she'd seen the glass double-doors in back down the hall while he had her standing against the wall so she made for that, turned and ran, she'd go through the goddamn doors glass and all and . . .

* * *

. . . Jennifer saw Ray falling, cursing and twisting and firing again twice and saw Katherine crash to the floor with a bloom of red spreading across the back of her shirt like red ink spilled from an inkwell, Katherine jerking facedown on the bare wood floor, jerking and then still.

She saw this all in an instant and couldn't understand how these things could happen, how they could be *accomplished* and so suddenly. The moment had changed everything and astonished her, left her quivering, twitching in its wake as though her body were crawling with spiders. She couldn't have moved from where she was in a million years. *Let alone hit him with a chair. Let alone run.* She was aware of the tangy metallic smell of *gun* and the echo in her ears which blotted out all other sound, aware that at some point during this brief lightning flash of time she'd peed her pants, a sudden voiding, she didn't even know it had happened.

The wife *Elizabeth, her name's Elizabeth for godsakes can't you remember?* was down on her knees on the floor with her husband. She had her hands to his wound, *in* his wound, like she was trying to hold some lost part of him inside. She was shaking her head and sobbing and Jennifer could dimly make out the sounds of her hysterical grief over the roar in her ears. She heard Ray say something to the woman but she couldn't make that out either.

She watched him glance slowly from one of them to the other. *His glance lingering on each.* Katherine didn't move. She lay on her side still cuffed and tied to the chair, one leg bent at the knee as though frozen in the act of running. The two middle spindles had snapped at the base during her fall.

Sally lay half propped against the wall. There was blood on her forehead.

When he looked at Jennifer she saw him notice how she'd wet herself and saw his lip curl in disgust and realized that she felt no shame in it, no thoughts about it at all, the peeing didn't matter.

He turned abruptly and walked away down the hall—that choppy, jerky walk of his—digging into his jeans for bullets to reload the gun and disappeared.

She still couldn't move.

She wasn't like the others. The others didn't know him.

They did now.

She was pinned to the spot.

The woman Elizabeth didn't seem to be aware of his leaving. Her eyes were shut against the steady flow of tears and she was shaking with hysteria and her hands were red with blood nearly to the elbow. She kept rocking him. Holding on to the ruined head. *Holding him in.*

Her skirt was sodden.

He was gone just a moment.

When he returned his eyes were wide and seemed to focus *outside* the room, not on her or any of them or anything in the room in particular but beyond or maybe inward, she didn't know. He drifted into the room like a ghost and his head turned for a long moment to where the circular mirror had left its clean impression on the wall and he had the gun in one fist and a serrated steel carving knife in the other.

He stared at the spot like there still was a mirror there and then he turned.

Light and dark swam together the second time for her that night and she clutched at the arms of the chair knowing she could not lose conciousness, not now or else she might never wake up again so she gripped the chair until her fingers ached and slowly the room and everything in it returned to her the way she needed it to return, blank pale walls and covered furniture. Sally against the wall. Katherine in the hall. She saw that he'd drifted past her, was moving slowly past to stand behind the woman kneeling with her husband on the floor. He shoved the revolver into his belt.

He raised the knife and held it above her pointed down and her hearing had returned enough by then for her to hear him mutter *do her just like Sharon, he was talking about Sharon Tate* and if the woman even knew he was standing there she didn't show it, she just kept holding on to her husband's head until the knife came down and entered her just above the collarbone and she yelped like a struck dog and blood spurted up and out and Ray pushed the entire length of the blade down into her.

Her arms flew up and clutched his fists on the handle of the knife and he pulled it out, a rough sawing motion and he reached for her shoulder and pushed her face-first across her husband, her blood already pooling on the floor as now the hands went to her own pulsing wound as before they had gone to his, *holding it in, holding in the life.* A high mewling and a gurgling sound were coming out of her and blood ran down her chin and Jennifer looked away, just closed her eyes and looked away until she heard a thump on the floor beside her.

She looked down startled by the sound and saw that Ray had rolled the woman over on her back and pushed her again so that she lay sprawled right at her feet, the thump was the back of her head against the floor. Instinctively she drew her feet in beneath the chair seat as though away from something dirty and polluted flowing toward her, away from what he was doing, cutting through the buttons of her blouse and unzipping the skirt and pulling it down around her thighs, cutting through the white padded bra while the woman choked on her blood, the woman staring up at the ceiling and coughing a thin, bloody spray at him up into his face which he wiped away with the back of his hand, the one that held the knife which then cut through the panties too, and Jennifer closed her eyes a second time.

She had to.

She was going to be sick. She was going to throw up again.

She knew what they'd done to Sharon Tate.

They'd cut out her baby.

And that's what Ray was mumbling about, that and all the other filthy things they did to her, toneless, mild, talking about *cutting her tits off and carving these words in her belly and blood on the walls and that'll give 'em something to think about absolutely, cut out the baby and put it in her lap, wrap the cord around her neck* and telling the woman to beg, *beg* for her baby and meantime he was stabbing her over and over god knows how many times she could hear the woman's tiny cries deep in her throat and thumping sounds like melons dropping, heard every impact, she could smell the blood in the air thick as the smell in a butcher shop, she could hear it fall like heavy raindrops on the floor, imagine it flowing pooling toward her feet.

Please stop you have to stop! she thought, *she was going to go crazy if he didn't, she was going to, it was going to happen, please, what you heard could* drive *you insane* and heard two footfalls and a crash, glass breaking and she opened her eyes and saw Sally standing over him, blood running down her cheek and holding the finial and harp and socket and part of the broken base of a white china lamp in her hands. She saw Ray covered with shards and china dust reel across the glistening naked body beneath him and throw out his hand for balance, saw it slide across the blood-soaked floor so that he came down hard on his elbow and she felt a wild surge of pleasure at his pain.

"BIIIITCH!" he roared and reached for the pistol in his belt, the rifle slung over his back clattering against the floor as he rolled but Sally just took another step forward. She could see that Sally was terrified to move

anywhere near him but she did, *she did it anyway!* and shoved the jagged base of porcelain into his face, hard against his forehead and cheek so she heard it scrape bone and suddenly he was screaming and bleeding, *Ray* was bleeding *not* somebody else, bleeding from his head and from his face, and Jennifer brought both her legs out from under the chair as fast and hard as she could and kicked him in the back of the head, aiming for the blood that already welled there.

The effort almost toppled the chair and her with it. She didn't care. It felt good. *It felt wonderful!*

She watched him fall forward over the woman's body, fall face-to-face with the woman, Ray staring down into her open dead eyes and open mouth just a moment before what was left of the lamp came down on him again, Sally not finished, not finished with him yet, going after him—then his hand shot out and gripped the base of the lamp and pulled it from her hands and sailed it across the room over his head and he staggered dazed to his feet. She saw Sally backing away and looking for something else to hurt him with but there was nothing, only boxes and crates and chairs and then the pistol was out of his belt and pointing at her ending all bravery and all resistance.

In the silence she heard two women cry out, a dissonant two-part harmony. One of the voices was hers.

Chapter Forty-five

Katherine

Do the dead dream?

Katherine did.

She dreamt she was in the workshop, her father's workshop, and she was doing what neither she nor Etta were permitted to do.

She was cleaning up.

And not just sweeping, either. She had the Electrolux out there, and the Electrolux was roaring, sucking up sawdust and shavings and chunks of wood like tiny bits of bone, sending them clattering up through the extension wand and hose, both of which almost seemed a part of her, like something abstracted from her hand and arm. She vacuumed workbench, vise, clamps, sawhorse, hanging tools and shelves and mason jars full of nails and screws arranged by size, vacuumed his power saw, his circular saw, his coping saw, his planer and sander and finally the floor a second time and it was amazing, she was moving like lightning, moving effortlessly and it was done in a flash, all this space of his spotless now. So that he could start in fresh. A clean slate. And get on with life.

Chapter Forty-six

Schilling/Tim

"Which way on Stirrup Iron?"

"The house is off to the left."

They had the kid in the cage in the backseat behind them and three state highway patrol cars following them, their headlights gliding along the winding road over shallow dips and inclines climbing gradually into the hills. The kid said he knew the way and which house though not the family's name or the actual address. Lenny Bess would have known because the kid said he'd worked for these people but the line to the Bess house was busy. The kid seemed absolutely positive he could get them there and pick out the place in the dark. Time meant everything. So by far their best bet was to take him along and just *get* there.

The inside of their vehicle felt like the lake on choppy water before a storm. Emotions swirled and eddied. Mainly tension. But fear was there, the one-on-one personal fear you'd have of any armed killer and anxiety for the women he had in tow was there in spades but there was excitement too. *Because they ought to be able to do this.* If Tim Bess was right in his description of the house Pye was in a place he *thought* he wanted to be in but didn't. Two entrances, front door and rear glass sliding doors. Isolated and easy to cover. No neighborhood civilians to worry about except Bess who would remain in the car well out of the way. They'd have surprise and darkness on their side and plenty of backup.

If the kid was right they'd get the little sonovabitch.

He glanced at Ed staring straight ahead at the lights on the empty road. He knew that look. It was grim and humorless and purposeful. It wouldn't falter. You could take that look to the bank. But he damn well knew better than to try to converse with it.

He looked at the kid through the rear-view mirror. The kid was shadow, a penumbra in the glare of headlights framing his head and skinny shoulders.

"Tell me about the girls, Tim. Jennifer and Katherine. What are they like?"

"I dunno. Kath's new in town. I really don't know her too well. She's kind of stuck-up I guess. Jennifer's just . . . god, I dunno. Jennifer's just *Jennifer*."

"Would either of them give him any trouble? Piss him off? Try to fight him?"

"Not Jennifer. Katherine? Man, I got no idea."

"Are they going to go ballistic on us when we go in there? Do they know enough to keep the hell out of our way?"

"I think so."

They drove in silence for a while, headlights sweeping a field, a group of houses, a dirty white dog barking in a fenced-in yard.

"Can I ask you something?" Tim said.

"Sure."

"Am I in a whole lot of trouble here?"

Schilling glanced at him. It was the first time he'd asked. Schilling figured it was a good sign if not quite an admirable sign that it had come so late in the game.

"What do you think, Tim?"

"I think I'm in deep shit. *Truly* deep shit."

He wasn't.

He'd been underage on Steiner/Hanlon and he was cooperating with them on this one. But Schilling wasn't necessarily going to tell him that his problems were only juvie. A good hook was one that had a barb in it. They still needed his testimony on Ray.

"Let's just worry about the girls for now, okay, Tim? Then we can worry about you getting a shovel."

It had dawned on Tim steadily that she might be dead.

It was like an ache in your head you're barely aware of at first and then it grows and grows and pretty soon the headache's blinding.

That this should be so was an amazement to him. Not a single person he'd ever known at all well had died before, only one distant uncle and who gave a shit about him. And now Mr. Griffith and Ray's mother dead in one night. But even between the two of them and Jennifer there was a huge difference. He had never *touched* Mr. Griffith or Ray's mother. Not once in his memory, not even to shake hands and he had made love to Jennifer Fitch and that seemed to him to make all the difference in the world. As though the touching *were* the knowing.

No one he had ever *touched* had died before.

No one he had loved.

Or at least thought he loved. Because once not long ago he'd have said he loved Ray like a goddamn brother but there was no love in him for Ray right now, not a fucking ounce of it, he didn't care if Ray lived or died. So what was love anyway? Something you turned on like a clock alarm and slapped off the minute you awoke, once it suddenly got too loud and noisy? He wondered if he would still love Jennifer after this was over. And if she did die, would he love her memory.

Was it even possible to love a memory?

He tried to picture her dead because he knew it just might happen and he felt he needed to be prepared for that. He tried to picture her shot like those girls, shot through the heart or through the head. Beaten to death or strangled. He tried to consider these things because all of them were possible. But then he'd remember the feel of her, of her flesh, her lips and breasts the smell of her hair and it just wouldn't come, he couldn't find the cold dead body inside the living body of Jennifer.

She *couldn't* die. How could she?

He'd *touched* her.

"Turn here," he said.

"I know, kid," said Schilling. "I know."

Chapter Forty-seven

Sally

You should have run, she thought. *You could have. You could have slipped right out the door.*

She didn't even know Jennifer, really. She could have left her. Just left her.

The woman on the floor was past helping

And then she thought, *what would Ed have done?*

It didn't matter. She'd done what the moment and who she was told her to do.

There was some satisfaction knowing that she'd hurt him—*marked* him. He was not coming out of this clean and unscathed. It was no longer possible for him to plead innocence or lie his way out of this no matter how he tried to cover up. When the police found him they'd know him, match his face to what she'd done to him and *know*. The bloody crown of his head. The deep gash across the forehead, the shallower half-moon slice across the cheek.

I got you, she thought. *Me.*

She watched him wipe the blood out of his right eye and across his chin and shake his head, blood flecking the wall. Watched him pick up the knife and walk toward her.

Here it comes, she thought. Oh god!

She pressed back against the wall. The wall was solid, firm. Reality.

He stepped to one side of her and put the gun to her forehead and smiled. There was a thin film of blood across his teeth. The hand that held the gun was slick with it.

"You fucked me up, you know that?"

He laughed.

"You really did. I mean, this *hurts*."

He dropped the gun away from her forehead and cocked his head and studied her. Blood pooled in his eye and he wiped it again.

"Man, have I got taste in women. I just knew you'd be something else. Just like Kath over there. I knew the first time I looked at you. Am I right, Jen?"

She glanced over his shoulder at Jennifer slumped in her chair, that single kick to the head draining all the fight she had in her. Maybe it was the fact that the kick had done nothing to end this. That it was still playing out his way, not theirs. She saw her eyes drift empty and lifeless from the woman's corpse at her feet to the man's body and back again.

He seemed all at once aware of the taste of blood in his mouth and ran his tongue along his teeth.

"You're sure something all right. I ain't seen you naked yet, though. Only one of my girls I haven't."

"I'm not one of your girls, Ray."

The smile disappeared like a quarter in a magic trick. The gun pressed cold and hurtful into her cheek.

"You are now, you little cunt. That blouse is a fucking mess anyway. You got your girlfriend's head all over it! Take the fucking thing off."

It was as though he'd physically slapped her. She saw it all over again. *Tonianne laughing with her in the car. Nibbling on a cheeseburger. Turning at his approach. The split second when everything changed and the world went haywire in one dark moment of explosion.*

She choked back a sob and then something composed itself in her as instinctive and fundamental as the sob had been, and she looked him in the eye.

"You're right," she said. "It *is* a mess."

Her fingers fumbled at the top button of her blouse but her voice was calm.

"You don't need the gun, Ray."

"Oh, you're all cooperative now?"

"I'll do what you want."

"You will?"

"Yes."

"You will?"

"Yes."

She unbuttoned the top button and then the second.

"You gonna show Ray your titties?"

"If that's what you want."

"You are?"

"Yes."

"Gonna show Ray your snatch?"

"Yes."

"Say it."

"What?"

" 'Gonna show Ray my snatch.' Say it."

"Gonna show Ray my snatch."

" 'Gonna show Ray my titties.' "

"Gonna show Ray my . . . my titties."

"That's *good!*"

He giggled like a little girl. Wiped more blood out of his eye. Lowered the gun from her cheek and held it at his side.

"I ain't fucked you yet, either."

"No. You haven't."

She heard a low moan and looked at Jennifer. But Jennifer was just sitting there shaking and staring down at the woman as before. And Ray had taken a step backward. He was looking down the hallway.

It wasn't Jennifer. *It was Katherine. My god.*

"You fucking believe it? That bitch is still alive!" He laughed. "I shot her good too." He shook his head. "Well what the fuck, we can get to that shit later. You were saying?"

"I . . ."

"You stopped at two."

"What?"

"Buttons. You got two more buttons left there. Let's go. Let's see 'em. You think I got all night?"

She released the third button and realized she hadn't wished for a bra since her mother'd bought her her first trainer. There was no way to know what to do anymore. He was standing close but not close enough. Katherine's moan, that single step back had defeated her, ruined the only thing close to a plan she had.

"You a good fuck or a bad fuck?"

Are you a good witch or a bad witch? The guy was crazy.

"I'm . . . I'm a good fuck."

"Who says so?"

"My boyfriend."

Her fingers picked at the fourth button.

"You got a boyfriend? Who's your boyfriend? What's his name?"

"Ed."

"Ed? Like in *Mister* Ed?"

"What?"

"The horse. He hung like a horse or something?"

"What?"

"Pull out your shirt! Pull out the shirt and lose the fucking button. *Now! Or I put you down like they put a horse down like I put my fucking mama down. Do* it!"

371

She had the shirt out and unbuttoned before he even finished, and it took her a moment to understand the last part, a moment for it to sink in, that he'd killed his own mother but when she did she felt something glide up her spine and start her trembling again. She was losing all control again.

If she'd ever had any.

That one step. That one step out of reach.

She felt a breeze from the open window like a ghostly hand across her stomach.

"*Ed.* Jesus! You are *so* full of shit, Sally. There's no fucking *Ed.* You aren't balling any Ed you rich-bitch fucking *dyke.* You think I don't know you? You think Ray don't know some queer when he sees one? You bull-dyke skanky *bitch?* Let's see those tits. I ought to let Jennifer suck 'em, bite 'em. Bite 'em off. Hey Jen, you want to suck some titty? Take off your goddamn shirt you fucking *bitch.*"

She closed her eyes and shrugged it off her shoulders. Felt it glide down over her bare arms and back like a fallen veil. She kept her eyes shut tight. She did not want to see *him* see her body. She did not want to look into his face. She knew her breasts trembled. *She* trembled. She couldn't help it. She did not want to watch him enjoying that. The wall felt cold against her back.

"Not bad. Pretty good in fact. Uh-oh. Got blood on 'em, though. Dried blood. Kinda gross, Sal. Messy. But they're good all right. Look at me."

No.

"Look at me!"

No.

"Open your eyes you little cunt!"

She did and he had it out of his pants, the knife stuck in his belt and his dick in his hand and he was working it, squeezing it, milking the thing and then jerking it rapidly and hard and then milking it again, then jerking, his penis red with blood from the palm of his hand, his mouth open wide and blood pooling in one eye and the other staring straight into hers and then she could see he was almost ready, he was coming this fast, the brow knitted, the mouth open wider and he took one staggering step toward her to throw his slime across her body, his filthy slime over her bare legs but that was what she needed, what she had prayed for and she brought her knee up hard.

He howled and fell to his knees both hands clutching his bloody groin and she ran for the door. Heard Jennifer scream something behind her. Flung open the door. Saw a fine, dear face at the threshold.

And never heard the gun.

Chapter Forty-eight

Anderson

One moment she was a sudden half-nude presence in the doorway, her expression terrified then excited at seeing him there and the next moment the right side of her chest seemed to explode in front of him. He tried to catch her but she fell reeling off the side of the porch and into the shrubs and it was a uniform behind him who leapt from the porch and got to her, and the cop in him simply took over then, the furious raging *man* in him took over, and he and Schilling were through the door and firing. Pye was firing too, his limp dick dangling out of his pants, trying to stuff it back in and shooting wild twice, three times, trying to back away down the hall where ahead of him somebody lay tied to a chair.

He heard a massive shattering of glass which would be the uniforms at the back double doors. Anderson's own shots went wild—goddammit, he was way out of practice—but out of the corner of his eye he saw Schilling take the position unflinching as Pye's fourth round cracked into the wall behind him and saw him fire and Pye went down screeching, grabbing for his right leg which had burst open at the thigh.

He felt a rushing white heat in his head and ran for him and Pye turned and fired but the pistol clicked on empty. He tried to unsling the rifle but Anderson was on him and the next thing he knew he was astraddle him and pounding at him, pounding at his pretty face and then suddenly the face wasn't pretty anymore, the face had burst, the face was a tangled mess of torn flesh, of bloody lips and nose and eyes beneath him. His hands ached and stung and he kept pounding, the kid wheezing squealing squirming under his thighs and he was aware of Schilling's hands on his shoulders and at the same time the kid trying to reach for the knife in his belt and then he felt Schilling release him, Schilling stepping over and stomping hard on the hand that wanted the knife, kicking it aside, standing on the hand and then grinding it to the floor.

He heard bones snap and the kid screaming, spittle and blood flying out of his mouth. His fist found the oozing eye socket one last time. And then just as suddenly as it had come over him his rage deserted him.

The kid didn't move.

He felt exhausted, drained, empty. His hands were raw and in his left hand something was maybe broken. He was shaking and it was entirely possible he might puke. He looked up and saw that he was surrounded by uniforms with their guns drawn. Mostly kids. The kids were looking at him with a kind of amazement, like he'd just stepped out of a spaceship, a big blue, bug-eyed Martian. The older hands looked grim. One of them slowly nodded.

Two of them were kneeling beside the girl in the chair. He heard one of them ask if she was alive. *Barely*, said the other. *Shot bad. Lost an awful lot of blood.*

Jennifer Fitch was wailing in the living room.

He got off Pye and stood. His legs were wobbly. He felt Charlie's hand on his back supporting him. Ed turned and looked at his face. The face was unreadable as a stone.

Charlie finally had got his man.

He wondered how it felt to him.

He turned and walked down the hall toward the door and heard Fitch's wail soar higher, louder as two of the uniforms approached her. *Jesus Christ* look *at this place* somebody said and then he was out the door.

They had gotten her out on the lawn by then and one of them was giving her mouth-to-mouth and working on her chest while two others stood over her and another approached from his squad car and Anderson heard him tell the others that the ambulances were on their way.

The ones who were standing parted for him and he knelt beside her and looked first at her, at her face and the terrible wound in her chest, and then at the young dark-haired patrolman who was working on her, doing it right, doggedly and by the book but looking as though he were only moments away from bursting into tears. There was a desperation about the boy and Anderson knew that something had occurred within the boy that would last and which in the full flower of manhood would turn him one way or the other, an event which had branded him. To be helpless in the face of death, at the hollowing and coring of another and to wish so mightily not to be was not one of the great favors god did man.

"Give us a minute please, will you?" he said.

The boy looked at him. And Anderson thought that he would cry then, because Anderson was telling him what he didn't want to hear, that it was futile, that it was over, to give it up. But he didn't cry. He just nodded and set her head down gently in the grass and stood and like the others, moved away to give him space. Anderson took the boy's place beside her in the grass and held her and rocked her and reached into her hair and only then did he feel the freefall tumble of his heart.

"Oh, Sally," he whispered. "Oh jesus, look at you. Jesus, what you could have been. What a fine, fine woman you are. *Oh christ,* what you damn well could have been!"

He saw the lights in the distance and heard the sirens of the emergency crews approaching and was half-aware of footsteps on the stairs coming and going, uniforms going about their business, doing their jobs, the kind of jobs he'd wanted never to have to see or do again and he held her and waited for her to go cold in his hands so that the cold could convince him it was finished.

Afterward

"What then must we do? . . . we must give with love
to whomever god has placed in our path."
—Christopher J. Koch
The Year of Living Dangerously

Flower Power

Do the dead dream?

Katherine did.

At the epicenter of her dream stood her mother as in a spotlight, a much younger version of her mother which Katherine had seen only in black-and-white stills in photo albums, the age perhaps of Katherine herself, her mother dressed in a pink silk chemise dress with spaghetti straps and matching turban, every inch the flapper and she was smiling, standing leaning against a bar surrounded by the empty chairs and tables of some unknown long-ago restaurant and drinking from a long-stemmed glass.

Behind her and to one side the barman appeared in white stiff shirt and gartered sleeves and as she watched him polish a glass the room was in an instant full, every chair at every table filled with stylishly dressed young people of that era all in their teens and twenties talking together and laughing and she had the strangest impression of floating toward her mother, not walking, of gliding by the diners and drinkers who partied together at the tables around her as though she were a breath of summer air, as though she were a ghost. But she was not a ghost, she couldn't be because her mother set the long-stemmed glass on the bar and embraced her, smiling. She could feel her hands light and gentle across her back and then felt the hands release her, her mother's young pretty face all serious now.

You're not me, her mother said. *You never were. There's nothing wrong with you at all. You're just fine, Katherine. You're absolutely fine.*

And as the lights in the room all went out at once and the bright gay laughter of the young suddenly stopped, Katherine believed her.

Schilling watched her go.

Watched her father sobbing by the hospital bed. In two weeks' time the man had lost everything he loved. There was nothing Schilling could say to console him.

All the same he tried. He did try. His words seemed to him to be the equivalent of dropping pebbles into a lake. From any height at all you could barely see a ripple. What could it possibly mean to this man that Pye would spend the rest of his life in jail? What could it possibly mean that no plastic surgery was ever going to get him back his arrogant pretty face? That he would never kill again? In the enormity of this man's loss these things were trivial. Pye was alive on the earth and his little girl was not.

End of story.

End of story for Schilling too. If Schilling was ever going to eat his pistol it was now. Today or very soon. Nights alone all this week waiting for her to die the enormous gulf between what he'd set out to do and what he'd managed to do yawned wide and cavernous. He was sober. He was afraid *not* to be sober. But sobriety brought no absolution for his cleverness, his rigid determination. Sobriety was an angel that came to him with empty hands.

He spent a couple hours each night at the hospital, spelling Wallace if Wallace would allow him to, urging him to go down for some coffee at least, a breath of fresh air. Most of the time he declined and the two of them would sit in a silence broken only by the man's occasional fragmented remembrances his daughter, which sometimes seemed to force themselves out of him despite himself. He spoke of his fortieth birthday party when Katherine had crept up behind him and mashed chocolate cake with strawberry filling and vanilla icing in his face and he'd followed suit, the image of a laughing little girl and grown man rolling faces smeared with birthday cake across a living-room floor. He spoke of her birth, her difficult delivery, of his wife's seven hard hours in labor, her refusal of a cesarean. He spoke of a defiant black dress at her junior prom.

He listened to all this and much, much more until he almost thought he knew her. Brought flowers nightly to her bedside and then she died.

The night she died Schilling left him there, left him reluctantly but because the man insisted, climbed into his car and drove not to his home but down through the mountains and flatlands to Barbara and Elise Hanlon's house in Short Hills. The house was dark and the driveway was empty. There was nobody home. He parked in front of the house and waited. He didn't know for what. Just waited. He sat for three-quarters of an hour in the dark and smoked five cigarettes down to the filters before it occurred to him exactly why he was there.

The Hanlon house was for him a kind of wishing well. A place where his mind might just possibly empty itself enough, divest itself of enough of what he knew of the real world and the way the real world worked to let feeling in, to let hope and trust and tenderness in.

He'd gone to the well the night Elise Hanlon died and the well hadn't worked for him. His coin had disappeared into the empty dark of what Barbara Hanlon had become since last he'd seen her.

But now he was trying it again.

Please, he thought.

In the morning he woke slumped against the wheel. The car smelled of cigarette smoke and ashes. His windshield was covered with dew. There was still no Ferrari in the driveway.

He drove back into the mountains.

The day they sentenced Ray for the murders of Lisa Steiner and Elise Hanlon was only the second time Tim had seen him since Ray had punched a hole in his bedroom wall and stalked away with a pound of hash in his fist. The first was the day he had to testify. That afternoon Ray was already seated with his attorney when Tim entered the courtroom. Today he was standing. And today, maybe because he wasn't so nervous, maybe because he had nothing to do but watch, he came to the realization that Ray had reinvented himself once again. The broken nose and flattened cheekbone made him look older, less the pretty boy and more mature, as did the sober blue suit, striped tie and shiny new brown loafers.

His hair was cut short and neatly parted on the right.

Without the boots and what Tim now knew was inside the boots he was shockingly small.

A little guy in a suit. How could he be capable of all this death?

The district attorney was taking no chances. He'd given both Tim and Jennifer immunity in exchange for their testimony and was trying Ray first on Steiner/Hanlon, then late next month on the seven counts of murder, five counts of kidnapping and three counts of assault with a deadly weapon for his August killing spree. Outside the courtroom the November wind howled. Snow would be coming early this year. Inside the courtroom it was warm and quiet but for the shuffling of papers on the desks of the attorneys, the occasional cleared throat and the shuffling of feet.

The judge read the jury's verdict.

Guilty on two counts of murder.

Ray smiled and shrugged as they led him out. Like to him it was no big deal.

Not once, not even when he was testifying against him, had Ray even looked at Tim. It was like Tim didn't matter, finally. He wasn't there. Even as Tim ratted him out on the stand. He didn't look at him now either. Though he must have known he'd be there.

Tim stood, his father beside him and saw Lieutenant Schilling rise a few rows back. Schilling and another, shorter and thinner man with dark circles under his eyes were helping a heavyset woman to her feet. The woman looked stricken, not relieved. Though he knew this to be Elise Hanlon's mother. He glanced quickly away from her so as not to meet her eyes.

He noticed that once again Ray's father was not in attendance.

He and his own father made their way out among the others amid murmured voices and he kept his head down staring at the trousers and shoes ahead of him because he knew that they were talking about him, some of these people and so did his father. His father had never accused him of anything nor had his mother, they had stood by him throughout. But the way they looked at him accused him. His and Jennifer's deal for immunity did not allow him immunity from that.

He would have to get out of there soon, out of the house and out of town. Go somewhere on his own and do something with his life.

The question was what.

He was trained for nothing.

He was alone.

Jennifer wouldn't speak to him. He didn't know if she blamed him because Mr. Griffith was dead or if she was just too busy taking care of Mrs. Griffith, paralyzed from the waist down the moment Ray's bullet nicked her spine. Or maybe Tim just reminded her of Ray and she didn't want to be reminded of Ray. She wouldn't explain. But the reason didn't matter much in the long run anyway. It wasn't going to change. Their speaking days were over. She'd been very clear about that.

So Tim was alone.

That was what he had to show for all his years with Ray.

That was the price he was paying for a moment's protection from a bully in a schoolyard.

For keeping his mouth shut about those girls.

There was nothing to hold him here.

Maybe San Francisco, he thought. *Tune in. Turn on. Drop out.*

Maybe the Haight. The Summer of Flowers had come and gone but maybe there was still a scene there. He didn't know.

He walked out into the parking lot with his silent father and buttoned his jacket against the gusting wind.

On December 9 in the town of Independence, California, at four o'clock P.M., Charles Milles Manson, aka Jesus Christ, a thirty-five-year-old transient self-described musician five feet six inches tall was charged with the murders of Sharon Tate, Jay Sebring, Abigail Folger, Voytek Frykowski, Steven Earl Parent and Rosemary and Leno LaBianca.

Ray heard about it in his cell.

Christmas was only two weeks away when Jennifer took the stand to talk about that August night.

Her first day on the stand was hard because even

though she'd gone through everything with the prosecutor Mr. Rothert and before that with his assistants it was still hard to talk about parts of it. Talking about it she kept seeing it. It wasn't just words. It was Elizabeth Wellman's butchered body lying at her feet. It was Kenneth Wellman tying her to the chair. It was Ray with the rifle at her house and Mr. and Mrs. Griffith shot right in front of her. The words flattened these images so that they were more like pictures on a screen than actual events but didn't erase them, they were crystal clear on the screen and sometimes wouldn't flatten at all and she'd feel the fear as fresh and present as though it were happening in real time all over again.

So the first day was hard. But the second day was harder.

It was like Ray's attorney Patrick Farley was trying to make it *her* fault.

"You were in love with Raymond Pye, weren't you?"

"Once, yes."

"But not that night."

"Not that night."

"Because you were angry with him over the ring."

"That was part of it. It was a lot of things."

"And he almost hit you out there in the parking lot, didn't he?"

"Yes."

"And his mother came to your rescue."

"Yes."

"And his mother Ray subsequently shot."

"Yes."

"And you were angry with him because he was cheating on you, is that right? With Sally Richmond."

"Yes."

"Who Ray also subsequently shot. Were you angry over Katherine Wallace too?"

"Not at that time, no."

"But you were once."

"Not really. A little. Once."

"Seems your anger has had its consequences, Ms. Fitch."

"Objection!"

"Sustained."

And then later, standing behind his desk, rattling his papers.

"Would you say you loved the Griffiths?"

"Yes."

"Did Ray know about that? Did he know you loved them?"

"I . . . I don't know. I guess so. I guess he did."

"But he shot them anyway."

"Yes."

"Shot them right in front of you."

"Yes."

"To get back at you, would you say?"

"Objection. Witness cannot know the defendant's state of mind, your honor."

"Sustained."

And still later.

"This affair you had with Tim Bess . . ."

"It wasn't an affair. We just slept together. It was only that one time."

"All right, just the one time. But Ray found out about that, didn't he."

"Yes."

"And Tim was Ray's best friend."

"Uh-huh."

"Excuse me?"

"Yes. Tim was Ray's best friend."

"Why did you sleep with Ray's best friend, Ms. Fitch? To get back at Ray?"

"I guess."

"You were angry with him again, am I right?"

"Yes."

"And Tim was Ray's best friend. They'd been friends for years, hadn't they."

"Yes."

"How do you think Ray should have responded to that? To your sleeping with Tim? In your opinion."

"He should have understood, I think. I mean, he should have understood where I was coming from."

"He should have understood? And not been angry?"

"Yes."

"But *you* were angry when he slept with Katherine Wallace, weren't you?"

"I wasn't *that* angry. Not enough to kill somebody, Mr. Farley."

"But you're not Raymond Pye, are you?"

"Objection."

"No further questions for this witness, your honor."

She knew what Patrick Farley was doing. He was claiming diminished capacity. Insanity. Ray's anger that night had driven him temporarily insane. Well, maybe it was true and maybe it wasn't but she had nothing to do with it either way. It wasn't fair to blame her, was it? Or Tim or anybody else. In front of a whole courtroom full of people he was blaming her. It was so unfair.

She was only glad that the judge said that their part in the killings of Lisa Steiner and Elise Hanlon was inadmissable in this second trial. Prejudicial, was what he said. Robert had been furious. But she was glad.

She didn't need to have *that* come out again.

She still had to live in this town. For a while at least.

Mrs. Griffith didn't know it yet but she was talking to people at a state clinic who said they thought they'd be able to take her once they had an opening. She felt sorry for Mrs. Griffith, having to go to a place like that, with strangers all around and everything. But she wasn't spending the rest of her life taking care of a cripple either.

She was reasonably good-looking. She was young. Men liked her.

As soon as she got Mrs. Griffith into the clinic she was out of here.

She was *gone*.

Jim "Jumma" Cole didn't think life was so damn bad at Rahway State Prison, no way near as bad as he heard. Some ways, shit, it was better than the street was. You didn't have to put up with some honky pig busting up your action, some Newark PD muthafuck busting the brothers' heads for no good reason except you're black and you're big and you give them *the look*. Didn't have to watch the neighbors' dirty kids starve. Didn't have to smell the garbage rot all summer. Shit, a lot of ways the joint was better than that.

Here's what Jumma *didn't* have.

He didn't have his ax, his conga. And he sure did miss that, he did miss his music. He didn't have Loreen and he missed her big black ass in his hands but not much more than that. He sure didn't miss the mouth on her. Bitch could skin you *alive* with the mouth on her. He didn't have his Pontiac Firebird and he didn't have much daylight and he didn't have his threads and he didn't have the street. And he didn't have his scag. He missed his scag. Missed his crib. Even missed the party thing, sharing the spoon and the matches and the needles with the brothers, all comfy and communal-like.

Okay. So here was what he *did* have.

Plenty of other good shit to take up slack from the scag. Black beauties, bennies, 'ludes, dope, hash. Take you up or take you down, you name it. He missed the needle's big long beautiful rush but he could live with that awhile till he found some source he trusted. He had three squares a day he didn't have to work up a sweat for. Plenty of Camels. Had a color TV in the dayroom with a twenty-one-inch screen.

He was one big mean nigger and he was in for murder two, so he had his respect and his safety in the yard and he had his bitch.

He remembered the day the bitch comes struttin' in. Little fella with an attitude. Face kinda fucked up but still pretty. Hoots and hollers from the brothers. Doesn't seem to bother him one bit. Walks into his cell like he owns the place which Jumma finds out later on, he does. This bitch ain't going *nowhere*. Seven fucking counts of murder, to run consecutively. Which is why the dumb bitch has got all the attitude. He's heard that in the joint the big thing's murder. You kill somebody you get left alone. Like you're this muthafucking animal or something. What he don't understand is that word gets around among the population exactly *who* you kill. And in the bitch's case it's four little teenage *girls* and a pregnant lady, only two full-grown men one of them this old fuck, and then the bitch's fucking *mother*. The dumb crazy shit has killed *his own fucking mother!*

Plus he's this little guy. Real *young* meat. In pretty good shape for a white fella.

Smooth skin. Kinda pretty.

He's *prime*.

He hadn't given Jumma any trouble for a *real* long time. Few good whuppings did him down to the bottom of his soul.

He'd bled some at first.

But his asshole was nice and wide now.

So life wasn't so bad in Rahway Prison. Only thing bothered him was, he wasn't one hundred percent these days. Goddamn flu or something. Probably caught it on the yard, but the fucker wouldn't go away. The doc's antibiotics just weren't making it. Jumma felt tired lot of the time, a little sick to the stomach, had the shits off and on, night sweats, swollen glands—both sides of his neck—the whole fucking thing. He could tell he was losing some weight too.

Jack Ketchum

The bitch said he was worried. Didn't want to catch the flu.

Fuck him. He caught it, he caught it.

And then three days ago he gets these funny little bumps, notices them in the shower, bluish purple, one on his left thigh just above his knee, the other right next to his left nipple. Didn't hurt or nothing but having them there, man, they bothered him. Marred his otherwise perfect beauty. The bitch hadn't noticed the spots yet. The bitch was too busy riding his dick.

The bitch was always faced in the other direction.

He wondered if these funny little bumps of his had anything to do with the goddamn flu, popped a bennie and a tetracycline and figured he'd ask the doctor.

It was late April of 1970 before Ed Anderson was able to get what he wanted for the house and begin the process of packing, going through the attic and basement and garage, through all the memorabilia of his years with Evelyn, a sometimes painful process but necessary because the house in Tom's River was much smaller, with no basement and besides, these were the times for such activities, the sorting out of the important from the merely nostalgic, the strong true memories from the frailer ones.

In the attic he found her high-school diploma and all her report cards stacked and bound with twine, read them through for what was probably the first time as far as he could remember and was unsurprised to find her a fine student, much better than he'd ever been, all *A*'s and *B*'s, with not a *C* in sight. He read them and threw them away. In the same box he found her birth certificate and their marriage license and these he kept. He found her favorite bookmark, a two-inch-wide length of ribbon, crimson edged with gold. He resolved to use it himself from now on. Each time he opened a book he'd have a little glimpse of Evelyn.

On the day before he was to leave, the first Thursday in May, he was around back in the garden planting it one last time. The new owners, he had a feeling, would appreciate the flowers. Zinnia, petunia, pansy, larkspur, Sweet William. He was slightly late with the pansies but that had happened before and they did just fine. He was down on his hands and knees in the rich-smelling earth beside the garage when he heard a car pull in and saw it was Charlie Schilling.

Over here he said, and Schilling walked around to him and laughed and shook his head.

"You're relentless," Schilling said.

"Yeah. You should talk."

And it was a measure of the degree to which the man had healed the past few months that Schilling didn't flinch at that one.

"I got to wish you weren't doing this, Ed."

"What? Gardening?"

"Moving, asshole. What am I gonna do Happy Hour at Panik's joint without your ugly mug in there?"

"Just what you're doing now. Coke with a wedge of lime."

He leaned into the dirt, patting it gently the way Evelyn had taught him.

The cat whose name was Gimp now approached from behind the garage, the cat still listing to the right as the vet had said she probably always would from here on in and attempted to take a bite of larkspur.

"Don't even think it," Anderson said and spritzed her lightly with the watering can.

The cat raced for the safety of open lawn and sat back on her haunches and watched him.

"Be honest with me. It's Bill and June Richmond, right?"

"Sure, partly it is. Town this size, I keep tripping over them. Bill especially. I'm never especially happy when

I do. I don't need the reminder. Neither does he. But you know what, Charlie?"

"What?"

He sat back and brushed off his hands on his khakis.

"It's not the Richmonds. Hell, it's not even that the whole town knows about what happened. I think Sally really taught me not to worry too much about that kind of thing. Fact is, I'm just a goddamn dinosaur. This town's just growing too fast for me. Too many tourists every summer and too much building to accommodate them going on all year 'round. Tom's River's just a quiet little place. A little deep-sea fishing, not much else. The place I've got, Gimp won't even have to worry about traffic. Will ya, babe? So I won't have to worry about Gimp."

At the sound of her name the cat walked over stepping gingerly into the turned earth. Anderson reached over and picked her up and stroked her back and scratched her head and the thick ruff of fur at her neck and Schilling could hear the cat's loud purr stir the open air even from where he was standing. The cat had quite a motor.

"Me and Gimp, we're a couple of survivors. But we like our peace and quiet. My cousin's happy down the shore. I think I will be too. How about you, old buddy? You figure yourself for a survivor?"

Schilling looked at him, then nodded.

"Yeah, I think so, Ed. I think that I must be."

"Good," he said. "You come visit us then. You'd like the fishing."

The cat's eyes blinked and shut.

Ed and Charlie talked awhile and Ed continued stroking.

Elizabeth Massie

Wire Mesh Mothers

It all starts with the best of intentions. Kate McDolen, an elementary school teacher, knows she has to protect little eight-year-old Mistie from parents who are making her life a living hell. So Kate packs her bags, quietly picks up Mistie after school one day and sets off with her toward what she thinks will be a new life. How can she know she is driving headlong into a nightmare?

The nightmare begins when Tony jumps into the passenger seat of Kate's car, waving a gun. Tony is a dangerous girl, more dangerous than anyone could dream. She doesn't admire anything except violence and cruelty, and she has very different plans in mind for Kate and little Mistie. The cross-country trip that follows will turn into a one-way journey to fear, desperation . . . and madness.

___4869-8 $5.99 US/$6.99 CAN

DOUGLAS CLEGG

NAOMI

The subways of Manhattan are only the first stage of Jake Richmond's descent into the vast subterranean passageways beneath the city—and the discovery of a mystery and a terror greater than any human being could imagine. Naomi went into the tunnels to destroy herself . . . but found an even more terrible fate awaiting her in the twisting corridors. And now the man who loves Naomi must find her . . . and bring her back to the world of the living, a world where a New York brownstone holds a burial ground of those accused of witchcraft, where the secrets of the living may be found within the ancient diary of a witch, and where a creature known only as the Serpent has escaped its bounds at last.

___4857-4 $5.99 US/$6.99 CAN

T. M. WRIGHT

Sleepeasy

Harry Briggs led a fairly normal life. He had a good job, a nice house, and a beautiful wife named Barbara, with whom he was very much in love. Then he died. That's when Harry's story really begins. That's when he finds himself in a strange little town called Silver Lake. In Silver Lake nothing is normal. In Silver Lake Harry has become a detective, tough and silent, hot on the trail of a missing woman and a violent madman. But the town itself is an enigma. It's a shadowy twilight town, filled with ghostly figures that seem to be playing according to someone else's rules. Harry has unwittingly brought other things with him to this eerie realm. Things like uncertainty, fear . . . and death.

___4864-7 $5.99 US/$6.99 CAN

Coming in June 2001
from **Leisure Books** . . .

THE BEAST THAT WAS MAX
Gerard Houarner

Max walks in the borderland between the world of shadowy government conspiracy and the world of vengeful ghosts and evil gods, between living flesh and supernatural. For Max is the ultimate killer, an assassin powered by the Beast, an inner demon that enables him to kill—and to do it incredibly well. But the Beast inside Max is very real and very much alive. He is all of Max's dark desires, his murderous impulses, and he won't ever let Max forget that he exists. The Beast *is* Max. So it won't be easy for Max to silence the Beast, though he knows that is what he must do to reclaim his humanity. But without the protection of the Beast, Max the assassin will soon find himself the prey, the target of the spirits of his past victims.

___4881-7 $5.99 US/$6.99 CAN